The
Sound
of
Crickets

A Novel

M.L. Mercy

Copyright

The Sound of Crickets Copyright 2022 M.L. Mercy

Trigger Warnings

This book may contain instances of abuse, drug use, pregnancy loss, explicit language, and sexual content.

AOS Publishing, 2023
AOS Fiction, 2023

ISBN: 978-1-990496-07-3

Cover Design: Lara Chauvin

Visit AOS Publishing's website:
www.aospublishing.com

Dedication

Darrin-
For your support
For your friendship
For your love

Come back in tears,
O memory, hope love of finished years.

O dream how sweet, too sweet, too bitter sweet,
Whose wakening should have been in Paradise,

Christina Rossetti
Echo

Prologue

 Hollynd

3:04 a.m. I can hear the faucet dripping in the kitchen sink. A ping of water hits the stainless steel once every eight seconds, but the tiny droplet of water might as well be a sledgehammer pounding through the wall. It's violating the silence just the same.

And then there's the breathing. In and out. In and out. Air pushing through his lips in a rhythmic way. I should probably find this comforting because, hey, at least I'm not alone. But I don't find comfort in the breath beside me, nor do I find warmth in his touch as the skin on his arm slides gently over my flesh when I roll away from him to face the darkness.

Because he's not the one.

Because the one is breathing with someone else right now. And somehow that causes me to be awake on nights like these at three in the morning.

I get out of my bed and creep out of the suffocating room and into the kitchen to deal with that dreaded dripping. I stand in front of the sink with my bare feet tingling against the cold linoleum, and my waist pressing against the counter. After tightening the hot and cold handles the dripping stops. I should be relieved, but I'm not. I reach up and pull the white curtain with tiny yellow flowers along its bottom seam; the one that hangs over the small window located over the sink. I take a moment to look outside and scan the night sky for an answer. But there is no answer out there, because I've looked a million times before. There are only the stars and the moon—that deceptive moon that heard his promises of forever and now mocks me every night as it shines down on the two of us. Separate but not alone. In love but broken.

Part One

Four Years Earlier

Chapter 1

Hollynd

Arriving early to my first class of the semester, I walk into a mostly empty lecture theater for English 289: Nineteenth Century Poetry. Judging by the size of the bowl-shaped theater, it looks like it could sit the mandatory first-year English class, rather than a second-year one. It probably fits close to one hundred students. The front of the theater is a raised stage equipped with a light oak podium and a matching rectangular table. The front of the room is lit up much brighter with a row of tiny spotlights glowing overhead.

After settling into my wooden seat near the back of the room, I take a moment to breathe. Even though this isn't my first year, I'm still feeling nervous about the first day of classes. I guess old habits die hard. Pulling my long, dirty-blonde hair back from my face, I toss it behind my shoulders. I feel its weight mostly in the hood of my burgundy hoodie as I gaze around the room, hearing only the sounds of rustling papers from the other students sitting a few rows down. The room smells like a combination of bleach and wood, like it has been thoroughly cleaned after sitting empty all summer.

I'm relieved to finally be in my second year at Creston College, but with a jammed-pack schedule of classes to get through, I know it won't be easy. However, once I get through this year of studies, I can transfer to Stranton University to complete my degree in journalism.

I've lived in the city of Brighten my entire life and it's been a wonderful place to grow up. However, it offers little for excitement and delivers even less. My imagination reminds me quite often that there has to be more out there. More to see, more to write about, more to experience, more to love.

Writing professionally has always been my dream. I have a strange fascination with the power of words. I love playing with their sounds, evoking emotions, and creating stories with them. There's magic in creating something out of nothing.

Unfortunately, it's been a long time since I've felt the urge to let my imagination back in—five years to be exact— since my father passed away. But something inside me is beginning to tingle again. A calling to write again. A calling to create. Something magical is on the horizon; something that's going to change everything. I can feel it, if only I can get out of the quicksand of the ordinary.

However, being a logical person and realizing I can't live off the musings of magic, I decided to pursue journalism over creative writing. Fictional writing will continue to be my hobby, and maybe if I'm lucky, one day I can make a career out of it. For now, however, my goal is a journalism degree.

As the minutes tick by, the seats begin to fill up as the other students make arrive for class. Eventually, the seat next to mine becomes occupied when a guy drops languidly into it. While I try to ignore him, it's his scent that catches my attention. It's a heavenly mixture of spices, like cloves with a mix of cedar. The smell alone gives me goosebumps. When I turn to see his face, my pulse jumps straight to my throat. *Beautiful.*

It's hard to tell how tall he is because he's already sitting, but his broad shoulders indicate that he's not a small guy. His black hair lays off to the side, and his eyes are the colour of the ocean at night. A dark blue. A deep blue. An addictive blue. His bottom lip is looped with a tiny silver ring, as are both his ears, while his short-sleeved T-shirt exposes his arms that are covered in tattoos. Thick black lines run together creating detailed images blended as one. In the quick glance I take over his left arm I can make out a lizard with its long tail wrapping itself around his forearm, along with the words *Plenitudo temporis* running alongside. I couldn't be sure, but it looks like Latin to me, though I have no idea what it means. But what I do know is although I've never thought of myself as the type of girl who would drag a stranger to a closet to ravage his body…that may be quickly changing.

"Hey," the seated Adonis says with a crooked smirk.

Clearly I'm staring, and he's caught me. *Ugh.*

He raises his hand and brings it to mine for a quick shake. "I'm Landry Hayles."

"Hey," I reply with my most chill and nonchalant voice, holding out my hand.

The moment our skin touches, I feel a strange sensation run through my body. *What was that?* As my eyes wander over the face of the man sitting next to me, a strange familiarity washes over me. My soul stirs.

"Hollynd Turner."

"Hollynd." Landry repeats my name, and the sound of it falling from his lips makes me shudder. "That's a beautiful name."

"Thanks, my parents gave it to me." *Oh my God, I'm such a loser.* I curse myself while my cheeks blush.

A slight laugh escapes Landry's lips. "Right."

"I'm sorry." I give a quick shake of my head. "That was stupid."

"Never be sorry for being who you are."

His dark eyes stare into mine and I can't bring myself to look away. The wildest thoughts are bombarding my mind. I try to keep myself grounded most of the time, but right now I'm anything but grounded.

For the next three weeks, I sit in the same seat at every English 289 class, and just as I'd hoped, Landry Hayles – my favourite stranger – continues to sit in the seat next me. Every day we make flirty small talk before class begins. It's my favourite part of the day.

By the start of the fourth week, my feelings for Landry are becoming more and more certain. I think about him all the time, I'm excited to see him, and the butterflies constantly in my stomach…well let's just say they're vivaciously active.

When Landry arrives and unpacks his books from his bag, he looks at me with the same adorable smile I've become addicted to seeing. Wearing a pair of dark grey sweatpants and a dark green hoodie, he looks like the sexiest, coziest thing I have ever seen. My imagination takes over as I picture myself curled up against his soft clothes, and what I can only assume is a hard body underneath.

"Hey, Hollynd." Landry breaks me from my daydream.

"Hi, Landry. How are you?"

"I'm alright. Although I would be better without all these poems we have to read in this freaking class."

"You don't enjoy poetry?"

Landry grimaces as he tosses his poetry textbook onto his desk. "No, not really. I'd much rather read a novel than a bunch of poems."

"What type of books do you prefer to read?" I ask.

"I like fantasy and science fiction, mostly. What about you? Let me guess, steamy romances with big-chested guys named Chet?" Landry flashes a devious smile.

"I like all sorts of books. Some romance, some not."

Which is mostly true. As for the other part, I will admit that I also have a thing for steamy romances, but not with big-chested guys named Chet. More like bad mafia boys named Giuliano, but I'm not going to share that information with Landry.

"And I bet you like this poetry stuff too?"

"Yes. Why?" I reply defensively.

"Because, Miss Hollynd, you just got a full-time study partner," Landry says with a wink.

"Who says I want you as a study partner?"

Landry leans closer to my chair and whispers in my ear, "You want me, Hollynd." Landry pauses for a moment before continuing, "As a study partner."

I'm rendered speechless as the first part of his sentence replays in my mind.

Landry leans back in his seat with a smile, knowing I have nothing smart-ass to say back as the instructor begins the class. For the next hour, I swear I can still feel Landry's breath on the back of my neck from his whisper earlier. It's all I can do not to reach up and rub the spot that's still tingling.

When our English class is over, we both stand and begin to clear off our desks. As I shove the last book into my bag and begin my daily fight with its very temperamental zipper, Landry asks, "Do you want to meet at the library later to go over these poems?"

"You were serious about wanting me as a study partner?"

Landry tucks his laptop into his backpack. "Of course. You're one of the smartest people in this class, not to mention one of the cutest too."

I roll my eyes out of instinct at the compliment, though I can't help but feel a little giddy inside.

"Okay, let's meet at the library around four."

"Sounds good, study buddy." Landry gives me a slight smirk before walking away.

I can't help but smile brightly the entire way to my next class. Four o'clock cannot come soon enough.

Chapter 2

Landry

For the past four weeks I feel like I've done nothing but think about Hollynd. It was a class I had no intention of enrolling in. Nineteenth Century Poetry has never been on my list of classes to take, ever. However, when one of my other electives fell through, it was the only class left with spots available. So now I guess you can say I'm a student of the roses are red, and violets are blue group, reluctantly.

Being in my second year of a Computer Science and Software Engineering degree, a random class in English literature was not in my plan. My plan is to lie low in class and cruise by. I want this year of studies to be over so badly, then I can finally transfer to a university to complete my degree. A university that's far away from my father and his tyranny. And if that means I have to pick up some random English class, then so be it. I'll take the stupid course and move on.

If I hadn't been so worried about partying, drugs, and getting laid during and after high school, I could've finished my degree by now. Instead, it took me two years to get my ass in gear and realize I needed something that would not only make me independent from my father and his money, but also become a responsible member of society.

Now I'm a twenty-two-year-old man in a class with a bunch of nineteen-year-olds. Most days I feel like I've already lived more than one lifetime. Watching these fresh-faced teenagers with their doe-eyed naivety guiding them through the university hallways, I can't help but feel twinges of jealousy. If I think back to when I was nineteen years old, I can only remember flashes of what my life had been like. Between the drugs, booze, and hangovers, I can't remember a lot. That's not to say I don't like to still party occasionally. After all, I'm twenty-two, not dead.

On the first day of English class, my goal was to find a seat in the back and go unnoticed by the professor. Luckily for me, there was a stunning girl who caught my eye also sitting in the back. Her dirty-blonde hair laid in waves over her shoulders as I watched her fumble around in her backpack. When she finally looked up, I could see her small turned-up nose and light pink lips. And then there were her eyes, a glowing green. Everything about her was sweet.

At first, I thought I was simply sitting next to a hot girl, which was going to make getting through that class more bearable. Once we began talking however, I found out quickly that she was not only beautiful, but also funny and adorable.

Sometimes, when we'd discuss topics she was passionate about, like books for example, I'd stop talking altogether just to watch her talk with her smile shining brightly with enthusiasm. Her hand would whip around in front of her, as her excitement couldn't be contained. Her passion was contagious and just being around her, I felt a galvanizing effect throughout my entire being.

Each day that I sat next to Hollynd, I could see more of her beauty than I saw the day before. Like how her eyes were not just green, but a sharp dark green with flecks of gold throughout. How she looked mostly innocent, but in her eyes she held her sad secrets. Secrets that I longed to find out, that I needed to find out. Or how she would stick her tongue out a tiny bit past her lips and furrow her eyebrows when she was in deep concentration.

By the third day, I looked forward to the stupid English class just so I could see this girl, talk to this girl, and simply be near this girl. *What the hell?*

Four weeks later and I've arrived early to our class together. I'm anxious to see her, again. I'm contemplating how I ended up here as I'm tapping my foot on the beige tiled floor in an anxious rhythm waiting for her arrival. The lecture theater is still mostly empty, except for three other students who are sitting many rows up from my usual spot at the back of the room. The sound of my tapping echoed throughout the back of the room.

While waiting for Hollynd to arrive I pull off my grey sweatshirt leaving only my deep red T-shirt on with my black jeans, despite being in the classroom our instructor always insists is the coldest on campus. I'm sweating more than usual and as much as I hate to admit it, I think it's these feelings I'm having about Hollynd causing me to feel like I'm about to spontaneously combust.

Typically, I'm not the type of guy to fawn over a girl. In fact, the idea of having a girlfriend seems more like a hassle than anything. Don't get me wrong, I enjoy the company of women very much, but in short increments. Only a couple of hours or a full night at most. I have a few regular "friends" that I rotate through as needed. However, these "friends" know that there's no long-term deal in our future. I'm not that kind of guy.

It doesn't make much sense to me, having only known this girl for four weeks, but I can't shake the feeling that there was something more. Something more than my dick leading my actions. There's something different about her, which sounds like such a stupid cliché. It all seems too instantaneous, but I can't control it. Every part of my being wants her, and that scares the shit out of me.

After setting my laptop onto the tiny table attached to my chair, I look up to see Hollynd walking up the stairs towards me. A smile crosses her face as she takes the seat next to me. Dressed in a light pink knitted sweater and dark denim jeans, she promptly begins to unload her books. Unlike me, Hollynd doesn't use a laptop, but rather takes her notes by hand. It works out well since I don't have room for anything else except my laptop on the tiny, attached table, so we share her textbook. Most days, my favourite part of sharing her textbook is that I get to lean in close enough to smell the remnants of her shampoo, which smells like tangerines.

By the end of class, Hollynd and I have made plans to meet at the library later today to work on an assignment together. This will be our first time hanging out together outside the classroom since we began school. I've never been so excited to go to a library in my entire life.

Our plan is to meet at the library around four o'clock. My last class ended a little while ago, so that gives me plenty of time to get each of us coffee before we meet up. I hope she likes French vanilla coffee, because that's what I got her. I prefer straight black coffee as I'm not really into sweet drinks.

With one coffee in each hand and my backpack slung over my shoulders, I head toward the library.

When I arrive, I eagerly glance around the open floor plan of the large rectangular space. The front half is a large study area for the students, while large wooden shelves holding thousands of books encompass the back half of the library. The area up front is lined with tables and chairs as the sound of other students' studying together buzzes throughout. Two librarians are chatting as they pass books back and forth behind the circulation desk.

The library is combination of old and modern with hanging frosted light fixtures throughout, matched with the modern glow from large monitors on the walls advertising campus activities and information. This isn't an old-fashioned library where you're likely to be reprimanded for talking despite the age of the building. It's much more welcoming to student study groups and socialization. The relaxing atmosphere doesn't suit the old décor.

When I spot Hollynd, she's sitting at a large, dark wooden table on the far side of the room. As I walk towards her, my rubber-soled shoes squeak against the dark wooden floor.

As I get closer to Hollynd, I notice her blonde hair hanging over her shoulders and around her face as her head is tilted forward over her phone. She's completely spellbound by whatever she's looking at. The satiny shine of the strands of hair hanging by her pink cheeks makes me want to reach over and brush them away. Her eyebrows are arched as she stares at the screen. I feel a tiny smile cross my lips. Her adorableness is killing me, but in a good way. Whatever she's looking at has her so engrossed that she doesn't see me arrive until I set her coffee down in front of her before taking the seat across the table.

"What are you watching?" I ask out of curiosity.

"I was reading, actually." Hollynd takes the hot coffee into her hands inhaling deeply over the steam rising out of it. "Thank you so much. It smells delicious."

"You're welcome." I reply as I begin to pull my English book and laptop out of my bag. "So, tell me what you were reading."

Instantly, Hollynd's cheeks go red with embarrassment. "It's nothing."

"Now you must tell me. Judging by your reaction, I need to know."

Hollynd bites softly on her bottom lip. "It's a romance book."

"Like a smutty book?"

Hollynd squirms in her seat. "More like passionate."

"Let me see." I reach across the table, hoping she will hand me her phone.

Hollynd quickly swipes her phone away and tucks it under her leg. "No!"

"Alright, I'll leave it alone for now. But eventually you're going to have to show me what you're into. I have a feeling it's going to be shocking."

Hollynd rolls her eyes and opens her binder up to the English syllabus our instructor gave us at the beginning of the semester.

"Okay, so did you read the three poems by Christina Rossetti?"

"I did," I reply while taking a slow sip of my hot coffee. "They were kind of depressing."

Hollynd nods in agreement. "They are in a way, but also, they speak so much truth about the reality of life. Love and loss. Loss and acceptance. Love that never really ends, even when it's over. I don't know, maybe I'm just a romantic idiot at heart. But somehow, I can't help but feel a tiny bit of hope somewhere in the background."

Hope. I'm not entirely sure why, but I like that she mentions the word hope.

"Which one was your favourite?"

"Echo." Hollynd answers quickly.

"Will you read it to me?"

"I thought you said you read them?"

"I did, but I really want to hear you read it."

Hollynd takes a quick glance around to make sure no one else is close enough to hear her reciting the poem. "Okay."

After opening her textbook to the page of the poem, the words begin to tumble out of Hollynd's mouth with ease. She doesn't take her eyes off the textbook page, and I don't take my eyes off her.

At first her voice sounds shaky, like maybe she's nervous. Small vibrations linger on the words as she reads them. Her eyes widen as the poem flows through her lips, and now I realize that it's not nerves she's experiencing, it's emotion. I feel my lips part slightly, as I watch in complete awe of this woman exposing herself through the poem. I take a deep breath and try to steady my thumping heart as her soft voice rings in my ears. *Oh my God, what is happening to me?*

When Hollynd finishes the poem, she looks up briefly, waiting for my reaction.

It takes me a moment as I continue to internalize all that I'm feeling after hearing her voice reciting words of lost love. It was magnificent and heartbreaking. I had read this poem a few days ago on my own, but shit, it didn't read like this my head. When Hollynd says the words *pulse for pulse* and *breath for breath*, I feel like it's the first time I'm hearing them. Is it possible to experience a love that's so consuming that its demise can affect you for a lifetime? It's something I've never given much thought to before now. It's wonderfully intriguing and unsettling. Finally, my mouth gives way to a smile, unable to articulate the words to express how I'm feeling.

"Which poem was your favourite?" Hollynd breaks the awkwardness of my non-verbal reply.

"That one," I answer without hesitancy.

Hollynd raises her eyebrows with suspicion. "Really?"

"Well, not until I heard you read it. But it definitely is now." I'm still smiling and for some reason, I can't seem to stop.

Hollynd smiles in return before looking back down at the textbook. "I suppose we should get going on this assignment."

"Yeah, you're probably right."

We continue to work on our assignment for the next two hours. However, once we finish it, I feel like I'm not ready to say goodbye.

As we are packing up our stuff, I find the courage to ask what I've been thinking about for the last couple hours. "Do you want to exchange numbers? You know, in case we want to set up another study session or something?"

"Sure." Hollynd nods before pulling her cell phone out of her pocket.

I do the same, and we exchange phones and input the numbers before giving them back.

As we make our way out of the library, walking side by side, each with our backpacks slung over our shoulders, I nudge my arm against hers. "Thanks for meeting me, I had a lot of fun."

"Me too."

We walk in silence through the parking lot outside of the library, except for the sound of the pavement grit under our feet. The quad beside the library is empty, except for the trees whose leaves have turned from green to golden yellow. The smell of autumn is in the air, sweet with a hint of the bitter ending of summer. But it's not so bad because though it's technically fall, the air is still warm enough to forgo jackets.

There are only a few cars left in the library parking lot and though we're walking in the opposite direction from where my black Mustang is parked, I don't mind. I continue to walk beside Hollynd in the direction of her car.

"Just so you know, you can text me for fun too, not only to study." I mention casually to Hollynd, hoping she hears me. "Or you can call me if you ever feel like reciting another poem."

Hollynd giggles, "You'll be sorry when I call you at midnight to recite *The Divine Comedy.*"

"I'd suffer through it for you." I laugh in return.

When we reach Hollynd's car she turns and wraps me into a quick hug before getting inside. "Thank you, Landry. This was great."

I'm pleasantly surprised by the small show of affection from Hollynd, though it was too quick for me to reciprocate. I'm not sure if she gave me a friendship hug or if it was something more. But I hope it's something more to her because I get the feeling that it's something more for me. Something much more.

I watch her reverse out of the parking spot before I turn back to walk towards my car at the other end of the lot. In my head I'm trying to calculate how long I should wait before I text her. I shake my head at myself as I unlock my car, not only for already thinking about texting her, but for already missing her.

Chapter 3

Hollynd

It's been two days since I met Landry in the library to study. This was also the day we exchanged numbers —and while our English class was this morning —Landry was absent, and I haven't heard from him.

I lean back on my bed where I'm sitting covered in paper and books. Nestled into my small loft room in my mom's house, I fidget with my phone while ignoring the work that needs to be done before Friday. I can't concentrate on poetry right now, not when I'm trying to come up with a casual text to send Landry.

Hollynd:
Hey, Landry. I took some notes from class today.
Do you want me to send them to you?
Hope you are well.

There, it's sent. Perhaps now I can put my phone down and concentrate on my schoolwork. As I try to control myself from looking for the three little dots notifying me of an immediate response, I slide my phone out of sight underneath my open orange binder that's sitting on my lap and return to my homework.

Ten minutes later, a buzz rings through the air and my heart responds accordingly, pounding fiercely.

Landry:
Hey Hollynd. Notes would be great. Thx.
I'm fine. What are you doing?

Hollynd:
Working on Friday's assignment.

Landry:
Good. Then I don't have to ;)

Hollynd:
Nice try.

Landry:
Want to meet up?

Hollynd:
When?

Landry:
Now.

It's already nine o'clock. Where would he want to meet up at nine on a Wednesday night? Ugh, who am I kidding? Obviously, I'm going to go. So, I can either sit here and think about not going for ten minutes, and then say I'm going, or I can say 'yes.'. *Just say yes.*

Hollynd:
Yes.

Landry:
Pick you up in fifteen.
What's your address?

Hollynd:
534 Clover Cres.

Landry:
K

Dress warm.

I only have fifteen minutes to make myself decent. I'm already in my pajamas and my hair is up in a messy bun. After changing out of my fuzzy red and white polka dot pajamas, I quickly toss on a pair of black yoga pants, a black t-shirt, and a black hoodie. I kind of look like a cat burglar or a ninja. What can I say, I have never been a girl with a colourful wardrobe. I pull my hair out of the messy bun that's piled high on my head and shake the long strands free. I use my fingers in lieu of a hairbrush to untangle any noticeable knots. Luckily, my daytime makeup is still on, albeit it's a little smudged. But for the amount of time I have, this is as good as it's going to get. I quickly spritz on some perfume and head to the door to meet Landry outside.

Despite being twenty years old, I still live with my mom while I attend college. Mom and I moved into this house about a year after my dad died, when I was still in high school. When it became Mom and I, she didn't think we needed as much space as we had in our old house anymore. Though I think now that it was all the memories of my father that she couldn't handle. We moved into this smaller house. A three-bedroom bungalow with buttercream yellow siding and white trim. Rachel, my sister and only sibling, lives with her high school sweetheart turned husband, Colin, a few blocks away.

Before heading outside, I peek my head into my mom's room where she's already tucked into her bed and watching TV. My mom, such a creature of habit. Early to bed, early to rise, as the old saying goes. Her room is the best representation of her gentle spirit. The grey bedding with pink cherry blossoms makes her bed look even more inviting. A flicker from the candle burning on her nightstand catches my eye, as the scent of lavender coming off the melted wax catches my nose.

"Bye Mom, I'm going to head out with a friend," I whisper trying not to interrupt her show.

"Okay, honey. Be safe. I love you."

"I love you too, Mom."

I leave my mother's bedroom and head out of the house to meet the beautiful stranger turned "study-buddy" from my English class. I hardly have a chance to notice the light breeze or the scent of our neighbor's freshly cut grass before Landry arrives.

I watch as excitement rumbles around in my chest as Landry pulls up in his black Ford Mustang. Landry barely has the car parked before I hurry down the sidewalk and jump into the car.

The grey seat feels warm as I sit down. I notice the light on the dash signifying the passenger seat warmer has been turned on. I can't help but smirk thinking about how sweet Landry is under his bad boy, tattooed demeanor.

"Hey," Landry looks at me with a crooked grin as the streetlight bounces off his silver lip ring. *I want to lick every inch of those lips.*

Landry is dressed in black from head to toe. From his black hoodie to his black jeans, he looks as dark as his eyes presented him to be. I can't help but smile to myself about how we are basically matching with our lack of coloured clothing and matching hoodies.

"Hey Landry." My smile can't be contained. I can't even hide my excitement or desire for him when we are this close and alone. "Where are we going?"

"I thought we could go down to the beach at Pebblestone," Landry's dark eyes land on mine.

"The beach? Right now?"

"Yup. I brought us some beer and a blanket."

"I've never been there this late before."

"I enjoy going there at night, you can see every star and it's quiet. There's literally no one there right now. I'll even let you tell me all about the riveting book you're reading." Landry smirks.

"I knew you were using me for my literature knowledge."

"Absolutely." Landry's smile grows as he looks forward, puts the car into gear, and heads towards the beach at Pebblestone Lake.

We arrive at the lake about ten minutes later. I'm carrying an oversized red plaid blanket, following behind Landry as he leads the way with a case of beer in hand. We walk silently on the sand towards the water. Landry is right, it is peaceful here when there's no one else around. The only sounds are the water rolling gently onto the shore and hundreds of crickets chirping in the distance. The wind blows slightly and feels cooler than it did at home as it comes off the water. I'm glad I wore my thick hoodie.

Landry stops a few yards out from the water and motions for me to lay out the blanket. After it's down, I sit on the right side of the blanket and face the water. Landry follows suit, though, sitting more in the center than on the left side. He's close enough to me that I can feel the material of his hoodie press against my own hoodie sleeve. I can't even tell where one of us ends and the other one begins. Nothing but the sound of the water moving gently onto the shore and the distance cricket chirps echo through the air. I close my eyes for a moment to take in the perfect peacefulness of this moment.

"Nice, right?" Landry asks, already knowing the answer.

"It's really nice down here. A little cold, but nice," I reply without opening my eyes, still enjoying the moment and the person next to me. I inhale the scent of nearby lake water, and it reminds me of summertime.

"I like it because it's so quiet and away from all the noisy shit of the world. Except those annoying crickets. I could do without them."

"I don't mind them," I reply with a shrug. "They are just doing what crickets do. It's comforting in a way."

Landry laughs. "You may be the first person I've ever met who thinks crickets are comforting."

I offer a cute smile and shrug my shoulders again.

With a grin, Landry leans over to grab two beers and hands me one. As I twist the top off and take a swig, I can hear Landry mumble to himself, "She likes the goddamn crickets."

After a few minutes of silence, and both of us staring out towards the black water, Landry turns to me with his piercing blue eyes.

"Ever since the other day in the library I can't stop thinking about that poem *Echo*. I've never read much poetry before, but that one really stuck with me."

"Christina Rossetti was a great poet."

"Yeah, I actually read some more of her pieces."

"Why Landry Hayles, I think you might be starting to like poetry."

"I think I might be starting to like you." Landry bumps my shoulder with his which causes my body to rock slightly.

"You're making me blush," I admit out loud.

"Good," Landry smirks while he reaches up and tucks a loose strand of my hair behind my ear. "What do you want out of life, Hollynd?" Landry asks while pulling his hand away from my neck and taking a drink from his bottle of beer.

"Is this your idea of small talk, Landry?" I try to laugh off the question.

"Small talk is bullshit. What do you want out of life?"

"Oh, I don't know. My degree, I guess. Hopefully, I'll find a good job when I'm done with school. Eventually, a family I suppose, though I'm not too worried about that right now. What about you?" I take another drink from my bottle as well.

Landry stares at me for a long time and I feel like he's trying to read me like a human lie detector.

"What's your major again?" Landry asks with narrowed eyes.

"Journalism."

"And that's what you really want to do?"

"Yeah. I mean, I like to write. It pays well. There are a lot of opportunities."

"That answer is bullshit. Bullshit and ordinary."

"Excuse me?" I look at Landry who's still staring at me with a scowl of annoyance.

"That's what you tell your neighbor or your guidance counselor what you want. Tell me the truth, what do you really want? I won't tell anyone." The corner of his lip offers a small smirk.

I move my gaze out to the black water. I don't know what it is about him, but I want to tell him everything. Confess my sins and whisper my fears. I want him to take it all from me.

We sit quietly for a minute. *What do I want? What is my dream? My passion?* I don't know if it's Landry's intense stare or the forceful questioning, but I can feel the words uncontrollably fall out of my mouth.

"I want to write books. Fiction books."

"What kind of fiction?" Landry urges for more.

"The kind that tears your heart out and leaves you wondering why your life will never be as good as the fake characters you read about. The kind that makes you believe that love and passion exist, but you know you'll never get to feel the way my characters do, because they now own your soul and will forever remind you that you are never going to be enough. The kind that is anything but ordinary!" I release into the night air with Landry Hayles as my only witness.

I'm out of breath. I feel shocked with my admission, yet I feel free.

"I love that!" Landry finally says after a moment of reflection. "Now that's an actual answer!" Landry turns to me with his lopsided grin and takes a drink from his beer.

"That felt kind of good!" I laugh out loud as I gather myself from my brief outburst. "Like really good! Fantastic even! But wait, you didn't answer me before. What do you want out of life, Landry?"

I look into Landry's eyes which seem to have become darker at that very moment, like he has an answer that is so close to the surface and it's itching to get out. Without breaking contact with my eyes, Landry brings his hand to the side of my cheek and pulls my face towards his.

Right before our lips touch, Landry whispers into my mouth, "*Everything.*"

As our lips press together, I can feel the coolness of his bottom lip ring against my own bottom lip. However, the cool sensation is quickly replaced by the warmth of his tongue as it nudges past my lips and caresses the inside of my mouth. Within an instant, I fall back and relax my body as I lay on the outstretched blanket. Our lips never separate as Landry lowers himself down and leans over top of me.

We continue like this for a few minutes while I question myself. *What am I doing? I barely know this person. I need to stop before I sleep with him right here on the beach. I kind of don't want to stop. No, I need to stop.* The battle continues in my consciousness.

At that moment, Landry lifts his head back while he tucks a strand of hair behind my ear. We stare at each other with our mouths slightly agape and our breaths in perfect rhythm.

Silence.

"What the hell kind of answer is 'everything'?" I blurt out to break the silence.

Landry bursts out in laughter as he rolls onto his back beside me. "Wow, you know how to kill a mood, Cricket."

"Cricket?"

"Yeah, Cricket. You're comforting to be around."

I look away to hide my silly girl smile from Landry. *He's too cute.* I quickly compose myself, and I turn my head to the side to look at him with the most serious face I can make while still riding the wave of his kiss.

"I'm not going to sleep with you tonight," I state firmly.

"I never thought you would. Though, to be clear, I would totally be okay with that." Landry offers with a wink.

"And I just wanted to make sure we're clear that it's not an option," I assert, with a slight hitch in my voice.

"Who are you trying to convince? You or me?" Landry laughs as he takes my hand in his and presses it to his lips. "You're beautiful, by the way."

"I think you're beautiful," I reply with absolute honestly.

Landry bites his lip with embarrassment. "I don't think anyone has ever called me beautiful before." A small laugh escapes his throat.

"Then no one's ever really looked at you."

"You're doing strange things to me, Cricket." Landry whispers as he shifts his head to look up into the sky, though my hand is held by his and is resting on his chest.

Lying side by side on the red plaid blanket, I can't help but release a smile as I turn my eyes towards the stars. I watch them twinkle, and wonder how many times they have heard some guy tell some girl she's beautiful. I wonder how many times they have seen two people laying together, wondering how this person who they hardly know makes them feel more alive than they have ever felt before. How many times have they watched a stupid girl fall in love with a darkness that would eventually be her demise?

After another hour of laying on the beach together, where we kissed each other more than we talked, we decide it's time to call it a night. We pack up the blanket and our empty beer bottles, along with four full ones since we spent more time making out than drinking beer, and head back towards Landry's car. While he throws our items into the trunk, I head towards the passenger door and climb into the grey leather seat. I immediately tuck my cold hands under my thighs and let out a tiny shiver.

Shortly after, Landry sits down in the driver's seat and starts the car. As he puts it in gear and drives back towards the main route, Landry gently places his hand on my thigh and slowly rubs it with his thumb. I lean my head back against the seat and close my eyes to focus on the sensation of his hand rubbing my inner thigh. As the tires slowly bump down the gravel road, I look over at Landry who notices the shift in my attention and meets my eyes with a dark look, the same dark look I saw earlier in the night, right before our first kiss.

Suddenly, something comes over me, much like before when I couldn't contain the words of my dreams, a sensation I cannot control. It's a fire in my soul that's beyond me and all the good sense that I ever had.

"Stop the car, Landry," I speak into the dark car.

"Are you okay?" Landry asks while he descends his speed and stops on the deserted road.

"Yes," I reply while I remove my seatbelt and lift my body over the middle console of the car while clicking the button of his seatbelt.

Stradling my legs over his body, I feel him release the seat and slide it towards the back half of the car. I lean my head down towards Landry and place my lips to his—which have now become a familiar feeling to me after just spending the last hour attached to them. I *WANT* more. I *NEED* more.

Our lips press and open while our tongues eagerly explore each other as though we are starving. I rest my hands on Landry's wide shoulders while I feel his hands rub over the curve of my backside before they slowly slip under the back hem of my hoodie and the shirt I have underneath. His fingers make their way up my spine before moving toward the front of my shirt and grip the bulkiness of my size C cup.

Immediately, a warm sensation fills my lower half as I grind my pelvis into his. I can feel his hardness underneath me growing more intense with each second. I tug at Landry's black hoodie to help him pull it off his wide shoulders. It's only then does he stop his exploration of my breasts to help me get his sweater off. I move my hands to his stomach, which feels firm and rippled. As I grip the bottom of his T-shirt, I pull it straight up with force. I want it off and I want it off now. Landry straightens his arms up for me so I can easily slide the material over his head and through his arms.

As I toss the shirt to the empty back seat, my eyes take in Landry's hard pecs, which are covered in a variety of black tattoos. The darkness of the car, with only the moonlight and dashboard lights, makes it difficult to see each design of ink. I also can't help but notice the single silver hoop hanging from his right nipple. My first instinct is to reach up and gently slide my fingers over the cold steel. Landry lets out a tiny gasp of air as I touch his nipple ring.

"Lay back the seat more," I demand, while I look into his blue eyes.

"Are you sure? I thought you didn't want this to happen tonight?" Landry asks.

"I changed my mind," I reply with a smile while I continue to play with his nipple ring; I couldn't have made myself wait longer if I had tried.

The pull I have towards this man is unlike anything I've experienced before. Even with past boyfriends, I've never felt this before. It's something beyond me, beyond this world, like something dominated by the stars themselves. I am at their mercy. I am at Landry's mercy.

With a widened smile, Landry lays the seat back as far as it will go and pulls my head down to meet his lips once more. I cannot help but let out a moan of pleasure as his hardness grinds back into my center. Instantly, I feel Landry pull my shirt up over my head while his other hand reaches around to unfasten my bra and slide it off my shoulders. The cool air is shocking to my chest, and I feel my nipples harden. Landry releases my mouth from his and moves his lips down my neck slowly, while his soft kisses and warm breath give me goosebumps along my arms and back.

I feel his hands tighten around my waist as he pulls my body up and forward as my breasts lift to meet his lips. The warmth of his tongue is a welcome surprise over my cold nipples. As he continues to kiss and suck, his hand slides down from my waist and pulls the elastic on my yoga pants. The material gives way and slides over my curves towards the bend of my knees, taking my underwear with them. I maneuver my left leg up to slide it free from the bunched pants and let the bulk of the material slide down to the bottom of my right leg.

I reach down towards the button and zipper of Landry's jeans and slide them low enough with his Calvin Klein boxer briefs to free him for my own pleasure.

"Hollynd, are you on birth control?" he asks, cupping my face with his hands.

"Yeah, but I don't have a condom, but I'm clean. I swear."

"Me too. I was just tested recently, and I always wear a condom."

"Yeah, me too," I reply, which is totally true.

Usually, the idea of not having a condom would be a total deal breaker for me, but tonight with Landry, I couldn't care less.

Landry pulls my face down towards his and our lips crash together again with a consuming eagerness and passion. As our tongues stroke each other, I move my hips up to bring him into my center and take all of him inside of me. We continue to explore each other's bodies with our hands and mouth, keeping ourselves joined in perfect rhythm. As our movements become more intense and forceful, I feel a warmth of pleasure throughout my entire body. It explodes inside me, coming out as weeping breaths. Shortly after, I feel Landry pant himself towards his own release as he lets out a sharp moan with his finish, his fingers are clutching my hips fiercely.

For a few moments, we just lay there still fused together. With our foreheads pressed together and our mouths breathing heavily into each other.

"You're unbelievable, Cricket," Landry whispers into my still panting mouth.

"I like that you call me that," I admit in the darkness.

As I pull back with a smile, Landry grabs the back of my head and pulls me back in for one of his life-or-death kisses.

"You're all mine now. You know that right?" Landry says while our mouths are pressed together. "Mine."

"Yes," I answer back quickly without a doubt in my mind. *His.*

Chapter 4

Landry

My alarm goes off at 7:09 a.m. as it does every day. However, today, I don't hit the snooze button. I'm quick to get up and get going. After my time with Hollynd last night, I can't think of anything but seeing her again. Well, that's not exactly true. I have no trouble thinking about last night and how she climbed on top of me in my car and totally took what she wanted from me. It was so hot!

However, my feelings for Hollynd are frustrating me, because she's not like most of the women I know, and not in a cliché chick-flick sort of way. Hollynd is smart and funny and doesn't put up with a lot of shit, which I like, but also, I don't know. She pulls me towards her, in a weird subconscious way. When I'm not with her I want to be, and when I am with her, I want to be closer to her. This is both confusing and comforting.

I was not expecting to have sex with her last night, and I was okay with not sleeping with her yet. It was so unbelievably sexy, the way she took over when she straddled me in my car and took what she wanted. I've never been with a woman who took control like that, ever. I allow my mind to wander back to last night in my car and I can feel my body reacting in a way that is demanding my attention. I can still feel her hands on my chest and her tongue flipping around my lip ring. And her moans, ahh her goddamn moans. Screw it, I have time for an extended shower, I'll take these thoughts with me.

After I finish my shower business, I hear Rob banging on the bathroom door. "Landry, hurry up!"

"Calm down. I'm just about done."

I open the door to find Rob standing there, still in his pajama pants and a T-shirt with bedhead, looking unimpressed with my length of time in the shower. He needs to have a shower and get ready for class, which starts in less than an hour. Rob pushes past me as I stand in my towel, in front of the mirror running gel through my hair. Although this is my ensuite bathroom attached to the master bedroom of our two-room apartment, the shower in the other bathroom is currently broken. The superintendent of the building promised us it would be fixed in a couple of days. That was three weeks ago.

"What the hell took you so long?" Rob grumbles.

"I had business to attend to." I reply without taking my eyes off the mirror. "Also, this is my bathroom, jackass."

"I guess that means your date didn't go so well last night, brother." Rob laughs too hard at his own joke. "What was the chick's name again, Holly?"

"Her name is Hollynd, and as a matter of fact, the date was..." I pause trying to think of the best word to describe our night last night without sounding like a romantic pussy or a douchey prick that just got laid. "Our date was memorable."

"Memorable? What does that mean?"

"It means I'm seeing her again, and if you're lucky, maybe you'll be able to meet her."

"Well, if you bring her around, make sure some of her hot friends come with her for your poor, dear brother." Rob smirks while reaching down to run the water for the shower. "Now, get out of here so I can shower."

Rob and I have lived together for the past few years. As soon as I turned eighteen, I had to get out of my father's house. I got my own place and quickly convinced Rob to move in with me, despite the fact that he was still in high school.

Rob is two years younger than me and is my *little* brother in every sense of the word. Standing four inches shorter than me at five foot eleven, Rob has light brown hair and hazel eyes. His features are softer than mine, as is his temperament. Rob's the type of guy everyone loves, well, apart from my father who can't love anyone but himself.

I try to stay away from my father as much as possible, though there are times he demands to see us. Even then, I resist seeing my father, if possible, but Rob is a lot more forgiving than I am and he usually guilts me into seeing him.

I love living with Rob in our small but functional two-bedroom apartment, and attending the same college. Unfortunately, my father pays for our apartment and college tuition because there's no way we could afford it on our own. I know my father prefers us not being in his house anymore. However, I also think that since he has paid our way for college, he thinks he has an ownership over us. The thought of that makes me want to puke my guts out.

I shake my father from my thoughts. This isn't what I want to be thinking about right now. I pour myself a coffee in a to-go mug and get one ready for Rob as well. After checking the time, I yell towards his room to see if he's ready. A few minutes later Rob arrives, ready to leave for school.

I toss him the keys to my Mustang. "You drive today, I got to do some shit on my phone before class."

"Oh, like text your girlfriend." Rob teases as I reach over and punch him in the arm. "Don't you know you have to wait for three days to text a chick?"

"Shut up, you don't know what you are talking about." I mutter as Rob locks the door behind us.

"Okay, but you seem pretty pussy whipped for a guy who has only been out on one date with this girl." Rob replies as we make our way down the three flights of stairs to the parking lot to my car.

Throwing my bag in the back, I hop into the passenger seat and send a text to Hollynd. We don't have class together today, but I need to see her. After last night, I think I'm going to need to see her more than I've ever needed to see anyone before. *What's happening to me?*

Chapter 5

Hollynd

It's already past twelve-thirty and I'm rushing to get over to the south wing food court to meet Landry. He had text me this morning asking if I would meet him for lunch. However, my bio partner and I had gotten held up waiting to ask the professor some questions about our current lab assignment, so now I'm moving at a pace across the campus lawn that's somewhere between a fast walk and a jog.

When I arrive at the food court, it's bustling with students on their lunch break. The air is filled with the scent of fried food from the eateries that line each side of the food court. The buzz of conversation is all I can hear as I scan the crowd in search of Landry. I see him leaning up against the wall near the small sandwich stand, his head down as he studies the screen of his phone.

Wearing a dark blue T-shirt that's fitted to show his broad chest and black board shorts, I notice a tattoo running down the length of his left leg. I never had a chance to see it last night. It was too dark, and I never got him that undressed. I make a mental note to inspect that tattoo the next time we're alone.

As I walk towards Landry, I'm still trying to catch my breath. I must look like a wreck with my backpack slung over my shoulder, my ponytail falling out and hair in my face after my brisk walk. I'm wearing a pair of tight light blue jeans and an olive-green Creston College hoodie.

"I'm sorry I'm late, and that I'm such a mess." I blurt out when I get close enough for Landry to hear me.

Immediately, his eyes raise from his phone screen and meet mine. They seem to light up when our eyes meet, though I'm not sure why considering the state I'm in. Landry quickly tucks his phone into his back pocket and reaches up to the stray hairs around my face, brushing them away. Moving his hands back to my cheeks, Landry gently pulls my face to his and presses his warm lips to mine. I can feel my stomach flip with excitement.

After a moment, Landry pulls back. "I don't care that you're late, and trust me, you're not a mess. You're the most stunning person here."

Instantly, I blush as Landry slides his hands off my face.

"What do you want to eat?" I ask with a goofy grin.

"You pick, Cricket."

"Are you really going to call me that?" I say with the same silly smile that seems to be permanently plastered on my face.

Landry runs his hand over the small of my back. "Yes. I like it and I like you."

"Well, I'm glad you like me. I was worried I was a little too...forward last night," I strategically word it as to save myself the embarrassment of saying I basically threw myself at him.

Slowly Landry leans into my ear. "You mean when you made me pull over the car so you could climb on top of me and use me for your own pleasure?"

Heat crawls across my skin. "Yup, something like that."

"Baby, am I embarrassing you?" Landry's warm breath tickles my skin. "Reminding you of how you whimpered against my mouth while you grinded against me?"

I'm feeling flustered as the flops in my stomach are moving down towards my core. Landry's mouth is still against my ear, but now his hand has wrapped around my long ponytail.

"Okay, you have to stop," I whisper, only loud enough for him to hear.

"Do you regret it?" Landry asks, while still holding my ponytail firmly.

"No," I reply without hesitation. "Do you?"

"Hell no! But you're right. I have to stop before I drag you into a storage room somewhere."

I laugh. "My thoughts exactly. Come on, let's get some food."

I grab Landry's hand and start pulling him towards a pizza by the slice place. After we each grab a slice and a water, we head to an empty table near a giant window that faces the campus. It's a beautiful view with its combination of green grass, trees whose leaves are shades of yellow and orange in the fall sunshine. Not to mention the stone pathways that lead to an assortment of educational buildings that must be at least a hundred years old.

Before we sit down, I remove my hoodie, so I don't stain it with pizza sauce. I would like to pretend that I'm not a klutz, but my many ruined shirts would prove otherwise. I have a light lilac shirt on underneath that rises, baring my stomach, as I pull my hoodie over my head.

"What are you doing this weekend?" Landry's question interrupts my struggle with my shirt.

"Nothing I don't think." I say with a huff as I finally sit down in the seat across from him.

"Will you come with me to a party?" Landry takes a bite of his lunch.

"Sure, who's party?"

"It's at my cousin Eddie's place." Landry continues to eat his pizza and I can't help but stare at his lips while he chews.

"Oh, meeting the family already. Are you sure about that?" I smile as I take a bite from my slice of pizza.

Landry laughs and shakes his head, "Oh, it gets worse because we're going with my brother Rob. Honestly, I'm more worried about you meeting them."

"Why?"

"Well, not Rob, he's great. But Eddie can be a little... let's say wild. But once you get past his wild side, he's actually a pretty good guy. He's had my back more than once."

"Well, I'm sure it will be great." I smile as I take another big bite out of my pepperoni pizza. So far, my shirt remains sauce free.

Landry grabs his phone out of his pocket to check the time.

"Shit, babe, I gotta run. I have a meeting with my professor right away."

I wave him off. "Yes, go. You don't want to be late."

Landry gathers up his garbage and walks it to a nearby garbage can to drop it in. He arrives back at our table and grabs his bag.

"Do you have any friends that you want to ask to come with us? So Rob doesn't feel like a third wheel."

"I could ask my friend, Sydney. She's always up for a party."

"Perfect, so now I can ditch Rob with Sydney and keep you all to myself," Landry winks and leans over to kiss me softly on the lips even though they're covered in grease.

I laugh. "Who says Syd and I aren't going to ditch you two?"

Landry moves his lips to my collarbone and gently kisses his way up my neck. It feels better than it should, considering we're in public.

"If I were to bet, I would say your perky nipples are telling me that you have no intention of ditching me." Landry whispers and then kisses the top of my head and walks away.

I look down at my very alert and betraying breasts pushing against my thin shirt material. *Son of a bitch.*

Chapter 6

Hollynd

The rest of the week flies by and before I know it, it's Saturday night. Sydney and I are on our way to Landry and Rob's apartment to meet up with them for a drink before we go to Landry's cousin's party. I must admit, I'm nervous about meeting Landry's brother.

Landry and I haven't been seeing each other for very long, less than a week, but it feels like it has been much longer than that. The feelings I'm developing for him, especially this quickly, are terrifying.

It's not like Landry is my first boyfriend. I dated a few guys throughout high school and a bit afterwards, including a long-term relationship with Andrew, which lasted for over a year. While I loved Andrew, I never felt the same feelings for him as what I'm feeling for Landry, right now. This is something almost indescribable. *God, I hope I don't get crushed by this.*

By the time we arrive at Landry's apartment, I'm grateful to have a friend like Sydney by my side to help calm my nerves. Sydney is a bundle of positive energy and has never been one to turn down an invitation to a party. Tonight, she looks the part perfectly with a black mini skirt and a bright pink crop top. Sydney's bleach blonde hair is up in a tight bun, and she has silver hoops hanging from each ear. In comparison to my dark denim skinny jeans, white tank top, and grey faux-leather jacket, Sydney looks like a rock star.

When Landry arrives at the door to let us in, I'm left breathless as I scan over his body covered in a pair of fitted grey pants with a button-down black shirt. A couple of buttons are open at the neckline to show off the tops of his tattoos that creep up onto his neck. His black hair is laying to the side in a messy sexy way. Landry's earrings, lip ring, and a few rings on his fingers are all silver. I can only assume his nipple ring is also silver. I add another mental note to check that later along with his tattoos.

Sydney elbows me in the ribs to get my attention. "Hey princess, stop drooling so you can introduce me."

Blushing, I introduce Landry and Sydney as we make our way out of the entryway. As we walk past the kitchen to the living room, I can see a hallway further on down where the bedrooms are bathroom must be. It's a simple apartment, but it's cozy.

Sydney and I take a seat on the dark brown leather sofa that faces a giant flat screen TV. Adjacent from us is a matching leather chair in front of a black coffee table. The walls are bare and there are no decorative touches anywhere to been seen. Clearly these men aren't interested in home décor.

"Can I get you ladies a drink?" Landry offers while gesturing towards the kitchen.

"Yes, please. I'll take a beer," Sydney smiles.

"Sure, me too." I reply. "Where's your brother?"

"Oh, he's still getting ready. He's kind of high maintenance," Landry jokes.

"I heard that," a voice echoes out from the hallway.

Landry leaves for the kitchen to get the beer while Sydney leans over to me.

"Your man is crazy hot!"

"Oh my God, I know!" I whisper.

Landry interrupts us. "Crick, can you come help me carry these drinks?"

Sydney drops a questioning look at me. "Crick?"

I smile with a wink and mouth the words, "My nickname."

Sydney rolls her eyes; she's never been a fan of the mushy stuff.

I walk to the kitchen, which is hidden by a wall from the living room, to see Landry simply leaning against the counter with no drinks in his hands.

"You don't need help," I smirk while placing my hands on my hips.

"No, but I need something." Landry reaches out towards me, grabbing my forearm, pulling me closer to him.

While I'm wrapped in his arms, I drape my hands around the back of Landry's neck. Being that he's six-three and I'm five-five, I have to stretch.

Landry looks in my eyes while his hands make their way up my back, underneath my jacket.

"You look beautiful," Landry compliments me.

"You're not too bad yourself," I respond.

Landry presses his lips into mine. I feel his tongue nudging its way past my lips in search of mine. Warm breath surrounds my mouth as my hands tighten their grip on the back of Landry's head.

We cut our moment short when Sydney yells from the living room. "Hey, you two, I can practically hear the moans from here. At least bring me my beer before you tear each other's clothes off."

Landry pulls away with a smile. "She's pretty subtle, hey?"

I roll my eyes as I step away from Landry's hard body and grab two beers off the counter. Landry gets the other two and follows me back into the living room.

As we enter, Rob appears from the hallway. Despite being brothers, Rob and Landry don't look that much alike. Rob is shorter and unlike Landry's very dark almost black hair, Rob's is a light brown.

"Rob, this is Hollynd and Sydney." Landry uses his beer bottle to gesture at each of us.

Reaching over to shake hands, Rob offers me a sweet smile. I like him already.

"So, this is Hollynd? I've heard so much about you." Rob takes a sip out of his bottle with a smirk. I blush while offering a slight smile of confusion.

Sydney, never missing a moment to razz someone cuts in. "Oh, you mean you heard all about the adventures of the parked Mustang, too?"

"Sydney!" I screech with sheer embarrassment.

Rob and Landry both release ripples of laughter that shake their bodies.

Wrapping his arms around me, Landry pulls me in for a tight hug still vibrating with laughter.

"Putting out on the first date and doing a little kiss and tell? Sounds like I might have my hands full with you." Landry growls quietly in my ear.

"Yeah," I smirk back. "Think you can handle it?"

Grabbing the hair on the back of my head, my entire body begins to vibrate with lustful anticipation. I have forgotten all about the two other people literally a few feet away from us as my body presses harder into Landry's body. I'm not sure if Landry has forgotten our audience or not, but honestly, I don't think he cares, anyway.

"You're a lot of talk for someone who's going to be on her knees before the end of the night." Landry's voice vibrates in my ear.

"Is that a threat?"

Pressing his lips against my ear and flicking my ear lobe lightly with his tongue. "That's a promise, Cricket." My legs wobble slightly.

"Seriously, you two, stop that!" Sydney bursts out again. "My God, you're going to either make me sick or horny."

While we all laugh at Sydney's comment, Rob's cell phone beeps, alerting him to an incoming text. After reading it silently, Rob hands the phone to Landry, allowing him to read it. He lets me out of his embrace to take the phone from Rob. Landry also reads the text in silence before he hands the phone back to his brother. I notice Landry's entire body tense up as waves of coldness radiate from him.

"Is everything okay?" I ask hesitantly at the two brothers, who are now eyeing each other.

Even Sydney, who always has something to say, must also feel the tension in the room because she sits back quietly while she nurses her beer.

Landry's face bears no emotion whatsoever. "We have to stop by my father's house on the way to the party."

"Okay," I reply nervously. Something feels off about this.

Breaking from his stare with his brother, Landry forces a small smile and turns back to me. "You don't have to meet him tonight, Crick. You and Sydney can just wait in the car. We won't be long."

"Okay," I weakly smile back.

While I'm relieved not to be meeting another family member tonight, I'm curious why stopping at his father's house was causing such turmoil in our plans. There's now a heaviness in the air.

Chapter 7

Landry

Stopping by my father's house is the last thing I want to do, especially tonight with Hollynd. I want to keep the worst and best thing in my life separate for as long as possible. I have been ignoring my father's texts all day. I'm in no mood to deal with his bullshit. Obviously, my father is aware that I'm ignoring him, hence the text to Rob to summon me over to his house. My father knows my weakness, and he never hesitates to use it.

David Hayles, my father, is not a good man. He's a founding partner of the law firm WALLS and HAYLES and he's an extremely successful defense attorney. As a lawyer, my father represents the worst of the worst; well the worst that can afford him, at least. He doesn't care if you are as guilty as Satan himself on a Sunday; he only cares that he wins and that his clients pay him abundantly.

For the first ten years of my life, I had gotten off lucky. Mostly, my father had ignored me. Being the first son with his second wife, his third son overall, I wasn't an important factor in his life. His two sons from his first marriage, Isaac and Joshua, are his pride and joy. Isaac is twelve years older than me, and Josh is ten years older than me. Growing up without their mother, who had died from cancer, Isaac and Josh were groomed to be exactly like our father.

Today, they are both ruthless and successful lawyers working with our father. Their arrogance wafts from them and is as rancid as my father's. Overall, though, I can ignore my older brothers in my day-to-day life. They have little use for me, and I have absolutely no use for them. Our relationship today is much like our relationship growing up – nonexistent – and none of us has ever lost sleep over it.

My father kicked my mother out when I was ten years old after she was caught sleeping with another man. This wasn't the first time my mother had been unfaithful. It was, however the first time she was caught with a rival lawyer.

My mother left quietly and made no attempt to take myself or Rob with her, but I know she had her reasons. As the years passed by, she never came back to see us, and we never went to see her. She was just gone. Mom would send us gifts on our birthdays and Christmas, so at the very least I knew she wasn't dead. I also knew she was living in Florida because our bullshit gifts usually were some sort of Florida tourist trinket. They were absolute garbage, but I've kept every single one.

After my mother left, my job had become to protect Rob. In fact, the last time I saw her before she left for Florida, she asked me to take care of Rob because I was all he had left. I didn't understand what she meant by that, but I would eventually. My mother knew the cruelty that my father carried with him. I didn't always know his meanness, but now I can't imagine him or my life without it.

It was after my mother left that my father went from ignoring me to berating me. I was nothing like my two older half-brothers, and my father never let me forget how much that disappointed him, with either his words or his fists. Eventually, I pushed everyone away. I looked for alternative forms of relief. Booze, drugs, and girls were easy to come by when you had a rich father and a broken moral compass.

Over the years, my father used a variety of tactics to get me to obey him. Using my closeness with Rob was his favourite source of control against me. It never surprised me when my father used Rob to get to me; he had been doing it for years.

As a child, Rob had always been softer and gentler than I was. He loved everyone, especially our mother. After she left, Rob seemed lost and starved for paternal attention. Rob did everything in his power to please my father. Like me, before our mother left, my father had mostly ignored Rob. Even after our mother left, my father continued to ignore Rob. Unless he needed to use him for something, then my father would use Rob's need for fatherly love for his own gains. Rob never seemed to notice. But I noticed. It was disgusting, and I hated my father even more for it.

We pull up to my father's house, which looks more like a mansion with its security gate driveway and thousands of square feet of lit windows shining at us from the parking area. *A way to show his worth, through the flaunting of his possessions.* This house is more than enough for a man who lives alone. After my mother, my father never remarried but paraded a variety of younger women in and out of his bed. Perhaps he needed the space for his inflated ego and arrogance? No matter the reason, I'm staring at this house and my stomach immediately knots.

Before getting out of the car, I turn to the backseat to Hollynd, where she's sitting with Sydney, giggling about over a YouTube video.

"We won't be long. Just wait here."

"Sure babe," Hollynd replies with her heart-melting smile as her eyes come up to meet mine.

Even in the darkness of the car, I can see her eyes glowing as the light seeps through the back window. I savor the moment and take a deep breath before turning back to face my father's house. I don't want to go in there. I want to stay here with this beautiful woman in my backseat. My father's house is so unloving and cold. Hollynd is the opposite of everything he is. She's what I *want*. She's what I *need*. I should probably be a better person and not drag her into my fucked-up life and let her go now. But I won't. I know this without a second thought, because I'm more of a selfish bastard than a saint. My best course of action is to keep these two areas separate for as long as I can, though I know when I exit this car, I will not return as the same person. Every moment I spend with my father, the more I lose my own light.

My oldest brother, Isaac, swings open the large white door before Rob or I have a chance to knock. Despite having different mothers, Isaac and I are undoubtedly brothers with the same dark hair and tall standing posture. Hell, we even have the same mole on our chin, though his is hidden under his stubble. Although it's Saturday, Isaac looks like he has been at work all day and is wearing a suit and tie. The only evidence that he's not still on the clock is that his tie is pulled loose, and he has a tumbler of scotch in his hand.

"It's about time you guys showed up," Isaac grunts.

"Piss off, Isaac." I push past him and smell the strong scent of his drink.

Rob lowers his head and follows in behind me. Rob's never been one for confrontation, and I admire him for that.

"Dad's waiting for you in the living room." Isaac instructs and follows us as we walk through the foyer.

The large house is silent on this Saturday evening. There are no staff here tonight. The house is cold and quiet.

I walk straight towards the living room. I want out of here as quickly as possible, not only because the longer I spend in this house, the more I can feel my anger growing, but also because Hollynd is waiting for me.

We enter the living room, which is a typical room designed by a man who wants to impress with his wealth. Rich brown leather furniture takes up most of the space, along with a giant oak armoire that is hiding a large flatscreen TV. With the scent of cigar smoke lingering in the air, I see my father sitting in a leather chair across the room.

Dressed similarly to Isaac, like he's been in the office all day, my father has yet to notice our arrival. While Isaac and I have some physical similarities, he is the spitting image of my father. Both are big men with dark features, although my father's hair is greyer than the dark brown it used to be.

I clear my throat when we enter the room to make sure we have his attention. Looking up from his iPad and over the top of his reading glasses, my father's glare burns into me.

"When I send you a text, Landry, I expect a reply in a timely manner."

"I was busy." I stare back with the same glare.

Glancing towards Rob and Isaac, who are still standing beside me, my father demands rather than asks, "Robert and Isaac, give your brother and me a moment."

Giving a slight nod, Rob and Isaac take their leave of the living room and head in the direction of the kitchen. It's not an uncommon request by my father to ask whoever's with us to take leave so he can unmask the monster that's lurking just below his shiny suit and expensive haircut.

Tossing his reading glasses onto the coffee table in front of him, my father rises from his leather chair and walks towards his bar. He pours himself another glass of scotch. I know there's no escaping this meeting, so I walk further into the living room to meet him at the bar. On a side table I notice the large vase of white lilies, and I wish I could smell them over the cigar smoke. My father always has fresh lilies in the house, though I have never known why.

"So, what do you want?" I lean against the bar facing my father.

"I'm going to be running for mayor." My father states before taking a drink from the crystal glass in his hand. "It won't be announced for a couple of months, but my advisors have told me that there can be no bad press before or after that time."

"Okay, what does this have to do with me?"

"I want to give you fair warning now. I will tolerate none of your shit, Landry. You will not take part in any of your past behavior. There will be no more calls from the cops telling me you're in the drunk tank, there will be no more fighting and assault charges I have to pay to get dropped, no more of anything from you. You will go to school, keep quiet, and keep your goddamn nose clean. Do you understand?"

"What's the matter, Dad? Worried your not so perfect family will be exposed? Did you tell Josh to make sure he keeps his dick in his pants? Or warn Isaac to stop his massive gambling trips to Vegas?"

"Josh and Isaac are upstanding men. They work hard and are making something of themselves. I wish I could say the same for you. Spending all your time with drunken losers and nobodies. It's no wonder you're such failure considering the company you keep."

"My nobody friends are better than you'll ever be, even if you do become mayor. Your money and power are nothing," I growl, as my rage grows deeper.

"You have always been my biggest disappointment. I've worked hard to build this life for myself, and I will not let your stupidity ruin any of it. I will be running for mayor, and you will fall in line." The rage in his voice echoes throughout the room.

"And if I decide not to play your game?" I ask in an uncaring tone.

Raising his hand swiftly while crashing his glass down on the bar's wooden top, my father grabs the back of my neck with enough force that I think there may be bruises tomorrow. I refuse to let myself wince in pain.

"Listen, I'm done with your attitude and blatant disrespect. You're my son, and you will behave accordingly. You will do this for me and for your brother."

And there it is, my father's trump card. The blackmail he has held over me for years. The secret my mother told me when she asked me to take care of Rob. It's all I can do to keep the vile in my stomach from rising.

I still don't know how my father found out that Rob wasn't his biological son, and I don't know how he found out that I knew this secret too. But once he found out I knew, he had his weapon to use against me for the rest of my life. I still don't know who Rob's real father is, and my mother never told me. But honestly, it doesn't matter. I love Rob more than anyone else in my family. My father knows this, and he uses this against me every chance he gets.

After our mother left, Rob relied on my father for so much support. He thought the sun rose and set upon the man he thought was his father. It would kill him to know the truth and I knew that my father would take everything away from Rob out of spite towards me and my mother.

To be honest, Rob is the best one of David Hayles' sons. Of course, that is probably because he has none of David Hayles' genetics.

Dropping my head, I know my father is right. I would do anything to protect my brother. Defeat washes through my veins. I hate these feelings. Feelings of being trapped by this man, feelings of never being good enough for him, feelings of being unloved.

Pulling away from my father's firm grasp, I back away. At least there is a bit of comfort knowing he didn't backhand me this time. I absolutely do not want to face Hollynd with a swollen cheek. It's going to be hard enough to hide my anger from her tonight.

"Fine," I grumble as I pull away. "Is that all?"

"For now." My father reaches back for his drink. "Also, there will be a lot of functions coming up that I expect you to attend."

I give a slight nod with my head still lowered. There's no need to reply, my father knows he's broken me again. I turn and head for the door.

"Rob!" I yell towards the kitchen.

Rob meets me in the entryway.

"Let's go," I growl without making eye contact.

"Okay, let me say goodbye to Dad first."

I can't help but grind my teeth as Rob jogs towards the living room. I take a moment to lean against the wall and take a breather. To gain control of my anger, I close my eyes for a moment and breathe in through the nose and out through the mouth—the way a former counselor taught me to do after one of my fights in high school. Aside from being suspended for two weeks, I had to attend mandatory counseling sessions. Years later and I'm still trying to breathe away my anger. After a few minutes, Rob arrives back at the door, ready to leave.

Chapter 8

Hollynd

Sydney and I are fixated with our YouTube videos when the boys arrive back at the car. Like before, Landry gets into the driver's seat and Rob sits in the passenger seat. But something has changed, something feels off. There's a tension in the air that wasn't there before. I don't know what happened in the house, but I know it must have been unpleasant. I'm getting an unsettled feeling in the pit of my stomach.

Sydney seems to notice none of this. "Are you guys ready to go to the party now or what?"

Landry remains in his stoic silence, but Rob offers a response, "Yes, definitely."

Landry puts the car into gear, and we drive off towards Eddie's house for his house party. The entire trip only lasts about fifteen minutes, but with the thickness in the air, I feel like it lasts much longer.

After we arrive at Eddie's house, which is an older mid-century home, Rob and Sydney head straight inside while Landry and I hang back outside the car for a moment.

Running my hand down the length of his arm I ask, "Are you okay?"

Landry doesn't answer right away. He leans back on the car while his fingers press against the bridge of his nose.

"My father's an asshole."

"What happened?"

"I don't want to talk about it." Landry's eyes are pressed tight together.

"Is there anything I can do to help?" I offer.

Landry remains silent for a moment. I'm not sure what he's contemplating, but I feel like it's somewhere between pushing me away or pulling me in. I can tell he's hurting, and I want to help, but I have no idea what to do.

Finally, he grabs my hand and pulls it up to his lips and kisses it softly. "No, Cricket. Let's just go inside and have some fun, okay?"

"Sure." I'm trying to remain cool, but for some reason, I have a gnawing feeling of doubt inside me that tonight is going to be anything but fun. Landry seems to teeter on the edge of something right now.

We enter Eddie's house to the sound of Machine Gun Kelly playing in the background. There are more people here than I expected there to be, but it doesn't take us long to find Rob, Sydney, and Eddie all gathered in the kitchen where the drinks are being poured.

"Landry, it's about time you show your ugly face here," the man I assume is Eddie, yells as we enter the kitchen.

Eddie is a skinny, six-foot-tall man, with platinum blond hair that's long on the top but shaved on the sides. He looks like he could be a runway model with his light blue eyes and sexy smirk. Wearing a sleeveless white shirt and torn black jeans, I can see Eddie has tattoo sleeves covering both his arms, as well as his neck.

Landry goes over to the blond male model and gives him one of those half hug, half handshake thing that guys do. I patiently wait on the other side of the counter for Landry to finish greeting his cousin.

Landry turns back and motions for me to come over to where he and Eddie are standing. Wrapping his arm around my waist, Landry introduces me. "Eddie, this is my girlfriend, Hollynd. Hollynd, this is Eddie."

Eddie stretches out his hand towards me. "Hollynd, it's fantastic to meet you. Can I get you two a drink?"

"Yes," Landry answers for both of us. "What do you want, babe?"

"Just a beer is fine," I say to Eddie.

"You got tequila?" Landry asks Eddie.

"Of course, I do," Eddie replies.

"Line them up," Landry says while he lets go of my waist and walks towards Eddie who's putting out a line of shot glasses.

Looking at Landry, Eddie mumbles, "Is this the first line of many tonight?"

Landry nods and Eddie slaps Landry's back. "Yes, sir."

I don't really know what they are talking about, but that unsettled feeling I had earlier in my stomach by the car has grown tenfold. For a moment, I contemplate leaving. Something is not right with him since we left his father's house, but even though we have only been together for a short time, I feel this overwhelming urge to stay with him. Aside from the anger he's radiating, I can also feel pain. Landry is in pain, and how can I leave him in that place?

It seems like Eddie has forgotten about my beer, so I move to the other side of the kitchen, where Sydney and Rob are standing. They are watching Eddie and Landry line up their shot glasses.

Eddie looks up at the three of us. "You guys in?"

We all reply with a nod and walk up to the counter where the glasses are lined up in a row. I stand beside Landry and ask, "Are there any lemons?"

Reaching behind him, Eddie grabs a bowl of sliced lemons and hands them to me. "Here you go, darling."

"Thanks," I reply as I set the bowl down in front of me.

Sydney takes it upon herself to grab the first shot, holding it up. "Cheers!"

We all follow suit and shoot back our drinks.

The taste of the tequila burns my throat and I quickly reach for a lemon. However, before I can grab one, Landry's hand shoots out and takes the bowl for himself. He selects a lemon wedge from the top of the bowl and brings it to my mouth, slowly rubbing the bitter juice across my lips. My tongue instantly darts out to lich the flavor I'm looking for to chase the flavor of the tequila, which is still burning.

When I try to grab the lemon wedge with my teeth out of Landry's grasp, he pulls it away with force and sticks it in his own mouth, sucking the juice out of it. I can't tell if he is trying to tease me or if he is being mean to me. His eyes give away nothing.

I give Landry a shove on his hard shoulder, his body doesn't even budge. Landry pulls the lemon out of his mouth and quickly grabs my waist and pulls my entire body into his, while his other hand pulls the back of my head until our lips meet. He tastes like lemon, my lemon. Landry's mouth is pressing hard against mine and I press as equally hard in return. I'm not sure if we are flirting or fighting. Landry's on edge, I can feel it in his firm grasp around my neck and the hard pressure of his lips.

After we finish our shots, we go into the living room and sit on the worn black pleather couch. Sydney sits on the other side of me as Rob and Eddie sit at nearby chairs. There are other people, all of whom I don't know, around the living room engrossed in their own conversations.

The small group of us visit and laugh together as the party continues. Rob and Eddie share stories of Landry as a kid that have me belly laughing while Landry only offers a slight grin. Something is definitely off with him.

After a bit, Eddie nods his head up at Landry. "Landry, you good?"

Landry takes the final drink of his beer before setting the bottle on the table in front of the couch.

"Yep," Landry replies and stands at the same time Eddie stands. Landry leans down and kisses the top of my head. "I'll be right back, Crick."

"Okay," I reply, unsure where Landry and Eddie are going, but I have an anxious feeling about it.

Landry and Eddie head towards a hallway leading into what I assume are bedrooms. I turn back to Sydney and Rob. Rob's eyes were also following his brother and cousin as they walk down the hallway. When he looks back to the remaining members of our group, Rob's eyes meet mine and there seems to be a sadness in them. A sadness I didn't see earlier in the night. Giving me a weak smile, I feel even less comfortable with Landry's absence.

What the hell is going on?

Chapter 9

Landry

I follow Eddie down the hallway, keeping my head down, staring at the brown carpet underneath my footsteps. Guilt is plaguing my insides for leaving Hollynd behind in the living room so I can sneak off to some bedroom in hopes of easing my demons. I don't look back towards Hollynd or Rob because the thought of them seeing me right now is more than I can take. I just need a little help to get through the rest of the night and take my mind off my father, and Eddie always has the best answers for my problems.

We enter a small bedroom that Eddie uses as a spare room from time to time. There's not much furniture in the dimly lit room with yellowed walls and black curtains over the window. A twin-sized bed is in the corner, heaped with unfolded blankets. There's also a small round table in the opposite corner with four folding chairs placed around it. That's where we head immediately upon entering the room.

In no time, Eddie produces a glass vial from his pocket and twists off the black cap. Slowly, he taps out enough white powder on the table that will make at least six lines of relief. While Eddie takes his time cutting the powder, I pull a five-dollar bill from my pocket and roll it tightly.

This is not the first time Eddie and I have found ourselves around this tiny table, ready to partake in whatever substance is available to get our mind off whatever we were running from. For me, it has always been my father. Taking drugs is not an everyday habit for me, but I always felt it pull me in when my father and I had gone a round or two.

When we were younger, I would come over to Eddie's house to escape the wrath of my father when he was on one of his tirades. Eddie and I would sit in his backyard, smoke a joint, and sit in comfortable silence. Eddie's parents were never around, so he had free rein to do just about whatever he wanted, and he did just that.

The first time I did cocaine with Eddie was when we were both seventeen. It was a Friday night, which was also the same night my father came home drunk after losing an enormous case. That was the first time my father beat the shit out of me. Not just a backhand to the cheek or hard grab by the scruff of my neck. I mean, really beat the shit out of me. I didn't know that after you've had a couple of fists pounded against your face at the hands of someone who you thought loved you, that a numbness would settle throughout your entire body. It does.

After my father left the room where I lay bleeding from my mouth and nose on the floor, I took a few moments to think about all the ways I would kill my father if given the opportunity. Admittedly, I took a liking to the idea of stabbing him in the throat the best.

It took some time to regain my breath before I left the house. I went straight to Eddie's house, looking for an escape. The stronger, the better.

For a drug dealer and an addict, Eddie was reliable. While his coping methods weren't always the most ideal way, they worked for me the first time, and have been working for me ever since. I've always felt that there were few people I could trust, but Eddie has never failed me. Loyalty through narcotics probably sounds insane, but hell, so does the thought of a man beating the shit out of his son, so what do I know?

By the time I finish rolling my money, Eddie gestures at the supply laid out on the table. "Be my guest."

Before I lean down over the table, I take a quick moment to squash my guilt deeper inside myself. It's hard to convince yourself that you're good enough for a woman like Hollynd when you're about to snort a line of coke while she's waiting for you in a stranger's living room.

Yet I plunge in and inhale every single speck of powder I can off that dirty brown table. *I'm a waste of flesh.*

After I pull back, Eddie takes his turn, and we continue this trend until the tabletop becomes void of powder. Eddie and I both take a moment to allow the substance to settle into our system before he breaks the silence in the room.

"Do you want to talk about your dad?" Eddie tips his head back.

"No." I reply as I lick the tips of my fingers to dab up any remaining traces of coke left behind on the table, just in case.

"Okay, do you want to talk about the hot piece of ass you brought with you? Hollynd." Eddie emphasizes the D sound at the end of her name.

"First, don't talk about her like that. Second, yeah, she's pretty fucking hot." I laugh while I use the back of my hand to wipe my nose.

Anyone else but Eddie talking about my girl like that would probably get a punch to the throat. I close my eyes and let the buzzing take over.

Chapter 10

Hollynd

Landry's not gone for long, maybe twenty minutes at most. I hear him and Eddie coming down the hallway. They are laughing loudly about something; I don't know what. When they arrive back to the living room, Landry quickly pulls me up off the couch and takes my spot while sitting me on top of him. Immediately, he's nuzzling his face into my neck and holding me with a tightness that's almost unbearable.

I wiggle myself free enough from his large arms so I can turn to face him. When our eyes make contact, I can see a change in them. They're brighter, more aware, and rounder. I place my hand on his left pec to feel his pulse, which is easy to find since it feels like it's going about a million beats a minute. *Oh my God, is he high?*

"Landry, what's wrong with you?" I ask, though I already know.

I'm not an idiot; I've been to enough parties to know what a person looks like when they are high, though I have never partaken in any drugs myself. Except that one time I smoked a joint with some high school friends, which left me in a dizzying haze of paranoia and not at all "chill" like they swore I would feel. But this wasn't a high that came from a little pot. This was something stronger.

"Nothing is wrong, baby. I just missed you, that's all," Landry mumbles as he grabs my jaw and pulls it towards him.

He kisses me with a stronger force than he had earlier in the night. It's more urgent, more desperate. Eventually, Landry's mouth moves off mine and makes its way down my neck.

I turn to look at Sydney for support, but she's currently making eyes at Eddie, who's leaning against the opposite wall, gesturing her to come over to him.

I turn my gaze towards Rob. Surely, he'll know what the hell is going on. Rob meets my eyes but looks away quickly. He's as uncomfortable as I am at this moment.

As time passes, Landry and Eddie are having the best of time. The jokes and laughter are ramped. Sydney is leaning on the wall next to Eddie, having a great time, without a care in the world. Sometimes I wished I could be more like her, more carefree. But I'm not that girl, I can only feel my stress rising.

Sensing my increasing discomfort as the evening unfolds, Rob finally comes to my rescue. "Landry, maybe we should just head home, yeah?"

"What? Really?"

By this time, Sydney and Eddie have headed down the hallway towards Eddie's bedroom leaving Landry, Rob, and I alone.

"Yeah man, the party's clearing out, anyway." Rob gestures to the room.

"You're not ready to go, right Crick?" Landry asks me.

"I think we should." I encourage Landry.

"Come on, baby, let's stay." Landry kisses my neck and grasp my backside eagerly.

"Landry, there are people watching us."

"I don't care. I just need you, Cricket. Right now." Landry moves his mouth from my thoroughly kissed neck up to my lips.

"Babe, I need you too, but this is not the place to do this. Let's go home."

"Will you stay with me tonight?" Landry pulls away from my lips and looks at me.

Despite knowing that Landry isn't in his right mind, with the mixture of beer, tequila, and whatever else he may have taken tonight, he's looking at me with a combination of hope and shame in his eyes.

I should feel furious with him, not only for ditching me, but for ditching me to go get high. But it's not fury I'm feeling, it's fear. I'm afraid of the drugs. I'm afraid of the man Landry is when he's on them. I'm afraid that I *love* him just the same, either way.

"Of course," I whisper while reaching up to move the hanging hair from his forehead. Relief flashes quickly across Landry's eyes before he kisses me again.

Rob, Landry, and I stand outside Eddie's house near Landry's car, which is staying here for the night, to wait for our Uber. Landry's arms are draped over my shoulders, wrapping my body in the warmth of his arms. I close my eyes and inhale the cool night air.

My eyes break open when I hear a car arriving a short distance from the three of us. It's not our Uber as I was hoping it was. The two people stepping out of the old green car are unfamiliar to me, one man and one woman.

"Hey Landry, looks like you found yourself a new little plaything." The woman with bright red hair and a tiny black dress yells in our direction.

"Shut up, Mel." Landry yells in response, letting me out of his embrace.

"Landry, you're such a piece of shit." The man with the red headed woman roars in our direction. He's a large man with a shiny bald head that bounces an orange glow from the streetlight overhead.

I turn my attention to Rob. "Who are these people?"

"Just some local junkies who buy drugs from Eddie. Landry used to party with them. But by the sound of it they don't seem to get along so well anymore."

"Huh, you think?" I reply sarcastically.

"You got a problem with me, Brett?" Landry says as he approaches the man.

"Yeah, you stupid asshole. You owe me money."

"I don't owe you shit." Landry and the bald guy are now face to face.

"You hit my car when you were pissed, so the way I see it is you can either pay for the damage or maybe..." The bald guy looks over Landry's shoulder in my direction. "Or maybe I can just take it out of that piece of ass you have waiting over there?"

Landry snaps. His fist swings back and connects to the man's nose with a cracking impact. As the bald guy stumbles back, Landry takes another swing, which also connects with the guy's face. Rob runs past me in a rush and grabs Landry's shoulders, pulling him back from the guy.

"Fuck, Landry!" I can hear Rob yell at his brother. "Why do you always have to cause shit?"

Meanwhile, the redhead is helping the bald guy up from the ground while she's yelling and swearing at Landry.

Thankfully the Uber that Rob had called arrives at this moment. Rob hauls Landry over to the backseat as I open the door for him. Landry's holding his hand up and I can tell it's already starting to swell. What a mess this evening has turned into.

Rob takes the front seat of the Uber car as I crawl into the backseat beside Landry. With his uninjured hand, Landry tries to tug me over to his side of the car. Instead, I angle my body so that my back is mostly on my side of the car and I lean against the closed door.

"Come here," I say to Landry, who leans his body into mine.

I wrap both my arms around his body, as he lays back into my embrace. The embrace is somewhere between that of a lover and caregiver, and by far the most intimate hold I've ever felt with anyone. The position makes seatbelts impossible. With my one free hand, I send Sydney a quick text to tell her we left Eddie's house.

Landry's head rests on my shoulder. His swollen hand lies on his chest. I reach my hand up to his left side like I did earlier. His heart rate's still high. This makes my heart rate elevate and my entire body tense up. Icy fear runs through my entire body and memories flood my mind.

"My father is on the floor.... I think it's a heart attack or something.... Please send help.... Yes, he is still breathing. ...I can feel his pulse, it's fast.... Please, just send someone.... I'm all alone.... I don't know what to do."

I try to push this voice, my voice, out of my head. Reminding myself that this is not the same thing. Landry is going to be fine. He's just high. *Did I just minimize being high?*

I distract myself by nuzzling my face into the top of Landry's head. His hair smells like shampoo, like a concoction of coconut and lime. It's comforting because it smells like the night we spent in his Mustang. How was that just a few nights ago? I feel like I have known Landry for years. *This is crazy. I'm crazy.* I stroke Landry's hair the rest of the way to his apartment, trying to stop myself from falling deeper into this man. I'm failing.

The slowing of the car interrupts my thoughts as it pulls up to Landry and Rob's apartment building. I tap Landry's shoulder to let him know we're at his place. He pulls himself off my body and I instantly stretch out my cramped muscles. Landry's not a small man and I feel his weight through my entire body.

After getting out of the car, Landry gives me his good hand to help me out of the same back passenger door. Once I land my feet on the ground and stand up, the chilly night air hits my face with force. It smells like there's snow in the air.

The three of us head upstairs to the apartment. Rob goes straight into the kitchen while Landry's pulling me by the hand, still holding it tight from the moment we got out of the car and pulls me into his bedroom.

It's a decent size bedroom. Probably the master bedroom between the two that are in the apartment. There's a queen-sized bed covered with a black comforter and a tall black dresser which holds a TV on top of it. The walls are mostly bare, as are the nightstands on each side of the bed, except for a small lamp and an alarm clock.

Landry shuts the door behind him and pulls me to the bed, where we both fall onto the soft surface. Facing each other, we kiss softly as Landry caresses my hair. When we pull apart, I see a sadness in his eyes that wasn't there before. Perhaps the drugs helped to hide it. But I can see it now and there's no doubt in my mind that Landry's pulsating with turmoil.

"I'm sorry, Cricket." Landry bows his head.

"For what?" I ask as I run my hand up his arm, careful not to touch his bruising hand.

"I screwed up. I'm a screwup."

I try to smile with some sort of reassurance. "No, you're not."

"I am." Landry's gaze shifts upwards to meet mine. "You should leave me, but I know I won't let you go. I'm a selfish person."

For the next few moments, we stare at each other.

Silence.

"Let's go to bed, Landry."

And that's exactly what we do. No more kisses, no more words. Not tonight. We strip down to our underwear and crawl under the covers. Our bodies wrap together tightly, holding on to the *hope* that we are perfect, trying to force away the *fear* that we will unravel.

I wake up with a slight pain as I try to swallow through the dryness of my throat. I look at the clock, and see that it's five-thirty in the morning. Landry's still sound asleep. After his cocktail of drugs and alcohol last night, I expect him to sleep for a while. I'm exhausted and I'm desperate for my bed. I can see his mangled hand and wince at the sight of it. It's purple and puffy. We should've put ice on it last night. I hope it's not broken.

Slowly, I crawl out of bed and slip back into my clothes from last night, which are in a crumpled pile on the floor. I tiptoe to the bedroom door and slip through to the hallway. I walk softly through the apartment and go straight to the door leading out. I'm sliding on my grey jacket when I hear a door creak open from the hallway. I look up to see Rob walking towards me, still looking half asleep with his tousled brown hair and flannel pajama pants hanging low off his waist and his white shirt is wrinkled.

When Rob approaches me, I apologize. "I'm sorry. Did I wake you up?"

"It's okay. I wanted to talk to you before you go about Landry's little meeting with Eddie last night," Rob begins. "Sometimes Landry doesn't make the best choices. But he's not like a junkie or anything, Hollynd. I just wanted you to know that."

I can see the love for his brother in Rob's eyes. He's worried about Landry.

"What was he on?" I ask because I'm still not sure.

"I assume coke. That's his and Eddie's usual choice. Sometimes it's only pot, but since we had just left our father's house, I'm sure it was coke."

"So, how often does he do this?" I ask as I lean back on the entryway doorframe.

"Honestly, not that much. It usually happens when he's super stressed out or angry. But Hollynd, believe me, Landry's not a bad guy. I don't want you to be freaked out. I know he really likes you and I don't want you to run away because Landry's an idiot, once in a while."

"Is that what you think I'm doing right now, running?"

"Well, it's five thirty in the morning and you're sneaking out of here, so yeah."

"How bad is it between Landry and your father?"

Rob lets out a breath of air. Now he's the one running his hands through his hair.

"Well, it's not great. My father's not an easy man to get along with, or to please. I mostly try to stay out of his way, but Landry has never been able to do that. He's so goddamn bullheaded sometimes, and he can't help but poke the bear, if you know what I mean? Ever since we were kids, Landry has always challenged my father." Rob takes a pause, like he's trying to choose his words carefully. "I know more than he thinks I know, so please don't go and tell him I told you this, but Landry isn't as tough as he likes to let on. Things haven't always been easy for him. He's a good guy, and I've seen him with girls before, Landry's different with you."

With that, I nod my head and turn to open the door. I'm too tired to think right now. That was a lot of information to take in this early in the morning, especially when I have a hangover headache and lack of sleep. I'll worry about Landry later. For now I need to go home and sleep before rest eludes me with its games it likes to play with me.

Chapter 11

Landry

I pry my eyes open long enough to look at the time on the clock, it's just after eleven in the morning. I close them again and reach for Hollynd. I don't remember everything from last night, but I remember crawling into bed with her and wrapping our limbs together. But reaching my hand across the bed, I feel nothing but cold blankets. It makes me sit up in a panic. *Where is she?* I'm hoping she's out in the living room or kitchen, but I'm fearing that she's left me.

I get out of bed, only stopping briefly to toss on a pair of black sweatpants, and head straight for the door. My head is pounding almost as much as my hand, and I'm so thirsty. I need some ice and painkillers. *Ice later, Hollynd first.*

When I get to the living room, I see Rob on the couch playing a video game. He's in there alone.

"Good morning, sunshine. How's the hand?" Rob smiles in my direction.

"Shut up," I growl. "Where is Hollynd?"

"She left." Rob watches the TV intensely.

"When?"

"I think it was around five thirty."

"Five thirty in the morning? Did you see her?" Now, I'm yelling.

"Yeah. Bro, I think your little stunt with Eddie kind of freaked her out last night. Oh, and let's not forget your fight with Brett. Seriously, Landry, I don't think Hollynd's the type of girl who likes to party like that and I for one am grateful. I can't stand those druggy chicks you used to bring around."

I can feel the bile rising in my throat. I'm terrified that I have fucked this up. "What did she say?"

"Only that she wanted to go home to sleep and asked how often you partake in that kind of partying." Rob replies with eyes still focused solely on his game. I walk around the coffee table and stand directly in front of the TV.

I cross my arms, trying to control my anger. "And what did you say?"

"I told her that you don't do that shit often and that you're basically a good guy. Though if you don't get out of my way, I'm going to tell her you're an asshole." Rob's maneuvering his head, trying to see around me. "Why don't you call her and apologize. Tell her you won't do it again, which I think is a good idea. You don't want to become a skinny loser like Eddie."

I don't bother replying to Rob before I stomp out of the living room, back to my bedroom. I grab my cell from my nightstand and sit back on the bed. It rings four times before she answers.

"Hello?" Hollynd sounds like she's still sleeping.

"Where are you?" I demand.

"Landry, why are you yelling at me? It's still morning."

I inhale a deep breath trying to rein in my temper. "I'm not yelling at you Cricket, but I woke up without you here and I was worried."

"I'm sorry. I didn't sleep well, and I wanted to be in my own bed."

"I want to see you."

"Now?" Hollynd says through a yawn.

"Yes, we need to talk. Can I come over?"

There's a pause on the other end of the line before Hollynd finally replies, "Okay."

"I'll be there in thirty minutes." I hang up without a goodbye. I'm too focused on getting over there.

After a quick shower, I chug some water, take some painkillers, and use a shitload of nasal spray. I throw on a clean pair of grey sweatpants and a white T-shirt. I don't want to bother with my wet hair, so I put on a black baseball cap.

When I arrive at Hollynd's house, she answers the door quickly. I step into the house and look around to see if her mother is home.

"My mom's not here," Hollynd reads my thoughts as she closes the door behind me. "She goes to church on Sundays."

A freshly showered Hollynd offers me a small smile. Her wet hair is pulled tight into a braid that's running down the front of her shoulder. Like me, she's clearly hung over, wearing black yoga pants and a green hoodie. My girl looks tired, but still beautiful. My heartbeat quickens.

Hollynd turns to walk us out of the entryway, but I stop her by grabbing her hand. "Can I kiss you?"

She remains silent and her eyes dart around like she doesn't know where to look, but it's clear she doesn't want to look at me.

"Please?" *Now, I'm begging.*

"Okay," she agrees in a hushed tone.

I reach up and lightly run my fingers over her jawbone and nudge her chin up towards mine which brings my mouth towards hers.

I give her a soft kiss, trying to test the water on her reaction. I feel a slight sense of relief as I feel her lips press back against mine with more force than I first offered. We pull apart after a few seconds. Still holding hands, she pulls me in the direction of the kitchen. Hollynd pours two cups of coffee, adds creamer to both cups even though I take my coffee black – I don't say anything – and she motions for me to follow her up the stairs. The stairs lead up to a loft area which must be her bedroom. There's a double-sized bed under a small window that is covered in a yellow sheer curtain. On the adjacent wall there's a mirrored dresser covered in photo frames with smiling people I don't know.

Hollynd sits on the bed and crisscrosses her legs. I sit down beside her and take the extra cup of coffee from her hands.

"Thanks," I mumble while taking a sip.

"You're welcome."

I decided on the way over here that I was not going to pussyfoot around the reason I'm here.

"First let me say this, I like you; I mean, I really like you." This admission causes the corners of her mouth to curl up slightly as she sips from her coffee mug. "But I need to know how freaked out you were about last night. Rob said you were freaked out this morning."

"I'm not like a prude who's never been to a party with drugs before. I mean I've tried pot once, but I didn't like it. It's just not my thing. I was shocked that you did coke, you know. I think I was just surprised."

"It's not really a big deal for me," I try to justify my actions. "I only do it sometimes to blow off steam."

"Because of your dad?" Hollynd interrupts.

"Yeah," I adjust my eyes downwards towards the floor.

"Is he that bad?"

"Yeah."

"Do you want to talk about it?"

"Not really." I mumble, keeping my eyes firmly pointed to the floor.

"So, what about that bald guy from last night?" Hollynd's voice remains meek.

"Brett?" I turn my gaze back up to Hollynd. "Ugh, he's just some loser I used to party with."

"But you beat the shit out of him. I mean, look at your hand." I lift my bruised hand as Hollynd pulls it over to inspect the damage. "So, where do we go from here? You don't want to talk about your dad with me. I get it. We've only known each other for a few weeks."

"No, Crick. That's not it at all. I feel like I have known you forever, but I don't want that shitty part of my life in this wonderful part of my life."

"But what about the coke thing? Are you going to run and get high every time he upsets you? I don't know if I can deal with that, Landry. Hard drugs kind of scare me." Hollynd looks down with embarrassment. She shouldn't be embarrassed though; her vulnerability is adorable.

"I don't want to see you hurt or sick. Your heart was beating so fast last night. I could feel it through your chest, and I didn't like it." She's biting her bottom lip and her gaze stays on the same patch of floor I was just watching. "But I kind of get it for you, using something to numb the pain."

"What do you mean?" I ask, trying to meet her eyes, though she's refusing to lift them in my direction.

Taking a deep breath in, I can see Hollynd having an internal debate inside herself.

"It's okay, you can tell me." I encourage her.

"So, you know my dad died a couple of years ago, right?"

"Right."

"It was just him and I at home when it happened. My dad was in the kitchen, and I was in the living room when I heard glass breaking. I thought he probably dropped a dish or something. I asked if he was okay, but he didn't answer. When I went to see what was going on, I found him lying on the ground, surrounded by broken glass. He was breathing heavily and grabbing at his chest. I called 911, but other than that, I didn't know what to do. I couldn't help him. I just sat there on the phone like an idiot watching my dad die. I put my hand on his chest and I could feel his heart beating so fast and his mouth was gaping open, though his eyes were closed tight. I tried talking to him, but I was sobbing at that point." She reaches up to wipe a stray tear that had found its way down her cheek. "Anyway, the paramedics came, but it was too late. He died on the kitchen floor.

"After that, I was a wreck. I couldn't eat, I couldn't go to school, I couldn't function for weeks. The worst thing was I couldn't sleep. Every time I closed my eyes at night, I would see his face with the gaping mouth and closed eyes. I had insomnia so terrible that I thought I was losing my freaking mind. Mom didn't really notice because she was a mess herself. But Rachel noticed. So, she took me to the doctor, and he put me on some antidepressants and sleep meds. The thing is, with antidepressants they take a while to work, but the sleep meds worked right away. They would numb me. I was dead to the world, and I liked it. Sometimes I would take them in the afternoon if things were feeling too intense and then again at night. But I knew I couldn't do this for long because my sleeping pill prescription was going a lot faster than it should. So, I tried taking half a dose of my sleeping meds in the afternoon, but I would chase it with nighttime cough medicine." Hollynd's shaking her head and laughing lightly.

"I know, stupid, right? It wouldn't really put me into a deep sleep, but just sort of trance-like state. Maybe I slept, I don't know? But I didn't think about my dad, which is what I wanted.

After a couple of months, people kept telling me it was time to get over my dad's death and get back to normal. I had already missed a ton of school, plus I had lost like twenty pounds. People said they were 'concerned' about me, but I didn't want to just get over it, I mean, he was my dad for Christ's sake, and I couldn't save him.

"Rachel ended up taking charge and helping me out. Mom tried, but like I said, she had her own shit to deal with. I had to tell her all about my afternoon routine with the cough syrup and sleeping meds. Rachel set me up with a therapist to help me figure stuff out. They increased my antidepressants. I had to go to summer school, and I had to see a nutritionist to get my weight back up. Also, it turned out I slept better when someone was with me, so Rachel moved back in for a while and she would sleep with me every night. For being a pain in the ass most of the time, she's a great sister.

"The point of this entire story is I get where you are coming from, trying to numb yourself. I think I get you more than you realize. I want you to talk to me and show me the ugly stuff, too. I have tons of ugliness, as you can see."

Hollynd pauses and takes a sip of her coffee. She's still avoiding my eye contact.

"But I think the drug stuff with you just makes me feel out of control, Landry. I have trouble with that. I'm scared, you know?"

"I know what you mean, Cricket. Do you still have trouble sleeping or have to take pills?" I ask.

"Um, no. Sometimes I have trouble sleeping, but I mostly have a handle on it now. Well..." Hollynd's voice trails off. "Most of the time. I hope you don't think I'm a psycho head case now or something because I kinda-sorta like you." Hollynd's cheeks have a pink glow.

I reach over and set my coffee cup on the nearby dresser before taking Hollynd's coffee mug from her hand and setting it aside as well. I come back to her bed and sit on my knees facing her, placing my good hand on her thigh.

"You kinda-sorta like me?" I smirk.

"Oh, shut up," she swats my arm in embarrassment.

"Why are you blushing, Hollynd?" I tease.

"Because you are embarrassing me, Landry." Hollynd tries to hide a small smirk.

"I'll make you a deal. I will not do any hard drugs for a while and you kinda-sorta keep liking me."

"Are you going to keep liking me even if I'm the killjoy of fun?" Hollynd's eyes pull back up to meet mine.

"You're more fun than any drug in the world, Cricket. Thank you for telling me about your dad. You're so strong. I wish I knew you back then so I could have helped you through it."

"Me too," she whispers back.

I lean in closer to Hollynd and I can hear her breath rising.

"Can I tell you a secret?" I whisper, while moving my hand up to the nape of her neck. "I don't just like you, Hollynd. I think I kinda-sorta 'something else' you, which is a lot more than just liking, but I can't say it yet. It's too soon and I know you scare easily. So, I'm just going to have to show you how I feel instead of saying something to scare you off."

Hollynd's breaths become more rapid, and I can feel heat rising off her body.

"What time will your mom be home?" I ask, as I lower her back to the bed.

"Not until three or so."

"Good."

Hollynd's lying flat on her back with her legs stretched straight out in between my knees. I slowly place tiny kisses along her collarbone and up her neck, her skin is so soft and smells like vanilla. With her eyes closed, she takes a deep breath in before she licks her lips which are begging to be kissed, but before I give in to her, I have one more thing to mention.

"One more thing, Cricket. If you ever sneak out of my bed and out of my house in the middle of the night again, I will kinda-sorta make you pay for it. You won't be able to walk straight for a week, and you'll love it."

I hear a slight moan escape her lips while her chest rises underneath mine.

"Is that understood?" I confirm.

"Yeah, but technically it wasn't in the night, it was in the morning."

I cut her off by slamming my hardened pelvis into her mound and tightening my grip on the back of her neck. She moans louder this time, and I'm thankful that her mother's not home.

"Is that understood, Cricket?" I ask again in a deeper tone.

I can see a tiny smile escape from her lips, teasing me even further. I grab her earlobe between my front teeth and bite with enough force to cause her to gasp and buck her hips against mine.

"Yes, I understand." She pants her agreement.

"Good," I whisper as I smash my lips into hers, which are already slightly spread. Her tongue wraps needily around mine and she moans again like she did before.

Pulling back a bit, Hollynd says with her mouth pressed against mine. "I kinda-sorta 'something' you too."

Yep, this is love.

Chapter 12

Hollynd

Being Landry Hayles' girlfriend is easy. Loving Landry Hayles is easy. Being loved by Landry Hayles is better than easy, it's phenomenal.

The first time he told me he loved me was one of those moments that was randomly ordinary that turned to unexpectedly extraordinary. After saying good-bye at the front door of my mom's house, I turned to unlock the door as Landry turned and walked back towards his car. He didn't make it to his car before he turned back to the house and came up running behind me. Wrapping his arms around my body from behind, he pressed his chest into my back. Landry lowered his mouth to my ear and whispered, "I love you, Cricket." He pressed a kiss into my temple before letting me go and headed back to his car. I turned around to stop him, but in a panic, I simply yelled, "I love you too." With a wink and a smile, Landry looked back at me from outside his car and yelled, "I know," before he hopped in and drove away.

After then, the words "I love you" had become second nature in our conversations. We talked often about our future together. Which university we might transfer to next year — provided they offered both of our respective studies, and what kind of place we'd get together. Our daydreams became entwined with our future together.

We've been dating for over three months. Since the little drug episode at Eddie's house, Landry has never once shown an interest in anything illicit. We still go to parties together, even ones at Eddie's house, but Landry seems much more content to partake in a few drinks and very content to partake in me. And trust me, I'm not complaining.

Rob and I have become fast friends, probably because I spend so much time at their apartment. Rob's easy to get along with. His gentle nature and kind spirit makes him truly lovable.

Landry and Rob have spent a lot of time with my family over the past few months as well. Including Christmas when David decided to take Josh and Isaac on the family ski trip, but neglected to invite his other two sons. My mom was happy to have the two extra guests for Christmas, and I was thrilled to have Landry with me the entire holiday.

Overall, everyone has gotten along well, even Rachel and Landry, which I was tentative about since I know exactly how hardheaded they both can be; but honestly, things are going great. This is the happiest I have ever felt since my dad died. I feel like my family is becoming happier again, too. I know there will always be an empty spot in my family and my heart where my father once held. However, this new family is helping fill the rest of my heart.

Chapter 13

Hollynd

It's New Year's Eve and Landry's father is holding an extravagant party to announce his candidacy in the upcoming mayoral election, which will be held in the spring. After much insistence from Landry's father by the way of constant text messages and phone calls, Landry gave in to the invitation for his attendance at the party. I'm not totally sure if he had a plus one invitation. However, Landry said if I couldn't attend as his date that there was no way in hell he would attend at all.

In the days leading up to the party, Landry's been in a foul mood. I assume it's because he knows he will have to see his father. Two days ago, I overheard Landry telling Rob that his father had warned him to be on his "best behavior" and to "keep his mouth shut". It shocked me that a father would berate his child like that. I had never heard a parent speak to their child like that before. My heart hurt for Landry, knowing that he never received love from his father as a child or as an adult.

I never told Landry what I had heard. There's no doubt that Landry's father wanted all his children in attendance for his announcement. Having a picture of a perfect family was almost always a necessity in the political games people play.

I'm getting ready for the event at my house and Landry's picking me up here. I thought he could use some alone time before tonight, and I'm more nervous than I want to let on. It's a black-tie event, and though I wasn't one for fancy clothes, I made myself go buy a brand-new dress for the occasion.

I kept it simple, choosing an eggplant purple silk gown. It's fitted against every curve of my body and flowed out slightly from my knees to the floor. Only my right shoulder bore a three-inch strap which was detailed with rhinestones. I'm wearing my hair down in waves which drape over my bare shoulder.

I pace around the kitchen while I wait for Landry to arrive. My mom's sitting at the dining room table with her camera in hand.

"Mom, this isn't the prom or something. You don't need to take pictures." I express through my nervous teeth.

"Oh, you never mind. It's my prerogative as a mother to take all the pictures I want. Plus, you look so beautiful. How could I not capture this moment?"

"I thought you said you were going out with Linda tonight?"

"We are but that's not until later."

Before I can argue anymore with my mom, the doorbell rings throughout the house. I scowl one last time at her camera as I walk to the front door.

Never looking more handsome than he did right now, is the love of my life, dressed all in black. Landry's black blazer is buttoned over a black dress shirt and a thin black tie. Black slacks and black shoes, of course. Landry's hair is brushed off slightly to the side. All the piercings in his ears and lip almost seems to shine a little brighter with the aura of blackness that surrounds them. I'm rendered speechless as I take in the man standing before me.

Before I can gather my wits, Landry's arms move swiftly around my waist, and I'm instantly pressed against his chest.

"You look absolutely ravishing," Landry growls in my ear. "I will give you a million dollars to skip the party and let me take you to Vegas right now to get married."

"You don't have a million dollars."

"Details, details." Landry presses his lips to mine, uncaring about the lipstick he's smearing all over his own lips.

I pull back and wipe the colour off his lips. My mother peeks around the corner and offers her greeting to Landry.

"Landry, you wouldn't mind if I got a picture or two before you left?" My mom is such a smooth talker.

"Of course not, Francine," Landry purrs in return.

My eyes instantly roll to the back of my head. "Ugh, you two are insufferable."

Landry and I turn together towards my mom to get ready for one quick picture, which is what I told them is all that I would allow. With his arm wrapped around my back I can feel Landry's hand creep its way down over my bottom and give a little squeeze. I look away from the camera and find him looking straight into my eyes. We gaze at each other with pure electricity sparking between us and I no longer hear the snaps of the camera. Clearly, my mother did not abide by the one picture rule.

Finally, I tell my mom that we must leave. After wishing her a Happy New Year with a kiss on the cheek, we say our goodbyes for the evening.

On the drive over to his father's house, I can feel the tension in Landry's body rising. I reach over and rub his thigh softly, hoping to help keep him calm. Landry says nothing about my touch, but also doesn't stop me from doing it either. He's trying very hard to keep it together. I know how hard this is for him. I tell myself that my only job tonight is to be by Landry's side and provide the strength he may need to get through this night.

Chapter 14

Landry

By the time we arrive at my father's house, the unsettled feeling I've had all day is slowly morphing into something much more painful. My gut is burning, and my nerves are sending shocks throughout my body, causing my fingers to shake which I'm trying my hardest to hide from Hollynd.

Hollynd and I are aware of each other's bodies and feelings. I know she's trying to keep me calm in the best way she knows how, with her never-failing support. This girl is my strength most days, making me want to be a better man just for her. That's why I have stayed away from drugs for the past few months. I tell Hollynd that it was easy to give them up for her, but the truth is that it was fucking hard. I still want to get high sometimes, especially after I have had to deal with my father and his bullshit.

Luckily for me, getting ready to enter the political spotlight has kept my father very preoccupied and thus more absent from my life than ever before. I'm very grateful for this. I was hoping we could skip this announcement and New Year's party tonight as well. However, my father made it very clear to me that skipping this event was not an option.

My father spared no expense for this party as we pull up to the valet service waiting for us at the front of the house. The house is glowing with clear, twinkling lights. Draped in red carpet, the stone stairs leading to the front door are lined with lights. People are making their way up the stairs dressed in their finest attire— that I had no doubt cost more than my last semester's tuition.

I loathe this lifestyle almost as much as I loathe the people in it. It's a bitter pill to swallow, knowing that I feel this way when I'm wearing a suit worth so much money. My father insisted that all his sons show up in classic Versace suits with black jackets, black pants, black tie, and a crisp white dress shirt. I swapped the white shirt for a black shirt mostly out of spite and because I liked it better. I know my father is going to be pissed off about my rearrangement for his chosen attire, and the thought of that pleases me greatly.

And then there's Hollynd, guaranteed to be the most beautiful woman in attendance tonight. I take her hand into mine after I open the passenger door of my black Mustang. The valet attendant tried to help her first, but I insisted with a non-negotiating look. It's my job to assist the woman of my dreams, no one else's.

Hollynd always looks beautiful, that is never a question. From the first thing in the morning to the moment she closes her eyes at night, her beauty never once falters. It doesn't matter if she's wearing Kmart or Haute Couture, she's always magnificent. Tonight, of course, is no exception. Her skin is glowing against the deep purple colouring of her dress. Hollynd's hair is like tresses of golden silk and solitary diamond stud hangs from each ear.

I continue to hold her hand as we make our way up the carpet covered stairs towards the front entrance. Before we reach the door, I feel myself pull back with resistance, knowing my subconscious doesn't want me to enter.

Hollynd must feel me stall as well, because she turns towards me and places her palm on the warmth of my cheek. "You got this baby, and I got you."

Her words and constant support causes my entire body to be pulled into her and our mouths meet with a gentle touch.

"I love you." My lips are pressing against hers.

"I love you." Hollynd's lips are still pressing mine.

We break apart and I open the front door. I enter the house where love was never given and never received, while the purest love I have ever experienced is by my side. The conflict of feelings inside me at this moment does not go unnoticed.

The first place we go to is the open bar, which is set up in the living room. Several strong drinks are in order tonight. It's where my father's original bar is located, with a section of counter space added to accommodate more guests. I order a whiskey straight for myself and a glass of champagne for Hollynd.

I survey the room, which is a mixture of familiar faces and strangers. The buzz of conversations and the light sound of jazz radiates through the air. I continue to scan the crowd after our drinks are in hand. I'm looking for Rob, who should be here by now. He's the only person, other than Hollynd, I intend to socialize with tonight. Before I find Rob, I feel a hand firmly press my shoulder. I turn to see my brother, Isaac, standing beside me offering an icy glare.

"You're not wearing the suit dad requested," Isaac grunts.

"Isaac, I wasn't aware you had such an interest in fashion," I murmur, as I take a sip from my glass.

"Don't be a little punk tonight, Landry. This is a very important night for Dad. I don't even know why he bothered to invite you, to be honest."

I can feel Hollynd's hand tightening around mine. I glance at her quickly to see a fiery anger setting in behind her eyes.

Catching sight of Hollynd's anger, Isaac backs down. "I apologize," he offers his hand to Hollynd. "I'm Landry's older brother, Isaac."

Hollynd nods with a slight smile. "Hollynd."

I bring my attention back to Isaac. "Trust me, I'd rather be anywhere but here. Some of us have a life outside of kissing Dad's ass all day."

Isaac's face flashes a glimpse of annoyance at me, but before he can fire back my other brother Josh and his girlfriend, Lindsay, walk up.

Josh and Isaac both resemble our father, with his large six-foot stature and broad shoulders. However, unlike Isaac's dark and angry features, Josh has lighter brown hair, big brown eyes, and a golden complexion. Josh is also less of an asshole than Isaac, though he can still hold his own if needed in the douchebag department.

Beside him, Lindsay's arm is hooked tight with Josh's arm. An attractive enough woman with long bleach blonde hair and big blue eyes. Lindsay and Josh have been together for about a year. With Lindsay's father being the president of Infinity Bank, there's no doubt that this couple is a match made in yuppie, socialite heaven. I know my father must happily approve of this arrangement and the powerful alliance it will secure him.

"Landry, you actually showed up." Josh offers his hand to me in a more formal gesture than a brotherly gesture. "And you actually look sober."

"Oh, you know me, I can never pass up a family reunion." My voice is dripping with sarcasm as I return the handshake.

"And you brought a date for the first time. An exquisite date indeed." Josh gives Hollynd a charming smile.

Josh offers his hand to Hollynd, who offers hers in return and gives a polite smile. However, I can still see the anger swirling around in the back of her eyes. She's on guard tonight. Meanwhile, Lindsay's eyes narrow in on Hollynd's hand in Josh's hand.

"Josh and Lindsay, this is Hollynd Turner, my girlfriend." I introduce Hollynd to the couple.

"An actual girlfriend, Landry?" Lindsay questions with cattiness in her voice.

From what I know about Lindsay, she's everything you would expect from a girl from a very rich family and had everything she had ever asked for simply handed to her.

Before I reply to the snide remark, Hollynd takes over.

"Yes, his girlfriend of about four months. Correct, Landry?"

"Yes, baby." I pull her in tight and press a kiss on the top of her head. "Four of the best months of my life."

"Ugh, you are such a pussy." Isaac interrupts.

"Four months and he hasn't brought you around his family yet? Hmm, that seems strange, don't you think? You brought your last little groupie home after a week, didn't you, Landry? Of course, she didn't last too long, they never do." Lindsay's trying to bait Hollynd. I will not let her be successful.

"Well, it's simple Lindsay, we really try to limit our time with assholes. Oh, and look," I gaze down at the invisible watch on my wrist, "Time is up."

I lead Hollynd away from my brothers and Lindsay, but not before I hear her say to Josh, "God, your brother's a prick."

Hollynd and I find a vacant spot in the adjoining sitting room where there are many guests mingling and talking. The serving staff is swooping back and forth, carrying trays of champagne and appetizers. I grab a champagne for myself as my whiskey is long gone after the interaction with my brothers. My agitation is palpable.

"So those are your other two brothers?" Hollynd asks while nibbling on a mini quiche filled with spinach and gouda cheese.

"Lovely, aren't they? Sorry to say this babe, you haven't seen anything yet. You still have to meet my father."

"Josh seems nice. But his girlfriend, she's a super bitch. Who knows, maybe your father will love me? Most parents usually do." Hollynd winks at me.

"Hollynd, my father loves nobody except himself." I lift my full glass of champagne and drink the entire glass back in one gulp and slam it on the table beside me. *Shit, this is going to be a long night.*

It's at this moment I hear the ping of silverware on crystal sing through the air, my father stands at the front of the room on a raised platform with a microphone placed in front. The crowds from both rooms gather around the stage all eyes fixated on the figure that stands before them. They seem in awe of my father's dominating presence. I'm disgusted by both his presence and the people's reaction to it.

Hollynd and I stay at the back of the room, away from the stage. From across the room, I finally see Rob, dressed in his dictated attire, matching my other brothers. Rob's eyes finally meet mine. I motion with my hands raised to my mouth tipping back an invisible glass to bring me a drink. Knowing exactly what I need, Rob nods and makes his way to the bar.

A couple of minutes later Rob arrives with a whiskey neat for me, another champagne for Hollynd, and a champagne for himself. The room is now lulled into silence as my father speaks into the microphone.

"Good evening, my dearest friends. I am so honored that you have chosen to spend your last moments of the year celebrating with myself and my family."

Little bouts of applause burst through the crowd. I can't help but roll my eyes and take a big gulp of my whiskey.

Raising his hand and nodding his head in gratitude, he motions to silence the crowd.

"I would like to call my four wonderful sons to the stage before I continue my speech because what I have to say tonight is because of their continuous love and support. Isaac, Joshua, Landry, and Robert, could you please come up here?"

Again, applause ripples throughout the crowd. Hollynd reaches over instantly and squeezes my hand. She must feel the anger that is radiating off my body and I'm sure my face is doing a piss-poor job at hiding it. Isaac and Josh are the first to the stage while I follow closely behind Rob, who practically had to kick my ass to get me to move. I clench my jaw the entire walk to the stage and continue to do so as we line up behind my father.

I feel like a zoo animal on display, forced to do tricks when the master commands. I look to the back of the room and see Hollynd's eyes placed firmly on my face. She's not looking at anyone else. Her eyes look worried, perhaps with a touch of pity. I hate that, I don't want pity from her, or from anyone. I glance away from her gaze and avoid her eye contact for the rest of the speech, though I can always feel her eyes on me.

My father continues his speech, but I don't hear a word of it. I'm locked inside my own thoughts of fury and rage. I know the moment he announces his intentions to run for mayor because the room erupts with clapping, cheering, and whistling. At least that means I can get off this stage soon.

Finally, the speech ends, and I'm free to climb off my father's platform and back to Hollynd, who's still waiting at the back of the room. Before I reach her, a tray of champagne floats past me and I grab another glass for myself.

I can feel the effects of my previous drinks tingling through my body, but it's not enough. I know exactly what would be enough or at least help, but I don't know how to get past Hollynd. For the first time in our relationship, I feel a twinge of resentment towards her. I know in my heart that she only wants what's best for me, but it's the monster that lives in the shadows that is gnawing at me tonight. He's been dormant for so long, and he's itching to come out and play.

When I get back to Hollynd, she reaches up to my face, pulling it towards her face. She's trying to get our eyes to meet. She's looking to comfort me. Her kindness and love know no bounds, and I should be grateful. I know Hollynd is the best thing I have in my life. Knowing this makes me feel even worse because I know I don't deserve her. She's worth so much more than the love I have to offer her, because my love comes with pain. Unfortunately, I know Hollynd is going to feel that pain tonight, even before the monster inside executes his plan.

"Baby, are you okay?" Hollynd asks while still holding my jaw towards her.

I soften my eyes because I know the shit running through my head is not her fault. Hollynd's the only light in the darkness right now. I lean forward and press my lips to hers. God, I love this woman. So much that it hurts my damaged heart. Caught in a moment of passion, I cannot help but touch the tip of my tongue to the seam of her lips. Opening her mouth slightly, I can feel her tongue meet mine. A quiet grunt releases from my throat, as I feel my blood moving away from my head. Not caring about the other people mulling around the room, I run my hand up Hollynd's bare arm. I can feel her skin blanketed with goosebumps. I'm ready to grab her by the arm, haul her upstairs, throw her down on my old bed and fuck her senseless. Until we are interrupted by a hand slapping against my back shoulder. A quick glance back confirms that it's my father's hand that's gripping my shoulder. I shoot a glare in his direction.

"Landry, please do me the honor of introducing me to your lovely date." His eyes are on Hollynd and a plastic smile coats his face.

Hollynd, being the sweet person she is, offers him a warm smile. A smile that could warm any dead and cold heart, but this bastard is heartless.

"Hollynd, this is my father, David. Dad, this is my girlfriend, Hollynd Turner." I robotically announce.

"Mr. Hayles, it's a pleasure to meet you." Hollynd offers her hand towards him. She's no stranger to playing the fake pleasantries game.

"Hollynd, please call me David. I must apologize for my son's lack of respect with keeping his father informed in his life." My father shoots a cold glare in my direction. "Landry has never mentioned the beautiful woman he calls his girlfriend. Tell me, how long have you and my son been seeing each other?"

"Four months, hey Landry?" Hollynd's trying to bait me into the conversation.

"Yeah, about that," I confirm, offering no more. I just want this moment to end.

"Well, I apologize that Landry's not better at keeping his poor old man in the loop."

The entire air now reeks with phony banter as my father pats me on the back in a lighthearted manner.

Hollynd nods her head with a smile and tucks her hand into mine. I can't bring myself to clutch it back, instead leaving it to hang loosely while she holds onto my limp fingers. Everything about this moment angers me, my father's fake humor and Hollynd going along with it.

"Well, I'll let you two get back to the party." My father is getting ready to take his leave, but first grabs me firmly by the upper arm. "I would like you to be in my office alone in forty-five minutes. There's a matter that needs to be discussed."

Before I can deny his request, my father walks away, leaving Hollynd and I on our own again.

"Well, that didn't go so bad," Hollynd says once my father is out of earshot.

"Are you kidding me? That man is so phony, Hollynd. Don't fall for his charm because it's all bullshit." Resentment seeps through my words.

"I know, that's what you said before, but I thought our first meeting would be some sort of shouting match or him telling me to piss off by the way you described him. All I'm saying is that I'm relieved that it was pleasant." Hollynd replies calmly, trying to defuse the situation.

I pull on the knot of my necktie, trying to get some more air into my chest. I feel like I'm being choked to death right now as my pulse is beating erratically. It takes a moment for my body to finally start calming down, at least enough to appease the woman standing next to me.

I return the grip Hollynd has on my hand and lean down to give her a small peck on the cheek. "Let's find Rob." I say as I pull her through the crowd of people in search of my younger brother.

I spot Rob in the adjoining living room leaning next to the fireplace, visiting with some elitist friends of my father's. Rob has always been the model son for my father. He's polite, kind, respectful, and knows his place. I wish my father could give Rob the approval he has always been searching for, but David Hayles would never stoop so low.

When Hollynd and I approach Rob, the couple he has been conversing with take their leave. I'm grateful to have sidestepped the small talk.

"That was quite the speech Dad gave, hey?" Rob says as we approach.

"Hmm." Is all I get out.

Now that I have found Rob, I can feel more comfortable leaving Hollynd for a few minutes. I need a moment to myself, well, myself and the monster inside. He has an idea.

I clear my throat. "I need to check something quick. Will you be okay here with Rob?"

"Of course," Hollynd shoots me a smile. "Are you okay?"

"Yes, I'll be right back." *I don't deserve this woman.*

I leave Rob and Hollynd together to talk, and I make a beeline for the foyer where the large staircase is located that will take me upstairs. Keeping my head down to avoid eye contact with everyone, I march up the stairs, which had been closed off from guests. When I arrive at the top, I take a right and head down the silent hallway. Three doors down the hall on the right, I arrive at my old bedroom.

I don't miss living in this house at all and have no sentimental feelings when I open the door to my childhood dungeon. After I moved out, anything that was personal left in the room was removed. Posters of my favourite band, gone. High school trophies from volleyball, gone. There's nothing left in this room that says I used to live here, except maybe for one thing, and that's what I'm hoping for.

I open the doors to my old closet, which used to be filled with my clothes and is now empty. I step just inside the sliding doors and reach my hand up to the overhang on top of the closet door. Running my hand along the trim, I touch until I feel the familiar hole that I had gouged out a long time ago. Reaching my fingers down in the hole until I feel the smooth glass of what I am looking for. An old vial I used to carry my coke with me in high school. I feel the edge of something else up there is the hidden hole. This feels more like hard plastic.

Using my fingers, I grab the glass vial first and then the plastic bottle where I can hear tiny pills jingling around inside.

I read the label to confirm what I had left behind. Xanax. A prescription I had used often for pleasure and bought illegally, years ago. I make my way into the attached bathroom with both bottles in hand. First, I tap out the cocaine that is left in the bottom of the glass containers. It adds up to one very generous line of white pleasure.

After inhaling my first attempt at relief, I decide to supplement the coke with the pills. Thinking the pills had probably lost a lot of potency over the years of closet hiding, I take a little more than I used to do, just in case. Before I pop the pills in my mouth, Hollynd's face flashes before my eyes and gut-wrenching guilt fills my stomach. I squeeze my eyes together in a moment of hesitation, but the hesitation doesn't last long. I pop the pills and scoop a handful of running water from the nearby sink and wash down the evidence of my failings.

After I dry my hands, I return to my bedroom and sit on the neatly made bed. I check the time and I still have over a half hour until I have to meet my father for God knows what. Rubbing my hands over my face, I hear a soft knock on the door. It opens slowly before I can say anything, and the woman of my entire world enters and shuts the door behind her. Her eyes are big, and her smile is mischievous. Guilt kicks my ass again.

Chapter 15

Hollynd

I know I probably should have waited for Landry downstairs and given him some space. He's been so moody tonight, which is normal for Landry whenever his father is involved. I wanted to make sure he was okay.

Rob gave me the directions to Landry's old bedroom to see if that is where he had escaped to, which was absolutely my only goal in coming up here, until I spotted him inside that room.

Sitting with his legs spread, elbows resting on his thighs, and his hands resting together, Landry's head hangs between them. But as he looks up when I enter the room, his dark eyes turn my insides into lava. He's truly a thing of beauty. His blazer is unbuttoned, and his tie is pulled even more loose than it had been downstairs, while strands of his dark hair hang down in front of his forehead.

Landry looks up at me with a cold stare. "Lock the door." His low voice demands.

I shut the door behind me and click the lock on the brass handle. I walk slowly to where Landry is sitting, knowing that my face is giving away all my secrets right now. As I approach the bed, Landry sits up tall and runs his hands up the backside of my dress. I bring my hands to his chest and pull back on his blazer, urging him to remove it. Landry removes his jacket and I pull his tie loose enough to slip it over his head and toss it to the side.

Landry's hands reach up behind my back again, only this time grasping at my hidden zipper. Pulling the silver tab all the way down my back, he peels the purple silk forward and releases my body from its hold, letting it drop to the floor.

Standing before Landry in only a black strapless bra, black lace panties, and silver heels, my heart races out of control. In one swift motion, Landry stands up, grabbing my thighs on the way and pulls them around his waist. Suddenly, my back is slammed up against the wall next to the bedroom door and Landry's mouth lands firmly onto my own. There's no tenderness in his kiss or in the grip he has on my thighs. I'm sure tomorrow there will be tiny bruises left behind by unforgiving fingertips. Landry uses his body weight to hold me against the wall and his hand reaches up and harshly pulls my bra down, exposing both of my hardened nipples. His mouth moves to the newly exposed skin, and I let out a groan of pleasure.

Everything that's happening right now is tumultuously vicious, and I'm loving every moment. My fingers move at a rapid pace, trying to get through to the line of buttons that are keeping Landry's dress shirt in place, while maneuvering around his head which is still sucking on my breasts. When I get to the end of the buttons Landry lifts his head. I can now run my hands over his smooth hard chest, which I do promptly. Landry releases the hold he has on my legs which allows me to let them fall and have my feet find their place on the floor. He backs away from me while I'm still standing pressed against the wall.

"Everything off, except the shoes. Now!" Landry speaks the first words between us since I entered the room.

I do as Landry commands while he unbuttons his cuffs and takes off his shirt. His eyes remain on me the entire time. He looks down at his belt, which is still fastened up tight, though I can see his hardness pushing against the material underneath it.

"Undo these for me and then get your ass on the bed."

I walk over to Landry, still in my heels and nothing else. As I pull the leather strap of his belt I mumble, "God, you're demanding."

Grabbing the hair on the back of my head with a tight grip, Landry dips his other hand in between my legs. "Do you want me to stop?"

I don't bother answering as I remove his belt and undo the rest of his pants. Landry turns me around, so the back of my legs hit the edge of the bed.

"You didn't answer me. Do you want me to stop?" Landry grits between his teeth.

He's going to make me beg for it. He's still rubbing his hand over my mound.

"No," I manage to whisper.

"No? Then get your ass down on that bed and spread those long legs open for me as wide as you can. I don't have the patience to be gentle with you tonight, Cricket."

I do as he says without a word. Part of me is afraid of what's coming, but a bigger part of me is in an aroused tailspin.

Landry removes the rest of his clothes and crawls on top of me. Keeping his eyes locked on mine, there's a flash of a stranger I don't fully recognize in his eyes. I reach up to place my hand on his cheek in search of my lover's eyes, but before I can express any tenderness, Landry rams his entire length into me with harsh force.

My voice moans with a mixture of pain and pleasure as Landry continues his dominating ways. I try to silence the whispers of shame that are echoing in my head. I shouldn't be enjoying this brutality, but I kind of am. A lot. Landry and I find each other's mouths and collapse them together.

Once my body has adjusted to the roughness brought on by Landry's dominance, I reach back to brace my hands above my head against the wooden headboard. My hands grip the surface as hard as they can as Landry shows no sign of letting up on his forceful pace.

As I try to wrap my legs around Landry's waist, my ankles are caught by his forceful grip and my heeled covered feet are brought up to his shoulders. There's no softness in his touch and no tenderness in his thrusts.

Releasing equal moans of ecstasy while our panting continues strong, the once silent room is now echoing with pleasurable sounds. Eventually, our breathing becomes calmer, as we both begin to come down from our sexual high.

"Fucking hell, Cricket. You're so unbelievable. God, I love you." My romantic Landry finally arrives as he presses soft kisses on my face.

I press my hands to his face and guide his mouth to mine for a softer kiss this time.

Pulling away, I say, "I love you too, Landry. More than anything."

A slight wave of sadness flashes in his face before he pulls up. "I'm so sorry, Cricket. I don't deserve you."

"For what, baby?" I'm confused.

Landry shakes his head. "I think I need to go meet my dad right now."

Getting off me, Landry makes his way into the bathroom and brings me a damp towel.

We both get dressed in silence, Landry finally speaks. "Do you want to wait for me here? I shouldn't be long and then we can go."

Landry's voice seems shaky, and I notice a few twitches in his shoulders.

"You don't want to wait until midnight for the New Year? It's almost ten o'clock."

"No, I would rather spend it alone with you, in your arms." Landry embraces me.

"Okay. I'll wait right here for you."

Landry gives me a quick kiss on the top of my head and exits out the bedroom door.

I take my phone out to swipe through my social media while I wait for Landry to return. I hope this meeting with his father goes quickly and smoothly, though my intuition is giving me an unsettling feeling in the pit of my stomach.

Chapter 16

Hollynd

My social media accounts are busting with people's pictures of their New Year's Eve celebrations. Some friends are out at clubs, some are at private parties, and some are at home with their families. I'm still in my slightly wrinkled purple gown, on a bed that I just remade after encountering the most passionate sex I've ever had. I probably won't post about that though.

Sounds from outside the door interrupt my mindless swiping. Loud voices, shouting voices. I open the bedroom door and listen for more sounds like those I just heard. They continue to rumble through the hallway upstairs. I recognize Landry's voice and the other voice must be his fathers.

I quietly make my way towards the door that's containing all the yelling and huddle up close so I can hear what is being said.

"You couldn't even follow one simple instruction, could you, Landry? I wanted all you boys dressed a certain way tonight, like upstanding men. Not like some two-bit gangster. It's bad enough that you've covered yourself in those ridiculous tattoos and piercings. You're such an ungrateful piece of shit." I flinch at David Hayles' words to his son. I want to barge in there and give him a piece of my mind. But I don't.

"You're right, Dave, I'm ungrateful. Thank you so much for all the times you punched my face and the times you kicked me in the stomach. Oh, and thank you for the all the times you told me just how worthless I am." Landry's bitterness is thick.

"Listen, this mayoral race is now official, and that means you're on notice. One mess up Landry and I will finish you and your brother."

What is he talking about? I wonder. And which brother?

Suddenly, I hear glass smashing on the other side of the doorway.

"Feel like a big man now Landry, punching a picture frame?"

"Better than a kid's face like you prefer, Father."

"I'm done with you for tonight. You are clearly drunk or high. Clean yourself up and leave my party and take that nobody of a girlfriend with you. Once you are through screwing around with this one, I expect you to date women with a higher status. Your father is about to become the mayor of Brighten, after all." David's smug tone almost makes me gag.

Nausea bubbles in my stomach. I can't believe this man is so cruel. After hearing David walking across the room closer to the door, I quickly dart into an open door across the hall and hide in the dark shadows of the half bathroom. I watch David Hayles leave his office, leaving Landry behind.

Once David is out of sight, I go into the office where Landry is left behind. I find him sitting on an upright chair, clutching his right hand while a steady stream of blood runs down it. His leg is vibrating erratically.

"Oh my God, are you okay?" I run up to him quickly.

The stench of whiskey fills my nostrils before I notice the overturned tumbler on the floor beside Landry.

His eyes are glossy, different from how they were only twenty minutes before. They look at me slowly. "I spilled my drink," Landry mumbles and tries to reach down to grab the empty glass. As he does, blood streams from his knuckles and down to the tips of his fingers.

"I'm bleeding, Hollynd." Landry holds his hand up and inspects the blood inquisitively like he doesn't know where it came from.

"I know, baby. Let's go clean you up." I pull on his arm to get him to stand with me, but he doesn't budge.

"I hate him, Hollynd. I hate him so fucking much." Rage takes over Landry's entire body.

I don't know what to do or what's happening. His entire body is shaking with tremors. This is more than being a little drunk, this is something else. Maybe his father was right when he said he was high, but I was just with him.

"I'm so sorry, Cricket. I don't deserve you." Landry's words from not long ago replay in my head. What was he doing in that room before I got there?

Before I let myself go into full panic mode, I grab for my cell inside my clutch. I text Rob quickly, telling him that there is something wrong with Landry, and ask him to come upstairs and help me.

A couple of minutes later, Rob barges into the room with Josh close behind him. Seeing the blood dripping off Landry's hand, the broken glass and family picture laying on the floor nearby, and me, a shaking girl in a purple dress with her eyes brimming with tears, Rob loses his cool.

"What the hell is going on, Landry?"

Landry slowly shifts his gaze to Rob. "Fuck off. Both of you," he shouts throughout the room at his two brothers. "Did you call them, Hollynd?"

I rub my hand over Landry's arm to calm him down, but a darkened stare pierces through me from Landry's eyes. "Don't touch me, Hollynd! I trusted you!"

Landry swings his arm away from me violently, which causes me to lose my balance in these stupid heels and crash down to the floor by his feet. Landry makes no move to help me up as he stares downwards at me, his dark eyes burning with rage.

"He's high," Josh says in a monotone voice. He doesn't seem surprised in the least.

"No shit." Rob sarcastically replies.

Walking over to where Landry is still sitting slouched over, I watch Rob grab his brother by the jawbone, forcing him to look at his face. I crawl back from the two men who are now face to face staring each other down.

"What did you take, Landry?" Rob asks his slouched over brother.

Landry says nothing and glares coldly at his brother.

"Landry, what the hell did you take?" Rob now yells directly into his brother's face.

Landry continues to glare at his brother. "Feeling tough, little brother?"

"Shut up, Landry." Rob shoves his jaw to the side and begins reaching into Landry's jacket pockets. "I'm so sick of your shit, Landry."

"Well, I'm fucking sick of your shit, Rob!" Landry yells back.

Finally, Rob pulls out what he's been searching for in Landry's jacket. After reading the label, Rob tosses it to Josh, who is standing nearby.

"Xanax." Rob says to Josh who catches the bottle and tucks it into his own suit jacket.

"And what else, Landry?" Josh growls from across the room. Though Landry doesn't bother turning in the direction of Josh, his eyes are still staring down Rob with rage.

"Come help me carry him to the bathroom. We'll clean up his hand and then we got to get him out of here," Rob says to Josh.

Josh walks over to Rob and they each grab an arm to haul Landry towards the bathroom. The entire scene is heartbreaking. Not only because I'm watching the love of my life behave like a total asshole while he's bleeding, but because I can tell by the way Rob is handling the situation that this isn't an unfamiliar experience for him.

Josh and Rob take Landry to the same bathroom I was just hiding in across the hall, while I pick the broken glass off the floor and toss it and the broken frame in the garbage. Picking up the family picture that is laying on the floor, I place it on the side of David Hayles' desk. I notice there are drops of blood on the carpet where Landry had been sitting. With a tissue from the box on the desk, I try to dab it up, but it's no use. The blood has already soaked into the fibers of the carpet.

Rob comes back into the room as I'm crouched on the floor, dabbing the blood in vain.

"Just leave it, Hollynd." Rob is clearly angry. "Are you okay to drive?"

"Yes," I confirm. "I only had two glasses of champagne and that was a while ago."

"Okay, Josh and I are going to take Landry home in my car. You follow behind in Landry's car. Once we get home, Josh will drive you back to your house."

"No! I want to stay with him, Rob," I argue.

"Hollynd, it's going to get worse. You don't want to be there for what's going to come."

"Rob, stop it! I'm staying with him!" The anger rises as quick in my throat as the tears do in my eyes.

Rob runs his hands through his hair in frustration. "Fine, but don't say I didn't warn you."

Rob and Josh work on getting Landry out of the house without being detected by anyone at the party, while I get the cars brought to the front of the house by the valet.

Twenty-five minutes later, we are back upstairs in Landry's and Rob's apartment. Landry is mumbling to himself when his brothers sit his body down on the couch. I head into the kitchen to grab him a glass of water and a damp cloth. I set the water on the end table beside the couch and kneel next to Landry, running the cool cloth over his forehead.

The glazed look is still present in Landry's hooded eyes, but they are firmly on me. The anger he showed towards me in his father's office has disappeared.

"You're so good to me, baby." Landry mutters in my direction while I watch his eyelids fall closed.

His muscles are still twitching underneath his suit. I try to pull off his blazer hoping to make my broken Landry a little more comfortable. Landry brings his non bandaged hand to my cheek, and cups it softly. This is a far cry from the man who told me not to touch him not long ago.

"Aren't you furious at him?" Josh asks as he walks in from the kitchen.

"Yes, I'm livid," I admit, not looking up from my task. "But me being mad in this moment won't help anything." Then I pause while I examine Landry's face. "And more than my anger is my love for him." My voice trails off and I run my fingers through his hair and a single tear escapes out of the corner of my eye. "I'll be mad at him tomorrow."

Josh and I sit in silence while I continue to remove Landry's jacket and his black tie.

"Where's Rob?" I ask Josh, again not looking away from Landry.

"He went to the store to grab Landry some Gatorade and other stuff. He needed to cool down." Josh replies while texting on his phone.

"Well, thank you for helping us." I mumble while I undo the top button on Landry's dress shirt. "I hope Lindsay doesn't mind that you left the party." I glance in Josh's direction.

Josh pauses his insistent tapping on his phone and looks up at me. His brow furrows deeply. "She's fine."

I can't tell if Josh is annoyed or indifferent. I say nothing and turn my attention back to Landry who's starting to thrash his head back and forth on the back of the couch.

"I'm so hot." Landry claws at his dress shirt and hooks his fingers, even the ones on his now bandaged hand, into an opening at the front of his shirt and pulls with enough force that buttons go flying around the couch.

Landry clearly wants his shirt off, so I help him out of that too. Sweat begins to glisten across his forehead as his breathing becomes more rapid.

Looking back at me, Landry says, "Baby, I'm gonna be sick."

I jump up off the couch and grab his arm while Josh jumps up from his chair and grabs his other arm. Together, we pull Landry into the bathroom that is attached to his master room. I lift the lid to the toilet and Josh places Landry down in front of it. Landry's body starts to heave so violently I can see every muscle in his back contract. I can hear Landry's stomach contents hitting the water in the toilet bowl. I sit myself down on the edge of the tub with my hands and elbows resting on my knees while waiting for the purging to finish.

Josh is standing in the doorway, watching everything unfold. "You can get out of here if you want. I'll stay with him."

"I'm not leaving him," I shake my head, moving my eyes back towards Landry's heaving back.

"Well, at least go get changed out of that dress," Josh suggests. "It's going to be a long night for you. The vomiting can last on and off all night."

Agreeing with Josh's suggestion, I make my way out of the bathroom and into Landry's room. I have been leaving clothes here for a while now, as I spend a lot of nights here with Landry. I pick out a pair of baggy pajama pants and an old tee shirt of Landry's; I need his smell with me right now. Not bothering to hang up my dress, I leave it laying on the bedroom floor. Between getting into it right after sex, and the possibility of it having either blood or puke on it, —or both— I think it's going to need multiple cleanings.

I return to the bathroom where Josh is still leaning against the doorframe, scowling down at his brother in disgust. I stand beside Josh for a moment and together we both watch Landry struggling to breathe through the gagging.

"You're too good for him," Josh says without looking away from Landry.

Anger is radiating from Josh's body. I can feel it despite not touching him. I can't figure out why Josh even helped us tonight when his disdain for Landry seems so apparent.

Before I can say anything, Josh turns and leaves both the bathroom and Landry's bedroom. It seems the vomiting has subsided for the time. Landry's sitting more upright and not hunched over the toilet. I wet another cloth at the sink before walking behind Landry and sitting down on the floor behind him. I rub the cloth on the back of his neck, wiping away beads of sweat that have seeped out of his pores. Landry shifts his body around to face me and lowers his head down to my lap. I wipe down his face, which is also covered with sweat as Landry's head rests on my thighs. His one arm wraps around the back of my waist, wedging itself between my body and the wall, and his other arm rests over my knees. I run my fingers through Landry's dark, damp hair, trying to silently encourage him to go to sleep. His eyes are closed, and his breathing becomes heavy.

Suddenly from the other room I can hear my cell notifying me of incoming text messages, pinging one after another. It must be midnight.

"Happy New Year, Landry," I whisper, and continue to stroke his sweaty hair as I hum Auld Lang Syne quietly to myself.

I never expected for the new year to begin like this. I knew I would be in love when the New Year rang in. Hell, I knew from the moment I met Landry I was going to be in love with him forever. Only I didn't expect for this love to hurt so much. I didn't expect to hold my love while his demons were holding him.

I don't know how to help Landry, and I don't know how to save him from himself. Honestly, I don't even know if this is my responsibility, but I find myself believing that's what I'm supposed to do. It's not a question of how much I love this man, but a realization that this is something more than love. At this moment, in this room, as Landry lays here, silently consumed by the chemicals he has taken and consumed by a pain he cannot name, I take all the pain that weeps from his soul and make it my own.

Landry had said earlier in the night that he wanted to spend New Year's wrapped in my arms. I don't think this was what either of us imagined it would look like. I let my eyes close, letting the moment be exactly as it is, lover holding lover, soul holding soul.

I wake up startled by the jerking of Landry's body beside mine. Using a folded towel on the edge of the tub as a makeshift pillow for myself, I must have dozed off. Looking down to see Landry's body heaving again, I use all my strength in my arms to lift his upper body up and towards the toilet. We almost make it to the toilet before the liquid flows out of his mouth again. Most of it hits the toilet. The rest hits the floor.

"I must really love you," I mumble to myself while I clean up as best as I can, trying to contain my own throat from gagging in disgust.

Rob must hear the ruckus going on because he appears in the doorway and comes in to help me out.

"Hollynd, take a break for a bit. Go lay down. I can take it from here." Rob offers and I don't refuse.

I'm exhausted, both physically and emotionally. I go to the other bathroom down the hallway to wash up before I crawl straight into Landry's bed. Before I drift off, I take a big whiff of the pillows. They smell like Landry, and even though I have spent all night with him—most of it on the floor of the bathroom, — I miss him so much at this moment.

I wake up hours later and I can feel a heavy breath against the back of my neck. Adjusting slightly to glance over my shoulder, I see Landry's face buried against my back, his entire body pressed up against mine. I'm not sure what time he got into bed and I'm not sure what time it is now. The last thing I remember is Rob taking over the bathroom watch and I came to bed. I think that was around two in the morning. I reach over to the night table to grab my phone to check the time. Hitting the side button causes the screen to light up and it reveals that it's 10:27 a.m.

Despite having slept an adequate number of hours, I still feel exhausted. I decide to get up to use the washroom and retrieve a glass of water. Then I'll head back to bed for a bit. We are scheduled to be at my sister's house at four o'clock, so I have all day to recover from the previous night.

I walk softly through the living room after I notice Josh stretched out on the couch, still in his dress clothes from the night before. His once crisp white shirt is now carelessly untucked and creased. His left arm is tossed over his head, while his other rests on his chest, which rises and falls in a deep rhythm.

Despite my attempt at quietness, I hear Josh's body shuffle on the couch. I wince in fear that I woke him up as I enter the kitchen.

While I stand at the sink letting the water get as cold as possible, I become mesmerized by the stream hitting the stainless steel of the sink and swooshing down the drain. I really need more sleep. I'm so much in my own head I don't hear Josh come up behind me.

"What are you doing?" Josh grumbles.

His deep voice causes me to jump and grasp my chest.

"Josh!" I take a few anxious breaths in and out. "You scared me."

Josh offers no apology for startling me, but instead stares at me while waiting for an answer.

"I'm getting a drink," I finally mumble in return when I realize he's waiting on me. "Do you want one?"

Josh responds with a slight grunt.

"Is that a yes?" I turn to glare at Josh, who's now leaning casually against the counter behind me.

I don't bother to wait for an official 'yes' before shoving my full glass of water at him and begin to fill another one for myself.

"Thanks. How are you feeling?" Josh asks before downing the entire glass of water.

"I'm okay, I guess. Tired mostly." I turn towards Josh while grasping my own glass of water.

"No, I mean, are you okay? I assume you must be pretty pissed off."

I stand silent for a moment as my mind recalls all the events of the previous evening. The party, the meeting of the family, the stupid hot sex in Landry's old bedroom, the blood, the drugs, the vomiting, the panic. Warm tears fill my eyes, and I silently will them not to fall.

Despite being overcome with emotion, Josh offers no comfort. He simply stands there watching me while I begin to fall apart in front of him.

"I'm sorry," I squeak out between sobs.

"What are you sorry for, Hollynd?" Josh finally speaks. "Landry's the one who fucked up. Landry's always the one who fucks up. Haven't you realized that, yet?"

I stare coldly at Josh now that my tears have slowed, and anger begins to set in. "Josh, why are you still here if you hate Landry so much?"

"Who said anything about hating him? In fact, I'm here because I care too much and believe me when I tell you that I'd rather not care at all. But whether I like it or not, Landry is my brother. It's just what brothers do." Josh glares at me with anger in his eyes, but I can't tell if it's anger at my questioning or anger at the responsibility he feels towards his brother.

I can't help but let out a snort at Josh's statement. "What about Isaac? He doesn't seem to have the same attitude regarding brotherly love."

Josh rolls his brown eyes and lets out a sigh while running his hand through his messy hair. "Isaac has his own issues, trust me. He's too messed up to help anyone."

We stand quietly for a moment. I'm not sure what to say to Josh nor why he's still standing here with me. Both our glasses sit empty on the countertop. I'm not sure what it is about Josh, he's not comforting me like Rob did the last time I found myself in this situation, and yet, I feel a comfort just being in the still silence with him.

I break our silence when my internal thoughts slip out of my mouth before I realize they had even left. "I don't know what to do."

"You are doing enough, Hollynd. Landry's so lucky to have you. Do you know that?" Josh's stern voice returns as he pushes himself away from the counter and stands up straight with his arms crossed over his chest.

I shrug my shoulders and turn to refill my glass with water before heading back to bed. As the water fills my glass, I can feel my tears threatening to return as my bottom lip begins to quiver. Josh stands there stoically, watching me.

Once my cup is full, I shut off the water and turn to walk past Josh and out of the kitchen. Before I make it past him, I feel his strong arms reach out to my shoulders and pull me in tight to his chest. The comfort of his warm body and embracing arms causes my tears to return in waves. My entire body begins to vibrate with sobs, while Josh takes my water out of my hand with his free hand. I hear Josh take in a large breath of air and exhale it slowly.

"Just don't give up on him, Hollynd. He needs you." Josh's voice rumbles over the top of my head. His words coming out almost like a whisper.

I pull back from Josh's arms and wipe my face free of the fallen tears.

"What do I do, Josh? I'm so angry right now!"

"I know you are, Hollynd. Landry's more broken than he'll ever admit."

Josh hands me back my water and leaves me standing alone in the kitchen. Once I hear Josh settle back down onto the couch, I walk through the living room back to Landry's bedroom. Before I close the door to the bedroom, I hear Josh's voice one more time.

"Goodnight, Hollynd."

"Night, Josh," I reply before slowly closing the door until it clicks closed.

The apartment remains pin-drop quiet for the next several hours as we all try to sleep off our exhaustion. I wake up again around two in the afternoon and I'm feeling better than I had earlier that day. Landry's beginning to stir beside me. I flip over to my other side to see if he's awake or not. I see his eyes slowly open, and he instinctively brushes his hand down the side of my face. Usually, I would lean into his touch, but this morning I feel my body wanting to pull away.

"Hey, baby," he says with grit in his voice.

"Hey," Is all I can manage for a reply.

We spend the next several minutes just staring at each other. I'm wondering how much of the night before he remembers. I don't know what to say right now. I'm torn between screaming at him, dropping into a puddle of tears, or professing my undying love to him.

"Do you need some water?" I break the silence.

Landry nods, so I sit up and reach for the glass I had brought in a few hours before. Since it's now empty, I take it to the bathroom sink and fill it up. Handing over the water to Landry, who is now half-sitting, he offers me a little smile. It's layered with shame, much like his eyes. Landry takes a giant gulp from the glass before setting it down on the table beside him.

Again, we are in a stare down in silence. I don't know what to say and he isn't saying anything. I've exhausted myself from taking care of him all night, and part of me feels resentful that he probably doesn't even remember.

Finally, I give into the silence once again. "How are you feeling?"

"Like shit," Landry says as he rubs his face with his hands.

"What do you remember from last night?"

"I don't know. Not a lot, bits and pieces."

I stare at him, waiting for something. A reaction or some remorse, I don't know. That anger I had declared the night before to save until today is finally making its way back to the surface. Landry must sense my anger rising.

Landry lays his head back down on his pillow and lets out a long breath. "What do you want me to say, Hollynd? That I messed up again? That I ruined our New Year's?"

"I don't know, Landry. But I want you to say something! Just sit up and look at me." I can feel the tears threatening to fall. "I want you to remember that it was me with you on that fucking bathroom floor last night, cleaning up your vomit! Maybe I sound like a bitch right now, but I don't care!" I stop to breathe for a moment.

Landry fills the silence with a groan through clenched teeth and runs his fingers through his hair in frustration.

"I'm just sad that I can't help you when you need help." I continue speaking, not caring if Landry wants to hear anymore or not. "That you feel you need to turn to a substance instead of me. Like I'm not good enough to be there for you when you feel like you're breaking, but I'm good enough to clean up the mess."

"Oh my God, Hollynd! Stop trying to fix me all the fucking time! Do you know how exhausting it is trying to be perfect for you?"

"I have never asked you to be perfect, Landry!" I toss my hands up in frustration.

"You have no idea how hard I have to try to be good enough for you. How hard I have to work to be a better version of myself so I can be good enough for you."

"When have I implied to you not being good enough for me? That shit's in your own head, Landry, so you can stop the pity party right now. All I've tried to do, time and time again, is help you. Help you, not fix you. But hey, if that's not what you want then maybe next time you can sleep by yourself on the fucking bathroom floor."

I stop talking and wait for a response. Something, anything. But there's nothing. Landry continues to lie there in silence, lost in his thoughts.

"Fine, whatever." I finally recede. "I'm going to shower."

I turn and head into the attached bathroom and close the door behind me. After a moment of leaning against the sink to catch my breath, I turn on the shower, undress, and get in.

I allow the beads of hot water to beat against my flesh while I inhale the steam into my lungs. My entire body is shaking in rage. I try to busy my mind with the task of showering, but the sadness is still very much present. I'm sad about everything that happened last night, I'm sad about my outburst, I'm sad that Landry said nothing.

After my hair has been shampooed and my body has been washed, I simply stand in the falling water, lost in thought. The sound of the shower curtain opening interrupts my peace. I turn to see Landry standing there. Looking at me with shameful eyes.

The words, "I need you, Crick," tumble from Landry's quivering lip.

I motion for him to come in with me. Landry peels off the only thing he's currently wearing, which is his underwear, and enters the shower. His hand is still bandaged from last night's collision with the glass picture frame. Dried rust coloured blood speckles the top of the white gauze. I begin to unwrap the fabric knowing that the wound probably wasn't cleaned very well the night before. Once I get it free from the band-aid, I survey the number of little cuts over Landry's knuckles. It's puffy, bruised, and stained with dried blood. I make a mental note to check it over for tiny shards of glass before re-wrapping it after the shower.

I pull Landry over to where I'm standing in the stream of water and move to where he was just standing. As the water begins to wet his entire body, I take the bottle of bodywash and squeeze a generous amount of soap on my hand and lather up his hard, thoroughly battered body. Then I make my way to his head and wash his hair, removing all the old hair products and sweat. There's nothing sexual as I wash Landry's body, this is simply an act of love. In a moment of mercy, I feel as though I'm washing away the sins of my lover. *Maybe I am?*

Landry's head hangs lower while I make myself his caregiver. I finally bring my hands up to his shoulders and over to his jawline. Nudging him softly to lift his head and bring his eyes to mine. When they finally meet, I see the whites of his eyes are now a burning pink and tears are dropping rapidly from his eyelids. I know that these are tears of shame, pain, and regret. I wipe them away in vain since the water leaves his face wet just the same. Without warning, Landry drops to his knees, which bang against the porcelain floor of the tub. His arms grab fiercely around my stomach and cross together on my back. Burying his head into the flesh of my upper stomach, I return the embrace wrapping my arms around his head and shoulders.

Silence.

We hold each other tightly in the forgiving silence. With heavy breaths and the slight weep of pain, we allow the water to act as a symbolic baptism as we both grasp onto the hope that our love will be enough to see us through and that we ourselves will not be the cause of our own ruin.

Chapter 17

Hollynd

It's been three days since Landry and I held each other fiercely in the shower. We have yet to discuss the events of New Year's Eve in depth, but rather we both seem to have fallen into an internal struggle of silence. Despite having spent nearly every moment together for the last three days, we've barely spoken. Only tiny phrases or generalities are the only words that fill the space. Things like "are you hungry," "should we shower," and "sweet dreams." The love between us feels stronger than it has ever felt before. Long, drawn-out words don't need to be said, at least not now. For hours upon hours we've been cuddled together watching TV, sneaking little kisses here and there, and finding moments for gentle and prolonged lovemaking.

Eventually, we would have to talk more in depth about what had happened and where we should go from here, but not yet. Like we're trapped in a bubble made of hope and denial, we keep the realities of life at bay for as long as we can. I know how much it can hurt to love someone like Landry Hayles, but I also know how wonderful it is to be loved by him in the same breath. It's both heaven and hell, and I never want to leave.

Rachel called this morning, which is our third "bubble day" together, asking if I would meet her for lunch. I had seen her a few days before at her New Year's Day supper where Landry, Rob, and I had all attended, though we were a little worse for wear.

Landry encouraged me to get out of the apartment, however a very large part of me didn't want to leave him. Call it fear or mistrust, I'm not sure.

Finally, I agreed to meet my sister. I told Landry that I would only be there for a few hours. However, he insisted that after my lunch that I needed to go spend some time with my mom since I had barely seen her since Christmas. To say I was terrified that Landry was trying to get rid of me is an understatement. I felt panicked, worried he was going to go get high or frankly that he was sick of me and wanted me gone. Trying not to be a complete psychopath, I told him I would go over to my mom's house after lunch. And that's where I would be until he decided he wanted to see me again.

I arrive at the small locally owned cafe before Rachel. It's a quaint little cafe with a small selection of tables that all have white linens and white chairs. Each table has a centerpiece of different coloured carnations. Now that it's winter and the outside flowers are long gone, it's nice to see the floral colours on the tables. The server seats me at the two-person table with three blue carnations in a small milk-glass vase. Our table is next to a large window that looks out onto main street. The sun is shining brightly, but it's still cold. A thin layer of snow covers the ground. As the people walk by, you can see their breath leaving their lips, which looks like tiny puffs of smoke.

Rachel enters the cafe to break my thoughts. Wearing a beige wool coat, a bright red scarf, and knee-high black leather boots, Rachel rushes over to the table.

"Brr, it's so cold out there today!" Rachel rubs her hands together as she takes her seat and removes her jacket. "I'm definitely ordering soup."

The server returns once Rachel arrives. We both order the soup and sandwich combos to go with our coffees. While waiting for our food to arrive, Rachel wastes no time with small talk. She's here to say something, and I'm going to hear her out, whether I want to or not.

"What was going on the other day at my house when you guys came over for New Year's supper?"

"What do you mean?" I try to play dumb though it never works with Rachel.

"Don't give me those doe eyes like you don't know what I'm talking about. You, Landry, and Rob show up all looking like shit and it wasn't a "party all night" look, it looked like you all were on the verge of a mental breakdown. You spent the entire night looking like you were about to burst into tears at any moment. Landry wouldn't look anyone in the eye, his hand was all bandaged up, and only talked when asked a question and even then, it was one-word answer. And Rob, God poor Rob, he was trying so hard to be his normal sweet self but looked like he hadn't slept in years. What happened?"

I rub my hands over my face with a long exhale. I really don't want to talk about this.

"Nothing happened. Basically, Landry's father was being a dick, he and Landry got into a fight. Landry punched a picture and cut his hand. We went home, the end."

"Wait, this was about his dad again? Last time he had issues with his dad, you told me he went and got high on coke."

I feel my face give an involuntary twitch and it gives a total tell to Rachel.

"What the hell, Hollynd? Did he go off and get high again?" Rachel's angry stare is burning into me now. Rachel detests any sort of drug use and never has a problem vocalizing her opinions about the dangers of it or her disgust with using it.

My silence confirms her question, so she continues speaking. "What was it this time? Coke again? Or maybe the asshole upgraded to heroine?"

"Rachel, stop! It wasn't like that." My defensiveness rises.

"Explain it to me then, Hollynd."

"I don't know what it was, Rach. All I know is it was bad."

"What did you say to him about it?"

"We haven't really talked about it yet."

"What do you mean you haven't talked about it yet? It's been three days, and you have spent every moment of those three days with him. How could you have said nothing? How are you not super pissed off right now?"

I keep my eyes down and focus on the swirling cream-coloured coffee and shrug my shoulders.

"Are you doing this shit too, Hollynd?"

This gets my attention and raises my anger. "What? No, of course not. Why would you even ask me that?"

"Well, you don't seem too concerned with Landry's behavior. I thought maybe it's because you are hiding something."

"No, I'm not doing drugs, Rachel. And I am angry with Landry, but it's more complicated than that. His issues with his dad are really hard on him and..."

Rachel cuts me off. "Oh please, do not start defending him! We all have daddy issues. Christ, Hollynd, our dad died in front of you!"

"Yeah, and it messed me up for a long time. I'm still messed up about it."

"But you're not running around getting high. You're dealing with it like an adult."

I give a sarcastic laugh. "If you mean sleeping meds, antidepressants, and therapy is dealing with it."

"You are doing great, Lynd. I'm so proud of how far you have come since Dad died. You haven't even used sleeping pills for a while now and there's no shame in taking antidepressants and going to therapy. I think you are brave."

Tears swell in my eyes, though I'm trying my hardest to keep them in. It was difficult after my dad died, more difficult than I like to admit. Like before, Rachel's trying to take care of me and save me. Except I don't need saving from Landry. I need to help save him from himself. It's my turn to be the savior. *I hope.*

"I don't want to see you get so lost in Landry's problems that you start being dragged down with them," Rachel continues.

There's no holding the tears in, anymore. I quickly grab my napkin to wipe them off my face. We're still in a public place, after all.

After I finish wiping my face, I say to Rachel, "I'm going to be okay, Rach. And I'm going to talk to him. But I know he's sorry, and he's trying. You don't even know how bad it is with his dad. Seriously, David Hayles is an asshole through and through."

"Well, I guess he won't be getting my vote then." Rachel offers a joke to lighten the mood. This helps and brings a smile to my face.

The server arrives with our food and places the soup and sandwiches in front of us. I keep my head down so she doesn't spot my tear-stained cheeks and red eyes.

While stirring her hot soup, Rachel says, "So tell me about what happened after the party on New Year's."

I begin the story over and don't skip the details. Hearing Landry's dad yell at him, his anger in the office, the bathroom floor sleep, the sickness, and everything else. If I'm being honest, it feels good to share this story with Rachel. I needed to get it off my chest.

Once I finish, Rachel says with a sigh, "You must really love him, Hollynd."

"I really do." I reply without looking up from the coffee cup clutched in my hands.

"Now what happens? Do you think he would go get some help? I mean, maybe you can suggest something?"

"I don't know how to approach that one. But you're right, we need to talk about it. The last three days have been nice though, even if they were clearly an act of avoidance, they were really nice."

Rachel and I finish the rest of our lunch, drama free. Afterwards, Rachel heads home to spend the rest of the day with Colin and the twins. While I'm going to spend time with my mom, like Landry suggested. I decide to give him a quick call before heading over there. Our conversation is short and Landry urges me to spend the night at home with my mom. I try to keep my anxiety to a minimum as my mind tries to lead me to the worst-case scenario about why Landry wants to spend the night away from me.

Chapter 18

Landry

I slept like shit last night. It was the first night after several of not having Hollynd in my bed and I hated every minute, but I knew she needed a night away. She's been on eggshells around me for the last three days. I wanted her to have a night for herself.

I could tell by her text messages last night that she was full of worry, and I can't really blame her, considering how I keep messing things up. But I don't want her to worry about me and my sorry ass. I want to worry about her, I want to be the one to take care of her. Hollynd deserves it more than anyone else. I still don't know why she's with me, but she is, and I will never give her up.

Also, I wanted to spend the evening with Rob. I knew we had to talk this crap over, and about what had happened on New Year's. It was a conversation we had had before, though I think Rob is getting to the end of his patience with me.

Rob reminded me that Hollynd is the best thing that has ever happened to me, and he's right. Then Rob showed me something that broke my goddamn heart. It was a picture on his phone that he had taken that night. Hollynd and I were asleep together on the bathroom floor. Her head was propped up under a towel and rested on the side of the bathtub.

Hollynd's face was red from crying and her makeup was smeared around her eyes. I was flat on the floor with my body curled up against hers. I'm shirtless because I had probably thrown up on it at this point. My arms are wrapped around her, and my head laid on her thighs. I look dead to the world. I didn't know if I wanted to cry or throw up after seeing that picture. I'm so ashamed of myself. I asked Rob to send me a copy of that picture, hoping that I can use it as a reminder of what happens when I act like an asshole and how grateful I should be to have that angel there with me. Hollynd is definitely too good for me.

Classes are going to start back up in a couple of days and I'm determined to spoil Hollynd rotten over the next two days. I owe her at least that much. I started working on my plan yesterday, that's why I pushed her to go see her mom. But one night away from her is enough. I'm ready to have my girl back in my bed, but first I have a few other things planned.

I arrive at Hollynd's house precisely at one o'clock and find her waiting impatiently for me at the door, so much so that I didn't even ring the doorbell before the door thrusts open and Hollynd jumps into my arms. She smells fantastic, like a combination of vanilla and cinnamon. I wrap my arms around her tightly and savor this moment. Even though I only saw her the day before, I feel like it's been much longer.

"I missed you, baby," I say, while wrapping my fingers in her long strands of hair which lays softly on her shoulders.

"I missed you too." Hollynd says while she perches up on her tiptoes to reach my lips with hers for a kiss.

What starts as a soft closed mouth kiss quickly escalates into an open-mouthed hard kiss.

"Is your mom home?" I cannot resist asking because this kiss has my blood moving south quickly.

"Yes." Hollynd mumbles while our mouths are still attached.

"Damn," I grumble as I pull away from Hollynd. "I guess this is going to have to wait until later."

"Hmm, I guess so." Hollynd plants a tiny kiss on my jawline. "Come say hi to Mom and then we'll go."

"Good idea, since the last time I saw her, I wasn't in the best shape."

Of course, I'm referring to our New Year's Day supper. Waves of shame wash over my insides when I think about it.

After removing my shoes and jacket, I follow Hollynd into the living room where her mother is knitting quietly while watching a movie.

"Mom, Landry's here," Hollynd says to get her mom's attention.

"Oh, Landry," Francine rises from her spot, setting down her knitting items. She comes over to me and gives me a hug. "I hope you are feeling better."

Hollynd and I give each other a quick glance, knowing she's referring to the supper where we tried to play it off as a wild night of too much drinking, rather than a violent night of mixing drugs and booze. I would hate for Francine to know the truth about that night, or the truth about me and my self-sabotaging ways. I want her to see me as being good enough for her daughter. Hollynd always tries to protect her mother and keep her in the dark when dealing with anything bad or stressful. She told me once that her mother took the death of Hollynd's father very hard, which is understandable. Hollynd, being the caregiving person she is, does everything in her power to take care of her mother and protect her.

"Yes, Francine. Thank you." I return the hug while realizing how much I needed that embrace.

Hollynd's mother is such a wonderful woman. Nothing at all like my mother. Francine radiates love, especially for her family. I can see it in her eyes whenever she talks to or talks about her family. Hollynd is so lucky to have a mother like her and their close relationship is something to be admired.

"Do you two want me to fix you something to eat or make some coffee?" Francine offers.

"Thank you, Mom, but I think we are heading out," Hollynd interjects.

"Oh course. You two lovebirds go and have a great day."

"Thanks, Mom. I'll text you later." Hollynd leans over and kisses her mother on the cheek. I follow behind and do the same.

"Take care of my girl, Landry," Francine says to me.

"Always," I promise without hesitation. *Always.*

Bundling up in our winter gear, Hollynd and I head to my car where I have two hot chocolates waiting for us in thermal mugs to make sure they remain hot. My entire car smells like chocolate.

"So, are you going to tell me what the plans are for today or am I going to have to follow you blindly?" Hollynd asks while I hand her a travel mug of hot chocolate.

Smirking her way, I give her a wink and drive away from her house.

The first place I want to take her is to our favourite spot at Pebblestone Lake. Though it's too cold for us to sit out on the snow-covered beach, it's still a beautiful view even from the car with the sun shining across the frozen water. It looks like a lake made of glitter. Plus, it's our spot. I want to take Hollynd there first so we can sit and talk. I made some decisions over the last couple of days that I want to share with her. We need to clear the air from the night of my dad's party. Though it's easier to leave that shit alone, I know we have to talk about it.

After I park in front of the beach, I keep the car running because it's too cold to have it not running. I take off my seatbelt so I can shift more comfortably in my seat and Hollynd does the same. I clear my throat before I begin.

"Hollynd, I think we need to talk."

A panicked look flashes in her eyes. "Are you okay?"

Such a selfless girl, of course Hollynd's worrying about me. I reach over and grab her hand, bringing it up to my lips, kissing her palm gently.

"We need to talk about the other night."

Hollynd shakes her head slightly and opens her mouth to say something, but I continue before she gets the chance.

"No, baby we do. There are things I need to say to you, things I should've been said days ago."

Hollynd looks down at her legs and fidgets her fingers. She's nervous. Hell, so am I. I keep her hand I had just kissed in mine and continue.

"I know I messed up the other night, again. I shouldn't have taken those pills. It was stupid of me and I'm sorry. And I'm sorry that you had to take care of my sorry ass all night. The thought of you sleeping on a bathroom floor makes me sick to my stomach. You're worth so much more than that, Cricket. The fact that you were there on that floor to help me, well, I never want you to do that again. I'm the type of person who belongs on a bathroom floor, not you. You deserve so much better than that. So much better than me."

I can see tears are now forming in her eyes and her bottom lip is beginning to shake.

"Are you breaking up with me, Landry?" Hollynd asks.

"Hell, no! I mean I should, it would be the best thing for you, but I'm far too selfish for that."

"Landry, don't say that." Hollynd shakes her head which ends up releasing a tear that was near the edge of her eyelid.

"It's true, Crick. I'm a mess. You saw me the other night, I shouldn't have taken that stuff. I knew that before I took it, but I did it anyway. I just, ugh, I don't know. When I'm high, I don't hear him or feel him anymore. I don't really feel anything, you know?"

Hollynd's still not looking at me but nods her head.

"But what it does to you and Rob, that makes it worse. You're probably the only two people in the world that care about me and I'm constantly hurting you. But I'm going to stop. From now on Hollynd, I swear to you I'm done with drugs."

"Landry," Hollynd's tone tells me that she doesn't believe me. I can't blame her.

"No, this time Hollynd, I swear to you. Yesterday I contacted a therapist and I'm going to meet with her to get this figured out."

"Are you serious?"

"Yes. I don't want to lose you and I know you won't put up with it forever. I won't let you. I want to do this for myself, for you, and for Rob."

"I think that's a great idea, Landry." Hollynd face now bears a smile, and she has turned to look at me. "I will help you anyway I can."

"Well, there is one thing I need from you right now."

"What's that?" Hollynd asks with hesitancy in her voice.

"Be honest with me. Let me have it again, like you did the other morning. Tell me all the gross feelings I caused you. I don't want you holding them in or thinking I'm not listening to you. I'm listening. Tell me!"

"I don't know. Sad, I guess."

"No, I mean it Crick. Tell me the whole truth. You were clearly angry with me. Did you think about why you were dealing with this bullshit? Tell me, please." My voice is rising probably more than it should, but I need her to freak out on me. I know she was feeling it, now I needed her to say it.

"Yes, I was mad at you Landry."

"How mad?"

"Really fucking mad. You promised me you wouldn't do that again and you did it, anyway. I felt betrayed by you. Were you high when you slept with me?" Hollynd asks with disgust in her voice.

"A little."

"Did you think about telling me that you were high?"

"No, I was too ashamed." Now it's me that can't meet her eyes and I'm looking out the window instead.

"You really scared me," Hollynd says in a meek tone. "The way your eyes didn't seem to recognize me, the violent heaving, the yelling at me. And you don't remember any of it?"

I shake my head, "Not really. I'm sorry. But Rob and Josh did a pretty good job of filling me in on how much of an asshole I was being."

"I didn't know you and Josh were that close." Hollynd mentions as she begins to chew nervously on her fingernails.

"Josh and I aren't that close."

"He cares about you, Landry. A lot."

"I don't know about that, Crick. He tolerates me."

"You need to pay more attention, Landry. There are people who care about you, and it might surprise you if you just let them in a little."

Hollynd's words tug at something deep in my chest. It's hard to let people in.

"Josh said I was too good for you." Hollynd continues without taking her eyes off her now torn fingernail.

"He's right." I answer without hesitation.

"Maybe," Hollynd says in a whisper, and I'm not sure if she is saying that to me or to herself. I feel a panic sensation begin to move in my stomach knowing I could lose her. "But I'm not going to leave you, Landry."

Slight relief settles in.

"That's all I need, Cricket. Just you."

I reach over to Hollynd, who leans towards me as I place my hand along the nape of her neck and pull her towards me. Our lips press hard and cling to each other desperately. *God, I love this woman.*

I pull away and say, "Let's go home. I have a surprise for you."

Hollynd smiles widely and nods in agreement. *I will fix this, Cricket.*

Chapter 19

Hollynd

I have no idea what Landry's surprise might be, but I can tell by the route we are driving that we are heading to his apartment. He tells me on the way there that Rob has left for the night with some friends on a ski trip, so we will be all alone tonight. My heart lets out a little leap, and butterflies are dancing in my stomach. My mind, on the other hand, is regretting not wearing matching underwear.

Once we get up into the apartment, Landry stops me in the entryway before we go in any further.

"I have a surprise for you in my room." Landry tells me, and I involuntarily roll my eyes.

"Oh, I'm sure you do."

Landry kisses the side of my head. "That's later. This is something else."

Landry takes my hand and leads me to his bedroom, opens the door and allows me to walk in first. I look around at the room I have spent many nights in. Everything is different. The bed has been moved against the far wall and is now covered in a new bedspread that is dark grey with deep purple stripes. There are matching curtains hanging in the window above the bed. Even the curtain rod has been replaced from the plain white rod that used to hold the plain black curtains to a chrome rod with intricate details of sparkling stones at each end. The globe light fixture has been changed out to a high-end fixture that matches the curtain rod. The entire room sparkles. On the wall opposite of the bed sits a brand-new desk and chair, along with a new light blue MacBook placed on top.

"Landry, you remodeled your room." I state in awe of the transformation.

"No, Crick. Our room. I want you to move in with me." Landry wraps his arms around my waist from behind me.

"Seriously?" Landry pulls my body around.

"Yes. I want you here with me every night." Landry's now facing me with his hands resting on each of my upper arms.

"What about Rob?"

"Rob's fine with it. I already asked him."

"What about my mom?" I chew my lip, wondering how my mom will take this news.

"Do you think she's ready to live without you?"

"I think so, I know she wants me to be happy."

"So, is that a yes?"

"Yes! Oh my God, yes!" I jump straight into him hooking my legs around his waist and my arms around his neck. Landry laughs with pure happiness while he hugs my entire body and spins us around. *This feels like home.*

After putting me down, Landry turns towards the new desk and new laptop.

"This is for you, Crick."

"What for?" I ask in confusion.

"It's your place to write. You said you want to write, and I want you to do everything you want to do."

"But Landry, I can't accept the MacBook. It's too much."

"It's not enough. I would buy you ten more if you asked for them. This is your dream, and I will do anything you need to help you."

"What about your dreams, Landry?" I ask while gazing up at him.

Landry looks down at me in all seriousness. "You are my dream, Cricket. Just you."

I reach up and kiss him hard. In one swift motion Landry spins me towards the bed almost crushing me as we both topple onto the new bedding. Landry does not stay down for long, but rather moves into a kneeling position in between my widespread knees. Landry tugs his shirt over his head, bearing his hard chest. That's when I noticed the clear covering over his left pec muscle.

"What is that?" I ask.

Looking down to where I'm looking, Landry grins. "Oh, that's a new tattoo I got yesterday."

I sit up so I can look at it closely and notice it is a simple sketch of a cricket.

"Is it because of me?"

"Well, I don't have any other insects tattooed on my body, so either I have a strange fascination with one of the most annoying bugs on earth or I'm completely and stupidly in love with this girl I know named Cricket."

I look up at him in awe, trying to figure out how I got so lucky to receive love from a man like Landry.

"I love you, Landry."

"I love you too, Cricket."

After a tiny kiss on the lips, Landry's patience has worn out. "Now lay down, because I'm not done with you."

An hour later, Landry and I are laying together in a peaceful silence.

"I really like your tattoo," I say while I nuzzle deeper into Landry's chest, the side without the new tattoo. "I think I want one."

"Yeah?"

"Yeah. I want something that reminds me of you too."

"Babe, you don't have to do that." Landry mumbles as he presses a kiss onto the side of my head.

"I want to. I want something I can look at any moment and think of you."

"Well, say the word and I can text my guy."

"Yes, text him please."

Two days later, I'm looking down at my first tattoo on the inside of my right wrist. A simple calligraphy typed L with tiny purple flowers wrapping around it. It's small, delicate, and perfect.

Chapter 20

Landry

It's been four months since Hollynd moved in with me and I have never been happier. School has been going great. I have my girl with me all the time, and now that my dad is mayor, I never have to see him. As I promised Hollynd and Rob, I have been attending therapy once a week. Though I would rather not sit and talk about my father or my drug tendencies to a stranger, I know it's important to Hollynd and Rob. Honestly, I think I'm fine, but everyone is happy, so I keep it up.

We still go out and party some nights but searching out drugs to numb my pain has been far from my mind. I do miss letting go and flying high occasionally, but I don't miss the nights on the bathroom floor or the next day full of shame. This life is better.

We are nearing the end of our last semester at Creston College. Since Creston is a college that is designed to transfer out of, in order to finish the program at a larger institution, Hollynd and I both applied and were accepted to the university in Elmerson.

Rob is a year behind us in his studies, so he will stay at Creston for his last year there without us. I'm worried about this, but Rob keeps telling me to stop being such a pussy and that he will be fine without his older brother around cramping his style.

I haven't told my father that I'm planning on moving, though I doubt he will care since it will mean I am out of his life. My father must sense that I'm doing well because it's on a beautiful May afternoon while Rob and I are sharing a couple of beers on our balcony when my text message notification goes off.

David:
You need to come to the house this evening.

Landry:
Why?

David:
Because I have told you to.
SEVEN O'CLOCK

Landry:
I'm busy.

David:
You will do as you're told.
Be here! Sober!

Slamming my phone down on the table beside me, I drink the remaining half of the bottle of beer I have in one gulp. I don't know what the hell he wants, but I don't want to go, though I have no choice. I have plans with Hollynd, and it seems if I must stop by my dad's house, I'm going to have to take her with me.

Hollynd and I arrive at my father's house just after seven. My father meets us at the entryway after we arrive, still dressed as though he's at the office with a three-piece suit on, though he's carrying a glass of brown liquor in his hand. This is a very different attire than the casual clothes Hollynd and I are wearing. Hollynd is in a pair of tight denim jeans and fitted hoodie that hugs all her curves, while I'm in a pair of black jeans and a grey hoodie. Our original plan is a night at the movies, which I still intend to do. I'm not letting my father ruin our evening this time.

"Hollynd, I didn't know you would be stopping by with Landry tonight. How wonderful it is to see you again." My father leans in and presses a kiss to her cheek.

I can smell the rank phoniness from here. Hollynd politely returns the sentiment, though I can tell by the tenseness in her shoulders and tight smile that she's not comfortable. After seeing firsthand how volatile the relationship I have with my father is, she's not distracted by his charm.

"David, I hope you don't mind me coming with Landry," Hollynd replies while tightening her grip on my hand.

"No, not at all. Please come into the living room, take a seat. I'll get some drinks."

Hollynd and I sit together closely on the leather couch while my father gets a glass of wine for Hollynd and scotch for me.

"Well, I hear congratulations are in order," my father says while handing us our drinks and sitting in the single chair facing the couch. "You both are accepted into Stranton University next fall."

"Yes, we're both very excited to move to Elmerson together." I sternly say to my father while I take a drink. I know he's up to something.

"Well, it's really too bad. I'm sure Stranton is an elite institution, especially for the Liberal Arts programs. And I know that's what you like to study Hollynd, but I hear that Oak University in Reddington is very strong in its technology studies. One of the best in the country. You know, Landry, the dean at Oak University was a good friend of mine during my days of university."

"Is that so?" I wait for the other shoe to drop.

"Well, I want you to consider Oak University before you make your decision. You know I was speaking with Dean Wess today and he thinks you would benefit from attending a university like his. Not only tech studies, but Dean Wess is very interested in state politics as well and you know what that could do for me in the future. It's such a wonderful opportunity for both of us, son."

"Well, Dad, there isn't a Liberal Arts program at Oak."

"Are you two committed to going to university together? I mean, a year or two apart wouldn't be the end of the world. You have lots of time."

I can feel Hollynd shift uncomfortably in the seat beside me as she sips on her wine.

"Hollynd and I have no intention of spending a year or two apart." I sternly say.

My father shoots me a glare before letting out a deep laugh. "Oh, I remember young love, you lose all common sense in it. Hollynd, what do you think? You wouldn't want to hold Landry back, would you?"

"With all due respect, David, I don't think Landry attending Stranton University would really hold him back. It's a great institution too." Hollynd is smiling at my father while rubbing the top of my leg.

My father clears his throat. "You know, I have spoken to Rob and he will go to Oak when he's ready to transfer and since I will be paying for both of your tuitions it would be nice to contribute to the same place."

"I don't need you to pay. I can get a student loan." I protest.

"Don't be silly, Landry. I'm paying for your education as I have done for all my sons."

We sit in silence for a few moments before my father asks Hollynd if she would mind going to the kitchen to grab the tray of snacks he had his housekeeper prepare earlier. He's trying to get me alone. Hollynd politely nods and heads out to the kitchen. Once she's out of earshot, my father sets his glass down firmly on the coffee table in front of him and leans towards me with anger in his eyes.

"Listen to me Landry, you will attend Oak University if I decide you are attending, and you won't fight me on it if you want me to keep paying for you and your brother's education."

"Goddamn it, Dad, would you stop it already? Stop trying to control my life. I'm so sick of it. I'm happy for the first time and I will not let you shit all over it!" My voice is getting louder.

"Happy? Why because you found a girl stupid enough to think she's in love with you? You're so pathetic to follow a piece of pussy around to her university of choice because she warms your bed at night."

Instantly, rage boils over inside me. I feel my fists clenching and it's all I can do not to grab my father by the throat and choke the life out of him.

"I'm your son, and I'm happy! Isn't that good enough for you? I'm so sick of this shit." Now I'm standing, and my hands are tugging at my hair in frustration.

I hear Hollynd return to the room with the platter of food. She calmly walks over to the table and sets down the tray. Then with a stern, though loving look she says, "Landry, I think we should probably go now."

Before I can respond, my father—forgetting to put on his phony mask— interrupts. "I'm sorry, sweetheart, but I'm not through talking with my son and he will not be leaving until I have decided, or he becomes out of control. He has told you about his anger issues, hasn't he? Oh, and not to mention the drugs?"

My father is being smug in his shaming of me thinking Hollynd will find this information shocking. But my girl is tough, and I can see her strength coming to the surface.

Standing tall with her head high, Hollynd turns directly to face my father. "David, I know all there is to know about Landry. I know that he's a good man who works his ass off every day to become better. If you would take one moment to stop thinking about yourself and look at your son in front of you, you would see that too." Her voice is completely steady.

My father and Hollynd are now staring each other down. I'm dumbstruck by the woman in front of me. No one has ever stood up to my father before, especially in regards to his feelings about me.

"I'm sorry to burst your little love bubble, but my son is nothing but a loser and it's only a matter of time before he messes up this relationship too. I'm not interested in your opinion on what's best for him. You won't be around much longer."

"Enough!" I finally find my voice. "Dad, we are leaving. Hollynd, let's go."

I grab her hand and pull her towards the door. We don't bother saying goodbye as I march us straight out the front down and slam it shut behind us.

"Landry, I'm sorry. I know I should have minded my own business, but hearing him say such terrible things to you, I couldn't stand it anymore."

Hollynd thinks I'm mad at her. I'm far from mad at her. In fact, I'm completely taken by her and her strength. I grab her fiercely and smash my mouth into hers. Hollynd instantly lets out a moan. I move my hands to the back of her head and around her waist.

"I love you so much!"

"So, you're not mad at me?"

"Hell, no! You're the first person to stand up for me. Do you know how that feels? I don't know how I got so lucky, but you're the absolute best thing that has ever come into my life. Do you want to skip the movies? I have a better idea."

"Sure. What do you have planned?"

I pull her towards my parked car without answering. "We have to make a quick stop. Well, I do, you have to wait in the car."

Tonight is the night everything changes. *This is forever.*

Chapter 21

Hollynd

I'm waiting in the car while Landry runs into the mall. The sun has set, and the parking lot lights are coming on overhead. I'm still trying to calm myself down after my altercation with David Hayles. I rarely speak out of turn like that, but I couldn't stand to hear him talk to Landry in that manner anymore. What a horrible man!

After twenty minutes, I see Landry returning to the car with a bag in hand. It looks like a bottle of something, maybe wine?

Once he's seated in the car I ask, "Did you get us wine?"

"Close. Champagne."

"Why? Are we celebrating something?" I ask, still confused where his thoughts are at.

"We will be soon." With his lopsided smirk, Landry starts the car.

Ten minutes later we are pulling up to our familiar spot on the shores of Pebblestone Lake. Opening the door, Landry gets out of the car and grabs the champagne and a blanket from the back. Together, we make our way down to the sand and sit where we spent our first date, only eight months earlier. Once we are seated, Landry goes to speak, but I hush him.

"Shh, listen," I whisper. In the distance, the crickets are chirping like mad. "Your pet crickets are calling for you."

Landry rolls his body onto mine in a wrestling move. "You're such a brat. You're the only Cricket I want to hear calling for me."

I can hardly catch my breath from my full belly laugh as Landry settles his legs in between mine and props himself up on one elbow beside me.

"Will you marry me?" Landry's voice echoes through the air.

"What?" I say in a shocked state, questioning if I heard what I think I heard.

"Will you marry me?"

"When?" I respond with a laugh because I'm not taking him seriously.

"Right now."

"How can we get married right now? We're all alone on a dark beach. Who's going to marry us?"

"Are you saying yes?"

"I'm saying you're crazy."

Settling his hand over my forehead and stroking the hair off the top of it, Landry stares straight into my eyes. "I'm serious, Cricket. Marry me right here, right now. Having a minister or a Justice of the Peace doesn't make it any more real for me. I will give vows to you, just between us and it will be as real as any traditional wedding. I want this, Hollynd, and I want you forever."

"You must be serious, you called me Hollynd," I note.

Landry smirks as he reaches down into his pocket and returns with a closed hand. When he opens his fingers he exposes two thin white gold bands. One larger band and a smaller one.

"This is what I was actually doing in the mall. The champagne was an afterthought," Landry confesses while staring at me, waiting for my reaction.

"You were buying us wedding bands?" I look down at the two pieces of jewelry.

"Yes."

"You actually gave this some thought; this isn't just you jabbering on in the moment?"

"No. I want to marry you and I have known that I wanted to marry you for a long time now. But I don't want to wait on the formality. We can do the whole big thing and follow the conventional traditions some other day, but for right now I only want you and me to do this because it's what we want to do."

I reach into Landry's palm and pick up the two rings and slide them both on my pointer finger to examine them more closely.

"Yes." I say as I gaze back at Landry, who's still waiting for me to answer. "Yes, I will marry you right here, right now."

Grabbing my face, Landry pulls me in for a deep kiss, only to break away with a bright smile. "Let's do this."

We both rise to our feet and turn to face each other. We grab each other's hands with the two white gold rings still laying loosely around my pointer finger.

Landry clears his throat and takes a big breath before he speaks.

"As the moon, the stars, and those goddamn noisy crickets as my witnesses, I promise to love you for as long as I have a breath left in my chest, as long as I have a beat in my heart, as long as I have a sin to confess. You have saved me in so many ways. This darkness in my head was killing me until I found you. You are not my everything, Hollynd, you are my only thing."

I look up into Landry's eyes through the blurriness of my own while he pulls the smaller band off my pointer finger and slips it onto the fourth finger on my left hand.

Landry's right, the darkness that always occupies his eyes is gone at this moment. Everything that had been suffocating him and eating away at his soul seem to be gone. He's perfect. His dark hair and piercing blue eyes, and that smirk that raises more on the right side of his mouth than the left. *Perfect.*

It's crazy to have fallen in love this quickly, but it was something I had no control over because once Landry Hayles had decided I was his, there was no coming back from his world. And honestly, I didn't want to come back. For as crazy and messed up his world could be, it was where he lived, and it was the only place I wanted to be.

I feel my hands beginning to vibrate in the palms of Landry's hands. I know this is not how I imagined my wedding would be. Out in the middle of the night, on a beach in the dark. There are no witnesses and no legal bindings, but I feel deep down in my heart that this is as real as it gets. I should probably say that I'm wishing my family were here to witness this too, but honestly, I'm okay with them not being here. This isn't about them, it's about me and Landry. It will always be about me and Landry.

I try to collect my thoughts as I take in my breath and look up into the eyes that are staring straight into my soul. "Landry," I start to speak, but a slight cry catches in my throat. I give myself another breath. "I have never thought I would get married in a place like this, alone in the dark, but I always knew that when I got married it would be with the other half of my soul. And my other half is you. None of this other stuff matters because my soul finally feels whole when it's together with your soul. So yes, Landry, I will be your wife and you will be my husband for all of time, because you are me and I am you."

Landry's eyes never once budge from mine, but I notice a slight hitch in his breath as I slip the ring on his left hand. Slowly he moves his head down towards mine and I hear his whisper, "You are me and I am you," as our lips press together, binding the words we spoke to each other.

I pull away to give myself a moment before I'm overtaken with emotion.

"I can't believe you swore during your wedding vows," I giggle and a slight shake of my head.

"It's just those stupid crickets are so loud," Landry replies with his hands still gripping mine.

"I like the crickets," I retort with a smug smile.

"I know you do, my Cricket."

"And I like you too, husband."

"And I like you. Now shut up and kiss me, wife."

I perch on my tippy toes and bring my lips to his. It's the same lips I have kissed a thousand times before. Our kisses are still pulsating with the same desire, the same eagerness, the same neediness of new lovers drunk on lust. Just like our first kiss, just like I know our last kiss will be at the end of time.

And with that kiss, we are married. Just like that. Well, by the laws of the moon and stars, as this was not a traditional wedding and anything but ordinary. It was out on a beach in the middle of the night. Just the two of us. No family, no friends, no justice of the peace, only us. But the technicalities and lack of lawmakers don't make it any less real, any less binding, because I know in my heart that this man is my husband, and I am his wife.

Forever...

Chapter 22

Hollynd

I watch the line of power poles fly past the car window one by one. In the distance, there are poplar trees covered in last summer leaves that are threatening to turn yellow any day now. I gaze out the window with a permanent grin on my face as I admire the beauty of the land passing by. My life feels more complete than it has felt before. Beside me in the driver's seat sits my husband of three months, Landry. I turn my attention from the outside scenery to look at him as he stares intensely at the road. He's a picture of perfection, with his black shirt and black cargo shorts. Wearing aviator sunglasses with his dark hair. I can't help but stare.

Landry must sense me admiring him from the passenger seat because as I'm watching him, he reaches over and grabs my hand, bringing it up to his lips and presses a kiss on my knuckles. His eyes never leave the road.

Landry and I moved to Elmerson only a few weeks ago. We found a tiny one-bedroom apartment on the fourth floor of an old brownstone building in downtown. It's close enough to campus that we are able to walk to class, although classes haven't begun yet. Landry's father has recently informed Landry that he will no longer pay for any of his school tuition or housing costs. Like me, Landry has to take out student loans to pay for school. We've both been working hard all summer to save money for living expenses. We are also planning to get part-time jobs when we begin school. Between school and part-time work, we know that our time together will be limited but we both agreed that it is better than the alternative of living in separate cities like Landry's father wanted. Now we are the stereotypical starving students, which means we will search for a modest apartment. Honestly, I don't care what type of place we live in as long as Landry's with me.

It's the long weekend in September which is why we are driving back to Brighten for the first time since we moved away. It's my nieces' birthday party today and our attendance is mandatory, or at least that's what the *My Little Pony* invitation demanded.

It will be two busy days as we have to fit in time with my family and with Rob. Landry has no intention of seeing his father. The plan is to spend the afternoon with my family and go out clubbing with Rob and our other friends in the evening. We are only planning on spending one night here in Brighten as we are both anxious to be back to our little life together in Elmerson.

Chapter 23

Landry

I wake up the next morning squished between Hollynd and the wall in her old bedroom. We were out late last night, and though my body would much rather be sleeping, my mind is keeping me awake.

I can't help but worry about Rob. He wasn't his usual self last night. From the moment I arrived at Rob's apartment to our time at the club, he seemed out of it. Something's bothering him. I tried to get it out of him yesterday, but he kept on insisting it's nothing.

I look at the clock and see that it is already nine o'clock. Hollynd's still out cold beside me. This girl is the master of sleeping in when she's tired. I'm surprised how hard Hollynd sleeps considering she used to have such a problem with insomnia a few years ago. Hollynd told me that if she wasn't majorly stressed out, her sleep was great.

I shuffle my way out of the bed without waking her up. I decide to have a shower and a shave before I head downstairs.

After my shower, I leave Hollynd a text telling her I went to Rob's for a bit and that I would be back by the afternoon. We're planning to drive back to Elmerson tonight after an early supper with her family.

When I get downstairs, there's no sign of Francine. I'm not sure if she's gone or perhaps still sleeping. Either way, I decide to be quiet in case she's still sleeping and exit the house without a peep.

After a quick stop at a local coffee shop, I arrive at Rob's apartment armed with six egg and cheese sandwiches and three coffees, in case Nick is there too. I still have my apartment keys, so I let myself in. When I walk into the apartment, I find Rob already up, dressed in blue sweatpants and a grey hoodie, and sitting on the couch staring mindlessly at the TV.

"Oh hey, you're up. I brought you and Nick breakfast." I set the takeout bags and coffees on the coffee table.

Reaching over for a coffee, Rob grabs a breakfast sandwich from the paper bag riddled with grease stains.

"Thanks. Nick's not here, though. He's on a twelve-hour shift." Rob takes a bite out of his sandwich.

"I couldn't imagine being an EMT driver. It must be a stressful gig." I take a coffee from the tray.

"Yeah, Nick told me some horror stories from the job." Rob takes another bite out of his egg sandwich. "Where's Hollynd?"

"Still sleeping. I wanted to see how you're feeling this morning." I sit on the chair beside the couch and take my breakfast sandwich out of the bag.

"Landry, would you get off it already?" Rob huffs.

"I can tell something's wrong, so if you could stop being such a baby about it and tell me, then maybe I can help you."

"Do you ever think that maybe I don't want your help, Landry? You can't barge in here and demand to take over all the time. I'm a grown man, you know."

"Shit Rob, I know that. But I'm your big brother, it's my job to look out for you."

"Okay, but if I tell you I don't want you to go all bullish and start stirring shit up."

"Fine, I won't." I lie while I raise my right hand like I'm taking an oath.

"I got a call from the college on Thursday. There's something wrong with my tuition funds, like a stopped payment or something. I don't know what's going on. I tried to call Dad, but he told me that maybe I should be more like you and get a student loan. Then he hung up on me. But when I looked into getting a loan, I was rejected because I'm still considered a dependent of Dad's. So basically, they won't give me a student loan because Dad has too much money. Now every time I call him, it goes to voicemail. Landry, I don't know what I'm going to do. I might have to drop out." Rob drops his head in defeat.

"Like hell you are dropping out of school, Rob!" I rise out of my chair enraged. "I'm going over to Dad's house right now and I'll straighten this out."

"Landry, no. You're not going over there. This is my problem, and I will deal with it."

"Listen Rob, Dad only does this stuff when he's pissed about something. Knowing him, it probably has something to do with me."

"Why would he stop my tuition payment because of you?" Rob tosses his hands up.

"Because he's a cruel bastard, Rob!" I'm now yelling and my voice echoes throughout the room.

"Landry, I don't want you to get involved. You have this great life going with Hollynd, and I don't want it getting messed up because of me. It's time for me to take care of myself."

"I promised Mom that I would always take care of you. I know that I haven't always been an upstanding person, but this is the one thing I can at least say that I'm proud of. I take care of my family. There isn't anything I wouldn't do for you, even if that means taking all the shit Dad has to offer. Don't worry about me. I'm going to go over there and figure out why he's being such an asshole about this. You're not dropping out of school, do you understand me?"

Rob rubs his face in frustration. "Fine, but I'm going with you."

Thirty minutes later, Rob and I are sitting in my father's living room waiting for his arrival. His longtime housekeeper, Jean, greeted us at the door. She told us he's currently in a Zoom meeting in his office but would be down shortly.

Rob sits on the couch, fidgeting with his fingers. Having changed clothes before we left the apartment, Rob's in jeans and a white button-down shirt while I'm still in my black sweatpants and black hoodie. I can't sit still like Rob is doing. In fact, I can't sit at all. I'm pacing around the room, and I can feel my anger rising by the minute.

Finally, I hear the heavy footsteps make their way down the staircase outside the doorway. Moments later, my father arrives with a look of annoyance on his face. Wearing a suit and tie, he's dressed for work. Even though it's a weekend, he's always in 'mayor' mode. My father stops just inside the doorway to look around and survey his ground before he attacks.

"Well, to what do I owe the pleasure of the visit from my two sons?" My father's voice booms throughout the room.

"What did you do to Rob's tuition payment?" I can't control myself and march straight over to him, so we are face to face.

"I assumed since you turned down my payment for school that your brother would like to take the same independent route." A flash of vengeance flickers in my father's eyes.

"Dad, I tried to get a student loan like you suggested but they turned me down." Rob says meekly.

"That's a shame, Robert." My father steps around me and walks over to the couch where Rob's sitting. "I'm sorry, son. I didn't realize it would cause such a hassle. The payment will be restored to the college on Monday."

Rob's looking embarrassed and rubs the back of his head. "Oh okay, thanks Dad. I didn't know what else to do aside from dropping out."

"Nonsense, you will not be dropping out of college, Robert. Isn't that right, Landry?" Dad turns his head to eye me up.

"I told him there is no way that's happening." I eye my father with suspicion. He gave in way too easy.

"Good, so this was all a misunderstanding. Now Robert, could you please give your brother and I a moment alone?"

"Sure." Rob answers hesitantly. He knows that every time my father and I are together, a fight ensues.

Rob leaves the room quickly as my father and I stare at each other. My father sits on the couch and motions for me to come over.

"Landry, come and sit." My father orders.

"I'd rather stand," I reply defiantly.

"Suit yourself. Look, we have a bit of an issue that needs to be resolved."

"Which is?" I cross my arms while still standing.

"You attending Oak University."

"Not going to happen. I have already moved to Elmerson with Hollynd, and I'm attending Stranton University. End of discussion."

"Well, not exactly. I have spoken to Dean Wess again, and he has expressed that he would like you to attend Oak."

"Why does he want me there? It makes no sense." I ask in annoyance.

"Apparently enrollment has been down in the Computer Science department and there is student quota that needs to be met. Plus, he seems to really like the idea of having students that come from notable families. Did you know that the daughter of Governor Cross attends Oak? I think there would be a plethora of great people you could connect with there. It would benefit everyone." My father leans further back in his chair and crosses his legs.

"And benefit you no doubt. What does this have to do with you?"

"Dean Wess and his colleagues have been very generous supporters of my campaigns in the past and have promised to do so for future runs I may decide to take. I need their support and I cannot risk losing it because you are hellbent on shacking up with some girl wanting to play house."

"I'm not going to Oak University!" I shout at my father.

"Here's the thing, Landry. I would hate to have to pull Rob's tuition money again from the college, but mark my words, I will do it."

"Why? Why would you want to have your son have to drop out of college just because you aren't getting your way with me?"

"Robert's not my son, you know that." My father has lowered his voice. "I don't really give a shit about his future, but I know you do. I know that somehow your whore of a mother made you believe it was your duty to take care of him."

My fists clench, and I can feel the rage rolling in my veins. "You're a selfish son of a bitch."

"No, Landry, I'm a successful son of a bitch. My biggest downfall is having a son like you. Someone who's ungrateful and defiant. Honestly, I would rather you not attend Oak either, because knowing you, you're going to make a fool out of me with your reckless behavior. But Dean Wess insists you attend, and I want my money!" The harshness of his voice deepens.

"What about Hollynd? I'm not leaving her!" My voice raises to match his.

"Well then, I guess you have a choice to make."

"Fuck!" I scream at the top of my lungs.

My hands raise to my head and I pull my hair as hard as I can. I feel like the walls are crashing down on me.

"Oh, keep your voice down. You always have such a flare for the dramatics." My father rolls his eyes and straightens his tie.

"Dad, please don't make me do this. Please." My anger has turned to desperation as panic is starting to set in as I plead to the monster that made me.

"I've made my mind up, Landry." My father's voice does not falter.

A rush of hot tears fills my eyes. I will not let my father see me cry, so I turn my back to him and walk over to a nearby table that's holding a bouquet of white lilies in a crystal vase. Backhanding the vase, I watch the flowers fly across the table and bounce onto the floor. The vase crashes onto the floor and breaks into three large pieces.

"I will never forgive you for this," I say with my back still turned to my father.

"I don't need your forgiveness, Landry. I need your compliance."

"I promised Hollynd I would be there with her. I promised her everything. Now I'm supposed to say I changed my mind and that I'm going to move out and live five hours away instead?"

"I don't really care what you tell her. Just be ready to start Oak on Wednesday. You can move back in here and make the hour commute each day."

"I'm not living here with you." I try to say with conviction, but the words reek with defeat.

"I think it will be for the best. That way I can keep an eye on you. Make sure you don't mess this up like you do everything else. One day you'll thank me for this."

My father rises to leave the room. Before he exits through the doorway, he pauses and looks over at me standing there, defeated, with my head hanging low.

"Clean yourself up. You look as pathetic as your mother did the day I kicked her out."

On that note, my father exits the room. He knows exactly how to twist the knife a little harder, even though it's been driven through your heart and death is imminent.

Several hours later, Hollynd and I are driving through the dark on our way back to Elmerson. I somehow made it through supper with her family, though it took all the strength I had to get the bile from rising into my throat every time I thought about the situation with my father.

I know Hollynd can sense something is wrong. I mentioned to her that I had seen my father but did not go into the details of my visit. We've barely spoken during the drive home, though we have kept our hands clenched together. Once in a while, I will feel her thumb stroke the tops of my knuckles, but she doesn't once let go. I'm grateful that it's so dark right now so I can't see her worried expression. Despite not being able to see her face, I can feel the waves of worry coming off her entire body.

I don't know how I'm going to tell her what happened with my father. How am I going to tell her that I'm leaving her to move back to Brighten and attend Oak University? Is it possible to explain that I have to do this for Rob's sake and that I have no other choice? How do I not break her heart by taking back all the promises I made to her and by shattering all the dreams we have planned?

I can't do it. Not tonight. Tonight, I just want to get home and go to bed with my wife and pretend this day never happened. I want Hollynd to rest well in my arms and not worry about what the days ahead are going to bring. I want her to dream in ignorance and believe for one more night that I'm not a guy who breaks all his promises and abandons her in a city where she has no one else. Where she will be alone. But that's tomorrow's problem. Tonight, I will swallow my guilt and cherish my only thing, one last time.

Chapter 24

Hollynd

I roll over to find a cold and empty bed beside me. Landry and I fell asleep almost immediately after we arrived home late last night. We both seemed too exhausted to even give into the temptation of being in bed together. There were only innocent touches, and a togetherness wrapped in love.

Until two a.m. that is. Awakened by the sensation of Landry's hands running over the smoothness of my breasts took me from my sleep. At first his touch was soft, but with each pass of his hand, his grip became tighter. Somehow, in the complete darkness of our bedroom, our mouths made their way to each other while our hands explored the other with gentle eagerness. It was wonderful, but different.

Landry's touches and kisses seemed softer and slower. It almost felt dreamlike with the way he slowly maneuvered his body between my open thighs. Whispers of "I love you" echoed through the air as he thrusted himself inside of me. I let out velvet moans as his pace quickened and finally, we both erupted in a perfectly timed finish.

I fell back asleep soon after our middle of the night lovemaking session until now. Sitting up in the cold bed, I listen to Landry moving around the apartment. I check the time which reads six a.m. I wonder why he's up so early.

I get up and toss on a pair of pajama pants and a shirt before heading out to the living room. I find Landry sitting on the couch, clutching a cup of coffee with both hands. He looks exhausted. Dark circles are under both his eyes and there's no light in them. They look somewhere between dark and broken. His hair is a disheveled mess and I notice that his hands on his coffee cup are shaking.

"Baby, what's wrong?" I sit beside him on the couch. Before he answers, I pull the large blue blanket that hangs over the back of the couch and lay it over both of us.

Landry's eyes meet mine and they're so dark, more so than I realized a moment ago. My panic sets in. Something is very wrong.

"Hollynd, I have to leave Elmerson."

"Why? For how long?" I ask, with confusion.

"I'm going to Oak University instead of Stranton. I begin on Wednesday."

"Landry, what are you talking about?" I giggle slightly out of nervousness.

"I met with my father yesterday and we decided that it would be best if I attended Oak to finish off my degree."

"Oh, you and your father decided. I should have known this had something to do with him." I toss my arms up exaggeratingly. "Landry, enough is enough. Say no to your father once and for all. You live here now, with me. Remember me? We're done with his bullshit, we agreed. He can't hurt you when you're here. He can't control you with his money."

"It's not that simple, Cricket." Landry shifts his gaze downwards.

"Well, then please Landry, enlighten me because from where I sit it sounds like you're letting your father control you; again. Or maybe that's what you want, it's an easy way out for you."

"For Christ's sakes Hollynd, don't be stupid!" His eyes burst up to my face, burning with fury.

"Well, what am I supposed to think? Two weeks ago, we moved in together and everything's perfect. And now you're telling me you're moving out? Leaving me to go to a school five hours away?" I get off the couch and pace around the room.

My heart feels like it's beating a million beats a minute. The vibrating I noticed before in Landry's hands begin to move in mine as well. *This can't be happening.*

"Trust me, Hollynd. I don't want to do this to you."

"Then why are you doing this? I don't understand." My bottom lip quivers uncontrollably and tears break free from my eyes.

I sob as I wrap my arms around myself in some sort of form of self-preservation. Landry stands up from the couch and walks over to me. His large arms wrap tightly around my arms that I use to hold myself. My entire body is shaking in his arms. I would probably collapse to the floor if he wasn't holding me up.

"I'm sorry, Cricket. It's just something I have to do. We will still be together. Wait here for me. I promise I'll come back to you. I'm still yours and you're still mine, my wife." Landry whispers into my hair where his face is nestled.

Anger surges through my body like I have never felt before. I twist myself out of his embrace and shove him away from me as hard as I can.

"No Landry, I'm not your actual wife and you're not my actual husband because an actual husband would not leave his wife because 'daddy' said so. An actual husband wouldn't tell his wife to sit and wait for him when he's the one choosing to leave. That's not fair, Landry! None of this is fucking fair!"

I march out of the living room towards our bedroom. When I enter the room, I turn and slam the door so hard behind me I'm surprised none of the pictures fall off the walls.

I lean against the closed door and slide down it until my butt hits the carpeted floor. My tears are flowing at a rapid pace. I use the bottom of my shirt to wipe my face dry, only to have it soaked again almost instantly.

Five minutes later, I hear the front door slam and my entire body flinches. Landry must have left the apartment. I don't know if it's for now or for good. Either way, I don't move off the floor for over an hour until I can no longer feel my backside. I crawl over to the bed and lay down underneath the blankets. I feel like someone has kicked the shit out of me. I'm not sure how long I lay there for, but eventually, I feel my eyelids begin their weighted descent over my eyes and sleep takes over where the tears left off.

Chapter 25

Landry

I'm not your actual wife and you're not my actual husband because an actual husband would not leave his wife because 'daddy' said so. An actual husband would not tell his wife to sit and wait for him when he is the one choosing to leave.

Hollynd's words pulsate through my head over and over. I'm driving recklessly through the streets of Elmerson. It's a good thing that it's only seven in the morning and there's very little traffic right now. I'm gripping the steering wheel so tight that I feel like the bones of my knuckles may tear through my skin. I can't help but wonder how good that might feel at this moment.

My entire body is coursing with rage when I think about my father and this choice he's forcing me to make. Rob's future or living with Hollynd. Protecting my best friend, my brother, or keeping my word to the love of my life, my only thing.

Every part of me wants to drive to the shadiest part of Elmerson and score some blow right now, but I can't go down that path again. Another promise I've made to Hollynd and Rob, and I cannot afford to break this one, too. *But I want to. God, do I want to.* Resentment starts to build.

Instead of snorting up some relief, I find a gym that's open early and takes walk-in clients. Maybe if I beat the shit out of a punching bag for a few hours I can get rid of some of this rage and curb my cravings for numbness. Soon, I'm hammering my fists against the black bag, which is currently a poor substitute for my father's face. Over and over, I pound my fists until there's sweat dripping from my forehead. It's a good thing I keep gym clothes in my car along with a pair of sparring gloves, otherwise blood would drip from my knuckles right now at the same rate as my sweat.

By the time I finish executing my rage, I can barely lift my arms. In desperate need of a shower before I leave, I decide first to use the gym's sauna for a bit. I'm not ready to go back to the apartment and face Hollynd. I need to get this shit figured out in my head. I need a clear mind before I talk to her again.

Once I'm seated in the sauna, I let the warmth from the stones and sweet smell of cedar take over my senses. I love the smell of the cedar wood. It helps to calm my mind. When my heart rate has slowed down and my adrenaline drops to normal levels, I turn my focus on where I should go from here.

I debate in my mind about telling Hollynd about Rob's situations with his tuition and how my father is holding that over me to get me to attend Oak University. I'm sure she would understand why I need to go with that reasoning. For a moment, I think about telling her the story of Rob's paternal father, but quickly decide against that. It's too risky. This is one secret I intend to take to the grave.

Closing my eyes tightly, I lean my head against the dark wood. I'm so tired, I haven't slept since I woke up in the night and made love to Hollynd. God, it was amazing, though I had a gut wrenching feeling it would be the last time.

With my eyes still closed, I think back over the past year that Hollynd and I have been together. It's been the best year of my life. I think about getting married under the stars, Christmas with her family, our first date and first time together in my car. *This girl is my only thing.*

Soon, however, I find my mind slipping into the dark memories of our past. The party at Eddie's house, New Year's Eve, and now this morning. So many times, I've hurt her. So many times I have caused her cascading tears and wretched sobs. Every time I've lashed out when my father became involved with my life, she's been there to pick up my broken pieces. I don't know when, or if, this turmoil will ever end. How can I do this to her over and over? Am I being selfish keeping her to myself? All the while knowing that she's going to have to endure my never-ending battles with David Hayles? How can I expect Hollynd to always be the one to pick me up after I have crashed and burned again because of my own selfish ways? Doesn't she deserve better than this? Better than me?

YES.

The answer pounds through my head over and over while my heart slowly begins to crack. Every part of my being is trying to fight this thought out of my head. I don't want to give Hollynd up, not now and not ever, but God, I'm not worthy of her.

I think I'm going to be sick. How do I make myself do this? How do I let her go?

A vision of Hollynd's face appears in my mind. A memory from New Year's Eve while I rested my head on her legs on the bathroom floor and she ran a wet washcloth over my forehead. Remembering little from that night, this image has stuck in my memory. There are tears in her eyes, a mixture of pain, fear, and anger. I did that to her. Me, the one person who promised to never hurt her and never leave her.

It's clear from my past actions that I have no problem breaking my promises to Hollynd and I will break this one, too. I will leave her. Not only move out and go to Oak University. No. I will give her up and let her go. She deserves so much more and if I can give that to her by letting her go, then that's what I will do. I will give her the best thing I can think of...my absence.

Chapter 26

Hollynd

I'm not sure how long I have been sleeping. I need to open my eyes to check the time, but they're sore and puffy from crying. Continuing to lay there, I'm trying to remember everything that occurred this morning. I'm hoping it was a bad dream instead. Still refusing to open my eyes, my ears hear a noise from the living room as I had earlier before everything went to hell. Landry is back. I can feel his presence back in the apartment. Slowly, I drag myself off the bed and head back to the living room to deal with the rest of this disaster. I'm terrified. My heart is beating so quickly that I swear Landry can probably hear it from across the living room as I walk down the short hallway.

Landry's sitting in the same spot he was earlier, though I notice he's wearing different clothes and he looks like he has showered. I'm still in my pajamas and matted hair. I must look like a mess, but honestly, I don't care. Between my pounding heart, turning stomach, and tremored limbs, I'm surprised I'm able to move at all. But I do and I sit down on the opposite end of the couch from Landry.

Silence.

"Are you okay?" Landry's voice finally breaks into the silent air.

"Are you still moving?"

Landry's face avoids eye contact. "Yes."

"Then no, I'm not okay." I keep my eyes held to his face. He may not look at me, but I'm sure as hell not letting him escape the burning of my eyes.

"Hollynd, I want to explain to you why I have to do this. I think it's important that you know the truth."

"Fine, give me what you got, Landry. Explain to me how anything else could be worth more than what we have right here."

"Baby, it's not about anything being worth more or less, it's about doing the right thing. You know my dad wants me to go to Oak, right? He told me that if I don't attend Oak, he won't continue to pay for Rob's tuition."

"Why would he do that? That doesn't even make sense."

"Because he's a selfish son of a bitch. You know that, Crick. The Dean of Oak University is insisting I attend his university. He and many other members of the faculty are large donors for my dad's political campaign."

"Landry, that doesn't make sense. Your dad is a city mayor, and not even the city where Oak is located."

"There's already talk of a state run after his term as mayor. That's what they are raising funds for now. Anyway, the Dean told my dad that he wants both Rob and I to attend Oak."

"Can't Rob get a student loan like you did, so he's not dependent on your father's money?"

"Rob tried to get a student loan, but he was denied. He's still considered a dependent of my father's, while I qualified as a mature student."

"Does Rob know your father is doing this to you?" I ask.

Landry finally looks at me with a stern coldness. "No! And you cannot tell him, Hollynd."

I rub my eyes with the palms of my hands as I feel a headache setting in. "Okay, let me get this straight. Your dad is blackmailing you to get you to attend Oak University?"

"Yes." Landry's head hangs low with his eyes focused back on the floor below him.

"So, you're going to move to Reddington and finish your last two years at Oak, and then what? Are you expecting me to sit here and wait for you?"

It's an empty question. I know for a fact that if Landry asked me to wait for ten years, I would, but my anger is pushing me to push him.

Silence.

"No." Landry's words come out as a sort of mumble. "No, I don't expect you to wait for me, Hollynd."

"What are you saying, Landry?" My voice cracks as he finally lifts his head and meets his eyes with mine.

"I'm saying that this shit with my dad will never end for me, Hollynd. It's not fair of me to drag you along for the ride. Not to mention all the other baggage I have weighing me down. I won't let it bring you down too."

"Why don't you let me be the one who decides what I can or cannot handle." Tears pour over the rims of my eyes again.

"No, Hollynd. I can't do this anymore. I'll leave you money, so you don't have to worry about paying for this place on your own. I don't want you to have to move; I know you love it here."

"No, Landry. I love being here with you! It wasn't about someone paying half the rent. I don't want your goddamn money." Rage penetrates my voice.

"Hollynd, stop fighting me on this. Take my money, it's the least I can do."

"No, I'm pretty sure the least you can do is to not be a bastard that leaves his wife all alone in a city where she knows no one, despite the fact that you promised to be here." My words are spitting fiercely out of my mouth at an uncontrollable rate. "You promised me forever and unless forever means four fucking months, then I would say that this is the absolute least and worst you can do!"

I can see the darkness increasing in Landry's eyes as my hate filled words slam into him. And I'm pretty sure at this moment I do hate him.

"Oh, you're back to calling yourself my wife now, Hollynd? Because a few hours ago you said that you weren't my wife. Which is it going to be? Do you want to play the role of the heartbroken wife or the girlfriend that didn't really mean that much to me? Because right now I will take either option as long as you get that I'm leaving, Hollynd. This is happening, and I want you to move on. So, tell me, what do you want? For me to leave you amicably and try to help you out as best as I can? Or do you want me to walk out that door?" Landry's voice booms through the air.

"Why are you yelling at me?" I yell back. "I did nothing wrong!"

The air is thick with tension as we angrily stare at each other.

Silence.

Slowly the dark of Landry's eyes softens, and he shuffles his body over to sit next to me on the couch. His arms reach around my back as he pulls me over to lean my head against his chest. It's warm and I can hear the pounding of his heart.

"I know you didn't do anything wrong. It's me, Cricket. I'm the problem. I didn't want it to end like this." Landry's voice is less harsh and cracks slightly. "But it has to end. I'm never going to be the man you need me to be."

"Landry, please." My words through my sobs are almost inaudible. "Please, don't do this to me."

"I'm sorry, Cricket. Hurting you was never my intention. I only ever meant to love you and give you everything you deserve, and you deserve more than me."

"Don't say that," I sob into his chest, making the front of his shirt damp. "I love you, Landry." I reach down to roll his wedding ring around his finger.

"I love you, Cricket. But it's not enough. I'm sorry I couldn't love you better than this."

Silence.

I hear a sniffle coming from the head resting on top of mine. I turn my face up towards his and see a slight trail of tears running over his cheek. As soon as our eyes meet, our lips do the same. It's a soft kiss that I wish would last forever. It doesn't.

Landry pulls away from me and before I can say anything, he stands and walks to the bedroom. Five minutes later Landry walks out of the bedroom, carrying a single duffle bag with what I assume are his clothes, or at least most of them.

"What about all your other stuff?" I ask, looking around the apartment filled with items that Landry purchased, including the furniture and electronics.

"Keep it. I don't want any of it."

"Can I at least call you?" I sound pitiful at this point.

"I don't think that's a good idea, Crick."

"Why?"

"Because I won't be able to handle hearing your voice."

"But I won't be able to handle not hearing yours, Landry."

"Cricket, you're going to be fine. You're the strongest person I know."

My sobs take over once again. "Landry, please don't."

Landry leans over with his black duffle bag in hand and presses his lips against the top of my head.

"Goodbye, Cricket," are the last words I hear.

Thirty seconds later, I hear the front door lock from the other side.

Silence. Again. Stupid, pin-dropping, cricket chirping silence.

Six hours later, I receive an alert from my phone notifying a direct deposit was made into my bank account of ten-thousand dollars. I text Landry to tell him I don't want his money. The text goes unanswered and the money stays.

Chapter 27

Hollynd

It's been a month and a half since school began and since Landry left. I must admit that I was a wreck for the first two weeks after he left. I hardly remember going to or from my classes. Thank goodness the first few weeks were mostly content review and there were no major assignments.

In the beginning, I was lonely, wandering from class to class, trying to hide my broken heart from the world around me. This was my typical day.

The nights weren't great either. Some nights were so bad, I would drown my sorrows in wine. Those nights I would usually try to call Landry, but the calls always went unanswered. I had officially become pathetic.

I even called Rob one night after being ignored by Landry once again. Rob at least answered my calls. Rob told me that Landry had been avoiding him, too, ignoring his calls and texts. Rob told me that Landry is living with his father and driving to college every day.

As the end of September neared, I decided I needed to get my life together. I tried to tell myself that it was time to get over Landry, though secretly I still believed we would get back together. *We have to, right? That's how happy endings work.* However, until then, I needed to move on.

I was fortunate to sit beside a girl named Eva during one of my elective classes, Sociology of Gender, during the first week of classes. She and I became fast friends. Eva's a tall girl of five foot nine with long straight brown hair and big brown eyes. She could be a model, and she has the sweetest personality to match. I'm not sure why she wanted to become friends with me, considering I was a zombie of a person when we met. I looked tired all the time and possibly had a caffeine addiction. But that didn't stop Eva from inserting herself and her brightness into my life. She has made this last month without Landry bearable.

Shortly after we began hanging out, Eva introduced me to her very handsome friend, Parker. Standing at an even six feet, Parker has blond wavy hair that looks like he walked straight off a beach somewhere in southern California. Though his slender body was not the result of surfing, it resulted from being a power hitter on the college's volleyball team.

Parker, like me, had just come out of a long-term relationship with a broken heart to mend. He and his boyfriend, Blake, had been together for two years until he caught Blake going down on a club bouncer named Michele. Parker and I became good friends quickly as we leaned on each other amidst our heartbreak. Eva made it her personal mission to help us move on with someone else.

These two people soon became my lifeline here in Elmerson. Instead of drinking wine by myself in a pity party for one, Eva and Parker would come hang out at my place in the evenings when I wasn't working. I was fortunate to find a part-time job in a local bookshop that was filled with used and hard to find books.

When I didn't have to spend all my free time studying or doing homework, I still liked to write fiction. I even began experimenting with an idea for a novel. Something to keep my mind off Landry.

It's finally Friday night and after a long week of classes, Eva, Parker, and I are together for the first Friday in a long time. Amazingly, I didn't have to work for once and Parker didn't have a game scheduled. Tonight, we're celebrating the end of midterms.

Gathered in the living room of my small apartment, each wrapped in our own blankets because a mid-October cold snap has this building showing its age. It's not well insulated, and the windows are old. Still, we are all happy to be together, and truth be told, I really do love this apartment.

After a few glasses of faux champagne— which is cheap sparkling wine— I pull the vodka out from the freezer. It only takes one drink with Eva before she begins planning the rest of our night.

"Let's go dancing!" Eva sings while Parker and I let out a groan in unison. "Come on, you bitches. I'm tired of your sad faces. Let's go out and celebrate!"

"I'm in if you're in." Parker clinks his glass to mine.

I roll my eyes and lay my head back. The last time I went dancing, Landry and I grinded to *Nine Inch Nails*. The memory makes me wince.

Eva grabs one of my hands while Parker grabs the other. Together they hoist me off the couch, chanting my name. "Hollynd! Hollynd!"

"Fine," I give in.

"Yes!" Eva declares triumphantly. "Let's go through your closet and find your sexiest dress. Tonight, we're going to find you a man to kiss, or maybe more."

"Don't push the girl, Eva. Let's be happy we got her to agree to go out."

"Thanks Parker. This is why you're my favourite." I wink at Parker, who blows me an air kiss. I'm so lucky to have friends like these.

A few hours later, the three of us are in the middle of the dance floor at Club X9. We have been dancing non-stop and sweat glistens on our foreheads. Despite Eva's dubious attempts to find me a guy to hook up with, or even dance with, I stay close to Parker, who's also not interested in trolling for fish.

The end of the evening comes quickly and soon the three of us are huddling together on the cold sidewalk waiting for our Uber to arrive. Parker and Eva are spending the night at my apartment, as they do most weekends. I don't mind and I know they prefer it to the dorms they both live in. They share the lumpy pullout couch and often argue like an old married couple about who hogs the blankets more.

"Thanks for talking me into coming out. I really needed it." I confess.

"No problem, my love." Eva responds. "I'm just sorry I couldn't get you a guy to take home or even get one tiny kiss from. I have failed as a wing woman." Eva hangs her head in shame.

"Awe, poor Hollynd. If you want, I'll give you a kiss." Parker offers with a laugh.

"Yes, do it. It'll be hilarious." Eva pulls out her phone and opens the camera app.

Parker turns to face me and cups my cheeks with his large hands. "Ready, baby?"

"Give it to me, big guy."

Parker plants his lips on top of mine as Eva snaps the picture. The kiss doesn't last long before we burst out laughing together.

"So, how was I?" Parker grins.

"You taste like tequila," I giggle while wiping my mouth of his slobber.

"This one is definitely going on Instagram. 'The beauty and the sloppy kisser.'"

We continue to laugh as our Uber arrives to take us home. It feels good to have the ache of losing Landry replaced with the joy of friendship, if only for a short time.

After we get home, Eva and Parker crash together on the pullout, while I make my way to my bedroom. After brushing my teeth and getting into my pajamas, I crawl into my cold queen-sized bed, covered with the purple and grey striped bedding Landry bought for us only months ago.

Still slightly buzzed from the alcohol, I reach over and rub my hand over Landry's cold pillow. Nothing smells like him anymore and I don't have any pictures of us together out on display. Though I know if I were to reach into the drawer on my nightstand and open the unused journal, a picture of us would fall out. My wedding ring is tucked away in my jewelry box. Out of sight, out of mind. Right?

And then there's my wrist. The 'L' tattoo I cannot hide, cannot tuck away in a drawer, cannot erase. It's funny what we'll do when we reach the point of desperation. The things we cling onto in order to survive. I reach my wrist up to my lips and give my inked spot a tiny kiss, like I have done every night for the last six weeks. It's my little secret, my little ritual, my own little piece of hope, hidden somewhere in the back of my incomplete heart.

Chapter 28

Landry

I hate weekends. At least during the week when I'm busy with classes I can pretend to be a fully functioning human, but once Friday night comes around, it's clear that I'm anything but.

It's Friday night, in the middle of October and while many of my classmates are off celebrating the end of midterms, I return to my father's house to partake in my Friday night ritual comprising of smoking a joint or two and watching old UFC fights. It's quiet and I'm alone. The pot helps to numb my brain from thinking about Hollynd. *God, I miss her, though.*

The first couple of weeks after I left were complete hell. It took all the strength I had to ignore her calls and texts. I even silenced all her notifications or alerts so I wouldn't go batshit crazy every time her name appeared on my screen. I considered that I could block her, but I couldn't bring myself to do it. Somehow, I found a slight comfort in knowing she's still holding on even though not responding to her was agony. That's when the frequent use of pot began. I know it wasn't the healthiest option but considering my past choices had been much more volatile, I justified it that way.

After a couple weeks, the calls and texts from Hollynd became less and less frequent. Which I suppose is a good thing, like maybe she's moving on. It's what I wanted, but it makes me sad.

Living with my father hasn't been the constant battle of avoiding him like I feared it was going to be. Luckily, he's busy with his mayoral duties, and when he's not busy in council meetings, he's out schmoozing with potential political donors, so much so that I rarely see my father at all. If we do cross paths, I try to make it as brief as possible. He asks me about my grades and if they appear satisfactory, he'll usually leave me alone.

I have been avoiding Rob these past six weeks, too. Ignoring his calls like I have been ignoring Hollynd's calls. I know that makes me an asshole, but I can't deal with him right now. I don't want to get into a lengthy explanation of why I'm attending Oak University and why I'm no longer with Hollynd. Also, I know Rob will have a problem with me partaking in my 'weed weekends,' as I like to call them in my head, and I can't deal with the nagging right now. All that matters is that Rob's in school, it's being paid for, and he's happy. My happiness can wait. Though I know in the depths of my heart, as I'm praying to a god I'm not sure that I even believe in anymore, that my happiness will wait for me.

I wake up on Saturday morning with a slight weed hangover, which is mostly brain fog. After I hack up half a lung trying to get out of bed, I make my way down to the kitchen for breakfast before I hit the gym. Unfortunately for me, my father is also currently in the kitchen. I was hoping to avoid him this morning.

"Landry, I'm glad you are up." My father sits at a small breakfast table. He sips his black coffee and sets down the newspaper he's currently reading. Dressed in golf attire, he must have a tee time soon.

"Uh huh," is the only response I can muster at this moment.

"Tonight, you need to be present for a dinner I'm hosting with the Prestons, and they're bringing Lindsay with them. She will need someone to chat with."

The Prestons are rich donors of my father's political career and long-time friends. Lindsay, their daughter, has been dating my older brother Josh for a while now. Honestly, I don't know how Josh puts up with her. She's spoiled, arrogant, and kind of a bitch.

"Why would she be coming with her parents for dinner? Josh isn't even in town right now and hasn't been for a few months. Are he and Lindsay even still together?" I ask with a clear tone of annoyance in my voice. I don't want to have supper with the Prestons and I sure as shit don't want to sit and visit with Lindsay Preston.

"If I were you, I wouldn't worry about Josh's affairs. Your brother's gone working with a very prestigious defense lawyer on a high-profile case. I could only wish you had some of his ambition and drive, then maybe you could make something of yourself too. And yes, you will be cordial with Lindsay this evening. She may be your future sister-in-law soon." My father says proudly.

My father gets up from the table, leaving his dirty cup behind for the housekeeper to clean up, and leaves the room.

I continue to eat my bowl of cereal while leaning against the counter. This was not how I intended to spend my evening. Though my only plans were to smoke a joint and watch a movie, I'd rather poke my own eyes out than sit through a meal with the Prestons.

I finish my bowl of oatmeal cereal. After placing the dirty dish in the dishwasher and I get ready to leave for the gym. I hope this day doesn't get any worse.

It's six p.m. and my father has sent Jean to remind me of supper in an hour. I decide to take my chances on my father's wrath and take a few hits off a roach before proceeding to supper. Anything to make tonight's supper bearable.

While sitting on a chair by the open window of my room, I reach for my phone and scroll through social media to kill time. I'm not big on apps like these, despite being a tech guy. I used to never use them at all. However, after I left Hollynd, I signed up to the same ones she had so I could at least catch a picture or a comment from her once in a while. It was my guilty pleasure watching her from afar, though I limit myself to checking up on her only once a day. I'm trying to remain on the good side of stalkerish behavior.

While my thumb swipes through Instagram, I see a picture tagged with Hollynd in it from someone named Eva Lange. A name I don't recognize, but it's not the name that has me sitting straight up and taking notice, it's the picture. It's Hollynd with her hands resting on some guy's waist while he's kissing her. *That motherfucker!*

The guy's tall and lean with blond hair. His hands are placed on each of her cheeks. The caption reads, "Beauty and the Sloppy Kisser." What does that mean? Who's this guy and why's he kissing my girl? My girl? *She's not mine, anymore.*

I put my joint out by dropping it into an old beer can. I can hear the cherry sizzle at the bottom of the can that has a few drops of liquid in it. Now that both hands are free, I can zoom into the picture to get a closer look. Hollynd's half kissing and half smiling. Her eyes are closed, as are the blond asshole who's cradling her face.

I'm angry. No, not angry. I'm enraged. My hands begin to shake, and my heart pounds rapidly. I scroll down the screen to read the comments made underneath the picture.

Hollynd: Awe, my knight in shining armor <3
Parker: See babe, I always leave them wanting more
Hollynd: Sounds like all talk and no action to me
Parker: I'll do anything to get off that lumpy pullout of yours ;)
Eva: I'm a master matchmaker, lol

I throw my phone across the room, and it bangs on the wall next to my door. I'm livid! Who's this Parker guy and why is he talking about sleeping on my fucking couch? Clearly, he has spent the night there before, in my apartment that I paid for, with my girl. My thoughts are irrational, I know, but I don't care. Also, despite knowing that I caused this entire mess and I'm the one that left, the jealousy inside me is pulsating through every limb and every vein.

Hollynd's moved on from me. I grab my hair hard enough to feel the pain radiate through my skull. Hollynd's moved on and I'm left with nothing. I messed everything up. What is wrong with me? What have I done?

It's all I can do not to grab my phone off the floor, which now has a cracked screen, and call her. I really want to call her. Better yet, I want to drive there, find that guy, beat the shit out of him, then go find Hollynd and get a goddamn explanation.

But I do none of this. Instead, I sit down on my bed, rest my head in my hand, and let the image of that picture melt from my mind along with the rage it was, to become what it really is, pain. Heartbreaking pain that seizes in my chest and beats her name over and over.

Ten minutes later, Jean reappears telling me my presence is required, but suggests I change out of my sweatpants before coming down. I opt for jeans and a navy button down shirt. Again, I hope this day doesn't get any worse.

I'm seated next to Lindsay at the large dining room table which is set with crystal and expensive china. Small bowls of soup sit in front of each of us at the table. There are eight of us in attendance. The Prestons, another couple that I have never met before, my father, Isaac, and myself.

I look around at the company I'm keeping in disdain. What I wouldn't give for Rob to be here with me. I remind myself to send him a text tomorrow, I've been an ass long enough. I've already driven Hollynd out of my life, I don't want to lose Rob too. Losing both would literally kill me.

The quick thought of Hollynd brings back the image of her and that guy. Instantly, I'm angry again. Even the few hits of weed I took before coming down here are doing nothing to help. I need something stronger.

My thoughts are interrupted by Lindsay, who's telling me about her last trip to the Cayman Islands. Every so often she flips her bleach blonde hair back off her shoulder and runs her fake fluorescent pink nail through it. I could literally care less. I nod along mindlessly. Seriously, I don't know how Josh puts up with this girl. Finally, she says something that gets my attention.

"So, Landry, where's that little girlfriend of yours?"

Before I can answer, Isaac, who's sitting across from Lindsay, takes over.

"You didn't hear? Poor Landry and his little Cricket broke up." Isaac sticks out his bottom lip and pretends to pout. "Landry, our heartbroken little brother."

"What is your problem, Isaac? Just because you have never loved anyone more than yourself, or better yet, had anyone love your sorry ass, you don't need to take your shit out on me."

A flash of pure rage flashes in Isaac's deep blue eyes before he shakes his head and picks up his drink in front of him.

"Wait a minute, did you say Cricket? I thought her name was Hollynd?" Lindsay begins to giggle.

I clear my throat. "Cricket is her nickname."

Lindsay bursts out laughing. "Oh my God, what kind of lame nickname is that? Is she seriously named after a gross, noisy bug?"

I can't stand this any longer. Despite being only in the second course of the meal, I stand up and toss my napkin onto the table.

"I'm sorry, I have to go." I shuffle my eyes to the members of the table. Luckily, my father and his dinner guests are so engaged in their own conversation they didn't hear Isaac and Lindsay's quips.

I leave the dining room and head straight for the front door. I grab my jacket from a nearby closet. Thank goodness my car keys are in my jacket pocket. Before I get my second arm inserted into the sleeve, I feel a tug on my shoulder.

"Where the hell do you think you're going? Do you know how much you embarrassed me?" My father says sternly in a hushed tone.

"I can't stay with those idiots any longer. I have to go."

"For God's sake, Landry, can't you do one thing I ask without some sort of drama?"

I laugh unapologetically. "Are you kidding me? I do everything you ask." I tear my arm out of his grip.

"I'm leaving." I announce, and before my father can say anything, I walk out the front door and let it slam behind me.

Jumping in my car, which is parked nearby, I take off with squealing tires and leave a layer of rubber on my father's driveway. I'm done with my father. I'm done with Hollynd and that blond guy. I'm done with assholes like Isaac and Lindsay. I'm done!

After a fifteen-minute drive, I'm knocking on the familiar white door attached to Eddie's house. Three intervals of knocks later, the door flies open.

"Dude, I'm trying to sleep. Didn't I sell you weed the other day?" Eddie's standing in front of me without a shirt while he rubs his tired eyes.

I push my way past him without waiting for an invitation inside and sit myself down on my cousin's brown couch. "Fuck weed. Let's go hard tonight."

Pulling on a green shirt that's lying abandoned on a nearby chair, Eddie sits down before asking, "How hard are you thinking?"

"You got any blow?" I raise my eyebrow with interest.

"Hell yeah, I got blow. What are we celebrating tonight?"

"We are celebrating me not giving a fuck anymore, about anything, about anyone." An image of Hollynd flashes in my mind.

"Alright." Eddie gets up to retrieve his stash while I lean on the top of the coffee table in front of me.

Moments later, the lines of white freedom lay before me. I feel a slight hesitation, self-fueled disgust filled with knowing that I used to have more to live for than what I do right now. I lost it all and I have no one to blame but myself. But God, this looks good too. Between my lust for the drugs and my love for Hollynd, I knew there was no surviving this without one or the other. And since she isn't mine anymore, I knew the only path left for me was one of destruction.

I lower my head with a tiny plastic tube in hand and face my demons cloaked in white. For a brief moment, the image of Hollynd's face, her green eyes, pink lips, and her angelic glow flashes before me. *3, 2, 1 sniff.* The image disappears. As I move onto my second line, the image of my brother Rob flashes. *3, 2, 1 sniff.* Again, the image disappears. My shame fills the space they used to occupy.

"More," I say to Eddie as I tip my head back, allowing the drip to begin its descent down my throat. It feels like freedom. Freedom and loathing. My monster returns. *Hello, old friend.*

It's later. How much later? I don't know. I'm still at Eddie's house because I recognize the brown shag carpet. More people are here now. Some I know, some I don't. I don't really care either way. Eddie's talking to someone I don't recognize. He's some blond guy. Like the guy in the picture with Hollynd. My Hollynd. I know it's not the same guy, but I hate him just the same. Anger and rage are eager to take over and someone has to pay the price for it. I think this guy will do.

I stare at the blond-haired asshole until his eyes catch mine.

"What the hell are you looking at?"

Perfect, he's egging me on.

I stay in my laid-back position on the couch, though the coke has left my left knee with a permanent vibration.

I give him a once over with my eyes. "Just thinking about how many hits it will take to knock you the fuck out. I'm willing to bet it's just one."

"What did you say to me?" Blond boy stands up and puffs his chest.

Eddie comes to a stand as well. He knows my tendency for causing shit when coke hits me on nights like these. If I choose violence, then I will have my violence.

"Landry, cut this shit out." Eddie warns as he pulls his cell phone out from his back pocket.

"Who is this guy?" Blond boy asks Eddie.

"He's my cousin," Eddie mumbles with annoyance and continues texting furiously on his phone.

Blond boy and I stare one another down. Anger is flowing throughout my entire body. Eventually the blond guy turns his attention away from me and begins talking to the guy on his right. I continue my stare down while I nurse my whiskey. What blond boy doesn't know is that once this drink is finished, he's dead.

"What the hell's his problem?" Blond boy scowls towards Eddie before he looks back in my direction to see me still watching him.

I take that as my cue to stand up, down the rest of my drink in one gulp, and show this guy exactly what my problem is.

I can feel Eddie's hand on my chest. "Sit down, Landry. We're not doing this tonight."

Only I don't sit down. I push Eddie out of the way and take a swing at the blond boy. Hitting with his jaw on the first swing.

I can hardly feel my hand connect, like I can hardly feel his fist connect with my mouth. I taste blood. I lick it off my lip with a grin.

It only takes a moment to have myself kneeling over him, taking my anger out on this poor bastard's face. I'm not there long before a couple other guys grab me by the arms and peel me off blond boy's body. I'm tossed back on the couch while Eddie's yelling at me, though I'm not listening. I'm fighting their hold on me, until I see a familiar face in front of me. Rob.

"Jesus Christ, Landry," my baby brother curses at me.

High as a kite with blood running out of my mouth and my knuckles pulsating as they begin to swell. For a moment, I feel the twinge of shame I had fought off earlier.

"Get him outta here!" Eddie snaps at Rob.

Rob sits next to me while he wraps my arm around his shoulder. "I swear to God, if you don't help me get you out of here, I'm going to have you removed on a stretcher."

I put some effort into standing up on my own and walk out the door with Rob as my support. Rob opens the passenger door to his car, and I let my body flop into place. Soon after, I hear Rob get into the driver's seat and start the car.

"What the hell is wrong with you, Landry?"

I still haven't figured out why Rob is even here.

When I ask him, he replies, "Eddie sent me a text the moment you started eyeing his friend. He knows that look on your face when you're going to start shit."

"So, the little brother has to come rescue his big brother?"

"Landry, this pity party you're having for yourself is getting really old. You've been ignoring me for weeks. Ignoring Hollynd...."

"What do you know about Hollynd?" I growl at Rob cutting him off midsentence.

"She called me a while back. She's worried about you."

"Right." I comment sarcastically. "Well, sweet Hollynd doesn't worry about me anymore and I couldn't care less."

"Really, Landry? That's why you were beating the shit out of some guy? Because you don't care?"

There's silence in the car as Rob drives away from Eddie's house. I use my sleeve to dab blood from my lip which continues to crack open.

After a few minutes, Rob continues with his lecture. "I know you're upset that you and Hollynd broke up, but that was your choice. Though I can't say I understand any of the decisions you have made lately, this has got to stop. Look at yourself, Landry. You're a mess!"

"What do you know about my choices, Rob? You know nothing." I spew angrily at an unknowing Rob.

We spend the rest of the car ride in silence, until we arrive at my father's house and Rob pulls up in front.

"Do you need help to get inside?" Rob asks but refuses to look at me.

I feel pathetic. "No, I'll be fine. Thanks for the ride."

Rob nods his head and lets me leave his car on my own.

I make my way into the house. Mumbles from my father's dinner guests are coming from the living room. No doubt the brandy is flowing like water by now. I quickly make my way past the doorway hoping not to be noticed. Before I head up to my room, I decide to make a quick detour into the kitchen. I dig around the pantry until I find a bottle of vodka perched on the top shelf.

I'm still feeling jittery from the coke and now I only want to sleep. A few shots of this will combat the stimulation coursing through my body. I don't bother with a glass; I clutch the bottle with my fingers and take it with me to my room.

Once I'm alone in my room, I drink. I bring up Hollynd's Instagram account to see if any new posts are up. There's nothing new. I drink some more. I finally feel myself come back down. Waves of drunkenness begin to overtake the electricity of the cocaine. I'm disappointed in myself, for my actions tonight and for my actions of the past few weeks. I need to do better, and I will do better. I toss my phone to the side and lie down on my bed. Slowly, my eyes force their way closed. Darkness takes over.

I smell something sweet. I don't know what it is, but it smells like roses. My room is pitch black, though I don't remember shutting off my lamp. I don't know what time it is or how long I have been out. I fade out again.

It's warm beside me, soft hands are touching me. And there's that goddamn smell of roses again. I can't open my eyes. My eyelids feel like they weigh a thousand pounds.

There's a hot breath on my neck, leaving tiny kisses in its wake.

"Pretend that I'm your Cricket, Landry. Your sweet little Cricket. I can make it all better if you let me." The voice hisses in my ear as fingernails softly run down my bare chest.

As soon as I hear the name Cricket, visions of Hollynd enter my mind. Her face, her body, the smoothness of her skin, the taste of her tongue. *My Cricket.* I *miss* her. I *need* her.

I pull the face beside my head towards my mouth and take the needy lips into mine. It's not the same, but it's not nothing.

I give myself back to my Cricket. Or whoever will have me in this moment, I give it all away.

205

Chapter 29

Landry

I squeeze my eyes tight before I have even given them a chance to open. I feel like absolute shit. Images from the night before flash through my mind. Eddie's house, punching some guy, Rob, the vodka, then nothing. Well, not nothing. Roses, I smelled roses, and touching and kissing. I rub my hands over my face. I wasn't alone. Someone else was here. I turn my head and make myself open my eyes. The brightness of the morning light coming through the window is torture. I glance through the tiny slits I make my eyelids form to see if there is anyone with me. I'm alone. *Thank God.*

I don't know who was here, but I know it was someone and my body is telling me we did more than kiss. I try to think back to Eddie's house and if there were any girls there that I might have been with, but I can't remember. It's all too fuzzy. Ugh, annoyance with myself begins to grow.

My phone vibrates from where it lies on my night table. Reaching over to grab it, I see an incoming text from Lindsay of all people. I think about ignoring it, but I don't. I open it to read the words that change everything.

Lindsay:
Thanks for the ride last night, Cowboy ;)

What the hell? My heart beats erratically in my chest, and I can feel the bile rising in my throat. I think as hard as I can. The roses, the hands, the waves of bleach blonde hair hanging down over my face. *No! No! No!* This can't be happening. What have I done?

I can feel the bile turn quickly to vomit. I jump from my bed and grab the garbage can beside my dresser and empty the contents of my stomach into the plastic bin. Did I seriously have sex with my brother's girlfriend? I think of Josh and how he's not even here right now. I'm wondering if I should tell him or if Lindsay is going to tell him.

I think of Rob and how disgusted he's going to be with me. I think of Hollynd and curse the fact that her body is not the last that has touched mine anymore. This last thought makes me the saddest of all.

After I give myself a few minutes to allow the initial shock to dissipate, I grab my phone to call Lindsay. After a few rings, she answers.

"Hello, you."

"Lindsay, what the hell happened?"

She giggles. "You sure woke up on the wrong side of the bed considering the night you had."

"Why did you come into my room last night?" I demand.

"After I saw you slink past the living room all alone, I thought you needed some company. Of course, I had to wait until I could make my disappearing act."

"What about Josh? Your boyfriend and my brother."

"Joshy's been gone for so long and a girl like me has needs. And I've had my eyes on you for a while now. Your whole dark and broody thing is sexy. Plus, with your precious Cricket out of the way, well come on, who could blame me?"

"Cricket. Pretend I'm your Cricket. Your sweet little Cricket." The words echo in my head.

"Lindsay, I was out of my wits last night!"

"Well, you didn't seem to mind when you rolled me over and pounded into me over and over."

"Shut up, Lindsay. It never happened; do you understand me?"

"Oh, don't worry, Landry. I won't tell Josh if you won't."

With that I hang up the phone and drag myself to the shower, though I feel like no matter the heat of the water I will never be able to scorch away the shame I'm feeling right now.

Chapter 30

Landry

It's been over three weeks since the disastrous hook up with Lindsay. If that wasn't a wake-up call for me, then I don't know what was. I knew it was time to get my shit together.

After recovering from my self-sabotaging weekend, I decided to get my mind and body in better shape. If I had to endure this living arrangement with my father and living without Hollynd, I was going to need help.

My brother Rob had always been one of the most reliable people in my life. A best friend like no other. I went to him and confessed everything, well, almost everything. I still couldn't tell Rob about my father's threat with his tuition money. That secret was my burden to bear, and I would take any pain away from Rob, even if it seemed dishonest. I am my brother's keeper; this role has never once changed for me.

I did, however, tell him about leaving Hollynd because I thought she deserved better than me. I told him about the drugs and sleeping with Lindsay, to which he was thoroughly disappointed with me and rightfully so. And then I asked Rob for help. Help to be a better person, help to be someone that could be worthy of Hollynd because I knew I needed her back in my life, someday.

I started seeing my previous therapist again. The same one I had seen for a few months after the whole New Year's Eve episode. Back then, I saw a therapist to make Hollynd happy and feel safe with me. I'm choosing to go back to therapy for myself. To be a better man than I had been. To be a better husband to a wife that I no longer touched or kissed, spoke to or laughed with, but one I will never stop loving.

Life has a funny way of turning you on your ass when you least expect it. I'm trying to be better, I really am. My grades are up. I'm feeling healthier and stronger thanks to joining a mixed martial arts class. And though I miss Hollynd like crazy, every day my heart is healing because I believe us being apart can't be forever. I won't allow it to be.

I have arrived home after an early evening kickboxing class and I'm preparing a protein shake in my father's kitchen. I had noticed a few extra vehicles outside when I arrived, though I haven't seen a soul since I came into the house. In fact, the house is quiet, eerily quiet.

After I chug the shake and rinse my glass, I hear a voice summoning me. It's Jean.

"Landry, your father has requested your presence upstairs in his office immediately."

I roll my eyes at Jean, though I know she's not at fault. I nod to relieve her from waiting for me and trudge my sore body up the stairs and down the hallway to my father's office.

When I enter the room, I'm met with five pairs of angry eyes staring at me. Mr. and Mrs. Preston, Lindsay, Isaac, and my father. Mr. and Mrs. Preston sit with Lindsay on the sofa against the back wall, while Isaac's in a wingback chair in front of my father's desk. I hesitate in the office doorway. I'm still in my workout clothes and I'm in desperate need of a shower.

Before I can ask what's going on, my father, who's behind his large oak desk with his arms crossed, leans back in his chair. "Sit down, Landry," he motions to the chair next to Isaac.

As I walk towards Isaac, his eyes are burning daggers into me. I feel nervous, like an injured zebra laying on the ground as the lions' stalk around him.

"Lindsay and her parents have informed me that you had relations with her recently," my father begins with no tact whatsoever while staring coldly at me.

I feel my heart race and my eyes widen as I look at my father then over to Lindsay. She said she wouldn't say anything. Anger takes over.

"Lindsay has something she would like to tell you. Go ahead, sweetheart." My father turns to Lindsay.

Lindsay looks nervous as she looks at me and bites her bottom lip. She appears different from her normal self. She does not have her cocky attitude on display, but Lindsay looks meek and tired. Even her expensive yellow dress isn't sitting right as she's slouched down on the sofa with her arms folded across her stomach.

Before she speaks, her eyes drop to the floor. "Landry, I'm pregnant."

Silence.

Everything around me stops. There's a booming sound in the hollows of my ears. My eyes begin to dart around. To the Prestons' who are glaring at me, to my father and Isaac who are seething with fury.

"What?" I eventually mutter out.

"The girl said she's pregnant, Landry. And since Josh has been out of town for a few months now, and you took it upon yourself to covet your brother's girlfriend, it appears you're getting what you deserve." My father's voice is booming through the office.

My breath becomes heavy as waves of shock flow throughout my body.

"Does Josh know?" I ask with my head lowered.

Isaac, who also plays the role of brother's keeper, interjects. "No, he doesn't, but when he does, you can guarantee he's going to kick your ass so hard that-"

My father clears his voice and takes back control. "We will discuss our own family issues later. Let's get things settled with our guests first so we're not taking up any more of their time." Gesturing towards the Prestons, my father continues, "Landry and Lindsay, we have decided that it's best if you marry by the middle of January at the latest. That way we won't have to worry about Lindsay showing yet. It's going to be enough of a scandal that she has the baby less than six months after the wedding, but we need sufficient time to plan a proper wedding of this size."

Mr. and Mrs. Preston nod in agreement.

"What the hell are you talking about?" I interrupt. "We're not getting married!"

"I assure you, you are getting married, Landry. After you have defiled this woman and caused this mess, you will do right by her and her family. Not to mention doing right by your own family. I will not let my first-born grandchild be a bastard. Do you know how that will look to my conservative supporters? It's completely unacceptable." My father's tone is heavy with contempt.

My mouth goes completely dry, and my head spins. I feel like I may pass out. This can't be happening. I look at Lindsay, who's still slouching, but when our eyes meet, I see a tiny smirk appear on her face. Is she happy about this? Did she plan this? What is going on?

My father and the Prestons continue to discuss how they are going to announce our engagement. I don't hear any of it.

Eventually, Lindsay and her parents get up to leave. When Lindsay passes my chair, she leans down and presses her lips to my cheek. In my ear she whispers, "I'll call you later," like we are some couple who does that. I pull away from her touch.

The Prestons' take their leave from my father's office, and I assume the house. It's just my father, Isaac, and myself alone. My father pulls at his tie, releasing the knot and slamming the burgundy silk material onto his desktop. His eyes are staring at me, so I keep my head lowered. Like a child ready to receive their punishment, I breathe in to take mine.

Before my father says anything, it's Isaac who stands up suddenly and swings a fist. It collides with my right cheekbone with brute force. The impact causes me to slip off the side of the chair and onto the floor. I feel a hand pulling me up by the collar of my shirt followed by another jab to the face. The pain is searing, and I can feel blood exiting my nose. My head rests on the carpet.

"All right, Isaac, that's enough." My father announces casually, like he caught him eating too many cookies, not beating the shit out of his other son.

Isaac's staring down at me and his sweat is making his forehead shiny. My eyes drift over to see my father's face also looking down at me. Both sets of eyes reveal hate for the body lying on the floor in front of them, my body.

"Well Landry, you've really done it this time, haven't you? Couldn't you have kept your dick to yourself?" My father's words pierce my ears and my heart. Mostly because I know he's not wrong.

"What are you going to tell Josh?" I sputter out through the pain and the blood.

My father continues, "I will handle Josh and you will handle your bride to be. You give her no reason to be upset, do you hear me? Her parents are very important members of this community, and you should be so lucky to become a part of their family. It's a much better outcome for you than that last little whore you brought around here."

Hollynd, he's talking about Hollynd.

I try to sit myself up as rage sets in over his words about Hollynd. "Fuck you!" I yell up at my father as the blood that has run over the bumps of my lip spatters. "Hollynd was the best thing that ever happened to me." I can feel the emotions dampening my eyes.

My father crouches down and grips my jaw with his hand. "You are my biggest disappointment, Landry. I should have let your mother take you when she left." He pushes back on my jaw as he lets go.

My father turns to Isaac. "Get him out of here. And tell Jean to come clean up this blood."

Isaac's hands hook themselves under my armpits as I'm raised to my feet and pulled out of the office. Isaac continues to pull me down while I stumble behind him. When we reach my bedroom, Isaac pushes me through the door. Before I can fall to my bed, he grabs my shoulder and turns me back to face him.

"Josh is a good man. How could you do this to him, Landry?" Tears of anger fill Isaac's dark eyes. I've never seen emotion like this from him before. "He is your brother, Landry.

The best one of all of us. He deserves better than this." Isaac scorns at me before throwing one more punch to my head. This one connects hard.

An image of Hollynd flashes in my memory of her casually tucking her hair behind her ear before everything fades to black.

My eyes slowly push themselves open despite the throbbing pain pulsating in my skull. It takes me a moment to gather my thoughts and remember that I was punched in the side of the head by Isaac, sometime ago. I have no idea how long ago it was. Minutes or hours, I have no clue. I can tell I'm on the floor of my bedroom as the fibers of the carpet scrape into the flesh of my face. A soft glow from my bed side lamp illuminates the space as my eyes begin to focus a bit better. I push my aching body into a sitting position as more memories of the beating I took on the floor of my father's office flood my mind.

From the other side of the room, I hear a throat being cleared. I turn sharply, albeit painfully, in the direction of the sound. Leaning against the far wall is my brother, Josh. Wearing dark denim jeans and a hunter green button-down shirt, he stands with his arms and legs crossed. His dark brown eyes are staring viciously in my direction.

"Well at least you're not dead." Josh's voice booms throughout the room.

"Josh, what are you doing here?" I say with a painful hitch in my voice from the simple movement of opening my mouth to speak.

"Well, when your father calls you to inform you that your brother knocked up your girlfriend, you take the time to give your congratulations in person." Josh's words are riddled with spite and sarcasm.

I can feel the bile in my stomach pushing its way up to my throat. "Josh, look I'm..."

"Shut up, Landry. You don't get to speak to me right now. Only I get to speak and you're going to goddamn listen to what I have to say. I don't care if you're sorry or that it was a mistake. I don't give a shit how you feel about any of this. You fucked my girlfriend! You're my brother, Landry! Doesn't that mean anything to you?"

Josh has long since pushed himself off the wall and is now pacing back and forth with his fists clenched in rage. I can't help but hang my bruised head low as Josh yells the truth at me.

"For years, I have watched you self-destruct. Doing one stupid thing after another. With the drugs and the partying, the fighting and the women, and I've said nothing. Maybe I should have, I don't know. But then you found Hollynd, and I thought maybe you had a fighting chance at making your life something worth living, worth fighting for, worth stopping all this shit for. But nope, you messed that up, too, didn't you?
And you know, I'm not so mad about you sleeping with Lindsay, that relationship was trash most of the time, anyway. But you did this to me, Landry! I would never do anything like that to you or any of my brothers. Never! But you did this to me!"

I hear a slight crack in Josh's voice as I bring myself off the floor to a standing position. Once I gain my balance, Josh walks over to me until we are face to face. Staring at each other, I know better than to speak. I know that there's nothing I can say to make this better.

After a few more moments of tension filled silence, Josh continues. "The thing is, you're done now, it's over. You're going to be trapped under Dad's thumb forever. You've spent your whole life trying to get away from him, and now you're trapped for good in this life. I should probably feel sorry for you, and maybe one day I will. But not today. You and I are done. I will play my part of happy family for the sake of Dad and his political shit, but other than that, we're done." Josh's finger presses firmly into my chest.

Josh turns to leave, but before he does, he places a firm grip onto my shoulder.

"Enjoy your new life, little brother." Josh spits into the air with his eyes still darkened with hate and a small smirk on his lips. Josh's exiting words slice through my entire being.

Josh walks out the door and slams it hard enough that the items on my dresser vibrate. I lower myself on my nearby bed. Without warning my body heaves recklessly, leaving all the contents of my stomach laid out on the floor in front of me.

What have I done?

Chapter 31

 Hollynd

"It's beginning to look a lot like Christmas!" Parker's booming voice sings as he enters my bedroom carrying three glasses of eggnog.

Eva's sitting on my bed next to the giant suitcase I'm packing for my trip back to Brighten for Christmas break. This will be my first trip back home since Landry and I went home together for the twin's fourth birthday party. That was also the weekend that he ripped my heart out. It feels like a lifetime ago.

Not having a car of my own, and with flights being so expensive, I couldn't travel home this fall. Even to make this trip home for Christmas, my mom had to send me money for a plane ticket.

I'm so excited to see my mom and spend some of the holidays with her. I think this is the longest we've ever been apart my entire life. And I miss Rachel and her family. Though Rachel and I speak on the phone or text almost daily, it's not the same as seeing her in person.

I look at my friends sipping their eggnog, and I realize how lucky I've been to have met them during my time here in

Elmerson. While it began in such a heartbreaking way with Landry leaving, I have found happiness with my friends.

The last few months have made me stronger and more independent than I have ever been. I realize that I can survive without Landry, and I still have my own dreams to fulfill. There's a life for me without Landry. This is not the end of my story.

Aside from classes and working part time for the used bookstore, I have been trying my hand at freelance writing. Submitting articles for online magazines and local publications, including our college's newspaper. This experience has been so rewarding and has given me more passion in my writing. However, I'm missing my fiction writing terribly, which I have abandoned, though I hope to return to it, eventually.

Time apart from Landry has opened my eyes to not only realizing that yes, I can do without him, but also, I don't want to do this without him. I know we are meant to be together. I know Landry's the missing piece to my puzzle. *He is me and I am him.* Even if it means living separately while we are together, so be it.

Eva has tried several times to get me to go out with other guys, but I'm not interested. My heart and soul belong to someone else, and I know this isn't over.

Coming to this realization meant I was going to have to fight for what I want, and fight I will. Despite not having spoken to him in over three months and hearing nothing about him either, I can still feel his soul reaching out for mine. Sometimes I will see him in my dreams, and I believe deep down that he's seeing me in his dreams too. While we have been apart in this existence, I know we have been together in another this entire time. It's time for our bodies to catch up to our spirits.

"You really think you are going to get lover boy back?" Eva interrupts my thoughts as she flips through a journal I had an article featured in last month.

"Eva, leave the poor girl alone. She wants her man back and you've seen his picture. Can you blame her?" Parker comes to my defense while swiping through his phone for a random hookup on his new dating app.

For weeks, Parker and I shared the bond of heartache. Recently, he has found his way to move on through online dating and casual sex. I have only found my way back to Landry.

"What's the plan, Hollynd? How are you going to get Landry to come crawling back?" Eva interjects.

"Well, that's why I had you bring over that blue gown of yours." I remind her. "Every year on December 23rd there's a Christmas banquet with the mayor. It's quite the social event. My brother-in-law's company always buys a couple of tables for their staff and guests. Luckily for me, Colin was able to get me a ticket at the table with him and Rachel."

"And you think Landry will be at this event?" Eva asks.

"I'm not totally sure, but I'm going to take my chances." I admit.

"I think it's a romantic idea. A Christmas gala where your eyes will meet across the room and be pulled together by some universal force. You will bring Landry to his knees by your beauty, and he'll beg you to take him back." Parker continues with his whole imaginative scene. "Maybe Landry will come back with you and bring his totally hot, gay best friend with him."

Eva and I both laugh. "Let's worry about me getting Landry back before we worry about whether he has a gay best friend."

"Oh no, I said hot gay best friend," Parker corrects me.

The three of us spend the rest of the night talking and laughing together before we head to our respective homes for Christmas break tomorrow.

My flight the next day takes off from the Elmerson airport without a hitch and has me back in Brighten by one in the afternoon. Rachel and the twins pick me up from the airport. After we grab my luggage, the four of us head to my mom's house.

By supper time, I'm beyond exhausted after playing with the girls for a few hours and then helping my mom with Christmas baking. Rachel and the girls go home for supper, leaving my mom and I to catch up alone for the first time in a long time.

After supper, we head into her cozy living room, each grabbing a quilt to curl up in. Mom sits on her reclining chair, and I find a spot on the couch.

We talk for a while about how things are going in Elmerson. My classes, my job, and my friends. Mom tells me about how she has been keeping busy volunteering at a local shelter and, of course, she still has her activities with her closest girlfriends. Fortunately, my mom didn't have to work after my father passed away because of his life insurance policy. However, she always keeps herself busy. I assume it's to help ease the pain of losing him. *I get it.*

After we catch up with what's new, my mom asks about the one thing we have never discussed in the last four months.

"Hollynd, tell me what happened with Landry?"

I bury my head in my blanket for a moment as I try to collect my thoughts because I'm still not sure I totally understand what happened with him.

"Aw Mom, I don't know. I mean, we were happy, like really happy. And it's not like there was some big thing that happened that made one of us angry or one of us cheated on the other one. He said that he had to go to Oak University and that he didn't think we should be together anymore. Oh, and the lame excuse that I was too good for him. Whatever that means."

My mom nods along and listens as I vent my frustrations over the entire situation and my new realization over the last few months about who I am on my own and who we are together.

I express my concerns for his father's role in what happened between Landry and I, and how controlling he is over Landry.

My mom shakes her head. "I've never cared much for his father to be honest. Seems like a dishonest politician if you ask me."

"I think you are right, Mom." I nod along. "He's mean too, but only in private. I don't trust him. But what do I do, Mom? How do I help Landry?"

"Honey, I don't know if you can help Landry with his father. That might be something he has to figure out on his own."

We sit in silence for a few moments before I ask the question that has been plaguing me for some time.

"Mom, do you think about dating again? Dad has been gone for four years now."

My mom shakes her head. "Honestly, I don't think I could be with another man after your father. He and I had a connection, a bond. From the moment we met all those years ago at that office Christmas party. It was like he was the other half of myself I had always been looking for, though I didn't even know was missing. If that makes any sense?"

"That makes perfect sense to me. That's how I feel about Landry. But I never say that because I didn't think anyone would understand."

"Most people won't, my dear." My mom tells me. "I don't think it happens for everyone."

"What do I do, Mom, if I can't get him back?"

"Hollynd, honey, you can only offer your love. You can't make anyone receive it. Landry loves you. I have no doubt about that. I've seen him with you. It's love. But if he has demons chasing him, he might not be able to receive your love. Sometimes things are bigger than what we have to give."

"I have to try," I whisper to my mom and to myself.

"Then try with your whole heart, but keep it guarded."

"How'd you get so smart in the ways of love, Mom?"

My mom winks at me. "By watching Hallmark movies."

Chapter 32

Hollynd

It's the night of the Mayor's Christmas Gala, which is being held at a large banquet hall located in a swanky downtown hotel. The room is overflowing with people dressed in their best formal attire.

The dress I borrowed from Eva is a royal blue slim fitted dress. Just under my breast line is a band of rhinestones that circle around my back. The neckline is cut deep enough to encourage a little bit of cleavage, but not too much. I had Rachel tie my hair up into a tight, high bun to show off the length of my neck.

Rachel's dress is a fitted black gown that goes straight to the floor. It's sleeveless with two-inch straps. She wears a bright pink scarf draped over the creases of her elbows, making the pink absolutely pop against the black. Rachel left her brown hair down in long waves. Her date—and husband—Colin, is wearing a classic men's suit, black with a white shirt, though his pocket square is the same pink as Rachel's scarf. They look perfect together.

I'm seated with Rachel, Colin, and some of Colin's work colleagues. As we sit at the table waiting for the obligatory speeches before supper, I scan the crowd for Landry. While I haven't seen him, I do see Isaac and Josh, though I make no effort for their attention. There are a few other familiar faces I see while I sip on the white wine Colin has brought me from the bar, but still no Landry. I consider that maybe Landry's not here, but it's too early to know that for sure.

Finally, in the far-off corner near the front of the room, I spot him. My Landry. He's standing with Rob. Both men are looking especially handsome dressed in similar suits. Landry's looks to be dark grey while Rob's is navy. I'm surprised to see Landry in a suit with a white dress shirt and tie. He always opts for the complete dark look, but tonight he looks very much like his other brothers. Landry's still the most handsome man here. His dark hair is styled back, and his eyes are still dark and breathtaking.

From where I sit, Landry and Rob look to be in a rather intense conversation. Rob gives Landry a pat on the back while they move towards their table at the front of the room. Landry doesn't see me. In fact, he doesn't even look around the room before he sits, keeping his head low. I think about going up to him. Every part of me wants to go running to him, but I know this is not the time. At least I know he's here; I'm relieved, excited, and nervous. Tonight is the night I'm going to get him and my soul back. I know it.

A few moments later, a woman walks up onto the stage and gets everyone's attention when she stands at the dark podium and speaks into the waiting microphone. I recognize her as being Landry's father's assistant, Claire. She's dressed in a long hunter green dress which suits her red hair and pale complexion well. She's thanking people, most of whom I don't know, though I assume they are donors or supporters.

Eventually Claire introduces Landry's father, Mayor David Hayles, to the stage.

David walks heavily and takes his place at the podium while the room applauds for him. I can't help the feeling of disgust that rolls through my stomach when I see him. His presence commands the room. Standing tall and confident, dressed in a black and white tux, David waits for the room to quiet before he speaks.

"Ladies and gentlemen, my family and I are honored to have you here with us to celebrate the festive season." The words roll smoothly off the mayor's tongue.

Bragging about all his accomplishments this past year while in office, David Hayles has done nothing but boast about himself, all while making people think they played a role in his accomplishments. I remember back to the time Landry told me that his father only cares about himself. If only these adoring voters could have heard what I heard last New Year's Eve as David belittled Landry with no remorse.

Eventually David begins to wrap up his speech, but first says he has a big announcement he would like to make. I'm sure it's another political move he is planning to make. I don't really care, but listen, anyway.

"It's my pleasure to announce the engagement of my son to the lovely Miss Lindsay Preston. Would the happy couple please join me on stage?"

I see Lindsay rising from her seat. Despite my dislike for her, she looks beautiful in a velvet red dress that has a cowl neckline. Lindsay's bright blonde hair is in a side bun.

I look to see Josh rise as well, only he doesn't. In fact, he's not even there at the table with his family. Rather, it's Landry who stands. My mouth falls open as I watch Landry take Lindsay by the hand and leads her up onto the stage. They both smile at the crowd as the applause and whistles echo through the building.

I can't blink, I can't breathe. I feel Rachel's hand press down on my shoulder. I don't understand what's happening.

David Hayles raises his wineglass and says into the mic, "To Landry and Lindsay."

The entire room follows suit and soon there's the traditional clinking of glasses like they do at weddings when they want the couple to kiss. And so, they do. Landry leans in and presses a soft kiss to Lindsay's puckered and waiting lips.

I can't take this anymore. It's all I can do not to throw up on the table or tip it over in a fit of rage. I whisper to Rachel that I'll be right back, which I don't think is true. How can I come back into this room with them, the happy couple? Rachel knows she must let me leave and nods with agreement. I try to rush out of the banquet room, but not too fast so as not to raise suspicion or bring any attention to myself.

Once I'm outside the room and in a long hotel corridor, I head to the left where I see a bright red exit sign signaling my escape. I barge through the exit doors and the cold December air cuts through me, reminding me that my arms and neck are bare. But I don't care. I can't go back into that room; I would rather freeze to death than watch Landry and Lindsay celebrate their engagement.

"I told you that you were too good for him." A voice growls from behind me.

I turn around to see Josh leaning up against the side of the building with a drink in one hand and a cigarette in another. Despite the deep scowl lines on his face and his bowtie undone and hanging carelessly around his collar, he's still a very handsome man.

"I take it from the look on your face you didn't know." Josh continues as he sets his drink on the ground while holding his cigarette in his mouth.

I watch in silence, my mind still racing, as he peels off his suit jacket and gives it to me. I don't say a word as I slip my arms into the long sleeves and wrap it around me.

"Thank you," I whisper as the warmth of the jacket surrounds me. It smells like smoke and cologne.

Without a word, Josh hands me his crystal tumbler filled with a brown liquid. Without asking what it is, I bring the glass to my lips and take a generous drink. As the liquid hits my tongue, I can tell immediately that it's scotch. I hand the glass back to Josh who then takes his drink.

"When did you find out about this?" I ask.

"A month or two ago," Josh replies as he tosses the cigarette butt on the ground, stomping on it with his black dress shoe.

"A couple of months?" My voice shrieks. "And you didn't think to tell me?"

"It wasn't my news to tell."

"You texted me three weeks ago to say happy birthday," I yell at Josh and swat at his arm with rage. "You could have fucking told me, Josh!"

I know I'm taking my anger out on the wrong Hayles' brother as I hit Josh's arm repeatedly, but I don't care. Someone is going to feel my pain.

"Okay, scrappy, that's enough." Josh grasps my swatting hand and pulls me into his chest.

"Josh, let me go." I continue with my rage fueled tantrum.

Josh doesn't let me go though, he continues to hold me tight with one arm wrapped around my shoulder and his other arm still casually lifting his glass to his mouth. It's a familiar scenario we'd been in before.

After a few minutes of silence, I begin to calm down slightly.

"I don't understand what's going on, Josh." The words tremble from my lips quietly.

"I know, sweetheart." Josh's words are whispered, but not quite enough to miss the threads of pain laced throughout. I feel him press his lips onto the top of my head.

"How did this happen?" I ask my comforter and fellow broken spirit.

"I don't know. I was gone all fall working on a case. I came home to find my girlfriend engaged to my brother. No one bothered to ask me about it, but I guess they felt they had to act quickly because of the ...."

The exit door swings open, and Landry comes barreling out into the cold parking lot.

Turning to meet my eyes, Landry looks panicked. "Hollynd, what are you doing here?"

"Hollynd and I were just catching up, little brother." Josh answers for me but doesn't loosen his embrace as Landry walks closer.

I continue to stare at Landry from Josh's arms, saying nothing.

"Hollynd, I..." Landry trails off.

"I guess congratulations are in order, Landry." My voice is steady, though permeated with spite as I push myself out of Josh's embrace and stand face to face with Landry. "Lindsay, are you kidding me? No offense, Josh."

Josh takes the last drink of his scotch before setting the glass on the ground and then tucking his hands in his pocket. "None taken. He did me a favor, taking Lindsay off my hands. I probably would have let him have her if he'd asked me. Getting her pregnant seemed to be a bit extreme. But you know our Landry, he loves to be extreme."

For the second time in ten minutes, I feel like a sledgehammer is slamming against my stomach as the news of Lindsay's pregnancy rings in my head.

"She's pregnant, Landry?" I ask, while I can feel teardrops warming my cold eyes.

Landry lowers his head the same way I have seen him do several times already tonight.

"I'm sorry. I have to go." Turning as fast as I can, I start jogging away in my high heels across the parking lot.

Josh's jacket is still wrapped around my body. I have to get away before I crumble to the ground. I hear Landry call after me in the distance. But I won't stop. I can't stop.

Chapter 33

Landry

When the kiss between Lindsay and I ended on the stage in front of hundreds of smiling faces, I saw her. Hollynd getting up from a table in the back and walking swiftly towards the doorway. It doesn't escape me the strange combination of complete beauty and complete agony she carries as she crosses the back of the room.

Finally, the crowd calms their cheers. Lindsay and I return to our seats. My father wraps up his speech and comes down from the stage. As the caterers bring trays of food and drinks out to the tables, I excuse myself to find Hollynd.

I can't believe she's here tonight. My stomach turns as I think of her listening to my father's announcement. I should have called Hollynd to tell her myself. I had thought about it, but always lacked the courage to make the call. A part of me thought that if I didn't make the call, then it was never truly over. The tiniest sliver of hope, as fictitious as it was. Of course, I knew it was far from the truth, especially now that Lindsay's pregnant. Still, I can't stop myself from chasing after the girl I've crushed more times than I can count. I'm not sure what good any of this would do, but I can't stop myself from getting to her.

When I rush out of the exit doors and see her and Josh together, my guilt becomes doubled. The two people I've hurt tremendously with my actions are standing face to face, bonding in common pain.

Five minutes later, I'm watching Hollynd running away from me across a dark and cold parking lot. Part of me thinks I should let her keep running. Getting away from me is clearly what she wants. But another part of me— my heart—makes me take off after her. I leave Josh standing there as I go after Hollynd. Because she's running in a dress and heels, it doesn't take long for me to catch up to her.

I come up behind her and grab her arm to stop her. "Hollynd, please wait."

When she turns to face me, I see bright red cheeks stained with frozen tears. Hollynd's tiny fists pound against my chest in rage. Part of me wishes she could hit me harder so I could take some of her pain. Instead, I wrap my arms around her entire body and press her into me as tight as I can.

"Shh, baby, listen to me. I'm so sorry." Hollynd's body is vibrating fiercely against mine.

"I'm so sick of your sorry's, Landry! I swear that's all I ever hear from you! How could you do this to me? To us?" Hollynd's still trying to push against me with her fists, her eyes are wild with rage.

"Cricket, I didn't mean for it to happen. It was all a mistake. I messed up."

"Seriously, Landry? Did you accidentally sleep with her?" Hollynd screams in my face.

"I thought it was you!" I can't help but yell back.

"What does that even mean, Landry?"

"Baby, I was so fucked up. I didn't know what I was doing."

Hollynd's body finally stops resisting my hold. "What were you on, Landry?"

I shift my eyes off her eyes in shame. "Coke." I mumble with remorse.

"Ugh, Landry." Hollynd's voice carries the weight of her disappointment in me.

We stand silently together for a moment, reflecting on where we are and who we are with.

"You're having a baby, Landry." Hollynd whispers. "With somebody else."

"I know," I reply, still cradling her vibrating body against mine.

Then strangely enough, she starts laughing and it shocks me.

"I came here tonight to get you back." Hollynd confesses. "What kind of stupid idiot am I?" I realize then that her laughter is out of disgust. "Here you are sleeping with other people the whole time and I'm sitting around waiting for you."

"Baby, it wasn't..."

Hollynd suddenly pushes herself out of my embrace. "No, Landry. I don't want to hear it. I'm not your baby anymore; I'm not your fucking Cricket either. This thing that once was us, is done. It's over. You broke my heart, again. But for the last time, I swear to God."

Hollynd turns to walk away from me, and I can't resist grabbing her hand. I put her hand on my chest over the tattoo of the cricket etched on my skin.

"Wait, Cricket, please. Just give me a minute." While I hold her freezing hand over my heart, I press my hand on top of hers.

Hollynd stands stoic with her eyes closed, and she breathes slowly and steadily. She's savoring this moment as much as I am. I feel as though this is my last chance to say whatever I need to say to the love of my life, before I go off to marry another. But how does one find the right words for an occasion such as this? How are words supposed to encapsulate the ending of everything?

In a feeble attempt to articulate all that I feel, I allow my words to flow without thought. A free flow of everything I shouldn't say but can't not say.

"There is nothing I can say that will make this better. I know that. I want you to know that all the best parts of who I am, was when I was with you. And if our short time together is all I get in this life, then at least I know I had the honor of being loved by the owner of my soul, and I don't think everyone can say that."

For a moment, she doesn't pull away from my chest. Hollynd holds on for one more beat before her green eyes shift up to mine.

"Pick me," a desperate whisper escapes her lips. It's so silent that it's almost inaudible.

"I can't," I reply with a hitch in my voice and a small death in my heart.

Hollynd removes her hand from my chest and turns to walk away.

I let her go.

Chapter 34

Landry

Seven Months Later

Today is July 20th. Today was my baby's due date, but God had other plans in mind because my baby died on May 11th. I hate today with a passion because it's a day that means absolutely nothing now, and yet its power to cause grief throughout my body is like no other power. I'm angry and sad at the same time.

I remember May 11th like it was yesterday. I received a phone call while I was in class from Lindsay's mother. Since her mother has never called me before, I knew it must be important. I snuck out of the class through the backdoor to answer my vibrating phone. When I answered, Lindsay's mother was panic-stricken while telling me she was taking Lindsay to the hospital because she had begun to bleed.

At Lindsay's three-month checkup and first ultrasound appointment we discovered that Lindsay had placenta previa, which meant that the positioning of the placenta was under the baby and had completely covered the cervix.

The doctor gave us strict instructions that if Lindsay noticed any signs of bleeding, she was to get to the hospital immediately. Since I was still in school full time, Lindsay's mother volunteered to come stay with us to help Lindsay with her condition and to help her get ready for the baby.

After our wedding in January, which was an over-the-top event, Lindsay and I moved to Reddington instead of staying in Brighten. I didn't want to live under my father's roof any longer and it was time to face the reality that I was going to be a father and husband. Or at least a husband.

Before we lost the baby, Lindsay and I had come to an unspoken understanding. Lindsay felt as much obligated as I did to enter into this marriage. Truth be told, we didn't know each other very well and our fear for our future together gave us a bond. We slowly got to know each other and even became caring towards each other through the mutual love of the baby growing inside Lindsay. I wouldn't go as far to say that we loved each other, but we accepted each other.

And then we lost the baby.

Once I could see Lindsay, I sat beside her for hours holding her hand. She looked so small and weak in that hospital bed. We didn't speak, we sat together in silence. The doctor eventually came in to talk to us about our lost child. We found out together that it had been a baby boy, a secret we had chosen not to find out about earlier.

We decided we would name our baby boy Raziel, after the angel who keeps secrets and mysteries. Since our boy was born to be an angel, and it seemed God needed him there more than we needed him on earth, he deserved the favored angel's name. Why he was never meant to grace the earth is a mystery I will never understand.

The days following the loss of the baby were quiet. When Lindsay was released from the hospital, she went back to her parents' place in Brighten to grieve with them. I understood her need to be with her family. While we were getting along, we were still not true partners.

I was alone for the first few nights after losing the baby and I experienced waves of different emotions, one right after another. One minute I would feel anger, which quickly turned to sadness. The sadness would turn to confusion because I was sad for someone I had never met, never touched, never held. How could I be at such a loss for something I had never really had? The confusion would turn back to anger. And around and around it would go.

I tried to find answers with the help of tequila, but to no avail. Soon, my sadness began spiraling more and more. The baby's death, losing Hollynd, my father's control, it all had me longing to escape the hell of my grief.

I had a choice to make—turn back to my old ways or call for help. I called Rob. Rob came and spent a few days with me after Lindsay left to be with her parents. We didn't talk too much about the actual crisis at hand, Rob was just there for me. The bond that we had as brothers, how we would take care of each other always without having to be asked, was exactly what I needed to survive this darkness.

Eventually, Rob went back home to Brighten, and Lindsay returned to Reddington. I finished my semester at Oak University while Lindsay filled her days with spending time with her friends or family.

I had been seeing a therapist back in Brighten after my last round with drugs and would still make the hour drive back once a week to see her in Brighten. Therapy has also been a very helpful thing for me to help process and accept the loss of the baby, without having to resort to using drugs to numb out my emotions. For once in my life, I finally felt I had better control over myself and my reactions to situations.

Sitting quiet and still in the back of my mind is always Hollynd. Even being several hours away and a memory at best, I wanted to be a better man for her. At least if we never saw each other again on earth, then maybe Hollynd would be proud of me one day in heaven; both she and my baby boy.

Accepting that it was over between us has not been easy, but I'm married now. Even when that little voice in my heart tries to tell me I was married to Hollynd first, I make sure not to indulge it. I've moved onto a Hollynd-free existence, save for the one picture. A picture of the two of us I had taken once while we were curled up together in bed. A picture that I never look at except for the nights when I can feel my soul calling out to me, reminding me it's still out there, somewhere. It's with the one I cannot have, the one I cannot quite let go.

Chapter 35

 Hollynd

Six months later

Watching the fan on my sister's ceiling spin round and round, mindlessly, I'm beyond exhausted, and almost to the point of disillusioned. I'm back home in Brighten for Christmas break, though I'm not feeling very festive this season.

Rachel's getting ready for the annual Mayor's Christmas Gala that she and Colin attend every year. I attended last year, and that night ended in an epic failure, so I have opted out of going this year. Instead, I'm staying at home with my twin nieces.

This entire past year seems more like a blur to me more than anything. After I returned to Elmerson with a broken heart, once again, things began to spiral out of control for me. Determined to get over Landry and ignore the pain of losing him for good, I would drown my feelings with the drinks strangers bought for me at the clubs in Elmerson. Eva, Parker, and I became frequent club hoppers throughout the last year.

I noticed that my sleeping trouble from my past resurfaced after my ordeal with Landry. However, I knew if I could drink enough, then eventually the power of the alcohol would lull me into a sleep that contained no dreams and no nightmares. It was black. It was silent.

Aside from the drinking and dancing, I'd seek out the warm bodies of men to keep me company, for a few hours at least. I didn't do this every time we'd go out, though occasionally, I would tire of my pleasure coming from my battery-operated boyfriend and craved the touch of another person. None of these men were Landry, and I admit, I compared each one of them. But they were at least real and not some distant memory of the person who left me. A face I had no choice but to make a distant memory of because my own survival depended on it.

However, this lifestyle of denial and resentment led to other consequences in my life that were not only hangovers or the walk of shame. I no longer submitted articles to the magazines I had freelanced in the past. In fact, I no longer wrote anything anymore unless it was school related. My grades had dropped significantly. I was still passing my classes, but I was most definitely not at the top of the curve.

Parker and Eva were still permanent fixtures in my life, and we were more like a family unit than friends. Due to a mix up with dorm allocations, Eva ended up moving in with me last fall, even though I still lived in my tiny one-bedroom apartment. We had discussed looking for a two-bedroom apartment but had yet to get around to it. Eva stayed on the pull-out couch and the close quarters didn't seem to bother either of us. I enjoyed having her there with me. When Eva was in the apartment with me and she slept soundly in the other room, the ghost of Landry didn't seem so real anymore. Though I can't say that it completely disappeared, as some nights that familiar bedfellow would appear.

It was nights like these I would have feelings of wakefulness and alertness stir in my body. Remembering the nights of my teen years where I spent hours staring into nothing, wondering why sleep refused to come, wondering why my father had to die, remembering that I couldn't do anything to help him. These feelings bubbled up slowly in the darkness of my room. Wondering why Landry got Lindsay pregnant, wondering if he was happy with her, wondering why I wasn't good enough, wondering if he was okay after I had heard that his baby had died. These thoughts broke my heart repeatedly, and with each passing night, I found the struggle to sleep more pressing.

Finally, by the end of October, I had to seek help to get my sleep under control. I found myself with a prescription for sleeping pills just like I had all those years ago. I felt defeated and embarrassed that I had been brought back to this state. I told no one.

Now I'm lying in an over exhausted haze on my sister's bed as she comes out of her attached bathroom wearing a floor length beautiful silver dress.

"Wow, you look amazing, Rach." I say as I break my fixation with the ceiling fan.

"Thank you. And thanks for watching the girls for us tonight."

"No problem. We have big plans to order pizza and watch Mickey's 'Once Upon a Christmas.'"

"Just don't keep them up too late. We have a bit of running around to do in the morning before we all meet at Mom's later."

"Can I stay here tonight and come with you tomorrow? I need to grab a few things myself."

"Absolutely." Rachel finishes getting ready with a few squirts of her perfume.

When Rachel and Colin leave for their party, the girls and I settle in for our night ahead. Cuddles, pizza, and Christmas movies are exactly what I need right now. Anything to take my mind off the fact that my sister is probably at the same party as Landry and his wife. Knowing that Landry is only twenty minutes away from me right now is tugging at my soul.

Chapter 36

Hollynd

The next morning, Rachel's house is buzzing with excitement. It's Christmas Eve today and the girls are non-stop giggling already. The noise is bothersome as I'm currently experiencing what I call my "sleeping pill hangover" which usually gives me a slight headache and a fuzzy brain. Luckily, it doesn't last all day. At least the strong smell of coffee in the air offers some relief.

After a quick breakfast, Rachel, the twins, and I all get ready to head downtown to do our errands.

It's a beautiful day outside with the full sun and only a small amount of snow that covers the ground. I finish my errands quickly while Rachel and the twins are still out and about. I choose to wait for them in a small coffee shop on main street and sit near the window so I can watch all the people rushing around to do their last-minute shopping.

There are a lot of frazzled faces which make me smile. Christmas is a merry time, but the stress it can cause on people in desperate search for the perfect gift is quite the opposite. Still, there's a strange magic in the air even amongst the chaos.

While I continue my people watching, I look across the street and the door to Abby's Flower Shop opens as a man exits the shop. It's Landry, carrying a small teddy bear and a single rose. He's dressed in black from head to toe, including a black wool jacket and black leather gloves. Landry pauses at the door, using his arm to hold it open as if he is waiting for someone. Lindsay, of course, follows behind him also dressed in a black wool coat, which covers what looks to be a black dress, and tall black boots. When she exits the flower shop, she stands right beside Landry. I watch as Landry leans down and presses a soft kiss to his wife's cheek. Together they walk away from the flower shop and the direction of the coffee shop I'm sitting in.

It's the first time I have seen them together since last Christmas and the first time I have seen them as husband and wife. They look like husband and wife. I guess I didn't know what I expected. But the shakiness of my hands tells me I didn't expect to see Landry with a wife that wasn't me. And yet here I sit, alone in a coffee shop, the wife who had no wedding and no legal bindings. Only some silly vows made to the moon and stars who do nothing more than mock me night after night, reminding me that if they can't sleep, then neither should I.

I fake my way through the rest of the day with my family. The food and drinks, the games with the girls, the exchanging of gifts, I fake it all. I smile and laugh, but my mind is still sitting in the coffee shop from earlier today.

This evening I'm sipping white wine, hoping it will help to relax me, but soon realize that even the wine is not helping. My mind is still racing while my fingers tremor. Even though it's only nine at night, I decide to take two sleeping pills, the maximum dosage, hoping that I can have an early night. Despite the labeling on the bottle warning me against mixing these pills with alcohol, I continue to nurse my white wine. I will do anything to help the images of Landry and Lindsay leave my mind tonight.

The wine must hit me harder than I expected because an hour later I'm sitting in the washroom, dizzy with confusion. I can't remember if I took my sleeping pills yet or not. Staring at the pill bottle that is rolling around in my hand, I watch the tiny pills shuffle loosely in the container.

I feel fuzzy in the head. Why can't I remember? Every part of my body wants to sleep, I would give anything to sleep. Taking two more pills, I tell myself that I will definitely remember taking them this time.

Moments later, I watch images of the bathroom, like the white tub with a teal shower curtain or the Paw Patrol bubble bath bottle fade into nothing. I fade into nothing.

I don't know what's happening. I have never been so scared in my life. There are sounds of machines beeping, people are yelling. I'm stretched out on a bed, but I can't keep my eyes open. They're forcing me to open my mouth, hands are grabbing at my body to hold me still. What is happening?

It's Christmas morning and I open my eyes to see a stranger leaning over me to adjust the blankets covering my body. She's wearing blue scrubs and has her black hair tied back into a tight braid. She's a nurse, and I'm in a hospital.

When she notices I'm awake, the nurse whose name tag reads 'Mary' asks me, "How are you feeling?" Her voice has a sweet accent to it, British perhaps?

"What happened?" I ask, though my throat feels wretched and dry. It hurts to talk.

Nurse Mary hands me a cup with some water. "Hollynd, we had to pump your stomach last night. Do you remember why?"

"Because of my pills?" I ask, though I know the answer.

"Yes. Why did you take so many?" Nurse Mary asks while checking my IV attachment.

"I don't know. I didn't do it on purpose," I confess. "I couldn't remember if I had taken any or not."

Nurse Mary, and probably everyone else, is wondering if I took that many on purpose and the truth is, I hadn't. I know I hadn't done it on purpose. I couldn't remember.

"The doctor will come and see you in a minute. She's just outside the door with your mother and sister right now."

I nod as the tears swell up in my eyes. "I didn't mean to do it." The words scratch out of my throat with pain to Nurse Mary, who offers a sympathetic smile in return.

A few minutes later, the doctor enters my room with my sister and mother following behind. The doctor is an older woman with short white hair and glasses.

"Hollynd, I'm glad to see you are awake. I'm Doctor Lucas. You gave your family quite a scare."

The moment I meet my mother's eyes, we both break into sobbing cries. My mother comes over and wraps her arms around me while she holds me like I'm her little girl and I cry like I just fell off my bike.

Rachel's eyes fill with tears as well, but also with anger. She's mad at me; I can tell this without even asking. I know Rachel's going to let me have it when I'm better. Honestly, I don't blame her. It's Christmas morning, and she's not at home with her little girls, but standing in a hospital room with her messed up sister.

After my mom and I finish our hug and wipe our tears away, the doctor speaks to me. Asking me a series of questions about how I got the pills, how long I had been taking them, if I was on any other medications, and so on. I answer all the questions honestly. My mother and sister had already discussed my past issues with insomnia and sleeping pills, so the doctor knows I have a history with this, though never to this extreme.

"Hollynd, I'm going to suggest you go back onto the antidepressants you were on in the past. They seemed to be quite effective in helping you sort out your sleep and manage your anxiety, and I believe they will be effective again. I also think you would benefit from seeing a therapist again. Your family said they have noticed a decline in your behavior and quality of life over the last year or so. Does this seem accurate to you?" Doctor Lucas asks me directly.

I nod without making eye contact. My eyes stay firmly on my fingers as I pick at my nails.

"Okay, I want you to do nothing but rest for today. I would like to keep you here overnight to make sure there are no complications from the gastric suction on your stomach. Buzz the nurse if you need anything and I will check in with you tomorrow morning before we discharge you."

"Thank you." I mumble as Doctor Lucas leaves the room.

"I'm sorry." I whisper to my mom and sister.

My mom holds my hand while my sister is pacing around the room.

"Why didn't you come to me for help, Hollynd?" Rachel finally asks. "I mean, you could have come to us for help. We've been here before with you and got you through it. We could have done it again."

"I'm sorry, I didn't want to bother you all with my stupid problems." I wipe the tears off my cheek.

"This is because of Landry, isn't it?" Rachel demands.

"Rachel, I don't want to talk about it right now," I argue back weakly through my tears and pain.

Rachel rolls her eyes. "Of course, it's about Landry. When are you going to stop letting that guy control your life? Hollynd, you need to get over it and move on. He's married for God's sake!"

"Rachel, that's enough." My mom interjects. "Hollynd's heart has been broken."

"Mom, stop babying her!" Rachel yells in frustration.

"Rachel, you have never lost the love of your life. You married your high school sweetheart and I thank the good Lord every day that you did. But Hollynd isn't the same as you and you have to understand that these things take time."

Rachel lets out a breath and walks over to my bedside. "I'm sorry, Lynd. I'm worried about you."

"I know Rach, and I'm sorry too. And we will talk about this more, but right now, all I want is for you to go home to your family and spend Christmas with them. Please."

Rachel nods her head and reaches down to give me a hug.

A short time later, Rachel leaves to go be with her family, leaving my mom and I alone. I apologize again to Mom and we both shed a few more tears. While I tell her about all I have been feeling over the past year. I tell her how angry I am at Landry, Lindsay, and even their baby in some weird way. I hold nothing back and my mom listens without judgment.

It's evening by the time I convince Mom to go home and get some rest. She has spent all Christmas day with me in the hospital, for which I'm feeling both thankful and guilt-ridden.

249

Chapter 37

Landry

It's well into the evening on Christmas Day and I'm sitting in my father's living room with my three brothers. We each hold a freshly poured drink in our hands and are engaged in small talk about sports. We're waiting for our father who requested to have all his sons over for a visit on Christmas day. Lindsay stayed at her parents' house as she doesn't like to be around Josh, nor does he like to be around her.

While in a heated discussion about who is the better player between Lebron James and Michael Jordan, Rob's cell phone buzzes with a text notification. I watch him read the screen with widening eyes before they dart quickly to me.

"What?" I ask, knowing something isn't right.

Rob shakes his head and clears his throat. "It's nothing."

I continue to look at him and he shoots me a look that says to me, 'now is not the time.' I leave it for now as my father enters the room.

Once he has poured himself a drink, my father hands us each a cigar as he does every Christmas. We sit with our cigars and drinks, trying to disguise ourselves as a genuine family. Most of the conversation circles around politics. Rob and I mostly stay silent.

Around eleven o'clock, my father, who has passed the point of being sober, requests Rob to go find some trays of food left behind by the staff. Rob, being the dutiful son he is, follows the orders without complaint. I offer to help him for my own purposes of finding out what the text message he received earlier was about.

Once we are alone in the kitchen, I ask Rob what's going on. Rob looks torn, like he doesn't know what to say. His brows are furrowed as he bites at his lip. This has me even more concerned.

"Rob, seriously, what's going on?"

"Okay, I wasn't sure if I should say anything because I don't want you to freak out."

"Just tell me." My patience is wearing thin.

"It was Nick who messaged me earlier. He was on shift last night."

I'm reminded that Nick, Rob's roommate, is an EMS driver for Brighten Memorial Hospital.

"Okay, so...?" I continue to press Rob for information.

"They took Hollynd to the hospital last night."

"What happened?" Every muscle in my body becomes tense as I wait for an answer.

"I guess she OD'd on some pills."

"WHAT?" I move into a full-blown panic. "Is she okay?"

"I think so, he didn't say. But they had to pump her stomach."

"I have to go." I turn to leave, but not before Rob grabs my arm to stop me.

"Landry, what are you doing? You can't go to her. You're not with her anymore, you're married to Lindsay."

Rob releases my arm as I run my fingers through my hair. "I know. I know. I know." I say to Rob and to myself. "But Rob," I look my brother square in his eyes. "I have to go."

Rob nods his head, knowing there's no way to stop me.

"Tell Dad I'm not feeling well, and I left."

"Okay," Rob agrees hesitantly.

Before I leave the kitchen, Rob stops me one last time. "Landry, make it right. Fix it. End it for good."

I say nothing and I don't nod. I leave with my heart beating hastily as fear takes over. My only thing is waiting.

Thirty minutes later, I'm at the reception desk of Brighten Memorial Hospital trying to find out Hollynd's room number. Despite that it's well past visiting hours, and I'm not technically family, the receptionist is an old friend from high school, and I somehow convince her to let me go up to see Hollynd.

I'm standing inside the doorway of Hollynd's dark hospital room. There's a slight glow from the window where lights from around the hospital exterior shine through. I walk over to her quietly and sit down in the chair beside her bed. I watch as her eyes slowly open and focus on my face.

Silence.

We stare at each other for well over a minute without uttering a single word. We simply watch and breathe.

Finally, Hollynd lifts her hand from the side of the bed and reaches over to press it against my cheek. I let her. Her hand is cold and clammy.

"Hi Cricket," I whisper as she holds my cheek.

"Hi," Hollynd whispers back.

"What happened?" I ask gently.

Her eyes are glossy, but never leave mine. "I can't sleep, Landry. I just wanted to sleep."

I'm instantly reminded of her struggles with insomnia and what she told me about her use of sleeping pills to escape.

"I took too many pills," Hollynd continues. "I didn't mean to, but now they all think I'm crazy and need help. Do you think I'm crazy, Landry?"

I look at Hollynd, she looks fragile and defeated. Her hair has lost its shine and she has lost weight. Hollynd looks broken. I broke her.

I reach my hand up to remove the hair off her forehead. "No baby, I don't think you are crazy."

"Why can't I sleep anymore, Landry? I just want to sleep." Tears leak slowly from Hollynd's eyes.

"You got to let go, Cricket." I whisper into the dark air.

"How are you okay, Landry? How do you do it?"

"Baby, I'm not okay. Seeing you like this hurts so much." I grab her hand and place it on my chest. "I think you're a little bit broken, and I think I'm a little bit broken too. But I think it's time we fix ourselves for each other. So we can move on and know that the other one of us is doing okay. We need to be strong for each other, so we don't have to worry anymore. Hollynd, I need you to be okay and I need you to be happy. Can you do that for me, please?"

"I can't, Landry." Hollynd presses her eyes closed which causes a cascade of tears to fall.

"Yes, you can. I know you can," I say as I gently run my thumb over her dampen cheek.

"I saw you." Hollynd's voice shakes. "Yesterday, with Lindsay outside the flower shop. Do you love her?"

I lower my head as I remember holding Lindsay's hand as we left the shop with a teddy bear and a rose to take to our baby's grave for Christmas. In grieving over our baby, Lindsay and I are stronger together.

"What you saw was two people going to celebrate their baby's first Christmas in a cemetery."

Hollynd's hand moves off my chest and reaches for my hand. In a hush Hollynd says, "Landry, you lost your baby." Tears now flow from both our eyes. "I'm so sorry, Landry."

I can only nod.

"I know I shouldn't ask this and that it isn't right, but will you stay with me?"

I look up to the desperate face of my love and can't imagine myself anywhere else. Without an answer, I stand up and remove my jacket and shoes while Hollynd slides over as far as she can in her twin-sized hospital bed. Lifting the blankets, I crawl into the bed beside Hollynd as our arms wrap securely around each other's bodies.

Eventually after whispers of half sentence apologies and regrets, we both finally fall asleep in each other's arms. It's the first time in a year and a half I feel whole again. Though it's a feeling that is not without mourning because I know it's not meant to last.

I wake up in the early hours and slowly get out of bed. I need to go before any of her family arrive. As I'm sitting on the chair putting on my shoes, Hollynd wakes up.

"Are you leaving?"

"Yes. I have to go, Cricket."

"When do I get to be the one to leave you for once?" Hollynd turns her head away from me and looks up at the ceiling. "When is it your turn to hurt for me?"

I stand up and lean over Hollynd laying on the bed, resting my cheek against hers, which feels warm and wonderful. I curl my hand around the back of her neck. Her breath hitches before I begin to speak.

"I don't want to go. And believe me, I hurt for you all the time. Last year outside the Christmas gala, I wanted to pick you. Every day I've wanted to pick you. I still want to pick you. But..." I whisper my secret thoughts.

"But..." Hollynd's voice echoes my sentiment of impossibility.

Silence.

We remain close for another moment before I pull away and continue to get ready to leave.

After I get my shoes and jacket on, I sit on the side of the bed and cup her cheeks with my hands.

"Remember what I said, Cricket. I need you to be strong for me. I can't handle worrying about you, okay? You will get through this, baby. I know you will. Do this for me."

Hollynd looks at me through her tired green eyes. "Okay, Landry. Then you have to do it for me too. If I have to take care of your soul, then you have to take care of mine. Deal?"

"Deal." I whisper in return.

I lean forward and give my only thing a deep kiss on the lips. I can't help myself, despite knowing it's wrong

When I pull away, I hear the words fumble out of my mouth, "I love you, Cricket."

"I love you, Landry."

I stand and head directly to the door. I have to leave immediately or else risk the chance that I'll never leave at all.

I don't turn around, not once. I walk straight to the elevator and leave my only thing behind.

Chapter 38

Hollynd

Before I begin to process what has taken place with Landry, the night we spent together, or how I was all alone, again, Nurse Mary comes floating through the door.

"Good morning, Hollynd." The kindness of Nurse Mary's voice floats through the room. "You're looking much better this morning, love. Could it be because of that sexy thing I saw sneaking out of here?" Nurse Mary shoots me a wink as she begins wrapping my arm with the blood pressure sleeve. "Is that your boyfriend?"

I move my gaze to the window where the sun is starting to peek over the horizon. Everything outside looks crisp as tiny sparkles of frost float through the air.

"No," I reply to Nurse Mary. "That was my husband."

"What? I didn't know you're married!" Nurse Mary sounds genuinely surprised.

"I'm not." I reply emotionlessly. My eyes stay fixated on the horizon.

Part Two

Five Years Later

Chapter 39

Hollynd

Looking down at the place where I found and lost everything in my once upon a time love story seems much less dramatic when I view it from ten-thousand feet above. Everything seems so tiny, so quiet, and just as soul-crushing as I thought it to be when I first left six-ish years ago to attend Stranton University.

Have I been back since then? Of course. My family is still here. I have been back for holidays, birthdays, and summer visits.

Honestly, I don't mind coming back to Brighten to visit. This is where I grew up, in more ways than one. So, no, I don't hate coming back here. However, I do prefer it when I'm prepared to come back and it's a planned trip—and trip that didn't involve hospitals. This trip is the exact opposite. I'm unprepared, feeling rushed, and don't know how long I'll be here.

When Rachel called me around late last night to say my mom had collapsed, broken her hip in the fall, and taken to the hospital, I caught the first flight I could get home. I can't complain about the flight, it's relatively short. I could have made the four-hour drive instead of flying, but since my car has been temperamental lately, I thought the short, though expensive flight, might be the safer way to travel. Also, I just wanted to get home to see my mom.

Bing Bing Bing

"Attention passengers, please return your seats to their upright position and fasten your seatbelts as we prepare for our final descent into Brighten City airport."

I move my eyes from the oval window and mindlessly follow the directions of the flight attendant. I'm dead tired. My eyes are burning from the lack of sleep I didn't get last night. I always have trouble sleeping when I'm stressed out, but thanks to years of therapy, I can combat my sleep issues in a healthier way than my past coping methods.

This is not how I intended to spend this Saturday. I had plans to sleep in, wander to my nearest Starbucks around noon, and search for treasures at a local flea market with my best friends, Eva and Parker. That has been one of our weekly traditions since the three of us finished university.

Eva is now an events coordinator and Parker is a fitness and nutritional trainer. Together, we have been by each other's side for the last six years. Like my family, we have laughed and cried together. Both friends offered to come back with me to Brighten, but I insisted they stay home and enjoy their Saturday without me.

Thankfully, being a freelance writer for a variety of websites, I can work from anywhere. Leaving Elmerson for a last-minute emergency trip did not affect my ability to work. I can take my work with me. Honestly, I have nothing desperately needing my attention back in Elmerson, unless you count my half dead spider plant.

Finally, we land at Brighten where me and my fellow zombified passengers filter off the plane. It's around eight in the morning and the smell of coffee is the first sign of hope I have felt for the last eleven hours after receiving Rachel's phone call. After I make my way through the arrivals area, I see my brother-in-law Colin sitting on a wooden bench typing fiercely into his cellphone. His head is down, which shows off his salt and pepper hair, which was once a dark chestnut colour, but I guess having three kids can do that to you. Colin spots me when he gives a quick glance up between messages.

"Hey, you made it," Colin says as he rises to his feet.

We give each other a quick shoulder patting hug before we turn to walk towards the luggage carousel. On the way over there, his phone rings about five times.

"That must be Rachel," I smile at him with a sympathetic eye.

"Who else?" he smiles back. "On the way home, we have to stop at the grocery store to pick up a few hundred last minute things."

"Of course. Just be thankful she hasn't mentioned Costco."

"Well don't jinx it, Lynd." Colin scowls in my direction.

We laugh together because of my sister's occasional bossiness. Having known Colin since I was thirteen, I'm like the little sister he never had. Sometimes we still act like children, both vying for Rachel's attention, but usually we are great allies in surviving her bossy ways.

It's about an hour and a half later when we make our way up the walkway of Colin and Rachel's two-story home. While built in the nineteen-nineties, you could never tell with its updated charcoal siding and sleek stone walkway lined with a beautiful array of shrubs and flowers. I don't know how Rachel does it. Three children, a husband, helping mom on a regular basis, and she still makes her home look like it's straight off an HGTV show.

Meanwhile, my tiny apartment on the fourth floor of an old brownstone building and my suicidal spider plant are clearly the fixer uppers. Who am I kidding? My life has always been the fixer upper in the eyes of my sister.

As we enter the chaotic noise of my sister's house, I wince with a slight headache. The noise, in combination with flight pressure and lack of sleep, is catching up with me.

"Auntie Hollynd!" I hear in unison as two ten-year olds rush towards me. Instantly, my arms reach out to embrace my nieces. I love these two girls so much that I almost forget about my headache.

"Hi girls," I say to my adoring nieces. "Oh my gosh, look at how tall you both are."

My once tiny little princesses are now resting each chin on each of my shoulders. With them both standing at five feet, I only have a few inches to go before they are my size. How did this happen? They are anything but the three-year-olds I still imagine in my head. Being almost identical twins, they both have wavy brown hair and dark brown eyes, just like their dad. However, everything else is their mom's. The sharp nose and beautiful smiles that could light up an entire forest at midnight. They are turning into gorgeous young women, and I laugh to myself knowing that is going to kill Colin when they are old enough to begin dating.

"Auntie, look at my braces," Maria says, while flashing her teeth in my face.

"Auntie, I repainted my room. You got to come see it." Madison tugs on my wrist.

"Girls, give your aunt one minute to get into the house and take the bags from her hands into the kitchen," Rachel's voice rings out.

Begrudgingly, my nieces do as they are told and huff their way to the kitchen on their left. Still standing in the entryway with a sunken living room to my right, Rachel makes her way over.

"Hey, how was the flight?" Rachel asks while pulling me into a quick hug.

"Alright," I say with a shrug. "How's Mom this morning?"

"I haven't heard from the hospital since last night, but she's supposed to have surgery for her hip this afternoon. We should get there to see her before then, so let's plan to leave for the hospital in an hour." Rachel confirms as she checks the time on her phone. "Do you want to come to the kitchen and get a coffee?"

"Got anything stronger?" I reply with a very serious curiosity.

"I got Baileys for the coffee."

"Oh, thank God," I sigh as I follow my sister into the kitchen.

When I enter the kitchen, I see my sweet little niece, Cassie, sitting in her highchair, playing with a handful of cheerios. She's happily swooshing them around while her sisters continue to unpack the groceries.

"Hi, my baby girl." I bend down to kiss the top of Cassie's head.

With a raspberry gurgle and giggle coming from the chair below, my heart fills with a love like no other. I take a deep inhale of that baby smell wafting off Cassie's peach fuzzed head and a genuine smile flashes across my face.

Despite being in the second half of my twenties, twenty-seven to be exact, I haven't thought too much about motherhood for myself. Probably because I have no current romantic prospects, so why would I worry about step four, when step one (the boyfriend), step two (falling in love), step three (moving in together) are clearly not coming to fruition? Nothing romantic since my breakup with my long-term boyfriend, Kyle— which ended over a year ago.

Plus, if I allow myself to think about this too hard, I can feel a slight ache in my stomach that has been there for years. I try to tell myself that it's an ulcer from too much coffee, but in the dark of my heart I know it's the scars of a different loss. I don't allow myself to think of that either, because if I do, I might find myself back at the mercy of my regrets. Back at the mercy of his ghost.

Chapter 40

Hollynd

It's early afternoon when we arrive at the hospital to see my mom briefly before she is taken in for surgery. Luckily, she's awake and lucid enough to have a quick conversation.

Although Mom's laying in a hospital bed, she still radiates beauty like no other. Her light blonde hair curls around her face and her rosy cheeks lift into a smile when Rachel and I appear in the doorway.

"Oh, my girls, you're both here." My mother reaches towards me in search of a hug. "Hollynd, how was your trip?"

"It was fine, Mom. But how are you? Are you in pain?"

"Oh no dear, I'm okay. They have been giving me the good stuff," Mom jokes as she looks up to her IV drip bag connected to her right hand.

"We'll be here when you come out of surgery, Mom," Rachel notes.

"Okay, dear." Mom takes a slow blink and is lulled back to sleep.

"They did give her the good stuff," I whisper to Rachel, who nods in agreement.

Four hours later, Rachel and I are in Mom's hospital room waiting for her to wake up from surgery and be brought back from the recovery ward.

"I expect your mother will be in the hospital for at least a week to two weeks to recover from the surgery. However, it may be longer since she has been experiencing dizzy spells, which ultimately led to her fall. We need to do some tests so we can find the cause of the dizziness. Depending on the outcome of those tests and her surgery recovery, your mother may have to stay here longer." The older doctor with white hair and glasses that are too small for his face explains to us, while our mom is on her way back up to her room from the recovery ward.

"Okay, thank you doctor." Rachel offers a handshake. "Well, we still don't know too much," she continues while turning to me as the doctor walks away.

"Hey, don't worry about me. I will stay as long as I need to," I assure my overly stressed-out sister. "I'll stay at Mom's house and look after Georgie." Georgie is Mom's ten-year-old cat. The black and white fluffy cat has been my mother's constant companion since our father passed away eleven years ago.

"It will be great. I can help you with the girls while I'm here, too. It will be nice to spend some extra time with all of you. It can get lonely in Elmerson," I reassure Rachel, who's pacing with worry.

"I'm looking forward to having you around too, Sis," Rachel says with a slight look of relief, knowing she will not be on her own to look after our mom.

Not long after visiting with the doctor, Mom is back in her room sipping on some broth. The nurse mentions to us that

Mom is probably going to be asleep most of the evening and throughout the night as she's still on heavy painkillers from the surgery. We tell Mom about the plan of me staying at her house to look after everything while she's in the hospital. She seems happy to know that her Georgie won't be all alone.

Shortly after her chicken broth supper, we say our goodbyes to Mom for the evening. Rachel heads back to her family as I go to spend the night at my mom's house.

The house is a small bungalow that has a quaint cottage feel to it with its wrap around white porch and butter cream yellow siding. The front door is off the kitchen and dining area, while the living room is to the back of the kitchen and on the left. On the right there's a short hallway with two bedrooms, one which is my mother's room and one that's now a sewing room, and the bathroom. My old bedroom in the loft still remains the same as it was when I lived here.

It isn't long after I arrive to my old home that I flop onto my old bed and fall into a deep sleep. It's been a terribly long day and the coziness of my old bed is a welcome reprieve.

Chapter 41

Hollynd

After my very welcomed–and very needed–first night back in my old bed, the next few days fly by. Between trips to the hospital to see Mom, trips to Rachel's house for pretty much every meal, and trying to get a little work done. My sleep has been hit and miss the past couple of nights, but it's comforting to be in my old house and my old bed again.

What a relief it is to hear that my mom is doing well in her surgery recovery, though the cause of her dizzy spells is still being tested. I try to spend as much time with my mom as I can, but she always insists on keeping our visits short. Mom says there's no sense in us hanging around the hospital to dote on her, and that as long as she has her soap operas to watch and her books to read, that she's fine. Honestly, I think she's more concerned I'm not spending enough time with Georgie.

It's Thursday evening, and we're cleaning up after another meal at Rachel and Colin's house. The twins and I are clearing the plates while Rachel washes dishes in the sink. Colin has taken Cassie up for her bedtime bath.

"Auntie Hollynd, do you want to stay and watch Dancing with the Stars with us?" Madison asks while drying dishes for her mom.

"I don't know. I'm not really into reality TV. Although back in the day your mom and I used to have great dance moves." I wink at Madison.

"Mom having great dance moves? I can't even imagine," Madison laughs.

"Hey, I used to dance all the time when I was young and went to clubs." Rachel gives her butt a wiggle. "We should totally go out dancing!"

"Are you crazy?" I roll my eyes at my sister.

"Yes! Let's go tonight. Colin can stay with the kids. I'll call Sydney and Michelle. We'll make it a girls' night out!"

"A wild girl's night on a Thursday?" I ask sarcastically.

"It'll be perfect because it's not a weekend, it won't be as busy. Please-please-please! I finished breastfeeding months ago and haven't gone out for drinks yet." Rachel bats her eyes with a slight desperation.

"Fine." I finally give in.

"Eek!" Rachel squeals in delight. "I'm going to call the girls."

Three hours later Rachel, Sydney, Michelle, and I are sitting together in a black pleather covered booth at a club called the Flagship, a dance club we used to frequent in our younger days.

The club is busier than I expected for a Thursday night, but what do I know? I never go to clubs anymore, not since my senior year of college. There was a time where clubbing and excessive drinking had become my lifeline. That was a bit after the …. *Nope, I will not think about that tonight.*

The four of us have always been great friends so it doesn't take long for me to forget about wanting to be at home in bed instead of enjoying the company of my dear friends.

Michelle has always been a kind girl with a smile on her face. Now she's a mother of four children, all under the age of ten, and she wears the same smile, with a bit more exhaustion. Since Michelle is still breastfeeding her newest arrival, she has volunteered to be our designated driver, which suits the rest of us just fine.

Sydney is the wild and outspoken one of the group, and she's always honest, even if the truth hurts. She's never afraid to call anyone out on their crap and though she has brought all of us to tears with her bluntness more than once, Sydney is a loyal friend. Sydney has always said she's not interested in getting married or having children until she is well into her thirties. Having recently broken up with her long-term boyfriend of four years, the newly single Sydney has changed her marriage age to forty.

Despite the club being much busier than I thought it would be for a Thursday night, I notice that compared to many of the younger women at the club tonight, I'm way underdressed. Most of them are strutting around in miniskirts and very high heels. I, on the other hand, am wearing a pair of distressed denim jeans, a plain black T-shirt, and black ankle boots.

After our first round of drinks, we decide that one round of tequila shots is in order. I volunteer to get a round from the bar. Shaking my head as I head towards the bar, I already know I'm going to regret this in the morning. I lean against the wooden bar and wait for my turn to gain the bartender's attention.

"Hey girl, what can I get for you?" the cute bartender, with black hair and a beard, leans forward to ask.

"Can I get four shots of tequila with the salt and lemons?"

"Yup, give me a sec." The cute bartender winks.

While I'm waiting for the drinks, I turn around to scan the crowd of people. The dance floor is a combination of drunk college girls grinding way too hard on each other while a clump of men watches from the sidelines.

As I continue through the crowd of unfamiliar faces when a set of very familiar eyes meet up with mine. Instantaneously, my heart jumps into my throat. *Fuck-fuck-fuck-fuck* is racing through my head as the deep blue eyes watch me with an intensity and darkness I haven't seen for five years. Landry Hayles.

Landry still shaves his dark hair on the sides and keeps it a bit longer on top. From where I'm standing, he seems bigger, maybe broader in the shoulders than I remember. Landry is, however, still blessed with a mass of muscles and is still stupidly hot.

I try to catch my breath as my soul is twitching as it recognizes the missing piece of itself in the eyes across the room. Landry's not smiling or waving, only looking at me, and it takes everything I have in me not to collapse right there at the foot of the bar.

As our eyes stay locked for what feels like forever, I notice the corner of his mouth curl up. My inner voice is screaming at me to smile back or turn away, or basically anything rather than stare at him like a raving psycho.

"Twenty-two dollars, love," the bartender yells at me over the booming music as he sets down my order of tequilas on the bar, breaking me out of my trance.

"Oh, sorry. Here you go," I mumble as I fish the cash out of my pocket and grab the tray.

Before turning towards my table of girls, I take one quick glance back at the table where Landry had been sitting and there's no one. He's gone. I feel a strange combination of relief and sorrow. Had I made it all up in my head? *No, my soul always recognizes its other half.*

"Lynd, you finally made it! What's up with your cheeks? They're very rosy," Rachel points out promptly when I arrive back at our table.

"I don't know. Hot in here, I guess." I lie, though it goes unnoticed by my friends who are already buzzing.

I don't want to tell Rachel about seeing Landry. I don't want to bring up any discussions of him and I, or our whole messed up past. It's bad enough I can hardly hold my tequila shot as my handshakes so hard that I worry I may miss my mouth entirely. I somehow down the entire shot with ease, though it burns my throat.

While the girls continue to visit and laugh about their night of freedom from children and husbands, my mind races with blurred images and questions. *Why is he here? Why did he disappear? Where is his wife?*

Chapter 42

Landry

That's Hollynd. My Hollynd. My Cricket. *My only fucking thing*. It's been over five years since I last saw her lying in that hospital bed, where it took every bit of strength I had to walk away from her, again.

Hollynd was the love of my life. Maybe she still is? Shit, I don't even know anymore. All I know right now is at this moment, she's standing at the bar looking like the most beautiful creature on this whole planet, and I'm here trying to remember how to breathe.

God, she looks great. Better than great, phenomenal. Her dirty blonde hair isn't as long as I remember it being, but still long enough that I could easily grab a handful of it and... *Down, boy.*

Dressed in the tightest jeans I think I have ever seen, every single one of Hollynd's curves are on display. Christ, I've missed those curves too. She doesn't see me right away, but I'm fine with it because I must look like a total idiot sitting here in shock.

I almost didn't come out tonight, having only come here after leaving a local sports bar with my brother Rob and some buddies. I was hoping to go home after the game, but these younger guys are always up for much more. Not that I'm that much older than them but being a man of twenty-eight and having already lived through more crap than most men double my age, I feel like I'm much older. Most nights I want to go home after work, watch TV, and go to bed. Work has been my only successful accomplishment in the last few years.

My brother, Rob, and I started working on software design and eventually app creation after we finished college. We were small at first, mostly designing apps for local businesses. Slowly, between the two cities of Brighten and Reddington, we have been able to grow our tech company with much success. For the last four years I have spent all my energy on work while my personal life went to shit around me.

About a year ago, I moved back to Brighten from Reddington as my personal life became a dumpster fire, again, and I moved back in with Rob.

Rob has been overseeing the business in Brighten while I covered Reddington. Thank goodness we have a well-rounded team that could take over the Reddington area in my absence. I couldn't stay in that city any longer. So, now I'm living with my younger brother, just like old times.

It's embarrassing being a grown man having to move back in with your younger brother, but frankly I was desperate and on the verge of complete self-destruction, once again. Rob has been my life raft more than once. Saving me from myself more times than I care to admit. Now that I'm back in Brighten, I feel like I owe him. When Rob says he wants to go out, I often agree to go with him.

I only now realize I haven't seen Rob in a while, but now that Hollynd is in my sights, Rob could be on fire beside me and I still wouldn't notice him. I don't know why she's here in Brighten. The last I had heard, Hollynd was still living in Elmerson, the same city I left her in all those years ago. Not that I'm upset that she's here, quite the opposite. I love that she's here.

Suddenly Hollynd's eyes veer in my direction and I can feel myself willing her to look at me. *Just notice me, Hollynd.* And then she does. Her eyes lock with mine in an instant. Neither of us moves or smiles or waves. We only stare.

What is she thinking? Is she angry? She looks kind of angry. I can't take this. My heart is beating so fast I feel like I may pass out.

I hear my name being called from a table a few yards away. I glance over to see Rob holding up shots beckoning me over to the table he's at with two of our buddies, Nick and Cam.

Hollynd turns towards the bartender, handing money over for what looks like an entire tray of tequila. She's obviously not here alone. What if she's with someone like a boyfriend or husband? Instantly, I feel unwarrantably pissed off.

While Hollynd is looking away, I take my opportunity to head towards Rob's offering of shots. I'm not near drunk enough to deal with Hollynd yet. Though I do plan on dealing with her, that is something I know for sure. Now that I know she's here within reach, every part of me is scratching to go to her.

As I arrive at Rob's table with purpose, I grab the first shot I see and down it in one quick gulp.

"Woah, you look like a man on a mission," Rob snorts. "What's up?"

"I saw Hollynd." I look back to the bar where she had been standing but is now gone.

"Shut up, you did not. It was probably some chick who looks like her." Rob tips back his own shot.

"No one else looks like her," I say, more to myself than to Rob.

"She doesn't even live here."

"It was her, Rob!" My eyes are burning at him now.

"Okay, okay. Calm down. I believe you. Here, have another shot."

I take another shot of the whiskey laid out before me. This time I feel its slight burn on the way down. I didn't feel the last shot at all.

"So, where is she?" Rob asks now that Nick and Cam have wandered off in search of more shots and probably prettier faces than mine and Rob's.

"I don't know where she went, but she's here."

"How'd she look? Still hot?"

Resting my forehead on my fingertips, I shake my head. "So, freaking hot."

Rob laughs at my complete melt down. However, he offers a quick pat on the back as his silent signal of support. Rob knows all about my past with Hollynd and how I'm my own worst enemy when it comes to her. He also knows that losing her before damn near killed me.

"Well, now what?" Rob asks while lifting his drink of cola and Crown Royal.

"Now I drink some more and then I'll go find her." I raise my glass and let it clink against Rob's glass.

"You know, you could not go find her. We could find a couple of girls to hang out with tonight that are for fun. No drama and no feelings." Rob nudges my arm with his elbow.

But I'm already scanning the crowds for my girl at this point. Not some random girl like Rob wants me to find. My girl.

Rob can tell by the look of determination on my face that I'm on a mission to find Hollynd again.

"Landry, are you sure you want to find Hollynd? Are you sure you want to open that can of worms again? Remember how messed up you became over her?"

"I'm still messed up, Rob. I'll probably always be messed up." Letting out a long exhale, my brother shakes his head, knowing I've already made my mind up. "At least if I have her, even if it's for a second, then maybe I won't feel so fucking dead inside."

Chapter 43

Hollynd

About an hour later and a couple of more drinks, my brain is still racing with thoughts of Landry. My glossy eyes continue to scan the crowds of people over and over. Still searching. Still nothing. Maybe I was hallucinating? Maybe it was someone who looked like him? *Ugh, I have to get some air.*

I excuse myself from the table where my friends are still drinking and laughing under the pretense of a washroom emergency. I bypass the washrooms, however, and head for the doorway that leads outside in front of the club. The cool night air is a welcome feeling against my skin that's slightly glistening from the heat of the club. I walk to a nearby planter ledge and lean against the cool concrete. Smells of cigarette smoke tumble through the air as nearby smokers laugh together.

Breathe, just breathe, I tell myself as I try to collect my thoughts and regain a bit of sobriety. I know that was Landry in there, every inch of my body knows that it was Landry I saw across the bar. Where did he go?

"Hey, stranger." A familiar voice echoes through the air. Every inch of my body tingles with excitement and fear. *You came back to me.*

As I turn my head towards the ghost I've been running from for the last six years, I'm taken aback by his familiar—though somewhat changed—good looks. *Still gorgeous.*

Landry makes his way over to where I'm leaning against a concrete planter to the right of the club entrance. Now that he's closer to me than he had been in the club, I can see his face is fuller with a jawline that demands attention with the bit of stubble that blankets it. His eyes are the ones that cornered me earlier, with a blueness that still makes my heartbeat rapidly. But they seem darker than they had been years before. Like the darkness of life had damped the brightness, somehow.

"You don't have your lip ring anymore." The random statement falls out of my mouth as I bring myself back to the reality that stands before me.

"No. I figured I was too old for that, once I had to get a job and be responsible." Landry shrugs his shoulders with his hands in his pockets.

Only wearing a dark grey T-shirt and black jeans, I can't stop staring at the tattoos that line each arm. Some are so familiar and some I have never seen before.

"I always liked the lip ring." I say with slight sadness as I glance up to meet his eyes.

Why does this make me sad? *Because he's not mine anymore.*

Finally, after a few silent minutes of us looking at one another, I remember how to be a functioning person who's able to continue a normal conversation.

"Why are you here in Brighten?" I ask.

"I live here now." Landry replies with ease. He makes this casual thing look easy as I'm squirming in my own skin.

"Really? Since when?" I'm so out of the loop, which has been intentional on my part. I had to know nothing, because I needed to know everything.

"About a year."

"Wow, I didn't realize." I look at Landry, still deciding if he's a friend or a stranger.

"Yeah, shit happens. Things change." Landry shrugs his shoulders still looking at me fiercely. "But I'm wondering why you are here. Don't you still live in Elmerson?"

"Yes, but my mom is in the hospital," I explain while his eyes soften with a slight sympathy. *There he is. Mine.* "She's okay, but she broke her hip. I'm staying at her place for a while to help."

"I'm sorry to hear that, Hollynd. Geez, I haven't seen Francine for ages."

Landry leans on the concrete beside me with a scowl of thought like he's trying to count the number of years that have passed since he last saw my mom.

Landry's close enough to me I can feel the cotton of his grey T-shirt rub on my arm. Without intention, I inhale as deep as I can, and I find the comfort of his scent once again. Calvin Klein's 'Eternity for Men' cologne fills my nose and butterflies dance in my stomach. *Mine.*

"Mom's the same, except for the newly acquired injuries." I continue my rambling. I'm filled with nerves and excitement. "What are you doing for work?"

Honestly, I hate small talk, but what else do you say to the man you haven't seen in five years? Five years of separation, though he still consumes your every secret thought, your every longing, your every breath.

"I work for a technology firm here in town."

"Really? That's cool! Good for you."

"Rob and I started it a few years back, mostly out of Reddington, but then we expanded here to Brighten as well."

"It's your own company? Wow, that's super impressive!"

"Thanks. But what about you? Still writing?"

"I freelance for a few different websites and journals. For the most part, I can work remotely. It's nice to have the flexibility. Especially in times like now, with my mom's health concerns."

I knew I could pull off this small talk stuff. A certain amount of pride filled my chest as I recall all the sessions with my therapist, Shannon. She and I would discuss over and over what I would do if I were to run into Landry one day and how I could not become a total mess or a raging psychopath. *Well, look at me now, Shannon.*

"Freelance sounds great and all, but...." Landry replies, like he doesn't quite believe my fictitious optimism. "What about your book?"

My book, my dream. Well, since I haven't touched my fiction writing in over five years, I think it's safe to declare it's dead in the water. Apparently trying to find time to fulfill a lifetime dream is easier said than done when you're in the depths of grief and barely hanging on. Not that I have been living in despair for five years, it's just sometimes when sparks inside you burn out, dreams go with them.

"That didn't really work out," I try to say coolly while crossing my arms and biting my lower lip as I can feel my defensiveness kicking in.

"Why?" Landry asks.

"I don't know. I guess I got really busy with my other stuff."

"That's bullshit, Cricket."

There it is. My old nickname, *Cricket*. The nickname Landry gave me shortly after our first date. I probably would have found his current use more endearing if annoyance wasn't slowly building inside me about him calling out my writing, or lack thereof.

"Excuse me?" My heart thumps with a combination of frustration, anger, and if I'm honest, a bit of embarrassment. "You're practically a stranger now, so I don't think you really get to give your opinion on my career."

How is it possible Landry still has the ability to take my emotions from zero to ten in a matter of seconds? I turn and shoot him my deadliest glare as he turns his body towards mine. Slowly Landry brings his mouth close enough to my ear that I can feel his breath graze across the skin on my neck. I can also feel prickles of stubble on my cheek. *Mine.*

"I'm no stranger, Cricket. I know you better than anyone," Landry growls in a dominating whisper.

I can feel his fingers running up the length of my arm, causing an internal shiver throughout. They run smoothly over my skin, and I love it through my denial.

"My name is Hollynd," I say with an angry mumble, looking straight ahead avoiding his eyes. "Cricket is dead."

I pull back to meet his eyes and now his lips that were mere centimeters from my ear are only inches from my lips. I glance at his lips while I subconsciously lick my own. We're both slowly creeping towards each other. Despite having once known every touch of this man's body, and despite still being able to taste him, I remind myself that he's not mine anymore. He hasn't been for so long that there are days I'm not even sure if it ever really happened. But God, do I want to make him mine again.

"How's your wife, Landry?" I ask with our lips barely touching.

Landry pulls his body back while clearing his throat and shoving his hand into the pocket of his jeans. "Lindsay and I are separated. That's another reason I moved back here."

"So, you're divorced?" I ask. *I hope.*

"Not yet." Landry looks down at the ground for a few seconds and then brings his eyes back up to mine.

I continue to lean against the planter with my arms still crossed against my chest and I put on the best bitch-face I can conjure up. It's a lost cause. My love always outshines my anger. We say nothing but in the *silence* of the moment, we admit everything.

For a moment, I'm taken away from the reality of the situation. I'm standing staring at the face I have longed for, and sometimes loathed, over the past five years.

"How can I know this is real? That you're really here in front of me this time?" My internal voice betrays me by letting out my inner secrets in a hushed whisper.

Landry reaches over to me and presses his hand to my chest, where my heart lays underneath. "Can you feel that, Cricket? Your soul is saying hello, the same one you gave to me all those years ago. Can you feel it?"

I can feel it and so I nod. The soul I left in Landry's care, I've missed it. *I've missed him.*

Silence.

"Hey, there you are! "A very drunk Rachel cries while Sydney and Michelle trail behind. Rachel suddenly stops in her wobbly tracks when she sees Landry.

Landry drops his hand from my chest, leaving a noticeable absent feeling inside me.

"Well, if it isn't Landry Hayles, as I live and breathe. What rock did you climb out from under?" Rachel clearly has some unresolved issues with the way Landry crushed me all those years ago.

Landry turns to face Rachel, who is stumbling towards us now. Watching my sister, Landry's eyes flash a wave of annoyance. There seems to be no love lost between them.

"Rachel, it's good to see you. You're looking stable and sober." Landry snarks sarcastically, knowing my very inebriated sister has to do everything in her power not to fall over.

"Shut up, Landry. Go back to wherever you came from and leave Hollynd alone!" Rachel fires back with a pointed finger while Sydney and Michelle are trying to coax her towards the car. "Come on, Hollynd," Rachel yells back in my direction.

I turn to leave, and not only because Rachel's barking orders at me and my ride is ready to go, but because we were at a standstill and neither of us will go down easily. I also know that deep down inside that I must leave because being in the same vicinity as Landry, if only for these last few minutes, has stirred something inside me that I have for so long pushed down. It's both euphoric and dangerous, and I know it might kill me if it fully awakens.

"Goodbye, Landry," I say almost robotically, and I don't lift my eyes to him.

"Wait for a second. Let me see your phone."

"Landry, let's just leave it alone."

"Cricket, I can't." Landry's voice softens almost to the point of a whisper. "I can't let you go. Not now, now ever."

I reach into my back pocket and retrieve my phone. I enter the passcode and place it in Landry's waiting hand. Landry taps the screen quickly before handing it back to me.

"I sent a text to my phone so now I have your number and you have mine. Call me, okay?"

I nod while I push my phone back into my pocket. My emotions swaying somewhere between excitement and defeat. I turn once again to leave and walk to the waiting car. I get into the backseat of the car with my passed-out sister. I look back at Landry one more time. I can't help it. His eyes stay fixated on me.

Breathe, Hollynd, just breathe.

Chapter 44

Hollynd

I wake up the next morning alone in my mother's house, except for Georgie, who's sleeping at the foot of my bed. I don't want to get out of bed as I squint uncomfortably at the bright sunlight filling my room. Having had a terrible sleep and dreams filled with Landry when I finally slept, I feel like complete garbage. However, Mom will expect to see us today for a visit. I'm not sure if Rachel is going to make it since I'm sure she's nursing one hell of a hangover, therefore I know I have to go.

It's well after ten a.m. when I arrive at the hospital, and I'm surprised to see Rachel sitting there in Mom's room. She looks awful. Her frizzy hair is tied back into a low ponytail and dark circles are under both eyes.

"Wow, I didn't expect to see you here this morning." I smirk at my sister while she sips on her coffee. "How are you feeling, sunshine?"

"Terrible. The baby woke me up at six this morning," Rachel groans.

"It couldn't have been the beer and shots from last night, then?" I smirk.

My mom lets out a little giggle as I rubbed in my sister's bad choices. Rachel glares in my direction.

"Actually, I was telling Mom about your run in with Landry last night." Rachel butts in, trying to avoid the embarrassment of her hangover.

"Rachel, leave it alone," I urge with a roll of my eyes.

"Now Hollynd, Rachel's worried about you. We know how much that boy hurt you in the past." Mom, always the peacekeeper.

"That was years ago. I'm not the same person I was then. It's no big deal," I argue with my mom and sister while pulling up a chair next to Rachel. I really don't want to hear about this right now.

"Well, I don't like him," Rachel intercepts. "Why is he even here? I thought he lived in Reddington with his wife."

"He said they have separated." I squeak out as I begin to bite at my fingernail.

Rachel rolls her eyes with disgust. "Of course, Landry shows back up when it's convenient for him."

"Rachel, I saw him by chance. I was there because you wanted to go there, and he didn't know I was in town."

"He better keep his distance. I'm serious, Hollynd." Rachel furrows her brow in my direction.

Rachel and I glare at each other.

"Girls, that's enough," my mother demands.

We all sit quietly while Rachel and I stew in our own thoughts. Finally, we resume small talk, though it's obviously forced between Rachel and me. Less than a week together and we already need a break from each other. *Yup, that seems about right.*

I decide to spend the rest of the day at my mom's house, alone. I'm exhausted, both physically and mentally. Seeing Landry again was like being blindsided with a mountain of memories. Memories of good and bad, love and hate, salvation and ruin.

I need to keep myself busy, so I clean the house from top to bottom and do some baking to freeze for Mom to have when she returns home.

Finally, around nine when there's nothing left to clean and nothing left to bake, I give in and pour myself a coffee mug full of wine. With my mug of wine, I head up to my old room and dig to the back of my closet to find my very own Pandora's box.

It's an old shoebox that I hid in the back of my closet where it's laid untouched for years. Photos, notes, poems, mementos of the time Landry and I were together. It's all here. My favourite photo of us is still in pristine condition since I have always kept it in the frame. It was New Year's Eve night, the same night I met his father. Landry and I are looking straight into each other's eyes instead of the camera. It's a capture of true love. It's perfect.

I continue to dig to the bottom of the box, knowing exactly what I'm in search of and exactly where I had left it. Finally, I see the white gold ring Landry had given me during our faux wedding. A few years ago, I made myself accept the fact that the wedding on the beach wasn't real, despite believing for so long that it was. Eventually, I made myself take the ring from my nightstand drawer in Elmerson and bring it back to Brighten to be packed away. I can't help but slide my old ring on my left-hand finger. It still fits, of course. Because everything between Landry and I fit together perfectly until perfect wasn't enough.

Chapter 45

Hollynd

Two days, that's how long I last before calling Landry.

I draw myself a hot bubble bath, light some candles, turn on Damien Rice, and take my wine with me to the tub. As Damien croons about his favourite faded fantasy, I lean back in the bubbles and sip on the chardonnay, letting each sip go straight to my head. As each minute ticks by I grow more and more anxious.

After an hour, I pull myself from the bath and wrap myself in a luscious royal blue bathrobe I had left hanging in my old closet. I gather my phone from the vanity and bring my wine, which has made me a little buzzed, and a little more confident. I settle myself on my old bed and dare myself to dial Landry's number.

It rings four times before his voice dominates my earpiece, and instantly my pulse escalates.

"Cricket," Landry says, and the old nickname takes my breath away.

"Hey," I reply casually, trying to remain cool and collected.

"I'm glad you called. How are you?"

"I'm good. How are you?"

"Better now," Landry says, while my inner self becomes giddy. "Where are you right now?"

"At Mom's place. Hanging out in my old room."

"How's your mom doing? Is she back home?"

"She's still in the hospital for a while yet, though she's doing better."

"I'm happy to hear that, Cricket." Landry's voice is gentle and kind.

"Thanks. Anyway, where are you right now?"

"I'm at my place. Well, mine and Rob's place."

"I can't believe you are living with your brother again." I can't help but laugh. "Do you two still fight over the remote like teenage girls?"

Landry laughs. "No, not too often, but not never either. But, come on, we had some good times in that old apartment."

"Yeah, you and Rob lived there for what, almost three years?"

"I wasn't talking about Rob and I."

I remain silent to absorb the sudden seriousness in Landry's voice as flashbacks of our time living together flip through my mind.

"Are you still there, Crick?" Landry asks.

"Yes, sorry I was..." My voice fails me.

"Can I come see you?"

"When?" I ask in a hush.

"Right now."

"Landry, I don't know if that's a good idea," I confess.

"I know, it's a terrible idea. But we're finally here, in the same city and it feels unbelievable. We're both sitting alone, and I feel like I have waited a million years for this moment. I don't want to wait anymore."

"Landry…." I use a warning tone.

"Cricket…" Landry rebuts with a much more persuasive tone.

We're silently debating one another. I know he's waiting for my answer. For me to give in to him like I always do. I'm torn between bursting excitement and complete disgust in myself.

"Okay," I finally let out.

"Good, because I just left," Landry laughs.

"Christ Landry, I'm not even dressed," I say in a panic.

"You know I'm totally okay with that."

"Shut up. I'm hanging up." I cut off the call and rush to throw on some clothes.

I find a black pair of studio pants and a tight dark purple shirt and quickly throw them on. My hair goes up into a messy bun and I head down the stairs with my cell and an almost empty bottle of wine in hand and wait for Landry's arrival. Thank God I bought more than one bottle of wine, I think to myself.

Ten minutes later, the knock I feel like I have been waiting for my entire life echoes throughout the house. I resist the urge to run to the door but make myself take sure and steady steps across the kitchen to the entryway. I open the door to my missing half. Everything I have been working on letting go of and all the steps I have taken to move on are completely disintegrating.

Landry stands before me in a pair of dark blue sweatpants that hang low enough on his hips that I know if I were to grab the edge of his faded mustard yellow T-shirt and pulled it up, I would undoubtedly see the band of his Calvin Klein's.

"Can I come in?" Landry breaks the silence and brings me back to some sort of sense.

"Yes, of course." I step out of the way to make room for his large frame.

Landry shuts the door behind him and kicks off his running shoes onto the entryway mat.

I turn towards the kitchen when a familiar hand touches my upper arm with enough force to turn me back around. Landry and I stand toe to toe in the entry of my mom's little house. He's looking down at me with a warmness that I haven't seen in years.

"A million years, Cricket," Landry says. "Please hug me."

Instantly, I wrap my arms around his waist while his arms drape over my shoulders. I rest my head against his chest, and he rests his chin on the top of my head. We stand in complete silence with only the sounds of heartbeats and breaths to pierce the air. It feels like we are both holding on for dear life.

I tell myself over and over not to shed a single tear right now while I fight with the aching lump in the base of my throat. Landry slightly shifts his head and I feel his lips press down on the top of my hair. Bringing his hand up to the back of my head, he runs it down the length of my spine. A mixture of ecstatic happiness and absolute sadness are bubbling through my veins. It's everything I've lived for and everything I've died for, here in this moment, in my arms. I'm my own savior and betrayer.

With his familiar touch, a single tear escapes my eye and runs down my cheek. Landry pulls me back a little bit and our eyes shift towards each other. Landry notices the dampness on my face. He takes his thumb and drags it across my cheek to remove the moisture.

"I know," Landry mumbles as I shift my eyes down.

I can't look at him anymore unless I want to fall completely apart and become a crumpled mess at his feet. We hold each other for a few more minutes in our familiar *silence.*

"Do you want a drink?" I manage to get out.

"Yes!" Landry exhales with relief.

We walk to the kitchen, where I shuffle through the cupboards to see if my mom has any other liquor besides the wine I purchased earlier. I find a bottle of rum in the back of the cupboard. Thank goodness for my mom's love of frozen daiquiris with her ladies' book club.

"I have wine or rum," I announced to Landry, who is leaning against the counter with his arms crossed over his chest and his feet crossed as well.

"Rum please."

"Okay." I set the bottle down on the countertop and reach for a tall glass. "Do you want to see if there's anything good to mix it with in the fridge? Oh, and grab some ice too."

"Man, you're still a bossy little thing." Landry quips as he makes his way to the fridge.

He finds a can of cola and grabs the ice tray from the freezer. As Landry brings them to me with my back turned to him, I feel each arm come around each of my own as he sets the items down on the counter. Only he doesn't drag his arms back once they have done their job. He simply presses his hands on the counter and brings his head to the base of my neck. I can feel his hot breath dance upon my bare skin and a familiar longing builds in my chest.

"I'm sorry," Landry proclaims as he backs away.

I don't know what to say so I quietly continue to make his drink. Once it's ready, I hand it to him and then pour myself another glass of wine.

"Should we sit in the living room?" I ask as I gesture in its direction.

Landry nods in agreement and follows me into the living room. There's a couch and loveseat placed on adjacent walls. Heading straight for the love seat, I stretch my legs over the entire piece. I think this will ensure Landry will not sit with me, I can't have him beside me right now, I'm not strong enough. Landry makes his way to the couch and sits at the end closest to the loveseat. A corner end table between the two pieces of furniture works as a buffer between us.

"So..." Landry begins, but then pauses.

"So..." I repeat.

"Five years. Tell me everything."

In classic Landry fashion, he forgets all conversational manners of small talk. He wants honesty, grit, and authenticity. He wants the truth.

I tell Landry about my job in Elmerson and my friends. Basically, the last five years. I skip the first years after we were apart because it's a bloody messy story that centers around me trying to recover from him and his new life that didn't include me. Besides, Landry knows it's not a pretty story, he saw where it led me to after our night together in the hospital.

In return, Landry tells me all about starting his tech company with Rob. How they had to work very hard, but finally found massive success when they began developing apps for local businesses here and in Reddington.

Landry talks a bit about his time in Reddington when he was married to Lindsay, but glosses over anything that goes into too much detail about his life with her. I'm grateful for this. Lindsay and his father are pretty much no go for topics of conversations with Landry tonight, even though their ghosts hang heavy in the air.

As the evening wears on, we become reacquainted with each other, at least on a surface level. However, the more drinks that are poured, the thicker the air between us becomes. I'm not surprised; it's always been like this with Landry. We can only hide ourselves from each other for so long before our souls rip through our bodies to find our way back.

I watch Landry as he's stretched out across the couch on his stomach while he rests his chin on the armrest facing me. His face is closest to my feet that are stretched out while my upper body sits upright against the other armrest.

"Crick, what happened to the idea of writing a book?"

"Ugh, I don't know. It just never happened." I shrug as I let down my messy bun.

"But you had started it, I remember. You were so excited about writing." Landry begins laughing. "Remember your first sex scene you were trying to write?"

"Oh, shut up." I can feel my cheeks redden.

"You said I was your muse." Landry's still laughing.

"I'm not talking about this, Landry."

"Okay, I'm sorry. But seriously, what happened with the book?"

"I stopped feeling like I wanted to write," I say with a shrug.

"Because of us? Because of me?" His voice suddenly becomes serious.

I don't bother replying as the question has become rhetorical.

"Did you ever think about me?" Landry finally asks with a slight flicker of hope in his eyes.

"Yes," I reply without meeting his gaze.

"A lot?"

"Yes," I admit to both him and I.

"I thought about you too, you know," Landry confesses, still burning me with his eyes.

I don't know what to say to that. Part of me wants to jump for joy while the other part wants to scream at him and ask if this was only when his wife wasn't around or did he think about me while he was with her. I don't do either of these things. I lower my gaze and pick at my fingernails. In reaction to my lack of response, Landry moves off the couch and kneels on the floor beside the loveseat.

"Crick, I thought about you all the time. Every single day." Landry's hand moves up towards my cheek and I can't help but tilt my head towards his hand. His touch feels rough against my skin, but it still feels like heaven. "I mean, how could I not think about you?"

Without thought, my hand moves to his face as well. I know I should stop, but no part of me wants to. The butterflies in my stomach become ravenous.

I lean into Landry and slowly press my lips against his. The lips I once knew so well are still strangely familiar. It feels like everything I have been searching for the past five years, everything I was needing to become whole again. Landry immediately strengthens the kiss between us and pulls me into him harder. His lips part and his tongue moves into my mouth. It's exactly as I had remembered. *Perfect.*

Before I can pull back and come to any sort of sense, Landry wraps his arms around me and pulls me off the loveseat onto him on the floor, where he swiftly pulls me over him and rolls us both over together. Instantly, I'm underneath him with our mouths still attached. Landry's upper body is raised up with his one arm while his other arm cups the back of my neck, lifting my chin towards his. I instinctively wrap my leg around his thighs and pull him in closer to me. Every part of me is feeling hot and achy. It's a feeling I haven't fully experienced in years. Even with other boyfriends and flings, I never felt the way I do when I'm with Landry. He makes me feel like I'm whole, happy, and alive.

I shouldn't be doing this. I know this, but I can't stop. He's still married for God's sake. *He was mine first.* I feel his hand slip under the hem of my shirt and his fingers brush slightly against the skin of my stomach. I don't want him to stop, ever. But I have to stop this, I can't do this to myself.

"Landry, we should stop," I finally convince myself to say.

Landry pulls his head away from me and his hand leaves my skin.

"I'm sorry. I've missed you so much, baby." Landry strokes the hair off my forehead. "It feels so right, doesn't it? You're here and I'm here and...."

"Landry, you're drunk."

"So are you, Crick." Landry shares his lopsided grin again.

"Yes, but I still have some sense in me, and I think we should stop. This isn't good for either of us."

Landry buries his head into my neck with a groan.

God, his breath on my neck feels good. I can't help letting out my own groan more like a moan. Every part of my body is screaming for him. My heart's booming pace is all for him. My stupid body is always betraying my mind.

"I know that sound," Landry whispers against my ear.

Landry kisses my neck softly and then slowly runs the tip of his tongue down the path he kissed on my neck. It feels so good as I close my eyes to indulge a bit more in the heat beneath my jawline. *It feels so right.*

"Landry, I'm not sleeping with you tonight," I say, more to convince myself than him.

"Where have I heard that before?" Landry says through a smile and gently places a kiss on the corner of my lips.

"That was different. I said that before so you wouldn't think I was a slut." I can't help but laugh recalling our first date, which was also the first night we slept together.

"But?" Landry kisses me again, but more in the center of my lips and I can't help but kiss back.

"Maybe I was kind of a slut?" I giggle while our lips are still pressing together.

Landry laughs, too. "Yeah, but I liked it."

Landry continues to nuzzle into my neck as he brings his hand back to the bare skin that has escaped from the bottom of my shirt. His fingers tickle my skin gently, and this time they move up towards my breast and roll over my hardened nipple.

This is everything I have dreamt about for the last six years and everything I have been running from. I know the highs and lows that are going to come if I continue this path tonight. I know that there's a good chance I will not survive Landry Hayles this time. This might be my demise, and it's these thoughts that instantly sober up my foggy wine brain.

"I'm not a masochist, Landry," I say seriously. "That's why we need to stop. Now!"

My voice is stern enough that even a drunken Landry understands it's time to pull back. And he does. He pulls his body off mine and rolls onto his back, onto the floor beside me.

"What do you mean, you're not a masochist?" Landry lets out a sigh.

"I mean that from my experience being with you ends with a lot of pain and hurt. I don't think I can do that again."

"Cricket, come on, that was years ago. We're different now, I'm different."

"Landry, I'm still angry with you," I admit, while staring at the ceiling.

Landry turns his head to face me as I turn my head to face him. Instantly, a flashback to all the pain and lies I experienced at the hands of Landry Hayles burst into my head. Darkness descends into my heart like it did all those years ago, and I can't go back there again.

"Crick, I'm so sorry for the past. It's just that...."

"No, Landry. Stop," I cut off his words.

My instincts for self-preservation begin to kick into overdrive.

"There's no point in any of this. We don't need to talk; we shouldn't be kissing. It's in the past, all of it. Maybe it's best if we leave it there." Again, I'm not sure who I'm trying to convince more at this point.

"It doesn't feel like it's in the past, Crick. That kiss didn't feel like it was in the past."

"Landry, I can't do this again." I turn my face away from his and stare back up towards the ceiling. "You and I... it just about killed me."

"I know." Landry's hand takes mine and places it over his chest. "I know it's scary and that you're scared. Believe me, I'm scared too, but it's you and me. How can we not take this chance?"

Silence.

Stomach bile mixed with wine begins to make its way up my throat as panic starts to pound in my chest, as memories of our past start to flick in my mind. My hands are trembling as my breath quickens. I haven't had a panic attack for a long time, a few years even. However, there's no forgetting the feeling of one once they begin. Tears fill my eyes and drops fall down the sides of my face rolling towards my ears. The gates are opening. *I cannot stop the words.*

"Why did you pick her, Landry? Why didn't you pick me?" I cry out with ragged breaths.

"Oh baby," Landry reaches up to my face to wipe the tears away. "I didn't choose her. I chose..." His words trail off midsentence.

I can feel the anger bubbling up in my throat. "YOU MARRIED ME FIRST!" My shout takes up the space of the entire room.

The tears are flowing freely from my eyes now and my face crinkles into a full out sob. This pain I tried to bury repeatedly is rising so much so that I roll back onto my side, pulling my knees to my chest. My arms reach around my knees, holding them tight to my chest.

"I'm sorry. How many times do I have to tell you that? You know all this already. We went through this years ago. Lindsay was pregnant, and I had to do the right thing. Then when she lost the baby, I couldn't leave her like that. You know all this, Hollynd. I had no choice."

My anger rises more. I look Landry straight in his eyes, though mine are still clouded with tears.

"No choice? For five years you had no choice? I'm so sick of hearing that you had no choice. I'm sick of convincing myself that you had to do the 'right thing.' And I'm sorry if this makes me sound like a bitch, but I don't care about Lindsay and how she felt, or how you had no choice!"

Suddenly, Landry raises to a seated position, though still staring directly into my eyes. Darkness appears in his eyes as Landry's anger matches my anger.

"What do you want me to say, Hollynd? I was wrong. I should have chosen you. Every day I hated myself a little more because I didn't choose you. I married a girl I didn't want because she was having a baby that I also didn't want. And then that baby died, and I felt like the biggest piece of shit that ever lived. That I still feel like the biggest piece of shit that ever lived. I failed you, and then I failed my child." Landry says while fighting his own tears.

Silence.

We stare through our own glossy eyes at each other. But before his tears fall, Landry jumps up from the floor. I remain curled up on the plush cream coloured carpet, crying into my hands like I have done a thousand times before; enduring the same pain I've endured a thousand times before.

After running his hands through his hair, Landry finally speaks. "I gotta go. I'm sorry Cri...." His voice cracks before he can even get my beloved nickname out. And then he's gone from my eyeline on the floor.

Landry leaves through the front door with a slam and I continue to lay in the living room, barely breathing through the sobs that rattle my entire body. *He left me, again.*

Chapter 46

Landry

I walk swiftly towards my car and hop into the driver's seat before I remember that I'm way too drunk to be driving. I open the Uber app and order a ride. It's going to be about ten minutes.

"FUUUUCK!" I yell as I repeatedly punch the steering wheel.

I left her laying on the floor sobbing. I'm such an asshole. No wonder Hollynd's pushing me away. I don't deserve her. I've never deserved her and yet I keep trying to pull her back into my messed up world. I'm drawn to her light like she's my goddamn savior. Honestly, I don't know what I was expecting to happen tonight. I knew from the moment I arrived that I wanted her in whatever way I could have her. Did I think she would forget the past and not bring it up?

I look towards the window of Hollynd's mother's house to see the living room light still glowing through the sheer curtains. *Shit, is she still laying on the floor?* I want to go back to her, but every part of me knows that it's a terrible idea. It seems that I've been having a lot of those ideas lately. I know I'll only make it worse for her.

Finally, after a few more minutes of watching the dim light through the window, my Uber arrives. I hop out of my car and into the waiting car. As the Uber pulls away, the light in the window goes out. My heart aches a little bit more.

By the time I arrive home to the two-bedroom condo I share with Rob, it's almost one a.m.

Our condo is a large wide-open concept, with view of the kitchen, dining, and living room immediately as you walk in. The wall facing the doorway has a sliding door that leads out onto a huge balcony that overlooks the downtown core. To the left of the living room is a short hallway that leads to Rob's master bedroom. To the right of the dining area is another short hallway that leads to my bedroom.

I walk in to see Rob stretched out on the couch watching a late-night talk show. Rob is usually up this late or later, so seeing him awake is no surprise to me. How this guy can function as well as he does on so little sleep is beyond me. I already know that between the dramatic breakdown with Hollynd, the too much rum, and the late night, I'm going to be dragging my ass tomorrow.

"Woah, look who's up way past their bedtime," Rob sarcastically fires my way.

"Shut up," I reply, in no mood for his snarky attitude.

"Where were you, bro?" Rob asks without breaking his concentration on the TV.

"What are you, my warden?"

Rob smirks. "I'm curious. Thought maybe you found a little something or someone to help you with that giant chip you've been carrying around."

I throw my keys on the kitchen island and walk towards the living room, flopping down onto the lazy boy chair next to the couch.

After a few minutes of silence as we both fixate on the music playing on the TV, I break the silence.

"I was with Hollynd," I mumble.

"Bro, are you serious?" Rob sits up to look at me.

I nod without commenting.

"What are you thinking?"

"I don't know," I run my hands through my hair in frustration.

"What happened?" Rob asks.

"Well, it was great, until it wasn't. We talked for a long time, laughed, started making out...."

"You didn't sleep with her, did you?"

"No, but I would have," I admit without shame.

"But?"

"But she stopped us and broke down over Lindsay and the baby. Then I freaked out and left."

"What did she say when you left?"

"Nothing. I felt like I was suffocating. Seriously, I couldn't get out of there fast enough." I pause for a second to inhale all my remorse. "She was crying on the floor."

"And you left her like that?" Rob yells in my direction. "What the hell is wrong with you? You have been moping over this girl for six years and you left her like that?"

"I know, I know! I don't know what's wrong with me. I couldn't hear it anymore. About how I didn't choose her and about the biggest goddamn mistake in my life." I can feel the anger rising in my stomach again.

"What are you going to do now?" Rob asks.

"Nothing. Right now, I'm going to bed. You are going to drive me over there tomorrow morning to get my car and then we are going to work. End of story. I'm done with the drama.

Between her and Lindsay I think I have had enough drama for a lifetime."

I get up and storm out of the living room towards my bedroom and slam the door when I get there. After wringing my hands through my hair and pacing around wishing for some sort of reprieve from this feeling, I grab my phone and click on Hollynd's info. It's all I can do not to send her a text. I feel like absolute shit. Instead, I decide to head for a quick shower and go to bed. I am done.

Chapter 47

Hollynd

I wake up the next morning with a massive headache. After too many glasses of wine and the buckets of tears I left on the living room floor, I feel like my head is going to explode. I get up to go to the bathroom in search of a painkiller and a glass of water. As I pass my bedroom window I notice Landry's car is no longer parked out front. He must have come by early this morning to pick it up. I turn back to my night-table and grab my phone to see if he texted me to tell me he was coming to get his car. There's no text.

I suppose it's just as well, considering how we had left things last night. I don't know why we thought it would be a good idea to get together. We'll never be able to get over our past with those nightmares that are still hanging over our heads. Every part of my brain knows this and understands the logic around it. Still, I can feel the tug on my heart at every thought of Landry and the possibility of having him in my life again.

I need to wash off the wine and Landry hangover, so I hit the shower. Afterwards, I braid my hair back and dress in a long sundress that's black with teal flowers. It's one of my favourite dresses and I'm hoping that it will help improve my mood. As always, Rachel picks me up right on time and we head to the hospital.

At the hospital we learn that Mom will be able to come home at the end of next week. While I'm relieved to hear that, the doctor notes that she will need to have someone stay with her while her hip continues to heal and to monitor her dizzy spells. The doctor is thinking it's a case of vertigo because no other tests have come back conclusive, and he still doesn't want her to be on her own yet.

After spending much of the morning at the hospital, Rachel and I head back to her house to relieve the babysitter from watching Cassie since the twins are at school and Colin is at work.

It's a wonderfully warm day, so we decide to sit on Rachel's back deck like we have done a thousand times before and enjoy the warmth of the fall sunshine. Cassie is napping in a nearby rocker while Rachel and I sip on fresh coffee.

I will myself to not text Landry and to not constantly check to see if he has texted me. I fail miserably at the checking part, but there's never anything there from him.

"Sis, are you okay?" Rachel asks while lying in the pink beach chair beside me in her floppy hat and giant black sunglasses.

"What do you mean?" I reply by turning my head on the back of my beach chair and pointing my face straight towards the sun. I'm enjoying the warmth on my face and resting my tired, tear damaged eyes from the night before.

"I don't know, you seem a little off today."

"I'm tired from work," I lie to Rachel without missing a beat.

"Have you seen or talked to Landry again?" Rachel asks with suspicion.

She has my attention and I turn suddenly in her direction. Rachel's looking at me over the top of her sunglasses.

"Why would you ask that?" I ask defensively.

"Because you seem down, and nothing makes you more down than Landry Hayles."

I exhale slowly, debating in my head whether to reveal my recent interactions with Landry to Rachel or not. I don't really want to hear what she has to say about me meeting up with Landry, since I know she won't approve. But I also hate lying to her, mostly because I know she can usually spot a bullshit story a mile away. I decide to give her half the truth.

"I have texted with him a little."

"And?" Rachel fishes for more information.

"And what?"

"Well, what did he say to put you in this mood?" I can hear the anger rising in Rachel's tone.

"Nothing. We talked about life stuff, nothing dramatic. All that stuff is in the past and that's where I want it to stay," I lie, with a slight hope that I can convince myself of the statement I made.

"What's with the mood?" Rachel continues her interrogation.

"I don't know. I've been thinking about how things could have been different between Landry and me. If the whole shitshow with Lindsay would have never happened, where would we be now?"

"But it happened Hollynd, and there's no point rehashing a bunch of 'could-have-been's' because nothing can change the fact that you two aren't meant to be together," Rachel rebuts. "Aren't you still angry with him? Hell, I'm still angry with him."

"Yes, I'm still angry, but I'm kind of angry with myself too. Maybe I should have fought harder for him?"

"Fought harder? He slept with someone else, Hollynd!" Rachel rips the sunglasses off her face completely.

"We weren't even together then, technically."

"I feel like you're making excuses for him. Landry left you Hollynd, slept with someone else right away, got her pregnant, and married her. Not you, he married her. Don't forget that. He's not the good guy in this story." Rachel's now sitting straight up.

I begin to chew on my fingernails, like I always do when I can feel my anxiety rising. I know Rachel's right, but I can't let it go. I have never been able to let go when it comes to Landry.

"But what if we needed to meet up again, like fate or something? We are both here and we are both single," I wonder out loud.

"He's still married," Rachel counters.

"Fine, but he's separated. What if we're meant to be together?"

Rachel gives me a roll of her eyes, "Lynd, it shouldn't be this hard to love someone."

"I know. I just wish..." My words trail off because I'm unsure how to finish the sentence.

"I know." Rachel offers a sympathetic smile and places her sunglasses back over her eyes.

After spending the entire afternoon and evening at Rachel's house I come home to my mom's empty house. I feel confused, lonely, and utterly exhausted. I decide to go to bed early and catch up on the missed sleep from the night before after my confrontation with Landry. Maybe things will look better tomorrow?

Slowly, I open my eyes and fumble for my cell phone. I'm in my bed but know that it can't be the next day because of the darkness of the room. Once I find my phone, I bring it to my face while hitting the side button to check the time. It reads 12:44 a.m. and notifies me that I have three missed text messages all from Landry.

Immediately my heart begins to ache as I flashback to last night when he left me lying on the living room floor. While I realized that I may have overreacted in my outburst, I still can't believe he left me, again.

I pull up my recent text messages to see what Landry has to say for himself.

Landry:
I'm sorry.
I freaked out.

Landry:
You were right about everything.

Landry:
What can I do to fix this?

I hesitate for a moment before ultimately replying.

Hollynd:
Fix what, Landry?
Last night or the last six years?

Landry:
All of it.

Hollynd:
Maybe it's not worth fixing.
Maybe it's better left alone in the past.

Landry:
Please don't say that, Crick.

Hollynd:
Landry, I'm a different person now.
I'm not going to let you crush me again.
I can't let that happen.
I won't let that happen!!!

I slam my phone back down onto the night-table. I think about shutting it off completely, but I know I would never actually follow through with that. What if he decides to text back? Ugh, I'm pathetic.

I eventually fall back to sleep and in the morning, I check to see if Landry did indeed text back. He didn't. I will not spend my day or evening moping around over Landry Hayles. He has already used up too much of my time. Today I will spend it with my family and tonight I'm going out for some non-Landry-related fun. I pull up my text messages and find Sydney's name on the list.

Hollynd:
You want to go out tonight?

Sydney:
Yes!!!!!
Where??

Hollynd:
Somewhere we can drink
and dance our asses off!!!

Sydney:
Sounds like a trip to the Flagship is in order!

Hollynd:
Yes! Come to my mom's around eight.
We'll drink and get ready there.

I hop out of bed and skip down to the kitchen with a renewed sense of purpose. Mission "forget Landry 2.0" is in effect.

Chapter 48

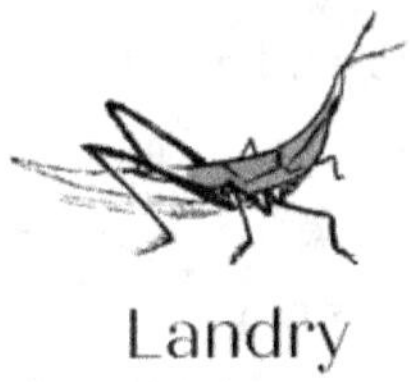

Landry

After my late-night text conversation with Hollynd, I slept like complete trash. Maybe I am being too much of an asshole. How could I expect her to want me back despite the last six years? Part of me wants to drive over to her house and beg her for forgiveness and promise to do anything she asks for the rest of my life, but that's just my heart thinking out loud. The smart part of my brain is telling me to leave her alone. After this many years apart, she doesn't need my sorry ass. She's better off without me. This is something I have always known, though I have ignored for the better part of my life.

I know even Lindsay is better off without me, even though she cheated on me several times over the years. I can't help but feel partly responsible for her behavior. It's not like I was the easiest to live with or being married to. While I never physically cheated on her like she cheated on me, I know that deep down she always knew that I would forever be in love with Hollynd. To be honest, she wasn't wrong.

Lindsay and I were never meant to be together. We were two people brought together by some seriously messed up twist of fate. While we both tried to do the right thing in the beginning of our marriage, there was no love between us. After we lost the baby, we found a bond in our grief, but eventually both fell into our own consuming darkness. Lindsay would search for comfort in other people. I would find comfort in either my memories of Hollynd or by throwing myself into work.

The last time I found out Lindsay had cheated on me, again, I knew it was time to end the charade we had been living with for years. While Lindsay wasn't upset about my leaving, she was, however, upset that her luxurious lifestyle might change.

The tech company that Rob and I had developed began to flourish. Hence it was a lifestyle that Lindsay was not eager to give up. After I told her I wanted out of our marriage, I ensured her I would continue to support her financially for as long as she needed me to. My guilt for being a shitty husband for six years would come at the cost of thousands upon thousands, if not more.

It's Thursday afternoon and I'm trying to be productive, or at least look productive in my office. I'm doing whatever work I can do to keep Hollynd off my mind. A knock on my door interrupts my thoughts, and I look up to see Rob waltzing in and taking a seat in front of my desk.

"What's the point of knocking if you're going to come in uninvited?" I growl at him.

"What's got you in such a terrible mood?" Rob sits down in the chair in front of my desk.

My office is nothing fancy. A basic black desk along with two basic black chairs fill the space. No pictures are on the walls, nor are there any on the shelves behind me which hold documents and binders.

"Ugh, it's these contracts. I feel like I've been staring at them all day," I grumble.

"I'm thinking since there's a basketball game tonight, we should head to Ted's Bar to watch it over beer and wings. Maybe after that we can hit a club and unwind?"

"Rob, I don't know. I'm exhausted today and my mood is garbage. Besides it's only a pre-season game, isn't it?"

"That's why you need this," Rob says with a grin. "I'll text Cam and Nick to join us."

"Fine." I finally agree as I turn back to the contracts on my desk.

I could use a pick me up.

Chapter 49

Hollynd

It's almost nine-thirty on Thursday evening. Sydney and I are already one and a half bottles of wine into our night. We have mutually agreed that we needed to find some good-looking distractions tonight and our mission was fun, with no drama. Sydney recently ended a long-term relationship with her boyfriend of four years. Since they had owned a house together, it was more like a divorce, complete with fighting over assets and animals.

Having spent the last hour blow drying and curling my dirty blonde hair, it's finally looking like I'd spent the day on the beach. Soft waves fall over my shoulders and down to the middle of my back. I thought since it looked like I had spent the day on the beach that I would pair my hair with a black fitted dress that's covered in pink swirls. The bodice of the dress is tight and fitted, which gives me a slight pop-over of cleavage. The fitted material flares out at the tip of my hips and flows to just above my knees. I cover my dress with a black cardigan, and wear black ankle heeled boots. After all, it is technically fall.

Sydney, on the other hand, went full out rocker chick. Her bleach blonde hair is pulled into a tight ponytail and large silver hoops dangle from each ear. In a short and tight deep purple dress and knee-high boots that has silver buttons running up each side, Sydney looks like a force to be reckoned with, as always.

We're sitting on my mother's couch waiting for our Uber as I empty the rest of the wine into our glasses. Sydney reaches over to grab her glass and raises it in a toast-like manner.

"To a drama free evening!" Sydney proclaims.

"Amen!" I practically yell as I tip my glass to my pink tinted lips and down the remaining wine with one gulp.

It's at that moment that Sydney's phone alerts us of our ride. We quickly gather our purses, lock the door, and head out for the night.

By the time we arrive at The Flagship, there are already a ton of people scattered around the entire club. The dance floor is hopping with people moving to the crushing beat pulsating through the air, and multicoloured lights flicker overhead on the ceiling.

As we get ourselves situated at a small table with drinks in hand, we both scan the crowd of people for either faces we know or faces we would like to get to know.

Within a few minutes I spot a tall guy with dark blond hair and piercing blue eyes. He looks vaguely familiar, though I can't quite place where I know him from.

"Sydney, do you know the guy over by the bar with the navy T-shirt, blond hair, and those fuck me eyes?" I can't help but add in the last part, drinking always makes my inside voice come out to play.

"I don't know," Sydney replies. "He looks familiar."

"Right? That's what I thought."

As if he can sense us talking about him, the blond man glances in our direction and makes direct eye contact with me.

He smiles, and I shift my eyes away quickly. But almost as quickly as I looked away, I look back again. The blond man is coming our way and I can feel excitement building in my chest. He's so gorgeous, in a Chris Hemsworth sort of way.

"Hollynd Turner!" Mr. Hemsworth look-alike says, as he arrives at our table.

"Yes?" I reply in more of a question than a confirmation.

"You don't remember me, do you?"

I blush and give an apologetic smile. "No, I'm sorry."

"It's okay. Miles Wilton from Bio 101 at Creston College."

"Miles! Of course! You were the best lab partner I had ever had," I blatantly flirt with the handsome man in front of me.

I jump up and wrap my arms around his broad shoulders, hugging him like he's my long-lost best friend. I'm blaming the booze for my forwardness.

"I'm sorry I didn't recognize you," I say as I release Miles from my hug.

"It's not a big deal, Hollynd. I mean, it has been, what, seven years?"

"That's hard to believe. Please join us," I gesture to the empty stool at our table. "Sydney, this is Miles. We met back at Creston College all those years ago."

Sydney reaches across the table as she and Miles shake hands and exchange greetings. After a few minutes of polite small talk between the three of us, Sydney excuses herself to see a bulky man with a man-bun and a beard sitting across the room.

"So, tell me about yourself Miles. What do you do?"

"I'm actually a high school science teacher now," Miles says, with a beautiful grin.

I laugh. "Of course you are. See, you were the best lab partner and possibly the only reason I passed Bio."

"Nah, you were a better lab partner than you think."

I feel my cheeks burn with shyness and his hand slightly brushes against mine on the top of the table.

"How about you Hollynd, what do you do?"

"I'm a writer, actually. I do freelance work for a bunch of websites and a few magazines. I live in Elmerson now. I'm only here for a bit because my mom had an accident, and I came to help out my sister."

"Oh my goodness, is your mom okay?" Miles' eyes soften.

"Yes, she's going to be fine. She's still in the hospital but should be home sometime next week. I'm staying at her house right now and taking care of her cat."

Did I purposely hint that I'm currently all alone at my mom's house? Yes. And did I purposely already scan his finger for a wedding ring? Again, yes. I can already feel my drama free night taking form.

After another half hour comprising of another round of drinks and more talking, Miles and I become more and more flirtatious.

Miles leans closer to my ear and whispers, "Dance with me?"

I don't even bother with a reply. I swiftly grab his hand and lead him to the dance floor. Knowing exactly what I want, there's no sense playing hard to get.

Miles places his hands on my hips and pulls me in tight to his body. I can feel his body heat through my dress. My left hand finds its place on his very toned pec, while my right hand wraps around the back of his neck. I can feel Miles' breath on the side of my neck as he leans in closer. I feel his lips softly touch the spot under my ear. Goosebumps emerge over every area of my skin and my insides tingle. I close my eyes for a moment to enjoy the tiny kisses that continue up and down my neck as Miles and I continue to move our bodies in one fluid motion together.

I open my eyes and look to the edge of the dance floor. I'm greeted by the look of pure darkness and jealousy.

Landry is standing there with his face like stone, staring straight at Miles. Landry looks like he's ready to beat the shit out of him. Wearing black jeans and a dark red button-down shirt with rolled-up sleeves, his multiple tattoos on display. Landry looks like a force to be reckoned with; a very sexy force to be reckoned with. His arms are crossed against his broad chest and his nostrils flared.

I feel my body tense up as my emotions play off Landry's vibes. Even from twenty feet away I can feel him like a ton of bricks. My body begins to stiffen, which is also felt by Miles who pulls away from me.

"Are you okay?" Miles asks regarding the change in my demeanor.

I glance back to Miles and slap on a fake grin. "Yeah, I'm sorry. I felt a little lightheaded for a second," I lie.

"Do you want to go sit down?" Miles asks with genuine concern.

"Actually, I'm going to go to the washroom."

"Okay. I'm going to go check on my buddies. I'll be over at their table by the bar." Miles gestures towards the left side of the bar.

"I'll come find you," I promise as I make my way off the dance floor in the opposite direction from Landry, who's still standing there with his arms crossed.

I walk down the short hallway that leads to the washroom. I'm grateful to find the entire bathroom temporarily unoccupied and lean against the sink. My pulse is slowly returning to normal after my Landry sighting. I turn to wash my hands as I look at myself in the mirror and shake my head. So much for my drama free evening. I can't help but feel a tiny smirk work its way across my lips.

Chapter 50

Landry

I watch as Hollynd pushes her way through the crowd towards the washroom hallway. I have a dozen different feelings pulsating through my veins right now. A mixture of rage and jealousy are by far the most dominant as I watch that guy rub his hands all over Hollynd's perfect body. *My body.* Every part of me wants to stomp out onto that dance floor and beat the shit out of that guy.

But aside from my egotistical alpha response, there's also a feeling of pain shooting through my chest as I watch Hollynd's eyes slowly close and enjoy this other man's touch. It makes my stomach turn and bile rise to my throat.

I shake off my unnerved feelings and walk towards the washroom hallway. I have to talk to Hollynd. As I walk across the bar, I'm silently cursing Rob for bringing me here tonight. The plan was to watch the game, drink some beer, and go home. But of course, after the game was over and Rob had already had half a dozen beers, he wasn't interested in going home and begged me to come out with him. I begrudgingly agreed, mostly because I didn't want to go home and hang out by myself. I've been feeling very anxious lately, and I knew that an increase in anxiety for me usually led to self-medicating methods of either pot, or if it was terrible, coke. Both of which I had stopped completely years ago.

I wait patiently against the wall outside of the washrooms, trying not to look like a total creep. Finally, I see the door of the ladies' room pull open and a defeated-looking Hollynd walks through the door. She stops immediately when she spots me leaning against the wall. Before I get a chance to speak, Hollynd raises her hand up to me.

"Landry, don't even start."

"Hollynd, wait. Give me a chance to explain." I stand up straight.

"Explain what exactly? Your psychotic stare down out there, or maybe that you left me sobbing on the floor of my mother's living room two nights ago? Or the random texts in the middle of the night?" I can see Hollynd's teeth are clenching as she glares at me.

Before I can answer, Hollynd marches straight up to me so we are face to face. Even angry, she's still so beautiful.

"I'm sorry I left you like that the other night. I didn't know what to say to make you hate me less than you clearly already do." I keep my eyes focused on her eyes.

"Look, I know I acted like a bit of a psycho with my breakdown the other night, but you took off. Again!"

"I never wanted to leave you, ever."

"You know Landry, you keep saying that to me, and yet, it keeps happening. So either I'm an idiot for believing you time and time again or you are nothing but a scared man who doesn't know what he wants."

Hollynd's now on her tiptoes and has her pointer finger pressed deep into my pec muscle. There are no tears in her eyes, only rage.

"I couldn't deal with you the other night, Crick," I grunt out in frustration.

"Oh, I'm sorry that I'm 'too much' to deal with Landry," Hollynd air quotes the 'too much,' which is dripping with sarcasm.

"For Christ's sakes Hollynd, why are you being so difficult? I'm trying to apologize."

Leaning in closer, Hollynd presses against me. "Awe, what's the matter, big boy? Can't handle a woman standing up for herself?" She says with widened eyes and a pouty mouth.

'Big boy,' the name she used to call me anytime she was trying to get under my skin. She knows exactly what she's doing right now.

"Do you want me to handle you, Cricket?" I play back.

There's silence between us as the air thickens. If there are people passing us in the hallway, they go unnoticed as we are in our own untouchable stand off right now.

"I have to get back to my friends," Hollynd announces but makes no effort to turn and leave. Instead, she continues to stare at me, daring me to take the bait.

"Who was that guy?" I demand.

Hollynd lets out a small laugh, like she can't believe I'm seriously asking about him. I can feel my jealousy rise again as I reach over and slowly rub my hand across the nape of her neck, because I know how much she secretly loves when I do this, and I pull her in closer.

"I'll ask again, Cricket." Our faces are only inches from each other. "Who. Is. That. Guy?"

I can see her fight flash through her eyes. That defeated look she had only moments ago has completely vanished. My vicious girl has come out to play, and it excites me more than it should.

"Oh, that guy," Hollynd says sweetly as she stares straight into my eyes. "That's the guy I'm going to take home and fuck tonight."

"Over my dead body," I respond as I pull her the slightest bit closer with my hand still placed on the back of her neck.

"We'll make sure not to trip over you on our way." Hollynd offers a sly smirk.

Goddamn it, she has such a sassy mouth, and she knows exactly how to push my buttons.

"You're coming home with me, Cricket," I demand, again.

Now she really starts laughing. "Oh, you think so?"

"I know so," I growl as our mouths suddenly crash into each other.

As quick as we come together, I feel Hollynd push herself away from me.

"Landry, stop!" Hollynd shouts as she reaches up to the top of my head and grabs a fist full of my hair. Pulling and twisting with an iron grip, she pulls my head down to her face. "I swear to God Landry, if you leave me or hurt me one more time, I'm going to freaking kill you."

I'm trying hard not to allow the smirk that is forming on my lips to break out. God, this girl is so full of spunk, she drives me crazy.

"Yes, Cricket. I promise I won't," I say while my neck is still twisted down to her.

"A promise isn't good enough. I want more."

"Anything you want, babe."

Hollynd releases me from her grasp allowing me to straighten my back and shoulders. Hollynd's shakes her head. "Landry, why can't I let you go?"

With my thumb, I press under her chin lightly urging it to tilt upwards. Our lips touch only briefly before our tongues desperately sweep through each other's mouths. I can taste the alcohol on her lips and it makes me bite gently down on her. She tastes amazing, like rum and cherries.

While my right hand moves back to her nape, my free hand cups her ass, pulling her closer to my body. Hollynd lets out a slight moan and I squeeze her tightly, reclaiming her body as my own. *Mine.*

We pull our mouths apart and I move my lips down her neck towards her collarbone. Her sneaky cleavage has been teasing me since I saw her on that dance floor. My mouth instantly salivates.

Before I give my lips the satisfaction of pressing against the top of her rounded breasts, I state again, "You're coming home with me."

Before Hollynd can answer, I press my lips down on to the top of her breast and drag my tongue over the curve. My right hand has now made its way down from her neck and is cupping the breast I'm currently tasting with my tongue.

Another moan escapes her mouth and I finally hear the answer to the question I didn't exactly ask, but rather demanded.

"Yes, Landry. Take me home."

Chapter 51

Hollynd

I knew the moment I saw Landry waiting for me outside the washrooms that I would be his for the rest of the night. As much as I love to act all tough and smug, resisting him has never been my strong suit. To be honest, I never really wanted to resist him, I only ever wanted him. Even the times when I was so angry with him and felt I could spit fire, I was drawn to him. That old familiar pull from a force that I cannot name was always nudging me towards Landry, and is still nudging me towards him now.

Both Landry and I are quiet on the way to his place. He says nothing as he pulls me into his body and wraps his arms around me. My head rests on his chest the entire way home, and I sit and listen to each beat of his heart. Landry strokes the hair on the side of my head with one hand while the other runs up and down my thigh. Everything is suddenly calm and peaceful. There's no drama, no painful anger, there's only peace. In the silent moments in the back of this car, our souls are basking in the glory of being together again.

Fifteen minutes later, the driver finally arrives at Landry's condo complex. It's an overwhelmingly large building with more floors than I can count. Its modern design and mirror reflection makes me question if we are even at the right place. Landry pulls my hand and leads me to the entrance of the building.

Once we reach the twenty-first floor, the floor his condo is located on, Landry continues to take the lead towards his front door and unlocks it. He holds the door open for me with an outstretched arm. It's so dark in the condo entryway I can't get a good look at my surroundings. Landry turns on the single light that hangs overhead as he follows me through the door, shutting and locking it behind him. Before I have a chance to look around the now lit space, Landry swiftly grabs a hold of my arms.

With my back now pressed against the wall, my hands are stretched above my head. Landry leans in, slamming his mouth to mine and I can't help but let out a little whimper. He runs his hands down each side of my arms in unison. Moving slowly over my extended shoulders, down my ribcage, and around my backside. It's in that instant I feel Landry's large hands lift me up, and automatically I wrap my legs around his midsection and let my arms come down off the wall to grab a hold of his shoulders. Our lips hungrily grasp at each other.

Landry walks us out of the entry way through a darkened area, which I can't make out due to the lack of lights and down the hallway. I assume he's carrying me to his bedroom. It's quickly after that I feel my back lowered down and pressed against a soft mattress as he's leaning over top of me.

Landry pulls his lips off mine and stands at the foot of the bed. Reaching towards a dresser on his left, Landry flicks on a small lamp that glows softly throughout the room. Standing up straight at the end of the bed, Landry grabs the bottom of his shirt and rips it off over his head to reveal a tattooed chest that is firm and muscley. There are more tattoos than I remember him having when we were younger. I want to look closer but decide to wait until a time that I'm not twitching with anticipation.

Landry extends his hands towards me, motioning me to take them in my hands. After placing his hands in mine, he pulls me until I'm sitting on my knees in front of him. Tugging my black cardigan off and tossing it to the side, Landry reaches back to the hidden zipper and pulls it down the length of my spine. This allows him to slide each strap of my dress off my shoulders simultaneously as I pull my arms up. Once my arms are free, my dress easily slides down to my waist where Landry pulls it further down over my hips and down towards my knees. Soon I'm in nothing but a black strapless bra and short hip-cut panties that allow the bottom half of my ass cheeks to be exposed.

Looking down to take in my entire form, Landry exhales with a smirk. "You're still so breathtaking, Cricket. Every inch of you is the most perfect thing I've ever seen." Reaching up to brush the hair off my shoulders towards my back, Landry continues his admission of praise. "Do you know how many times I have dreamt of this moment?"

Landry places a hand under my chin to tip up my face towards him with a gentle tug before continuing. "How many times I imagined those needy eyes looking up at me, silently begging me to take back what was always mine? Tell me baby, am I right? Are they begging me to take you back?"

"Yes," I whisper through my parted lips, which are dry as my heart slams in my chest.

Lowering his head closer to mine, though still tilting my chin up and staring straight into my eyes, Landry matches my whisper. "Tell me who you belong to. Tell me who you have always belonged to."

As my legs shake and my breath becomes shallow, I reply, "I belong to you, Landry."

"No one else. Ever." Which comes out as a statement rather than a question.

"Wait, are you asking me if I have been with others since you? Because obviously I have," I confess as I press my hand on his chest.

Landry grabs me swiftly around the back of my neck. "I'm not asking about the losers you may have fucked, Hollynd. I'm asking, who have you always belonged to?"

"You, Landry," I reply softly.

"Say it louder!" Landry demands as his grip on my chin tightens, almost painfully so.

"FOR GOD SAKES LANDRY! I'VE ALWAYS BEEN YOURS!"

Landry leans in and whispers, "And who do you think about when you touch yourself?"

I feel my cheeks burn with embarrassment from this last question. Holy hell, I've forgotten how intense Landry could be when he wanted me. It's a familiar scenario and conversation I had had with him in the past, but I don't remember him being this gritty.

Not allowing me to hide my reaction to his last question, Landry takes his hand that was on my neck and slides it to the back of my head where he grabs a fist full of my hair and jerks my head back up forcing me to meet his eyes.

"Tell. Me." Landry demands harshly.

I can feel my body lingering somewhere between overwhelming desire and anger. Landry is being much more demanding than I remember. I'm not sure I appreciate being manhandled and bossed around like this, or maybe I do? It's hard to tell right now as my body and brain fight for my attention. Landry's much darker and more jaded than I remember.

My response comes out much more heated and layered with anger than I intend it to be, but I have always had trouble keeping my emotions in check with Landry. Between waves of anger and passion, every part of my body is screaming to get to him.

"You, alright! It's always been you, Landry! Every time I close my eyes, you're all I see. You have always been all I see, even when I didn't want to see your face anymore. It's burned into my goddamn soul."

A devious smirk appears on Landry's face as he pushes me back onto the bed and leans his entire body over mine, holding himself up by his arms, but slowly lowering himself towards me.

Right before our lips touch he whispers, "I've always belonged to you too, Cricket. I'll always belong to you. Never doubt that. You are me."

I respond without hesitation, "And I am you."

Instantly, our lips meet again, for the—I don't even know how many times that night—only that this time I know it will be the kiss that leads us too far. There is no going back this time, and if we fail each other and ourselves again, survival will be impossible. For both of us. But we *will* take the risk, because we *must* take the risk. There is no other choice for us, and there never was.

Chapter 52

Landry

Hollynd lets out a soft whimper as I move my lips from hers and trail them down her neck. Reaching around her back, which is now pressed against the mattress, I unhook her bra and tug it away, throwing it carelessly to the side. Making my way down Hollynd's body, the familiar sweet scent of vanilla radiates off her flesh. It is the smell of my only thing.

I'm not sure why I felt so possessive with her a moment ago. I couldn't help myself. Having her within reach for the first time in so many years made me feel insane with want and jealousy. Between seeing her dancing with that guy and thinking about all the others who have had her over the last six years makes me want to reclaim every inch of her. It's all I can do to not sink my teeth into her soft pink skin and mark her.

My blood is pulsating through my veins and I'm doing my best to keep the beast within me at bay. I guide my fingers down Hollynd's smooth stomach towards her mound as her breathing becomes erratic, and her legs move apart as an invitation. Her wetness is substantial, and I work her with my fingers, at first slowly in circles before I add more pressure as I pump one, and then two fingers in and out of her.

"Landry," Hollynd cries while her head tips up towards the ceiling. "You should stop, or I'm going to come."

"That's what I'm expecting, baby," I say, while taking her hardened nipple into my mouth and tugging it gently with my teeth.

Hollynd's moans become more and more boisterous. I feel her insides clenching around my fingers. An increase in moisture flows over my inserted fingers and begins to run down the palm of my hand. I push my body back up to the top of the bed to meet her mouth as she's panting through her release.

Kissing Hollynd hard as she struggles for air, her hands reach up to my hair and she pulls it hard to ensure she has my full attention.

"Landry, I need you. Now!" Hollynd demands before pulling my head back down so her tongue can wrap itself in mine.

I pull away to meet her gaze, which is glossed over from her recent liquified explosion, and give her a half smirk.

"Yes, ma'am." I smirk before releasing my hold over the top of her body to reach my nightstand that holds a pack of condoms.

As I pull myself upright to slide the condom over my keen dick, I watch Hollynd watching me with her bottom lip held down with her teeth and eyes widened in anticipation. I feel that beast inside me bursting to take over, to consume every inch of her tender body until she screams for mercy and vows before every god and every devil that she is mine forever. I'm her only master.

Hollynd's dirty blonde hair is fanned out over my black bedding—which also makes her skin look as pure as snow. Except for the devious grin on her face and the rosiness of her cheeks from erotic euphoria, she could easily pass for an angel.

I grab her thighs, pressing my fingers into her flesh fiercely, and drag her body to the edge of the bed. This allows me to stand on the floor and take her as hard as my legs can thrust in their dominant position.

"Are you ready, Cricket?" I ask while towering above her, as her panting breath causes her rounded breasts to rise and fall rapidly.

"How did you put it the other night? It's been a million years, Landry. Get inside me right now!" Hollynd's demanding voice echoes through my room.

It's possibly the greatest sound I have ever heard— the sound of Hollynd's voice demanding me to claim her as mine again. *Forever.*

I waste no time inserting every inch of myself into her and lose my breath for an instant, knowing that we are finally together as one again. The way we were always meant to be together.

Living without this woman for the past six years and believing it was entirely my fault has left me living in a darkness that I thought I'd never be able to escape. But now, there's a light to be seen, as Hollynd lays underneath me with her arms stretched up above her head, giving herself to me completely. Again.

I take her hard without hesitation. It's like a redemption for the monster in me through the touching of this angel's flesh, a redemption that I do not deserve, but will take greedily and without remorse.

Chapter 53

 Hollynd

It's been two days since I spent the night with Landry. While I haven't seen him since that next morning, we've been texting all day, every day. Our texts throughout the day usually begin sweet and flirty to downright dirty by the time night has rolled around.

Having spent the last couple of days with Rachel and my mom at the hospital, I can tell Rachel is getting suspicious of my constant vibrating phone. Rachel scowls at me every time I text furiously on my device. I know it's killing her not to know who I'm talking to.

We're sitting in the waiting room of the hospital waiting for our mom to get back from her last in-hospital session of physio on her hip. The doctor said she will be able to go home tomorrow, which is such a relief. Mom will need to continue outpatient physio and use a walker for a while.

As for the dizzy spells, the doctor has prescribed some vertigo medication, which seems to help a lot. I have offered to stay longer to help my mom around the house while she is still recovering. And while I do truly want to help my mom, I also know that part of offering to stay has to do with Landry. Of course, I have not mentioned this to either my mom or sister.

The text message notification buzzes on my phone again and interrupts my thoughts. I already know who it is before I check it. Still, I can hardly wait to read it.

Landry:
I want to see you tonight.

"Who the hell keeps texting you and why are you always smiling? It's unnerving," Rachel's voice booms beside me.

"No one. Calm down." I try to act relaxed, though making sure my screen is angled away from Rachel so she can't read it over my shoulder.

"Seriously, you have been on that thing nonstop. You're as bad as the twins." Rachel shifts in her seat.

"What's gotten into you today?" I glare at my sister.

"Nothing. It's just…" Rachel lets out a long exhale.

Buzz. My phone interrupts us again, only this time Rachel grabs it out of my hand before I have a chance to hide it from her.

After reading the screen where Landry's name appears, Rachel's eyes turn to ice, and I can see her anger growing in her body.

"Are you kidding me?" Rachel says while turning my phone screen towards my face so I can read the screen.

I quickly grab my phone from Rachel's hand and shove it in my purse.

"Is this who keeps texting you? Landry? I should have known." Rachel's annoyance is palpable.

"Keep your voice down Rachel, we're in a hospital," I remind her.

"Is that who you were with the other night?" Rachel demands.

I don't answer, but chew on my bottom lip. I don't need to answer. Rachel already knows.

We're silent for a few minutes. Finally, Rachel softens her tone and turns to look at me with a much more caring stare. "Lynd, what are you doing?"

Still chewing on my lip and refusing to make eye contact, I reply, "Rachel it's fine. It's no big deal."

Rachel lets out a sarcastic quiet laugh. "No big deal? Do you remember what he did to you? What you did to yourself?"

"Of course, I remember." I sigh.

"How can you let him back in?"

I can feel the tears forming in my eyes, though not falling over the edges. I know Rachel cares about me, and I know deep down she's afraid for me, but she also doesn't know the bond between Landry and me. She doesn't know all the times we took care of each other. She doesn't know that I already promised myself to him forever. I don't intend on telling her any of this now, but I tell her one thing.

Turning my head so our eyes meet, mine still glistening with tears and her eyes still filled with pity, I whisper, "I love him."

Rachel looks away and simply shakes her head in disbelief. I feel as though I have let her down. I don't know, maybe by saying that I love him out loud, I feel like I have let myself down too.

We remain quiet for the rest of the time we wait for our mom. We know we're at an impasse with each other, so it's best if we don't say anything. After a few minutes, I get up to use the restroom and allow myself some privacy to reply to Landry's text.

Landry and I make plans to meet up later that evening after I get my mom's house ready for her arrival home tomorrow.

After I return from my faux trip to the washroom, I see my mom has returned to her hospital room. Rachel is sitting beside Mom talking in a hushed whisper.

I enter the hospital room with hesitation, and I get the distinct feeling that they are talking about me.

"Hi, darling." My mom greets me when she sees me enter the room.

"Hi Mom, how are you feeling?" I ask as I offer a hug.

"Great. I'm a little tired but I'm excited to go home tomorrow."

"That's good, Mom. I was about to go home and get the house ready for you. Are there any specific grocery items you want me to stock up on?"

"Lots of fresh fruit, please. Oh, and maybe ice cream." Mom gives me a wink.

Rachel is sitting there quietly with her arms crossed defensively. She's angry about our previous conversation regarding Landry. Well, that's fine. Rachel can be angry all she wants. The fact remains that I'm a twenty-seven-year-old woman and I can make my own damn decisions. Hell, I had been doing this for the last six years in Elmerson on my own. There was no Rachel or Mom there to check up on what I was doing. I was fine there without their input, and I will be fine here without it. Though I'm not entirely sure how long I will stay here in Brighten. I push the thought out of my mind for now.

Deciding I can't stay around Rachel's tension any longer, I tell Mom that I will be back tomorrow morning to pick her up. Rachel doesn't bother to ask me if I would be coming over to her house later. She already knows she will likely be given a false excuse. She knows who I have been texting with and that there's no point in trying to save the unsavable.

It's well past dark by the time I finish cleaning the house. Everything smells fresh and clean. I hope Mom will be happy when she gets home tomorrow.

I realize that I have missed supper completely and decide to order some takeout. I'm trying not to think of the fact that I haven't heard from Landry since earlier today, but I guess he kind of left the ball in my court to get a hold of him. Thinking that since this is my last night alone in my mom's house, I should make the most of my time, and by that, I mean the most of my alone time with Landry.

Before I place an order for food, I give Landry a call.

"Yeah," Landry abruptly answers the call after multiple rings.

"Landry, it's me."

"Give me a sec." Landry replies with tension in his voice.

I wait quietly on the other end of the call, and I can feel my pulse rising. I knew this Landry, the one that can be angry and abrupt. This Landry can take your feet right out from under you and leave you lying in a pool of your own disarray and pain. I hated that place.

A few minutes later, I hear his voice once again, only this time it's much more relaxed and calming.

"Hey baby, sorry about that."

"What's wrong?" I ask nervously.

"Nothing," Landry huffs.

"Landry, I know that voice. What's going on? Where are you?"

After a long pause, I hear an exhale echo through my earpiece. "I'm at my father's house."

"I see." Instantly, my stomach turns.

I know the type of relationship Landry has with his father, and I know what it does to him when he's around his father. I haven't seen David Hayles in years, but my hatred for him has never once softened.

"Do you need me, Landry?" The familiar words tumble naturally out of my mouth like it hasn't been years since I have spoken them.

Silence.

"Yes, Cricket." His voice, which sounded so strong only a moment ago, is now timid.

I could never turn my back on Landry when he was like this, even when he turned his back on me.

"Okay. I'm on my way." I end the call and grab the keys to my mom's car. With my purse and jacket in hand, I go to find my other broken half.

Chapter 54

Hollynd

When I pull my mother's car up to Landry's father's house, I see Landry sitting on the front steps with his head in his hands. When he lifts his face at the sound of my stopping tires, he looks older than I remember, even from the other night. Landry's eyes look tired and there are dark circles around them. Landry rises to his feet and walks down to my car and hops into the passenger seat. We sit there silently for a few moments, both of us not sure entirely what to say. It's like a warped deju vu moment.

I speak first. "Where are we going, Landry?"

"To our beach," Landry says without hesitation.

"Alright, to our beach." I nod as I put the car into gear and drive forward.

Our beach, the spot of our first date. The spot of our first kiss. The spot where we got married in our own secret ceremony.

We drive in silence the rest of the way to the lake. When we arrive, I park facing the black water. It's so dark out tonight that I can't see anything, and there must be a cloud cover because I can't see the moon or the stars either.

Neither Landry nor I reach for the door to exit the car. Instead, we sit there looking out into the nothingness in front of us.

"Thank you for coming to get me," Landry finally says.

"You're welcome. Do you want to talk about it?" I ask quietly.

Letting out an exhale, Landry responds, "No, not really."

I nod in the car's darkness, though I doubt he can even see me. I'm not surprised Landry doesn't want to talk about what's bothering him. He has never wanted to talk about his relationship, or lack thereof, with his father. I know not to push the subject either, though I do feel a slight annoyance and frustration that after all this time we're in the same spot we have been a thousand times before. A sense of hopelessness begins to seep into my heart. Maybe nothing has changed. Maybe this isn't a new beginning for us, but a repeat of the story that left me with nothing in the end. Can I go through this again? Do I want to go through this again? Is it time to face the fact that there will always be a part of Landry that I cannot reach? And without having all of him, can I truly have any of him?

"When I was nine years old and Rob was seven, my mother somehow convinced my father to take a day off work and go to the beach with his family." Landry's voice echoes through the car. I can tell he's not looking in my direction, but simply staring straight ahead into the darkness.

"It wasn't this beach. It was one about two hours north of here where a lot of his country club friends had their summer homes. Anyway, it was a great day. I remember Rob and I seeing how deep of a hole we could dig in the sand, playing frisbee, and swimming. My mom sat quietly on her beach towel pretty much all day and watched us play. My dad made his rounds visiting other beach goers he knew.

"At some point I had the idea that we should play frisbee in the water. So, we did. Rob had this one crazy throw and the wind caught it and it fly far out into the water. I thought I was a good enough swimmer to get it, but I didn't realize how strong the waves were the further you got away from the shore. I started to panic, and I couldn't touch the bottom. Rob screamed at my mom, who then screamed for my dad. When my dad saw me, he came running into the water, out to where I was, and pulled me to the shore. I threw up a shit ton of water when we got there. All these people kept coming up to see if we were alright. Dad held me tight and thanked them for their concern. And while I was terrified that I had almost drowned, I was so happy that my dad had been there for me because it must mean he loved me. I always thought he didn't care because he usually ignored me, but there I was, on the beach where he showed me, he really loved me for the first time."

Landry stops to take a few breaths. I'd never heard this story from Landry before. He rarely ever talked about his childhood when we were together. I reach over and rub his arm to offer some comfort and encourage him to keep talking. Landry grabs my hand and holds it gently in his. He turns to me to meet my eyes, though it's hard to see each other, I know he's looking at me.

"When we got home that night and everyone had gone to bed, my dad came up to my room. He never tucked me in at night, so it was a surprise to see him. Instead of saying goodnight or sweet dreams, he came over to my bed and grabbed my upper arm and yanked me to my feet. When I looked at him, I could see nothing but pure rage and hate in his eyes. He said that if I ever embarrassed him like that again, like I did at the beach, that he would beat my ass so hard that I would have wished I would have drowned. Then he threw me back on my bed and left my room. I had finger bruises on my arm for a week after that. I told everyone it was from when he saved me. My heroic father who saved his drowning son."

We both remain silent for a moment before Landry continues. He's still staring out into the blackness of the night.

"When I was fifteen, I asked him why he even bothered pulling me out of that lake that day, that his life probably would have been better if I had drowned. You know what he said? He said that he couldn't stand the thought of people looking at him with pity if he had a child that died, because if they pity you, you lose your power over them. Can you believe that? It was never about saving me; it was always about him.

"How many times did he backhand me or punch me because I wasn't good enough? Or because I messed up, again. And for some stupid reason I thought maybe he still loved me somewhere deep down inside of him.

"Why do children do that? Always wanting love from their parents when clearly there isn't any to be given? I thought maybe when I had my own child..." Landry's words trail off as he reaches up to wipe his cheek. "I thought maybe I could show him what it meant to be a real father, a good father. But even after we lost the baby, all my dad said to me that it was probably better off, since I would have made a terrible father anyway because I screw up everything I try to do."

Landry's now squeezing my hand hard. There's so much tension in his face and his entire body. I pull my hand free and hold it to his cheek.

"I'm so sorry that happened to you. But can I ask you something?"

"Sure." Landry turns his head towards me. The pain in his eyes is unbearable to look at.

"Why do you put up with him? I mean, all these years, I couldn't figure it out. At first, I thought it was because maybe you needed his money, but you have your own now. You don't have to deal with his shit."

Landry inhales slowly. "I do it for Rob; it's always been for Rob."

"What do you mean for Rob?"

"You know what, it doesn't matter." Landry tries to change the subject.

"But it does kind of matter, Landry. Because it's hurting you, he's still hurting you."

"But I have you again, Crick. And you make it better."

"I can't save you, Landry. Believe me, I've tried to save you. It's never been enough. Besides I can barely save myself most days."

"Maybe we can save each other?" Landry murmurs as we stare at each other, not even wasting a moment to blink.

Silence.

"Come." Landry reaches for the door handle and exits the car.

I follow him out my door, though I don't know what we're doing. Landry walks around to the front of the car and waits for me there. He extends his hand out towards me, wanting me to take hold. When I do, Landry leads me away from the car, closer to the water's edge. The sand is soft beneath my rubber soled converse shoes. The cold air is numbing on my skin and seems to get cooler the closer we get to the water, but neither of us seems to mind that much.

Landry stops when we arrive a few feet from the water and pulls me into a tight embrace. His arms collapse over top of me, and we face each other with our chests pressed firmly together. My face is leaning against his chest while he rests his chin on the top of my head. I can feel the motion of his chest moving in and out with each breath he takes. It's comforting.

"This is the spot we got married." Landry mentions out loud.

"I know. There are no crickets tonight though," I say remembering the sound of the crickets the night of our first date and when we got married.

"Well, you're here, and you're my favourite Cricket of all, you know?" I can hear the laughter in Landry's voice before beginning a more serious note. "I would do it again."

"What's that?" I ask.

"Marry you. I would do it all over again if we went back in time."

"Me too," I admit with a slight smile.

"I would do it again now."

Instantly, butterflies circle frantically in my stomach. Technically, he's still married to Lindsay. Of course, he knows this. Maybe he's being sentimental.

Before I can respond, Landry continues. "And I would fight harder for you, for us. If I could go back in time."

"Me too."

"I'm going to fight for you this time." Landry pulls back from our embrace and plants his hands firmly on my arms.

I tilt my head up to see his face while he looks down at mine. Landry's eyebrows are scowling with seriousness.

"I swear to you, Cricket. I won't stop fighting for you ever again, and I know after all this time and all the shit I have done that I don't deserve you. I have never deserved you. But I want you and that might make me a selfish bastard, but I don't care. I know that you're still angry with me. Hell, I'm still angry with me too, but I will make it up to you. I will prove myself to you. I want you to be mine again. In fact, I have never thought of you as not being mine. No matter where you were or where I was, a piece of me was always with you. I haven't been a whole person in years. You're not my everything Crick, you are my only thing. You've always been my only thing."

By now, the tears have begun to drip down my cold cheeks. The added moisture has made them even colder. But honestly, I could care less because for six years I have fantasized about this moment when I could have Landry back. I didn't believe it was ever possible, and yet this is it. This is real.

Am I afraid that I might lose him again? Absolutely. But more than the fear and more than the anger I have, there is the love that I still have for Landry. Even after all this time and all the tears spilled over his memory. Our love never went away, and it never disappeared. It simply got lost, like Landry and I lost each other. Never forgotten, only lost.

Chapter 55

Landry

There, I did it. I let it all out, and it feels good. No, better than good. Fantastically freeing. Except that Hollynd's crying. That was not my intention and I truly hope they are tears of happiness, relief, or even overwhelmed emotions, anything but anger or regret.

I reach my thumb up to her cheek to wipe the line of tears. Hollynd's face is freezing.

"Baby let's go back to the car. It's too cold out here," I suggest.

"No, wait." She stops me from turning towards the car by placing her hands on my chest. There's a pause as Hollynd furrows her brows and bites her bottom lip. She's so goddamn adorable.

"Losing you was one of the worst things that has ever happened to me. Well, aside from losing my dad. But the difference was he didn't choose to leave me, Landry, but you did, and that just about killed me. I'm so afraid of getting hurt by you again because honestly, I don't know if I will survive it this time or not. And I'm angry, Landry. I'm so angry with you." Hollynd's eyes glare fiercely at me as panic sets in.

"Cricket, I'm so sorry...."

"Stop. I'm not finished." Hollynd takes a deep breath before she continues. "I'm angry with you, but more than my anger and more than my fear is something else. It's you. Your place in my life and in my heart has always been just that, your place. That's never changed. Even when I told myself that I hated you, I didn't really hate you. I don't know, maybe I told myself that for self-preservation, or maybe because I thought hate could replace love. Either way, I have always loved you more than any other feeling I've had towards you. It took me a long time to accept that, but that is what it is. My heart cannot decipher the difference between you and love anymore. Whatever else I may remember feeling once upon a time with you, love will always overcome because that is who you are to me."

This woman standing before me is unbelievable. I don't know how after all this time no other man has claimed her heart as their own, but I'm so grateful they haven't.

I lean down and press my lips to hers. Her face is freezing as the cool wind off the water continues to blow against our bodies.

"Come on, let's go back to the car." I tug at her arm, and this time she follows my lead.

I climb into the driver's seat and Hollynd gets into the passenger seat, despite it being her mom's car. She has always preferred when I drive.

We sit quietly for a moment while the heat from the vents begin to warm us up.

"Can I come home with you tonight?"

Hollynd nods as I back the car away from the dark lake. We drive in silence for the first bit of the trip before Hollynd finally speaks.

"Landry, if we're going to do this you have to be honest with me."

"What do you mean? I have been honest with you."

"I mean about everything, Landry. Your father and Rob, what happened with you and Lindsay. I need to know everything. For six years, I have lived with questions about why things turned out the way they did. I don't know how to get over it."

I think for a minute about what it will mean to tell Hollynd everything, especially the truth about Rob's real father. Will she understand why I have kept this from him for all these years? I know she is right though; she deserves the truth.

I reach over and grab her hand that's resting on her thigh.

"You're right, Crick. You do deserve the truth, and I will tell you everything. But let's not do that tonight, okay? I only want to be with you. Let's deal with all the other stuff tomorrow."

Hollynd looks over at me with a smile.

"Okay. But at least tell me what was going on with your father tonight."

I exhale deeply before getting into the newest demand David Hayles has for me.

"He wants me to give Lindsay another chance."

"What?" Hollynd screeches.

I can't help but laugh at her reactions. "Relax, babe. I told him there's not a chance in hell I'm taking her back. Even if you hadn't come back into my life, Crick, I still wouldn't be taking her back."

"Why does he want you two back together?"

"Why do you think? The senate race is next year, and he wants her father's money. Lindsay's father wants us back together, so David wants us back together."

"That's messed up, Landry. Your dad's an asshole."

A full belly laugh echoes through the car. "Yes, he is," I agree.

"What did he say when you said that you wouldn't get back together with her?"

"The same old song and dance he always gives me. How I'm such a disappointment and a loser, blah blah blah."

"Ugh, maybe if you won't tell him to fuck off, I should go over there and tell him myself!"

I can't help but bring Hollynd's hand up to my lips. This woman has always been on my side, my biggest champion. Even when no one else was, including myself. I don't know how I could have let her go all those years ago.

"Thank you for trying to protect me, Cricket."

"Always," she replies without taking her eyes off the road.

Finally, we reach Hollynd's mom's house. Once we get inside, Hollynd offers to make a pot of tea to help warm us up, but I have a different way in mind.

"Take me to your old room," I mumble into her ear as she fills the kettle at the kitchen sink.

After setting the kettle aside, Hollynd turns to face me while wrapping her arms around my waist.

"You're insufferable," Hollynd says while she perches up on her tippy toes to kiss my neck.

"And you're irresistible." I rub my hands over her backside.

"I want to dance with you," Hollynd says.

"Here? In the kitchen?"

"Yup." Hollynd leans over to reach her phone which is on the counter and turns on an old song, "Iris" by the Goo Goo Dolls.

She presses her body back into mine and we start to sway to the slow song. I place one hand on the back of her neck and place the other back on her rounded ass cheek. Her soft hands enter the bottom of my T-shirt and run up my bare back. Suddenly, I feel my shirt being pulled up from my torso and over my head.

"What are you doing?"

"I want to see your new tattoos. There are more than I remember."

Hollynd's fingertips graze over the black ink as she inspects the designs with her eyes. When she sees her familiar Cricket tattoo on my left pec, she stops to press her lips lightly against it. After she pulls back, she continues her viewing, but then stops again to examine the letters that run down the left side of my torso.

"Who's Raziel?" Hollynd asks while she examines the cursive writing.

I clear my throat. "That's my son's name."

"Landry, that's beautiful. What does it mean?" Hollynd's voice softens to almost a hush.

"Raziel is the angel who keeps secrets and mysteries. Why he was never born on earth is his secret to keep with God because I will never know."

Hollynd says nothing. She continues to circle her fingers over Raziel's name. As she did with her Cricket tattoo, Hollynd leans in and dabs her lips against the letters of my son's name. As she pulls back, her fingers run along the letters I hear her whisper so quietly that I almost don't hear her at all. "Sleep well, little angel."

I feel my eyes beginning to moisten as I watch the love of my life speak to my angel in heaven. What a precious thing to witness.

After a few more minutes of examining the ink on my chest and back, I feel a tug on the belt loop of my jeans.

"Let's go upstairs." Hollynd pulls and I follow eagerly.

Chapter 56

Landry

I wake up early to the sound of Hollynd's breath beside me. The best sound in the world. I lean over to check the time, and see it's just after eight. My body is used to getting up earlier than this for work, so I feel like I have slept in enough and my body is calling for coffee. Hollynd's still out cold, so I slowly get out of her bed in an attempt not to wake her.

After I'm up, I slip on my pants from yesterday and head down to the kitchen to make coffee. Once I'm in the kitchen, I realize how long it has been since I have spent the night in this house. I think back to the Christmas I had here and what it was like to be around a real and loving family. I want that again and I feel like I'm so close to getting it, that is, if I don't mess it up this time.

The coffee finally finishes dripping when I hear the front door to the house open. Rachel's voice rings through the entryway.

"Mmm, is that fresh coffee I smell? I'm dying for a..." Her words stop when she sees me standing in the kitchen. It's obvious she was expecting Hollynd.

"Where's Hollynd?" Rachel asks offering no greeting.

"Upstairs sleeping," I reply while I pour myself a cup of coffee. "You want one?" I hold up the pot towards Rachel.

Rachel doesn't answer me but stands there with her hands on her hips. "What are you doing here, Landry?"

"You know what I'm doing here, Rachel." I stare at her as I put the pot back on the burner and take a sip of my coffee.

"Okay, then maybe I should ask why are you here? Why are you doing this to her again?"

"Doing what?" I murmur.

"Landry, you can't weasel your way back into Hollynd's life now that your wife left you or whatever."

I can feel my back straighten as my defenses rise. "That's not what this is about, Rachel. I'm not weaseling my way back in and my wife didn't leave me. I left her, not that it's any of your business. None of this is your business."

"It is my business, Landry, because it involves my sister. You weren't the one who had to take care of her last time. You didn't have to watch her lose weight, almost fail out of school, and OD on sleeping pills. Did you know that she almost died? No, because you weren't there for her. In fact, you're the one who caused all of it to begin with. So yeah, it is my business!" Rachel's eyes are burning with anger towards me.

Rachel doesn't know that I went to see Hollynd when she was in the hospital after the sleeping pill incident. Hollynd never told her. I can still see her lying there in that bed, looking so weak and tired. I need to diffuse this situation with Rachel, for Hollynd's sake.

"Rachel, let me ask you something. If someone asked you to choose between Hollynd and Colin, who would you choose?" I set my coffee cup down and place both hands firmly on the countertop.

Rachel rolls her eyes. "Landry, what are you talking about?"

"Seriously, say you had to choose between Hollynd and Colin. Who would it be?"

"This is ridiculous." Rachel's glaring at me.

"See, it's not so easy is it, Rach? When you are given the choice between the two people you love most in the world, all you can do is try to do the best that you can with what you are given and hope to hell it doesn't hurt too badly. Only it hurt, badly. It ended up hurting Hollynd, and it ended up hurting me. But I made my choice, and even though it took me a long time to accept that, I had to because that's how life is sometimes.

"Now, for some unknown reason, I have another chance with Hollynd, and I'm not letting you or anyone stop me this time. I love her so much, Rachel, I don't even have the words to describe it."

Rachel's body remains stiff, still doubting my words. "What about Lindsay? You loved my sister so much that you married someone else?"

"Nope, I'm not doing this with you, Rachel. I owe you nothing. The only person I owe an explanation to is upstairs sleeping."

"Well, I'm not sleeping anymore." Hollynd is walking down the stairs while rubbing the sleep out of her eyes. "What are you two fighting about?"

"You," Rachel replies.

Hollynd walks over to me as I hand her a freshly poured cup of coffee.

"Okay, look," Hollynd sets down her cup before even taking a sip. "You two can stop this right now. You don't get to fight about me. I get to make my own decisions because I'm an adult.

"Rachel, what happened with Landry and I is in the past, and whatever happens in the future is between Landry and me. And Landry, Rachel's going to worry and be cranky because that's who Rachel is. Sure, it's annoying, but it comes from a place of love."

This last comment seems to soften Rachel's hardened expression and sends a wave of pride through my body. My girl is sexy when she's tough.

"Hollynd, I'm worried about you. Tell him about the last time. Tell him about the sleeping pills," Rachel grimaces.

Hollynd rolls her eyes. "Rachel, he knows. He was there."

"What?" Rachel asks with widened eyes.

I nod with Hollynd's admission.

"Landry came to me in the hospital and stayed with me." Hollynd moves closer to me and wraps her arms around my waist. "He's the reason I got better. He saved me."

I lean down and kiss the top of Hollynd's head, completely enamored with the woman holding on to me. "You saved me," I whisper against her hair.

I can't know for sure, but it feels like Rachel finally understands. There's no fighting Hollynd and I this time. I may not have fought for us before, but I'm sure as hell going to fight for us this time. Even if it costs me everything.

Chapter 57

Hollynd

Mom has been home for a full week now. I have been with her almost 24/7, making sure she's getting around okay with her walker and that her vertigo meds are working well. Being my mom's caregiver has been both fantastic and exhausting. I love spending so much time with my mom. After living apart for the last six years, I feel like we are getting to know each other all over again, now as two adult women. It's a fortunate gift to spend this much time with her, despite the circumstances that brought me home in the first place.

I've shared my news about Landry and me with her. My mom has always been my biggest cheerleader and seems genuinely happy for us.

Landry and I have been trying to spend time together, but between me taking care of Mom and his work, it has been difficult. We talk more through texts than anything, though I know the time is coming soon. We need to see each other and talk. I mean, really talk. First there's the issue that I don't live in Brighten anymore and I will have to go back to Elmerson, and soon.

Second, there are the secrets surrounding his father that Landry has promised to share with me but hasn't yet. However,

I don't expect that whatever he could tell me will change what we have between us. It will be nice to know there are no more secrets and that we are really on a united front this time. Whatever it is, I know that it's a fight Landry has battled alone for far too long.

After ten full days with hardly any alone time, Landry and I have a date planned. Rachel and the twins are going to come and spend the night with Mom so I don't have to worry about anything. After our kitchen confrontation a couple of weeks ago with Rachel, she has been much more accepting of Landry and me. This is a tremendous relief to me.

Landry is picking me up from Mom's house at seven to take me to dinner at our city's most popular Italian Bistro. I can't remember the last time I even ate at a real Italian restaurant, and I'm beyond excited.

I'm in a black dress that is completely fitted from chest to knees. There is a bright red thin belt around the upper waist. I pair the dress with black heels. Knowing Landry, he will wear all black as well, so I'm sure we will either look like a power couple or a goth couple.

Landry arrives right on time carrying a bouquet of a dozen red roses. Landry's such a classic romantic. As I expected, he's wearing a black suit with a black shirt and black tie. Power couple or goth, either way, my man is hot.

I take the roses and put them in water while Landry catches up with my mom and the twins in the living room. Rachel is in the kitchen with me.

"You really love him again, don't you?" she asks as I fan out my flowers in the vase.

"Rach, I never stopped."

With a nod of understanding and a smile, Rachel finally seems to get it.

A half hour later we sit at a quiet table in the back of the bistro. The atmosphere is cozy as soft light and candles encapsulate the area. The tables are far enough apart that I hardly notice any of the other patrons. For all I know, it's only Landry and I here tonight.

After the server brings us a bottle of champagne—at Landry's request—and takes our order, we are finally alone.

"What's the occasion?" I ask as Landry fills each of our glasses.

"I just got the love of my life back, what's not to celebrate?" Landry smirks and places the bottle back in the bucket of ice to the side of the table.

"Do I know her?" I quip with a smug smile.

"I'm keeping track tonight, Cricket," Landry grunts.

"Keeping track of what?"

"Every time you make a smart-ass comment, the dirtier your night is going to end."

I lift my glass to my mouth. "Is that a threat or a promise?" I wink at Landry.

"That's two." Landry sips his champagne.

We spend the rest of the meal talking about our week. I tell him about Mom being at home and taking care of her, and he tells me more about his work. Somewhere in between our main course and dessert, which Landry insisted on cheesecake, a favourite of mine, I finally find the courage to bring up the topic I have been dreading.

"Landry, I need to talk to you about something."

"Shoot," Landry casually replies while refilling our champagne.

"Well, it's that I don't live here, and you know that eventually I will go back home to Elmerson."

Landry's face is stoic while he nods along.

"I guess I'm wondering about what happens then, with us I mean?" I watch his response carefully, feeling nervous about my decision to bring this up now.

Landry sits up straight in his chair and clears his voice before he speaks. "Well, it's quite simple, Cricket. I'll come with you."

"Are you serious?" I'm shocked by his abrupt answer.

Before Landry can continue, the server brings by our cheesecakes, which are dripping with cherries. Once he leaves, Landry continues.

"Yes, I'm serious. I told you I'm fighting for us this time and if that means I have to move, then I will move."

"What about your job? No, not just your job, your company?" I hastily ask.

"Well, I will either find a way to run the company remotely or I'll sell my half."

"Just like that? It's that easy?"

"Yes. Look Crick, I don't care about the company or where I live. I care about you."

"What about Rob?" I wonder out loud.

"Rob will have the option to buy me out or one of the top guys might buy my shares. Honestly, I don't even know what shares I will have left. Lindsay's fighting for half of my shares in the company and if she gets what she wants, I will only have a quarter of the shares left, anyway."

"She's trying to take your company?" My anger rises.

"Yes, that's why the divorce isn't finalized yet. We can't agree on a settlement."

"Oh." I sit quietly while I process this information. "Tell me what happened to you and her."

Landry leans back in his chair and lets out a huge sigh. "You sure you want to hear about it?"

"I do," I reply.

I'm not insecure about Landry's relationship with Lindsay anymore. I don't like that it happened, but that doesn't change the fact that it did happen.

"Well, neither of us really wanted to get married. That was all on our parents. It was basically like marrying a stranger. Our first few months married were awkward. She spent most of her time at her parents' house and I spent most of my time at school or high."

My eyes widen with his statement, Landry immediately notices and corrects himself.

"It's okay, Crick, relax. It was pot, mostly." Landry reaches over to my hand and rubs the top. "Baby, seriously, it's okay. I don't do that shit anymore."

I nod but stay quiet to allow him to continue.

"Anyway, when we lost the baby, two things happened. First, we both lost our shit for a while and then second, I think we both realized that we needed each other to get through our grief. We tried to become better people, both of us. I worked harder at school and Lindsay decided to try some online classes. We lived together full time and basically tried dating, which I know sounds strange, but it's true. For a year or so we got along well. But we were more like friends than anything else.

Eventually, she told me she wanted to try for another baby, but I said no. At this point, I was starting my company with Rob and work was my focus. Also, after losing Raziel, I wasn't even sure if I wanted kids anymore. Losing him just about killed me, and I didn't even know him.

"It pissed Lindsay off that I didn't want a baby and I was too busy with work to notice. Sometime after that was when I found out about the first affair she was having, with our accountant of all people." Landry stops to roll his eyes and take a drink of champagne.

"The sad part is that even after I found out about her and the accountant, I didn't really care." Landry continues. "Basically, for the next couple of years I built up my company while she had affairs with other men and spent my money."

"What happened that finally made you leave her?" I can't help but wonder out loud.

"She told me that if I wouldn't give her another baby that she was going to get pregnant from someone else. Which is fine if that's what she wants, but I don't want to be a part of that mess. It's one thing to ignore a person spiraling out of control, but if they try to bring a kid to their mess, that's too much."

"Yeah, that makes sense."

I never realized that Landry's marriage with Lindsay was so messed up. All these years I thought he must be happy with her since they were still together. I assumed I was the only one struggling.

"But enough about that, what about you? In the last five years you must have dated other guys."

"Yeah, I dated some here and there. But I only really had one long-term relationship."

"Tell me about it, but first let me get more champagne in me." Landry reaches for the bottle and tops up our glasses.

"I seriously just sat through your story about your marriage, Landry. You can hear my nonexciting story about Kyle."

"Kyle," Landry repeats me with a roll of his eyes and sip from his glass.

"Kyle and I dated for just over a year. He was okay, super nice. He's actually a sports journalist so we got to watch a lot of pro games together which was fun."

Landry's eyes form a scowl. He has always been the jealous type.

"Anyway," I continue, "after a year together, Kyle asked me to move in with him, but we couldn't agree on where to live. I didn't want to move out of my apartment, and he didn't want to move in there, so we eventually broke it off."

Now Landry's scowl had turned more into a confused look. "You couldn't pick a place to live? Why wouldn't he move in with you if he really wanted to be with you?"

"Because he said that there was too much baggage in my apartment and that it was strange that I refused to give it up."

"What's so special about your apartment?" Landry still looks confused.

I lower my head and bite my bottom lip. "Because it was our apartment, Landry."

"You still live in our first place in Elmerson? That tiny apartment in that old building?"

I nod, but don't look up as a wave of embarrassment passes through. I probably look like a pathetic girl who was holding onto an old boyfriend for too long.

"And you still live there?" Landry confirms.

Again, I only nod.

"Cricket, look at me."

I lift my head to see a smiling Landry.

"You're telling me you broke up with a man that you were serious with because you wouldn't leave that apartment?" Landry's eyes are searching mine.

"Well, when you put it like that, I sound pathetic." I roll my eyes back at him.

"No, I love it. I love that you kept that place. And I love that I get to move back into it with you." Landry offers a wide smile.

"Seriously, you don't want to move back there. We'll find a nicer place when you move to Elmerson."

Landry shakes his head. "Nope, I have daydreamed about our time together in that place for the last six years, and I want to be there again with you. Maybe not forever, but who knows, maybe it will be? If you still love it there, then I will love being there too. I don't care where we live as long as we're together."

"Perfect. Well, might I suggest we go to your current place right now together. I have cheesecake to work off." I flirt with a grin.

Landry signals for the bill which is brought over swiftly. "And you have a debt to pay too, don't think I have forgotten about that."

"What are you talking about? I have been on my best behavior. I didn't even make a joke about Rob being the brains of the business when you said he could take over." I smirk.

Landry doesn't even look up as he totals up the tip to the bill. "That's five."

"Five? What happened to three and four?"

Landry stands up from the table and reaches for my hand to help me out of my chair. When I stand, he pulls me close to his body and growls in my ear, "Kyle happened."

I'm in so much trouble, and I love it.

Chapter 58

Hollynd

"Seriously, Landry, are we taking all these *Star Wars* books?"

I'm currently sitting on the floor of Landry's bedroom, surrounded by books everywhere. We are packing up his belongings to move to our apartment in Elmerson.

It's been over two weeks since my mom returned home from the hospital and her recovery is going great. While homecare will continue twice a week, and we finally convinced her to hire a housekeeper, Mom told me she's ready to be on her own again. While I will miss being with her, I'm so excited to begin this next stage of my life with Landry. I think we have waited long enough.

"Yes," I hear the snark in Landry's voice coming from the walk-in closet. "It's a collection, Cricket. You don't bring part of a collection."

I scan the piles of books, wondering how we are going to fit all these in the small apartment. There's only one tall bookshelf in the living room there and it's currently full of my collection of books.

"You know, there are *Star War* movies you could watch instead of reading all these books." I love antagonizing him.

Landry marches out of the closet and leans against the door frame. He looks extra sexy this morning with his low hanging grey sweatpants and white T-shirt. His hair is still messy from the night before. Landry is imperfectly perfect.

"The movies are not the same as the books. Don't even go there, Crick."

"I liked the movies," I say while I raise myself off the floor and move to the bed, where I kneel on it and crawl across it slowly. "Kylo Ren is pretty hot, you know?"

Landry struts over to the bed and stands directly in front of where I have crawled to as I remain on all fours. However, before Landry can make his argument further we are interrupted by the doorbell.

"Ugh, are you kidding me?" Landry throws his head back in frustration.

I can't help but giggle and get up from the bed. "Take care of that light saber in your pants, Ren. I'll get the door."

Landry shoots me a glare as I skip out of the bedroom.

I arrive at the door, still grinning ear to ear, as I swing it open only to be met with the cold stare of Lindsay.

Lindsay's bleach blonde hair is back into a high and tight ponytail, while her deep red lips grimace at the sight of me answering the door. Wearing a very slimming black dress with red heels, she looks like she's off for a night on the town, not a morning stop at her soon to be ex-husbands.

Suddenly, I feel very inadequate with my black and grey plaid pajama pants and a Jim Morrison T-shirt on, not to mention the messy bun thrown together on the top of my head.

"I should have known you'd crawl your way back into Landry's bed once I was tired of it." Lindsay's still a cold bitch.

"Lindsay, won't you come in." I widen the door for her to enter as my voice drips with sarcasm.

"Where's Landry?" Lindsay snaps as she stomps her way into the apartment, only stopping once she reaches the kitchen island.

"I'll get him." I roll my eyes and turn to leave.

"Wait, before you go Hollynd, I have something I've wanted to say to you for a long time." Lindsay glares at me with pure hatred.

I take a deep breath and stare at the woman I have loathed for so many years. I can't help but imagine how my hands would look wrapped around her slim neck.

"What?" I place my hands on my hips.

"I thought you should know that you're the sole reason that my marriage failed."

"Excuse me?" I pull my head back with disgust. "Weren't you the one sleeping with other guys during your marriage?"

"I was looking for comfort and love from those other people because my husband couldn't even give me the basic courtesy of being a proper husband. He never cared about me or how I was doing. He was in love with his precious 'Cricket,' so much that my existence meant nothing to him. Trust me when I say he was unfaithful to me long before I was unfaithful to him."

"I never fucked anyone else." Landry's booming voice echoes through the kitchen as he walks out of the hallway that leads from his bedroom.

"Landry, how nice of you to join us." Lindsay bats her fake eyelashes at him. "I was just telling Cricket here how much we missed her over the last few years. Although it was like she never really left though, wasn't it? Did you tell her about the time I let you have sex with me and pretend that I was her for you?" Lindsay smiles brightly.

"Shut up Lindsay!" Landry yells across the room while I'm trying to process what the hell I just heard. "Unless you are here to sign the divorce papers, get out of my house!"

"I told you that either you give me half of your shares in Landro Tech or I'm not signing!" Lindsay screams back at him.

"I gave you the house in Reddington, the BMW and the Lexus, and half of my investments," Landry screams with anger.

"You know, both our fathers think we should get back together. We could forget all this ugliness and give this another try?" Lindsay bats her eyelashes again.

Did she say that in front of me? This woman is unbelievable!

The anger in Landry's eyes is raging now and he clenches his fist tightly, while Lindsay remains leaning against the island with her arms crossed.

"Lindsay, us getting back together will never happen. Get that idea out of your head right now. I would rather give up everything I have for you to disappear from my life."

"Then give me half of your shares!"

Landry looks over at me as I stand in complete shock and silence, wishing I was anywhere but here.

"Fine," Landry says to Lindsay, but still looking at me. "Have your lawyers add fifty percent of my share of Landro Tech to your settlement."

Lindsay's face breaks into a vindictive smile, knowing she has finally gotten her way. "I knew you'd finally come to your senses, Landry."

"Get out, Lindsay!" Landry yells.

"Fine, fine. I'm going." Lindsay lifts her hands like she's pretending to surrender. "Enjoy my used trash, Hollynd." She shoots me a wink before walking to the door.

Landry marches back down the hallway in a rage and I hear his bedroom door slam which causes me to flinch.

As Lindsay opens the front door to leave, I call her name to stop her. I march up to her, face to face for what I hope is the last time.

"If I ever hear you refer to Landry as trash or hear that you have bad mouthed him or bothered him in any way again, I will end you."

Lindsay immediately begins to laugh. "Oh Hollynd, please, what are you going to do to me? Write a nasty letter to me? I think you should remember who you are talking to, Cricket, and remember who Landry actually married."

"He was never yours, Lindsay, and I think that kills you inside. Landry has always been mine. He was mine before you were married, after you were married, and now, well look who it is slamming the door on your pretty little face." I blow her an air kiss as I swing the door closed while Lindsay stands there with her mouth agape.

I give myself a moment to breathe as I lean against the closed door, hoping for my adrenaline to drop before I go to check on Landry. After a few minutes with my eyes closed and every deliberate breath in and out, I head down to the closed door of Landry's room. I do that thing where you knock and enter at the same time, though I intentionally open it slowly, still wary of what I may find when I walk in.

I open the door and enter the room, finding Landry sitting on the edge of his bed with his back slouched over and his arms resting on his knees.

"Are you okay?" I ask as I slowly sit down on the bed beside him.

Landry lifts his head and looks at me with dark eyes. "Is she gone?"

"Yes."

"I'm sorry you had to see that."

"Oh no, Landry, I'm fine. But are you okay? You told her you'd sign over half your shares of Landro Tech. Are you sure you want to do that?"

"If I don't do it, she will never sign the divorce papers and I want it to be over. How can we ever move on with her still lurking around making demands?"

"But Landry, that's your company."

Landry sits up and shifts his body so he's facing me with his one leg now laying on the bed.

"Don't you get it, Crick? I would give up everything for you. If she would have asked for all my shares, I would have given them to her. I told you, I'm fighting for you this time. I'm fighting for us. That is, as long as you're okay with the fact that you're stuck with a very poor man once this divorce is final. Aside from what Lindsay is taking and the lawyer's fees, I'm not going to be as financially stable as I am now."

"Oh, baby. You know I don't care about that stuff. I've been poor for forever, it's not that bad. We can live off ramen noodles and love, and we can go thrift shopping together. Plus, we get to find other ways to stay warm to keep the heat bill down." I offer a smirk to my sad man, who's wearing the effects of the Lindsay storm that just passed through.

Finally, I see a small smile appear at the corner of his lips. "Tell me more about how we can keep warm."

"First, did you know it's easier to stay warm if you keep bodies uncovered, but still together?" I rise to my knees as I pull Landry's T-shirt up from his waist and over his head.

"Hmm, is that so?" Landry raises his arms straight up to allow me to release the shirt from his arms.

I toss the shirt to the side of the bed while I feel Landry's hands clasping at my T-shirt and pulling it upwards. Soon my shirt and my bra find themselves piled on the side of the bed along with Landry's long-forgotten shirt.

Moments later my legs straddle Landry's waist as our bare chests pressing firmly against one another and my arms wrap around his broad shoulders.

"Tell me more about being poor," Landry says while his hands travel down the bare flesh of my back and dip inside the band of my pajama pants.

"We have to find ways to be active at home, so we don't have to pay for gym memberships." I giggle as I grind my hips into his hardened center.

"Yes, I can keep you active at home." Landry begins to nibble on my neck. "What else?"

"Well, if you really get sick of ramen noodles and Kraft Dinner, I can always offer you something else to eat that won't cost us a thing." I run my one hand through his hair.

"Mmm, what's that?" Landry mumbles into my neck.

With a tight tug of Landry's hair, I pull his head back to meet my lips with his. "Me." I say with our lips pressed together.

In an instant I'm flipped off his lap and my back slams hard into the mattress below. Landry's body hovers over mine, but only for a moment before he moves lower down my body.

"Deal!" is the last thing I hear him say before his head disappears between my thighs.

I close my eyes and let the rapid sensation take over my body. Yeah, I think we'll be okay without Landry's money. This man is made for me.

An hour later, Landry and I are snuggled together in his bed, still enjoying our post sex glow and have completely forgotten about our earlier encounter with Lindsay. Knowing we should probably get up and continue with our current job of packing Landry to move, we're both procrastinating and taking our time to just be with one another.

Around the time I think I should get up, Landry's phone buzzes with a text message notification. Landry reaches over to his nightstand, where his phone is located, and lays back down beside me before he checks the message. Together, we read the message that lights up his phone.

David:
Landry, get over here.
ONE HOUR

I hear Landry under his breath, "Shit."

"Do you think this has to do with Lindsay being here earlier?" I sit up to face him.

"I guarantee it."

"Well, what can he do about it? Nothing. You're an adult; he has no say over any of this. Tell him to screw off and get it over with once and for all."

"It's not that simple, Hollynd." I can hear frustration building in Landry's voice.

"Landry, that's what you always say about your dad. But what if it is that simple? Tell him to fuck off and go away. You want me to go there and tell him? I will, you know. I will march straight into that house and tell him exactly where to shove that pompous attitude of his." Now I can feel my frustration growing.

"Ugh." Landry groans loudly while he rubs his hands over his face.

"What can he possibly do to you if you don't give him what he wants, Landry? Nothing."

We sit quietly for a few minutes before Landry also sits up.

"There's something I have to tell you, Hollynd."

This catches my attention immediately. I know it must be serious because Landry uses my real name which he rarely ever does.

"Okay," I reply and then wait for him to begin.

"You know how my mom left when I was ten and Rob was eight, right?"

I nod.

"Before she left, she asked me to take care of Rob for her. We couldn't go with her when she left, my father wouldn't allow it. She told me it scared her for us to be with our father, especially for Rob. When I asked why, she said it was because Rob had a different father than I did. Some man from one of her numerous affairs, I guess. Mom told me I could never tell Rob though because it would make him sad and that my father would be livid.

"It turns out my father already knew this and told my mom to leave his house without us, even Rob. Dad knew how much it would hurt her to be without us and he wanted to make her suffer. He said that if she left Rob with him, he would never tell Rob the truth and would give him the same financial opportunities as myself, Isaac, and Josh. So, my mom left both of us. She asked me to write to her and let her know how Rob was doing. From then on, I decided I would do whatever I had to protect Rob from my father and the truth. Eventually, my father learned I knew the truth about Rob and blackmailed me with it whenever I didn't do what he wanted." By the time Landry finishes his story he's out of breath.

"That's why you transferred to Oak?"

"Yes. My father stopped paying for Rob's university and would only continue to pay for it if I did what he wanted. I couldn't let him take that away from Rob. Rob deserved the best life and the best opportunities."

"Why didn't you tell me this then, when you left me?" I ask, with confusion.

"Crick, I was so confused and scared. I felt like complete shit for leaving you alone in Elmerson. You deserved better than me, after all I had put you through with the drugs, and my dad, and now I was leaving you. Also, I thought you would hate me for keeping this secret from Rob. You deserved to be with someone who was worthy of you. Who I was at that time, was not a man worthy enough to be with you. Part of me thought it would be better if you found someone else, but a bigger part of me hoped you would wait for me to finish university and then I could come back for you. But..."

"Lindsay got pregnant," I interrupt with my own recollection of events.

"Yeah," Landry nods. "Lindsay got pregnant."

"And your father made you marry her?"

"Yes."

"Would you have married her anyway, even if your father wouldn't have made you, because she was pregnant?"

Landry stops and looks me deep in the eyes. "No. Would you have taken me back if I had been a single dad?"

I look down to pick at my fingernails, an old habit which comforts me. "I don't know." I whisper as I continue to look down. "Probably," I admit with a shrug. "But there is one thing I need to ask. Why did you sleep with her, of all people?"

Landry runs his hands through his hair. "Honestly, I was so high that night I hardly remember it. I think I thought it was you."

"What about Josh? Did you and him ever reconcile?"

Landry nods slowly. "We did, though we never really discussed my marriage to Lindsay. A few years ago, I noticed he needed help. Josh was hurting and he was heartbroken. It was a hurt I knew like no other, it was the kind of hurt you experience when your heart is smashed into a million pieces. It was the kind of hurt I felt when I lost you. Josh had been broken like I had, and it sure as hell wasn't from losing Lindsay. Lindsay never had his love."

"But he was broken?"

"He was." Landry nods.

"And you helped him?

"I did. And now we're better. Not great, but better. But that's a different story."

We sit in silence for a long time, both lost in our own thoughts.

"Do you hate me for keeping this secret?" Landry hesitantly asks.

I look up at Landry sharply. "Not at all! Oh my God, Landry, you were a kid. Your mom asked you to take care of your brother when you were a kid yourself. As for your dad, don't even get me started on him. But baby, I think it's time to end it, it's time to tell Rob."

I nod in agreement as I can feel warm tears pool in my eyes. "I know it's time. But what if he hates me?"

"He might, Landry. But he deserves to know the truth about where he came from. He doesn't need your father's money anymore."

"I don't want to lose him, Cricket." A single tear escapes Landry's eye and makes its way down his cheek.

I reach over and wrap my arms around Landry's body. "I know, baby. It'll be okay. We can tell him together. I will be here for you. It might take some time, but I think he will eventually understand."

"And if he doesn't?"

"Well then, at least you know you did your very best to take care of him for as long as you could. You've been a terrific big brother, Landry. Rob is lucky to have you."

We sit silently for a minute.

"Well, I better get ready to go to my father's house." Landry pushes himself out of my embrace and stands up.

"Hold on," I jump up out of bed. "You're not doing this alone. Remember, we fight for us, together."

Chapter 59

Landry

After telling Hollynd about the secret I've been carrying for years regarding Rob's real father, I feel like a tremendous weight has been lifted off my shoulders. It terrified me that Hollynd would be angry with me or disappointed in me for keeping this secret, but I should have known better. Hollynd has such an amazing heart, that not only did she hear me out without judgement, but she also helped me understand why it's time to give up this secret. It's time to tell Rob the truth.

There was a time I thought I could always protect Rob from my father and still make sure he was provided for, if I could only keep this secret from him and keep my father happy. Now I see that this is an impossible goal. My father will never be happy with me or my choices, so unless I want to live completely under this rule for the rest of my life, it's time to get everything out into the open.

As soon as I saw the text message from my father on my phone, I knew exactly what had transpired in the last few hours for him to send me that message. I can almost guarantee that Lindsay left here and called her parents to inform them I had finally settled on giving her half my shares. That led to her father calling my father to tell him that the divorce papers would be finalized soon, which means that a divorce could tarnish their perfect family name, especially if Lindsay's infidelity came to light.

Of course, this caused an outrage with my father since he knew if the Prestons were angry about the divorce then their financial contributions for his senate campaign would be in question. This would be unacceptable for David Hayles, hence the text message I received which demanded me to be at his house in one hour.

So now here I am, freshly showered and getting ready to head to my father's house with the same sense of dread in my stomach. You would think now that I'm in my late twenties this feeling would have subsided, but unfortunately my father's wrath is never to be taken lightly.

However, a huge difference between this meeting with my father compared to past meetings with him is having Hollynd by my side. As soon as she saw the text from my father, she told me I was going, and she was coming with me. Hollynd promised to be by my side, so that we could deal with him together. I think this is the first time in my life that I have had someone on my side. It's a strange feeling, like courage and hope mixed in with a bit of fear of letting down your biggest supporter.

Thirty minutes later Hollynd and I park outside of my father's house. The sky is a dull grey and it feels like it's threatening to snow at any moment. Before we exit the car, Hollynd reaches over and takes my hand.

"Babe, if you want this can be the last time we ever have to come to this house again. Your father no longer has control over you. His vile words and threats can't hurt you anymore, I won't let them."

I look into Hollynd's beautiful green eyes, staring at me in all their seriousness. She looks like a freaking lioness ready to take down her prey. As embarrassing as it seems, I need her strength right now to help me get through this. In the past, I would use an exuberant amount of booze or some sort of drug to help me through, but I'm not that man anymore. I'm the man who is worthy of this woman sitting beside me.

"Thank you. Let's go." I give Hollynd's hand a squeeze as I pull it up to my lips for a tender kiss.

Together we walk hand in hand up the stairs to the front door of my father's house. It's finally time to end the years of secrets and abuse. It's time to set myself free.

My father's housekeeper, Jean, greets us at the front door and offers to take our coats. She then directs us to my father's office upstairs. Hollynd and I continue to hold hands up the staircase and down the hallway to the office. We are a united front.

I don't bother knocking on the office door but enter unannounced. My father is sitting at his large oak desk. Wearing a suit, as always, but with his tie pulled loose and a tumbler of scotch nearby, he looks more stressed than political.

My father's eyes shoot an icy glare in my direction; however, they change as soon as he notices Hollynd by my side.

"Well, isn't this a nice surprise." My father's fake political voice is in full force. "Hollynd, I didn't realize you were back in Brighten."

"Only temporarily," is all Hollynd offers for a reply.

"I see. Well, my dear, if you don't mind, I would like to speak with my son alone for a moment. You're more than welcome to head back to the living room and help yourself to a drink."

"No David, I think I will stay right here with Landry," Hollynd replies, never once dropping eye contact with my father.

I can see the annoyance building in my father's eyes as he clears his throat. "Very well, though I don't think you of all people are going to want to hear what I have to say. Come and sit." My father gestures to the two wingback chairs in front of his desk.

"Landry, I just received word that you and Lindsay have come to some sort of agreement with your divorce settlement?"

"Yes, that's correct," I reply coldly.

"Well son, I believe that we had discussed you two calling off this silly divorce thing and giving your marriage another shot." My father looks towards Hollynd. "I know how much you must miss Lindsay; she was such a good wife."

Hollynd doesn't offer any expression as my father tries to goad her.

"No, Dad. It's not happening. Lindsay and I are getting a divorce, and for the record, she was a terrible wife. She cheated on me constantly."

"From the way I understand it, it was you, my son, who was the one who couldn't get your act together after this one here." My father gestures with his head towards Hollynd.

Hollynd lets out a sigh of disgust.

"Dad, that's enough," I warn sternly.

"You're telling me, Landry, that you would rather give up shares in your own company, give up millions essentially, so you can have a little slut like this back in your bed?"

"For fuck's sake!" I yell, but before I can get up, Hollynd's hand reaches over and presses on my arm.

"No, Landry. He's right." Hollynd's eyes meet mine for a second before they turn back to my father. "You are giving up millions to be with, what did you say David, a slut like me? Here's the thing David, Landry and I are going to be together. In fact, we should've been together this entire time, but you couldn't let him be happy, could you? You have spent Landry's entire life making sure he knew just how worthless he was. Do you have any idea how messed up that is? You're his father, for God's sake! You don't deserve to have a son like Landry in your life. He's a good man; a better man than you'll ever be."

My father begins to laugh, though it is latent with rage. "Where do you get off telling me how great my son is? You have no idea all the shit he has pulled over the years. The drugs, the fights, the arrests, the many other women before you. He has been a failure and disappointment since he was born. Landry has the opportunity to do the right thing and I will not let someone like you lead him astray."

My father turns his attention to me. "You will stay with Lindsay, and you will get this terrible woman out of my house immediately. I mean it Landry; you will do what I say. For yours and your pathetic brother's sake."

"No!" I respond and stand in front of my father's desk. "I'm done. It's over. I'm going to tell Rob everything. He needs to know the truth and I need to be done with you."

My father immediately stands and marches around his desk, so we are face to face. His hand reaches up and grabs me at the base of my throat. "Why you little piece of shit..." I can feel flecks of scotch scented spit hit my cheek.

Before I can react, I feel Hollynd's body wedge her way in between the two of us.

"Hollynd, what are you doing?" I yell at her, terrified she's going to get hurt.

"Get your hands off him now, David. If you try to hit him, you're going to end up hitting me too, and I doubt it would look very good if the media found out that the future senator hit a woman in his office. So, I will say it again, GET YOUR FUCKING HANDS OFF OF HIM! You're done hurting him." Hollynd's voice radiates through the entire room.

My father finally releases my neck and backs away. I immediately grab Hollynd and move her behind me. There's no way in hell I'm letting her get hurt.

"We are finished, Dad. It's over." I say standing in front of Hollynd.

"I swear to God, Landry, if you walk out that door, I will never give you or your brother a single penny for the rest of your life. You are out of the will; you are out of everything," my father threatens.

I can't help but crack a smile. "I don't care, Dad. I never wanted any of this shit anyway, I just wanted a dad, but if you are my only choice for a father, then I would rather not have one at all."

I reach back and grab Hollynd's hand. "Come on, Cricket. Let's go."

Hand in hand, we leave my father's office and my father's house the same way we entered, as a united front. From now on, we fight together.

Chapter 60

Landry

It's eight p.m., and it's been hours since I left my father's house for what I'm telling myself is the last time. I'm sitting on the couch in the condo that Rob and I still share, waiting for him to get home. After work, Rob told me he was going to hit the gym and have a quick supper with some buddies. I'm on my second beer, waiting patiently.

After we arrived home from my father's house earlier today, Hollynd and I decided that I had to tell Rob the truth tonight about everything regarding his real father. It's time, and I wanted to make sure he heard it from me first. Although Hollynd offered to stay with me while I talked to Rob, I felt it was best to do this on my own. I wanted to do this on my own. A nightmare I have been running from for the past seventeen years is finally ending, and no matter how messy and horrible it may be, it's time for it to end.

I think back to the times I lied to Rob, well, lied through omission, trying to keep my word to my mother while trying to appease my father's demands. I hope Rob will see that I did what I thought I had to do out of love for him, to protect him.

Finally, around eight-thirty I hear the front door open. Rob is home. He knows I'm wanting to talk to him, but before he comes to meet me in the living room, he stops by the fridge in the kitchen to grab himself a beer while bringing an extra one for me.

"Hey," Rob says while he hands me my beer and sits on the chair adjacent to mine. "Are you sitting here in silence? The TV isn't even on."

"Yeah, I didn't want the noise. I need to talk to you about something important."

"Okay? You're freaking me out." Rob smirks while he takes a swig of his beer.

I set my newly opened bottle on the table in front of me and grab the manilla envelope lying beside me.

"First you should know that I have agreed to sign over half of my shares of Landro Tech to Lindsay as part of my divorce settlement."

"What? Are you kidding me? I don't want that woman to have any say in our company."

"I'm sorry, Rob, but I had to. It was the only way to get her to sign. But this is for you." I hand the envelope over to Rob.

"What is it?"

"I want you to take my other half of the shares. This will give you seventy-five percent control of all the shares of the company. You will still have control over everything."

"I'm not taking your shares, Landry," Rob argues and tosses the envelope back to me.

"Rob, listen to me. I need a clean break from Lindsay, and I'm leaving, anyway. Me being some sort of silent or distant partner is going to be a shit show. Just take the shares and do what you want with them. Hell, sell the company. You'll make millions and you will be free of everything too."

"Landry, you are not handing over millions of dollars' worth of shares. Have you lost your mind?"

"It's already done. I had my lawyer draw up the preliminary papers this afternoon. I'm out, Rob. Plus, you deserve this, I owe this to you."

"What are you talking about?" Rob asks in confusion.

I lay my head on the back of the couch and close my eyes for a quick second before I sit back up and look at my baby brother.

"There's something else I have to tell you. Something big."

"Spit it out, Landry!" Rob's voice is sounding nervous.

"David Hayles is not your father."

"What the hell are you talking about? How many beers have you had?" Rob jokes as he takes another drink himself.

"When Mom left us when we were little, she told me you and I did not have the same father and that she wanted me to take care of you since she was leaving you behind with me, to live as my full brother, as David's son. Mom said that Dad had told her if she didn't leave both you and I with him he would make sure you would have nothing. None of his money, none of his connections, nothing."

"So, she left me? Just like that? This doesn't make any goddamn sense."

"I guess he wanted to be cruel to her for cheating on him, so he took away her kids as punishment."

"Is he your father?" Rob questions me.

I nod.

Rob stands in frustration and begins pacing around the room. "Okay, so let me see if I got this straight. David Hayles is not my father, but Mom left me with him anyway for his money. And you're telling me that you knew about this the entire time?"

I lower my head as I feel the shame of the years of my betrayal beginning to turn in my stomach.

Rob laughs out loud, though it's a laugh of disbelief rather than finding the wave of information humorous.

"Wait, so who's my father then?" Rob laughs nervously. The laughter isn't really laughter. It's fear.

"I'm not sure, Rob. Mom never told me and neither did Dad."

"Oh, so this is something you and Dad have discussed frequently, I see. Did you two laugh about it together? Joke about the poor bastard kid no one wanted and that you two were stuck with?" Rob yells in my direction.

This makes me stand with panic. "Rob, no. That's not what happened. Dad tormented me with this information for years. He blackmailed me and threatened to take stuff away from you if I didn't do what he said. Like remember when there were issues with your college tuition, that was only to get me to go to Oak University instead of Stranton. That's why I moved back, that's why I left Hollynd."

"You are blaming me for your shitty choices, Landry?"

"No, that's not what I'm saying, Rob. I'm saying that I gave it up for you. I gave up everything for you, because I love you and I only wanted to protect you. Mom asked me to take care of you and that's what I did, the best way I knew how."

Rob's face is blazing with anger as he continues to pace around the living room. I stand with my arms folded across my chest, waiting for a response.

Finally, after a few minutes, Rob stops pacing and stands with his hands placed on his hips.

"I have spent my entire life trying to get that man to notice me. To love me the way he loved Isaac and Josh, or at the very least, give me the attention he gave you. I would have preferred to be yelled at constantly rather than Dad ignoring me all the goddamn time. All I ever wanted was to make him proud, but this makes more sense now. He saw me as worthless."

We stand silence for a moment.

"You should have told me." Rob stares at me with rage.

"I couldn't." I lower my head in disgust with myself.

"You could have. But you were a coward. Shit, maybe you enjoyed knowing I wasn't as special as you."

"Rob, you know that's not true."

"Honestly, Landry. I don't know what's true anymore. But what I do know is in the last ten years, I have had to take care of you and your shit more times than I can count. Landry's high again, Rob will take care of him. Landry's heartbroken over Hollynd, Rob will take care of him. Landry knocked up some other girl, oh quick, call Rob to help him. Landry's marriage is shit, and he has to move out, he can move in with Rob. Well fuck you, Landry! You say you have done everything for me, well, I have done everything for you too. But worse, you lied to me for years. So how about this big brother, not only am I done with our 'Dad,' but I'm done with you. Actually, I am done with every single one of you."

"Rob, come on. You don't mean that." I'm staring at Rob, hoping to see some sort of hope or forgiveness in his eyes, but there are neither.

"I do mean that Landry, I want you out of here. Finish packing up your shit to move away with Hollynd and get out of my house. I don't want to be anywhere around you, and I don't want you to come back here, ever. I know it's only a matter of time before you fuck things up with Hollynd again and you're on your own this time."

"Rob, I'm sorry." I can feel the tears threatening to fall. I try my best to keep them at bay.

"I don't want to hear it, Landry. I WANT YOU GONE, NOW!" Rob shouts as he walks towards his bedroom and slams the door hard enough that I can feel the vibrations of the impact on my feet.

This is exactly what I feared would happen when I told Rob the truth. He's so angry with me and I feel like there's nothing I can do to make things right.

I pull my phone from my pocket to text Hollynd to let her know that I'm on my way to be with her at her mom's house. Obviously, I can't stay here tonight, I can't stay here ever again. In one evening, I lost my brother and best friend. *I'm sorry Mom, I failed him.*

Chapter 61

Hollynd

Finally, it's moving day! Landry and I are officially ready to return to Elmerson together. Honestly, I never thought this day would come. If someone would have told me that four weeks ago I would return home with the only man I considered my home, I would have never believed it.

It's been three days since Landry's fall out with Rob. I wish I could have been there for Landry and Rob, but I get why Landry wanted to do this on his own. Landry has been quiet the last couple of days. I don't ask, but I can tell he's deeply saddened by the way things went with Rob.

For the last few days, Landry and I have been going to Rob's condo to pack up the remaining items in Landry's room. We have been intentionally going while Rob has been at work to give him space. Landry told me he has tried to text Rob a couple of times but has never received a reply.

Landry and I are planning to leave for Elmerson in the afternoon. We spent the morning at Rachel's house having brunch with them and my mom, who's health has greatly improved. This makes me so happy, and since it's a Sunday, everyone was home. I'm going to miss my family so much.

Landry's lawyer has asked him to meet him after lunch to finish signing off on the paperwork to give Rob Landry's shares of Landro Tech. Landry told me that signing these papers shouldn't take too long, so I decided to wait in our packed-up car for him. He offered for me to come in with him but honestly at this point I'm tired and want to get home to Elmerson.

While I'm waiting in the car killing time while scrolling through my social media accounts, I'm startled when my phone rings in my hand. It's Rob.

"Hello?" I answer quickly after seeing Rob's name pop up.

"Hey, Hollynd. Sorry to bother you."

"No, Rob. I'm glad you called. Are you okay?"

"Honestly? I don't know. I'm pretty pissed off." Rob's voice sounds gritty and tired.

"I can't say that I blame you. It's that Landry…"

"Hollynd, please don't defend him to me. I can't hear it right now."

"Okay." I pull back. "Then why did you call, Rob?"

"I heard you guys are leaving today?"

"Yeah, we're heading out right away."

"I wanted to ask you," Rob's voice cracks as he takes a pause. "I want to ask you to take care of him for me, Hollynd."

Instantly, I feel my own eyes fill with tears.

"Hollynd?" Rob asks, to make sure I'm still on the line.

"Yes, of course I will take care of him, Rob. I will always take care of him, you know that."

"I know that. I'm glad you two found your way back together."

"Do you think you will ever be able to forgive him? Landry, I mean."

"Honestly, I don't know. I don't know what's going to happen."

"I understand. But Rob, know that no matter what happens, I love you, and Landry loves you too."

"I know. I love you too, but listen, I got to run."

"Okay. Bye, Rob," I whisper in sadness for both brothers.

"Bye, Hollynd," Rob murmurs before he disconnects.

Wiping away the tears that have stained my cheeks, I take a breath. I know how much these brothers care for each other, and it breaks my heart to see their relationship being torn apart by a vicious man's lies and hatred. I can only hope that in time they will find their way back to each other, like Landry and I did. *Sometimes things are meant to happen, in the fullness of time.*

Chapter 62

Eight Months Later

I make my way through my apartment door with an arm full of groceries. Before I can call for Landry's help, I notice him stretched out on our lumpy pull-out couch, sleeping, with our orange and white kitten.

It's been eight months since Landry and I moved in, or should I say, moved back in together, into our tiny apartment in Elmerson. Our kitten, Kitty Ren, who's named after Kylo Ren, my favourite Star Wars bad boy, was my Christmas gift from Landry. However, now it's those two who are as thick as thieves. I suspect Landry had secretly wanted the kitten for himself, despite being adamant that the kitten was for me.

It's a Sunday afternoon and I'm happy to see Landry resting. Last winter Landry began school at Stranton University in their graduate program. He's working towards his Master's degree in Computer Science. However, unlike the last time Landry went to university, his father's not paying his tuition. We're back to being the stereotypical "starving students" who have a ton of student loan debt. Though I'm not a student anymore and I'm still working steadily as a freelance writer, the money isn't great and I'm still trying to pay off my student debt from before.

We're not living the life of luxury; however, we're as happy as can be. We spend as much time together as Landry's busy schedule allows. It took us some time to get to know each other again, and it turns out I might love him more than I did before.

Landry still hasn't heard from Rob, which I know weighs on his mind heavily. He has given Rob the space he requested and hopes that one day Rob will find it in his heart to forgive him for the secret he kept from him for all those years.

I'm trying to unpack the groceries as quickly as possible to not disturb the sleeping buddies on the couch in the next room. However, I didn't silence my cell phone, so when my text message alert goes off, the sound echoes through the apartment.

"Crick? Are you home?" I hear Landry mumble from the next room.

I leave the groceries and wander into the living room. I'm met with outstretched tattooed arms reaching high above Landry's head as he stretches off his nap. This has made the bottom of his blue T-shirt ride up and expose his hard abs which disappears under his low rising grey sweatpants. Instantly, I'm excited. Kitty Ren is performing his own stretch on top of Landry's chest, where he had been sleeping before he jumps down off the couch to run over to my legs and weave his way in between them.

"Hey, big boy," I say as I walk over to the edge of the couch.

"Mmm, come here." Landry's arms are now reaching forward to my waist. As his hands grip my waist, I'm pulled on top of his lean body.

"Hi," Landry greets me when we are face to face and softly kisses my waiting lips.

"Hi," I reply after our kiss.

Landry moves his hand from my lower back and cups my bottom as his lips make their way down my neck.

I can't help but let out a slight groan when my phone alerts me again to another text message.

"Who keeps texting you? Don't they know you're busy?" Landry grumbles.

"It's Parker. He and Manuel are coming over for supper, remember? He keeps hounding me about what kind of wine will pair best with our meal. I told him we aren't picky when it's free."

Parker and Manuel have been together for three months and I couldn't be happier for them. Parker had a tough go with a relationship for the last few years, but finally met the love of his life while taking a cooking course at the local learning annex. Manuel was his teacher and Parker was Manuel's worst student.

"Ugh, I forgot it's double date night." Landry reaches up and rubs his tired eyes.

"Oh, come on. You always have a good time when Parker and Manuel come over."

Landry scowls at me while I type away on my phone.

I'm so happy that Landry has become friends with my close friends here in Elmerson. Parker and Landry even have gym dates together, which Manuel and I love to tease them about thoroughly.

Landry and Eva have also taken a liking to each other, but with her still living the carefree, single lifestyle, we don't see her as much as I used to.

After I finish replying to Parker, I toss my phone to the end table nearby.

"You know sometimes you have to share my attention with others." I lay back down and wiggle my body between the side of the lumpy pull-out couch and Landry.

"But what if I don't want to share you? What if I want to keep you all to myself?" Landry grumbles into my ear.

"Well, I can arrange that for the next three hours until the guys get here. Hmm, what can we do for three hours?"

"I can think of something." Landry turns his body to the side, so we are face to face.

"Me too. I was thinking you could vacuum while I start to prep supper. Then you can clean the bathroom while I set the table."

Landry's fingers go straight for my ribs and tickle me fiercely. "That is definitely not what I had in mind."

I laugh hard while his fingers continue to pester my body. Landry's hands move from a tickling motion to a pawing motion as our lips find each other through our laughter.

"Okay, well I guess we have a little time before we have to get ready for our company," I mumble into Landry's neck and slowly circle my tongue against his smooth skin.

"You gave in pretty quick there, Cricket."

"Must be your power of seduction." I continue to nuzzle into his neck.

"You better tell me more about how you can't resist me." Landry's mouth is hovering over my ear.

"Don't you ever tire of hearing how sexy and handsome and wonderful I think you are? Oh, and of course, let's not forget your modesty," I tease sarcastically.

"Never!" In one swift motion, Landry has me flat on my back on the couch and his body is hovering over top of me.

Slowly, Landry brushes my wild hair off my forehead. "You're still my wife, you know that right?"

"I don't know. We haven't really talked about it since, you know, you were actually married to someone else."

"Nope, you are still my wife. And I'm not 'actually' married to anyone anymore, but I would like to be. If you will have me."

I can't help but feel a smirk form over my lips. "Landry Hayles, are you proposing to me?"

"Well, not really proposing since we are already married, but more like doing it again, but officially."

"Don't you think this is too quick? I mean, we've only been back together for six months."

"Cricket, we have been together for eight years. From the first day that I saw you in that classroom at Creston College, our first date on the beach at Pebblestone Lake, and our first wedding under the stars. You've been mine and even when we were apart, I have always been yours. Nothing and no one ever changed that. But I want to do it again and I want to do it right. You are not my everything, Cricket. You are my only thing."

I reach my hands up and place them over Landry's stubbled face. "Oh, baby. I love you so much and of course I will marry you again, but I have one request."

"Anything."

"I want it to be us again. Well, except for the Justice of the Peace and a witness, but that's it."

"What about your family?"

"No, I get it, I want to celebrate with them, and I know they will want to celebrate with us too. But we can plan a party or something with them. But when you and I get married, I want it to be us, like it was the first time. It isn't about anyone else, Landry. It never has been. You and I have something that no one else would ever understand. Hell, I don't know if we understand it fully ourselves. But this pull, this longing, this completeness I feel when I'm with you is something that words will never do justice in trying to describe it. You feel it and I feel it. It was never about anyone else; it was only ever about us."

Chapter 63

Landry

I finally submitted my final paper for one of my graduate classes. I never thought I would go back to school after I finished my degree six years ago. It was Hollynd who encouraged me to pursue my Master's degree after I expressed an interest in teaching Computer Science at the post-secondary level.

At first, I was hesitant to go back to school, knowing that the amount of student debt at the end of my studies would be huge. For the first time in my life, I'm living without access to large amounts of money, and it has been an adjustment. Thank goodness for Hollynd's positive outlook on life. She helps me see that life doesn't need to be bought in order to be happy.

I'm arriving at our little apartment earlier than usual since I didn't have any classes scheduled now that the semester is over. My goal for the rest of the afternoon was to search for a summer job until I begin my next semester in the fall.

As I arrive at the front of my apartment building, I'm shocked to see the familiar face of my younger brother Rob leaning against the brown brick building.

"Rob, what are you doing here?" I ask, still in shock.

"I wanted to talk to you. Can I come in?"

"Yes, of course." I unlock the main door to the building and hold it open for Rob to enter, as I follow behind. We don't talk again until we are up the stairs and into my apartment.

The apartment is empty, except for Kitty Ren, who meets me waiting at the door. Hollynd's gone this afternoon for a meeting with one of her editors.

"You have a cat?" Rob asks, now experiencing his own shock.

"It was Hollynd's Christmas gift," I explain as Kitty Ren circles my legs.

"You two are looking pretty close there, brother." Rob laughs and I instantly feel a wave of relief flow through my body.

The last time we spoke was during our blow out over the secret of his paternity. That fight was eight months ago now. I haven't heard from him since.

"Can I get you something to drink?" I offer as Rob and I make our way into the living room.

"In a minute. I need to talk to you first," Rob says, and I take a seat on the couch while I sit down on the chair.

"I wanted to talk to you about our fight and I wanted to apologize," Rob confesses while he's looking down at his own hands.

"What are you talking about, Rob? You did nothing wrong. I'm sorry for keeping that shit from you."

"After you moved from Brighten, I took a trip down to see Mom in Florida."

"Seriously?"

"Yeah. I needed answers. She told me everything. About her marriage to David, his abuse and threats, getting pregnant with me, my real father. She confessed it all."

"Holy shit," I say with my mouth agape.

"She also showed me all the letters you sent her. Reporting to her about how you were trying to protect me and take care of me like you promised her."

"That still doesn't excuse what I did, Rob."

"Landry, don't you get it? You've been the only one on my side. My entire life, as messed up as it is, it isn't nearly as bad as it could have been if it hadn't been for you."

"So, you forgive me?" I ask hopefully.

"Landry, there's nothing to forgive. You took care of me my entire life. I realized how lucky I am to have a brother like you."

"What about seeing Mom? What was that like?" I ask with a strong curiosity.

"Oh man, it was bizarre. She's still batshit crazy. Only now she's into healing crystals and voodoo ointments." Rob laughs.

"What did she say about your real father?" I ask hesitantly.

"Well, I'm relieved to report that it was not the pool boy. He was one of David's interns, of all people."

"Are you going to try to find him?"

"I don't know. I don't think so." Rob bites his lip looking unsure.

"Seriously? That's crazy." I can't help but rub my hand through my hair.

"Tell me about it. I think we need a beer now. Then I have some more news to share with you."

I get up to retrieve two beers from the kitchen. "As long as you don't tell me you are going to move to Florida and become a palm reader."

Rob laughs. "Well, with a mother like ours it wouldn't be that shocking."

When I return to the living room with our beer, I notice an envelope that was not there before sitting on the table.

"What's that?" I ask as I hand Rob his beer.

"That is for you," Rob replies before taking a drink. "I sold Landro Tech, well technically Lindsay and I sold it."

"What?"

"Yup, we got an offer from DMR Technologies, and I couldn't refuse. I guess I could have, but honestly, I didn't want to. It wasn't the same now that you and I aren't doing it together. Besides with what we made from the sale, I can now do anything I want."

"And what's with the envelope?" I ask as I pop the top off my beer bottle.

"That's your share of the profit." Rob smiles.

"No, I gave you my remaining share."

"I know, but after I sold the company, I didn't think it was right that you had nothing. You and I built this thing together, and I want you to have it. Lindsay took her twenty-five percent cut, without hesitation I might add, and I split the remaining seventy-five percent in half between you and me."

I sit there silently, not knowing what to say. I'm staring at Rob while he smiles. Rob reaches over and grabs the envelope and tosses it my way.

"Open it," Rob urges with excitement.

When I do, I see a cheque with my name on it with more zeros than I can count in one glance. "Rob, I can't accept it."

"It's not an option, Landry. It's yours. Use it for your schooling, to build a life with Hollynd, or whatever you want."

"How did you know about my schooling?" I ask.

"I still keep in touch with Josh, and I know he still checks in with you occasionally. You know, between him, David, and Isaac, he's probably the best one."

I scowl at Rob. Poor Rob, still trying to see the good in people. But he's right, Josh is the best one.

"I'm not saying he's not a douchebag. I'm just saying he's the least douchy of them, that's all." Rob takes a drink of his beer.

Looking back down at the cheque, I shake my head.

"Rob, I don't know what to say. Thank you! And thank you for understanding why I did what I did. That means more to me than this cheque."

"You're welcome. Now what time is Hollynd home? We need to go celebrate being free from David Hayles and Lindsay Preston forever."

Chapter 64

 Hollynd

"Holy moly, I didn't expect it to be this cold for the start of May." I wrap my black wool coat tight around my waist. I'm happy I opted for the warmer jacket when Landry told me that tonight was the night.

We'd already been visiting Brighten this weekend for baby Cassie's birthday party. However, we drove down a few days earlier to get the paperwork started with the Justice of the Peace.

Although the Justice of the Peace told us he was currently booked up for the next while, I guess a cancellation happened because the Justice of the Peace called to see if we wanted this Sunday night spot. Landry took it without asking me, not that I minded. I was so ready to be Mrs. Landry Hayles officially.

We're standing on the beach huddled together as the icy wind blows off the lake. Landry insisted this be the spot where we would get married, again.

Finally, in the distance, I can see the headlights of the Justice of the Peace's car heading towards us.

"Are you nervous?" Landry leans down to ask me.

"Nah," I reply. "You?"

"Nope. I have never wanted anything more."

Soon, the car arrives at the beach and parks beside our car.

The Justice of the Peace is accompanied by his wife, who will act as our witness for the ceremony. Part of me is feeling a twinge of guilt knowing that my family isn't here to witness the moment, but not enough that I would change or stop what we are about to do.

"Well, are you two ready?" Peter asks.

Landry and I both nod with a smile. We turn to face each other, much like we did the first time we got married.

"Today we are here to join Landry Hayles and Hollynd Turner in matrimony. I understand that you have both decided to recite your own vows. Is that correct?"

In unison, Landry and I nod.

"Very well, Landry, go ahead."

Landry clears his voice before he begins and reaches forward to grab my cold hands.

"Hollynd, my Cricket, it's been a long road for us to get here again. We've gone through a lot to get here, some good and some bad. Ours is a story I thought would never get its happy ending, yet by some miracle, it has. You're here tonight with me, and you're becoming my wife. I have no idea how I got so lucky to have you with me, to have a part of me, to have you loving me. I promise that this is forever."

I'm smiling brightly as my eyes stay focused on Landry's.

"Hollynd, go ahead," Peter announces, breaking me from my daze of pure love.

"Landry, seven years ago, I stood here with you and promised to be your wife. And for seven years I always thought of myself as your wife, no matter how far apart our paths led us. You told me once that I had your soul, and it was the only way I ever survived without you, because I always had a piece of you with me. And now, by the grace of God, I have all of you here with me again. Nothing will separate us again, Landry, because when we fight, we fight together."

"You are me." Landry finishes my thought.

"And I am you." I whisper in return.

"Landry and Hollynd, please present your rings."

We each reach into our own pocket where we had placed our old wedding bands earlier in the evening. Only when Landry pulls out my band from his pocket, I see it's pressed up against a square cut aquamarine stone surrounded in diamonds.

"Landry, repeat after me. With this ring, I thee wed," Peter says before I can say anything about the ring I have never seen before.

"With this ring I thee wed," Landry repeats while he slides the two rings onto my left-hand ring finger.

I look up from the sparkling ring to see Landry's face beaming brightly with pride. He knows he's done well.

"Hollynd, repeat after me. With this ring, I thee wed."

I slide Landry's wedding band on his finger and repeat the words, "With this ring, I thee wed."

"Now, by the power vested in me, I now pronounce you husband and wife. Landry, you may kiss your bride."

Peter does not even get the word "bride" out before Landry's hand reaches up and cups my face. His lips press firmly against mine, like it is the first time we are kissing. And even though we've shared thousands of kisses before, this feels like our very first one. It is the kiss that officially seals our fate, the fate that our souls have felt all along. We have a love that is bigger than our own understanding, and bigger than all our mistakes. It is a love that will stop at nothing, built from two souls who will never stop fighting for one another, because when they are together, they aren't everything... they are the only thing.

The End

Epilogue

Landry

Three Years Later

Every part of me wants to go to bed. I'm daydreaming of the king-size bed Hollynd and I purchased after moving back to Brighten over a year ago. That was also the same time we bought our own home down the street from her mother's house.

After Rob dropped a money bomb on us, I finally convinced Hollynd to move into a larger apartment in Elmerson. One that had a spare room for guests, an office for her writing, and enough space to have as many bookshelves as we desired. Hollynd, though still attached to her tiny apartment in the brown brick building, finally agreed.

We spent two years together in the new and bigger apartment while I finished my Master's degree at Stranton University. Now that money and student loans are no longer an issue, Hollynd takes on less freelance work and spends more time at home working on her dreams of being a fiction writer. Watching Hollynd work tirelessly at her stories allows me to be a witness to someone achieving their dreams, and the fact that it is the love of my life achieving her dreams is a gift like no other.

After I finished my Master's degree, I was fortunate to land a job at our old alma mater, Creston College, as an associate Professor in the Computer Science department. Hollynd was ecstatic to move back to Brighten as she had been missing her family a lot lately.

In the last three years I have had no contact with my father who is now a senator and has moved out of Brighten, so I don't have to worry about seeing him around now that we are back.

Isaac is still living here and took over the partnership in my father's law firm. I don't see him too often. Our relationship is still a work in progress, but it has improved.

Josh and I have grown closer in the last few years, which surprises the hell out of me. Maybe it was when my father finally moved that he began to feel a sense of freedom. There's no doubt in my mind that Josh has been on the receiving end of David Hayles' wrath more than once in the past, just as I have.

Rob spends most of his time travelling around the world. I think he's still searching for his own identity after losing the only identity he had ever had, which was being David Hayles' son.

Now Hollynd and I are back in Brighten in a modern four-bedroom house. There's enough room for each of us to have our own office, a large living room for entertaining, and as I had been daydreaming about, a bedroom with a large king-sized bed I'm dying to get into. Yet here I am on the floor of our attached bathroom, rubbing a cold washcloth on Hollynd's forehead. Hollynd's head is resting on my lap as she breathes sharply in and out of her mouth.

"Landry, I don't want to throw up again," she manages to get out between breaths.

"I know, baby. But if you need to, I'm here for you," I reassure my love.

"I want this to stop. When is it going to stop?" I can almost hear the sobs escape her throat.

My poor girl, the nighttime routine of laying on the bathroom floor together has become our ritual for the last few weeks. I can't help but remember the night Hollynd laid on the bathroom floor with me all those years ago. Only the difference is that I was strung out on Xanax and cocaine while Hollynd is giving me the greatest gift—the gift of a baby.

To say we were trying for a baby wouldn't be totally accurate. We were simply not not trying to get pregnant. It had been the morning sickness that had first tipped Hollynd off she might be pregnant. When Hollynd told me she was pregnant, I was consumed with a joy that I never got to experience the first time I was told I was expecting a baby. For years I have been working through my guilt over the loss of my first baby and I hope that the arrival of this one will be my chance at redemption.

"Okay," Hollynd taps my leg, "I think I'm done now."

She lifts her head off my lap and tries to sit up.

"There's no rush, Cricket. We can stay here as long as you need to."

"You're pretty good to me, Mr. Hayles."

"Well, I learned from the best, Mrs. Hayles."

"Help me up so I can brush my teeth and then we can go to bed."

I help Hollynd to her feet and leave her to brush her teeth as I get her a glass of ginger ale and a pack of crackers to put on her nightstand. Another one of our nightly routines.

Once we are back in bed, tucked in and getting ready to stream our favourite show, I take one last look at the woman beside me. I still don't know how I got so lucky to have a woman like Hollynd love me. But I do know that her love has made me who I am today, just as I know that my love has made her who she is, too. Now together, we are making a whole new life inside her and it's a life I will cherish with every fiber of my being. Hollynd will forever be my only thing, but this baby will be my everything else.